GREENLAND

Norwegian Sea

Trondheim

NORWAY

DISKO I.

ICELAND

North Sea

Vesterbig

EINERSFIORD
Osterbig
ERICSFIORD

Blue Shirt

R E T U R N

SCOTLAND

IRELAND

ENGLAND

FRANCE

NDLAND

O c e a n

SPAIN

AFRICA

LEIF ERICSSON'S JOURNEYS

← *Leif's journey from Iceland to Greenland*

← *Leif's journey in search of the New World*

Miles

0   100   300   500

map by palacios

BOOKS BY EDISON MARSHALL

HERO NOVELS

West with the Vikings A tale of the Northmen's discovery of America.
Earth Giant A tale of Heracles (Hercules in Roman myth).
The Pagan King A tale of King Arthur.
The Viking A tale of Ogier the Dane.
Great Smith A tale of Captain John Smith.
Caravan to Xanadu A tale of Marco Polo.

HISTORICAL NOVELS

Yankee Pasha The adventures of a young American frontiersman from
Salem to Tartary after the Revolutionary War.
Benjamin Blake A tale of the bastard son of an English squire in the
South Sea Islands in the period of our Revolutionary War.
American Captain A tale of a young mariner in Maine, Malta, North
Africa, East Africa, and England at the turn of the eighteenth
century.
The Gentleman The adventures of a Charleston gambler at home, in the
West Indies, and in South Africa prior to the Civil War.
The Upstart A tale of strolling players in England about 1730.
The Infinite Woman A tale inspired by the life of Lola Montez.
Gypsy Sixpence A tale of a young Lancer on the Afghan frontier in
India, his character and his story suggested by those of Richard
Burton.

GOTHIC ROMANCE

Castle in the Swamp A tale of the Carolina Low Country in the nineteenth
century.

REGIONAL NOVELS

Princess Sophia A tale of Alaska in the period 1898–1918.
The Inevitable Hour A tale of Martinique in the period 1890–1902.

BOOKS OF SHORT STORIES

Love Stories of India.
The Heart of Little Shikara Stories of animals of forest and jungle.
The Elephant Remembers A jungle book.

MEMOIRS OF BIG-GAME HUNTING

The Heart of the Hunter A looking-backward over hunting trails in
Canada, Alaska, Africa, Indo-China, and India, and where they led.
Shikar and Safari A factual and objective account of various big-game
hunts.

WEST WITH THE VIKINGS

EDISON MARSHALL

WEST WITH
THE VIKINGS

1961

DOUBLEDAY & COMPANY, INC., GARDEN CITY, N.Y.

With the exception of actual historical personages, the characters are entirely the product of the author's imagination and have no relation to any persons in real life.

DEDICATION

To

J. Riis Owre, Dean of the Graduate School of Miami University, a descendant of Vikings, and my good friend;

and to

Doctor Jose Balseiro, poet, essayist, and Professor of Languages of the Graduate School of Miami University.

CONTENTS

AUTHOR'S FOREWORD

Despite the declaration of Frudtjof Nansen, Danish explorer, statesman, and Nobel Prize winner, that the Icelandic and Greenlandic sagas are mainly fiction, I have borrowed from them freely in writing WEST WITH THE VIKINGS. In the first place, Nansen never doubted that Norsemen reached the North American continent five centuries before Columbus sailed, and almost all students of the period agree that the discoverer was Leif, son of Eric the Red. I too hold this view, but after poring over the *Flatey Book* as well as the *Saga of Eric the Red,* I came to the conclusion that a convincing adequate story of the Viking discovery of America never had been told.

The novel ends with what purports to be a letter from a priest accompanying Cortes to his spiritual guide in Spain. No such letter was written as far as I know but such a letter could have been written. Except for Carlos P. Lamar, physician and savant of Miami, Florida, I would never have heard of the Viking theory of the origin of the Aztec god Quatzalcoatl, a theory accepted by many historians and respected by all.

I am forever obliged to Doctor Lamar for giving me the suggestion out of which grew WEST WITH THE VIKINGS.

/s/ E.M.

CHAPTER ONE

THE NEW DREAM

I

My name is Leif. I am the son of Eric the Red, who was born near Stavanger, Norway, and who was a great thane of Herald Graycloak. And because his wrath waxed as red as his beard, and because he could never learn to strike a short or softened blow, hardly less than a blow to kill, he was sent into exile by the Lawmen, whereby it came to pass that I, Leif, was born in far-off Iceland. There smiths live in the bowels of mountains, whether giants or dwarfs, I know not, and their forges hurl up masses of molten rock, and smoke, and steam, and flame.

A holy man in a white robe, born in France, and in the service of the Christian Bishop of Ireland, made the long journey to Iceland solely to bless a little church that some of our islanders had raised. By his reckoning the year was 985 since the birth of his God Kris. He spoke to the people in the tongue of a Westman, as we Norse used to call the Irish, and he declared that the fiery outbursts, and the earth shaking and quaking, and great rifts in the ground, and crags being split asunder were not the fault of dwarfs or giants either. Instead these things were caused by prodigious fires stoked by the Devil, the enemy of Kris, and their purpose was to torment the dead who had died without acknowledging Kris as their God.

Yet I, a younker of fourteen winters, knew this was not true. We Icelanders believed that if a piece of iron, of due weight, were lowered into or left by one of the steaming, boiling, or smoking vents in the earth, in a few days would be found there a wonderfully fashioned piece of smithery, often decorated with precious jewels. It so chanced that such a vent lay at a lonely place near Ericsholm, our home acre. There I lugged an ingot of iron weighing ten pounds, which I had taken from my sire's abundant store. I thrust it into the vent, and when I returned

there, two days later, against a piece of black rock leaned a naked
sword.

Young as I was, well I knew that no smith in Iceland could
have forged it. Its blade was not long, but sharp on both sides
as the fang of a sting ray, and in the middle was a groove which
we called the blood channel, to cause a gushing wound. One
feature puzzled my unschooled mind. The hilt was ancient walrus
ivory, lustrous black from ages' immersion in the deep sea, such
as is sometimes washed up on our beaches. At first I wondered
where the subterranean smiths had got it. Then, after recalling
how the ocean pours over an endless precipice into Hel beyond
the Poison Sea, I reckoned that no few old tusks had been carried
down.

My thought was to show it first to my brother, Thorstein,
three years older than I and the favorite child of Eric, our father.
He had nothing to compare with it in shining splendor, although
his iron-pointed sealing spear, which he could hurl with great
skill, was very fine. Instead, I brought it to Thorhall Hunter, our
father's reeve. Thorhall had begun life as a Viking and ever
complained of the dullness of his present life; even so, it was the
most exciting on our island. No one could match him in spearing
monstrous whales; and I dreamed of the day, soon, when I
could go with him in his boat and be hauled swifter than a
salmon's run through our berg-strewn sea. When no whales
blowed, he hunted walrus for their thick hides and blubber and
precious teeth, and only when our pantries leaned instead of
bulged would he stoop to harpooning seals. Most of all he loved
to hunt the huge snow-white bears that sometimes visited our
coast on their great iceboats adrift from the dim north. These he
chased with a spear and sometimes dared attack them with bow
and arrow.

Keen-eyed strangers knew him for a hunter by the look of
him. He stood straight as a birch and his skin was almost the color
of birch bark, from snow glare and iceblink and windburn. Despite
his big frame his movements were sudden and violent.

"Leif, what have you there?" Thorhall asked, his voice as deep
as the muttered rumble of pack ice breaking up far away at sea.

"Why, it's a sword."

"Now how did you come by it, Leif Ericsson?"

"I found it leaning against a rock near Weland's Stew Pot." This last was our name for the boiling vent near Home Acre.

"I missed a ten-pound ingot of iron from Eric's store. You left your track in the ashes from our forge, and I had a mind to cane you, but the thought came to me of what you wanted of it, so I let you make the trial, hit or miss."

Until I turned fifteen, at which age I would be counted a full man, Thorhall had every right to cane me at his inclination. In the first place he was a thane in his own right, forsaking his barren holdings to become my father's eater. In the second place, Eric had appointed him to the office, not trusting his own temper not to flair and break some of my bones.

"Well, it was hit, not miss," I told Thorhall. "Have you ever seen a finer sword?"

Thorhall took the shining thing in his two hands and bent down the point and the hilt until the sweat burst out of me in fear that the steel would shatter. But it sprang back straight, with a little *ting* that was music in my ears, like the bell of the Elfin King that we sometimes heard far off as he summoned his band. Then Thorhall looked at the hilt, examining closely its workmanship, and then at some tiny marks engraved on the blade.

"Aye, I've seen better Drinkers of Blood," he said, "but not many."

I could not speak for happiness.

"What do you make of the little marks?" he went on.

"I can make naught of them."

"You can't read runes? By the God of the Nine Runes, you'll learn to, or I'll whale you black and blue. I'm not a great rune reader myself, but I can make out these. They say, 'My name is Wolf Fang. Thrust me deep.'"

"Well, I will."

"Well, how can you, when you've got all the makings of a Christian? Your mother, Thorhild, is turning you into one, and Eric can't stop her. You'll never shout over your shield in battle, you'll never find the Berserk's Way. You'll count sheep, drive cattle, geld bull calves to break their spirit, cast accounts, or maybe you'll be a greasy merchant, who can talk only of the price of tar, rope, and hides, and of walrus tusks that never hooked over your gunnels and well-nigh sunk you. How old are you? Close on fifteen but you're big enough to be eighteen and still growing fast. But what good will your big hulk do you? Tell me this, Leif. Was it your mother's God Kris or any of his angels that forged that stolen lump of iron into a wondrous sword?"

"No, it was dwarfs or giants, servants of Thor, who toil deep under the earth."

"Servants of Thor, you say. You know no better, or I'd smite you. In my grandsire's time, Thor was the God of seed planters, thralls, and slaves. I was named for Thor, so was your mother, because even then, before the coming of the white-robed priests to Norway, our race was turning into a pack of farmers, instead of marauders on the wide seas. Our grandsires loved gold, silver, shining jewels, and bright-faced maids; they got their meat by strand slaughter; they stayed up at night to hold wassail, not to help gravid cows drop their calves. Eric the Red is a Thor's man. That's the most you'll ever be, and 'twill be a wonder if you don't start following Kris, begging people who hit you on one cheek to hit you again on the other. But the dwarfs, led by Gruenelo who forged Agrament's Ring, and who fashioned you this sword, they're not Thor's creatures. They've been imprisoned in Hel, as great Loki is, and your mother's God Kris might have had a hand in it, I'll not say he didn't, for he's got a tough old sire to help him, but they're still faithful to Odin, God of the Winds, Rider of the Eight-hoofed Horse, God of Battle; and they can still raise Hel, as you well know. And I, Thorhall, am faithful to him, too."

My face burned, but I saw my mother's face in a vision, and I spoke up for her God.

"Thorhild told me that the giants and the dwarfs are in rebellion against Kris, but he will conquer them at last, and conquer all other Gods, and be king of earth and heaven."

"Who'll be king in Hel?"

And with that, Thorhall hurled my sword like a battle ax

against a wooden door, piercing the board with its point and driving it half through. Then, turning his back on me, in the burly trot with which he always moved, he went out of the hall and down to the strand and sat in his boat.

2

My mother, Thorhild, descended from Harald Bluetooth, one of the greatest of the Vikings. She had never told me so, and I knew of it from Eric's taunts, picturing her ancestor holding rouse in Valhalla with his mighty mates, all of them laughing to crack their ribs at a Norse woman of the true breed kneeling before pale Kris. They themselves had never knelt even to Odin. They had shouted to him, and at times danced before him but their knee joints lacked grease for deep bending.

Young as I was by counting, yet I was old for my years. Icelandic boys were made to stand watch over sheep in our windy pastures at age six. Hence I believed not by love alone, but by comparing her with other mothers, that she was the prettiest woman on the island except perhaps for dark Ellen, the young wife of one of our thralls and born in Ireland. Not very tall, my mother was finely fashioned, and she moved as lightly as a skimming tern. Yet it was her glowing pale-hazel eyes that most fascinated mine, and it was the lovely expression that came into her face when she spoke to all children, the very old and all humble folk, that I most loved.

"It is a magnificent sword," she told me, not putting her hand on it, "and it is very like one my grandsire showed me when I was a little girl. But what is it for?"

"Why, for fighting."

"For fighting whom? There are no wars in Iceland except blood feuds, desperately wicked. If you had said for killing other men, young men most likely, better fit for frolicking and making love and hunting and strong toil, than for lying stiff and cold in the Cold of Weird—if you had said that, you would have hit it better. What other use has it? It is no good for killing the great white bears that drift to our shores on the ice. Its reach is not long enough; you would have a better chance with a cheap spear. Now if this was a gift of love from some good God, or even from a kobold, it would have been a wondrous harpoon, with a long beak of the finest steel. With that you could hunt the great bears, and the long-tusked sea hogs, and even whales. More likely it is a bribe from the King of Hel, forever the enemy of gentle Kris, to get you in his power."

"Our old God was not Kris, but Odin," I answered, my neck prickling.

"Odin has been defeated, perhaps chained with the very chains that bind Loki, and Thor will soon go down. Kris will reign forever, world without end."

"How could he? You said he was a carpenter, little better than a thrall, not a warrior. Even our old God Weland was a smith, who stands higher than a driver of pegs into wood."

"Would you like to hear again the little that I know about him?"

And my mother spoke so softly and sweetly that I could hardly hold back tears.

"Yes, I would."

"He is God and man both. His father was a great God, far greater than Odin, greater than the Devil; and some say there were no other Gods until Kris was born, but that I do not believe, because my own sire saw Odin in his gray cloak, two ravens perched on his shoulder, two wolves dogging his heels. His hoary beard was blown by a strong wind, but the leaves of the aspen trees hung still in a great calm. My sire saw him on an island near Stavanger. The name of Kris' father is—but I do not remember. His mother was a virgin who lived, I think, in Ireland. A spirit came to her and told her she would bear a child, and it so chanced that when she had finished swelling she went into a city called Baile Atha Cliath, which we Norse call Dublin. It is said that she went there to pay tribute to the king, but that too I cannot believe, because the greatest king of all huddled, ready to be born, in her blessed womb. And because the guest houses were filled, she and her husband—aye, she was a virgin, yet married—took refuge in a cattle shed, and there, on lowly straw, came forth Kris. And he grew up, and performed wonders never seen by men, and preached on the mountain, and fed a multitude of his hearers from one basket of fish, and perhaps a few wheat cakes."

"Thorhild, what are wheat cakes?"

"We ate them in Norway. They are like the rye cakes you have sometimes tasted. Listen to what else Kris did. He stood up for the poor, the sick, and the maimed, and the lowly, and for little children. But the soldiers hated him because his soft words were mightier than their swords, and a Law Speaker named Pail, which to us means the pilot of a ship, washed his hands of the matter, and one of his followers named Jude betrayed him for thirty silver groats, and he was caught and sentenced to be nailed on a wolf tree, and so he died."

"Why did not his father, whom you called a great God, come to his help?"

"I do not know. Perhaps it was in Kris' fate to so die, and no man or God either can fight his fate. Kris died without lifting his hand in his own defense."

"By the Thunder God of the Red Beard, if I had been there, I would have defended him with this sword. And I would have sworn by Odin too, if I had dared."

"Hear the end of the story. In three days Kris rose from his grave, and he did not go down to Corpse Strand at the door of Hel to be devoured by monsters, nor was he borne to Valhalla by the Helmed Maidens on their white steeds, there to hold wassail and fight. Instead, he ascended to heaven, where there is no death and no darkness, and forever happiness and light."

"I love our dim winter days, and the long nights when the stars shine so bright, and our fires blaze. I would miss the seal hunting, too."

"There would be other joys, even greater than being towed in a longboat by a harpooned whale. And Leif, I have saved to the last the greatest wonder he did. It was only to speak some words. Those words were that all men are brothers, thanes and thralls alike, and they must not prey on one another, or kill one another, and instead all must do to others as they want others to do to them. When his kingdom comes and all men obey him, the earth will be like heaven. And now I have a present for you, Leif. I meant to keep it locked in my chest until you were fifteen for fear that in your stripling awkwardness you would break it, and no man in Iceland could mend it, and its like could not be gotten, short of a long journey across the seas. Perhaps it is a richer gift than a king's sword."

Then with an iron key my mother unlocked and opened an oaken chest, studded with copper nails, that she had brought from Norway, and took out what appeared to be a tube of about my arm's length, made of some polished wood with gold and silver inlay. I noticed that nine holes had been bored in it, one, nearest the end, larger than the others, and eight holes in line.

Now nine is the magic number. There were Nine Runes for which Odin made a nine-day journey into hell, and every ninth year was the Vikings' year of sacrifice, when every thane slew nine of every animal and bird that he could catch, as well as nine slaves. So I could not doubt that the wooden tube had been a gift of Odin, perhaps to Harald Bluetooth, and it too was a magic thing.

"What is it, Leif?" came my mother's quiet voice.

"I do not know."

"Listen. What you will hear is almost a mockery of what you would hear if a master brought it to his lips. What skill I had I have mainly forgotten."

My mother put her mouth to the larger hole in the tube and put her fingers over the smaller holes. When she blew across the larger hole, her fingers rose and fell in some lovely pattern. And into the air, into this room with earthen walls, under a turf roof, a room well-furnished by Icelandic counting, with a bed, a loom, a few benches of wood brought from Norway, and a hard-beaten floor of dirt, there rose strains of music, beautiful past all telling, perhaps such as the Lorelei makes on the shore of the great river that flows into Frisia, whereupon the pilot drops into dreams, and the master stands mazed, and the rowers ply their oars in madness toward their death doom.

My mother took the tube from her mouth and held it out to

me. "That song is also very old," she told me. "It was the welcoming song of the Danish women when the Viking fleets returned from their far and bloody raids, so it must be wicked. Still —I wish I could play it better."

"If I could play it half as well, I think—I believe——"

But my voice failed.

3

When I asked Thorhall Hunter if he would school me in the use of the beautiful broadsword, I feared an angry refusal. Instead he grumbled a little about wasting time on a Christian flute tootler, then set about the chore with great eagerness. To my surprise he also had a broadsword, made by a smith at Dorstaad, although not to compare with mine in workmanship or the edge and the sheen of its steel. I supposed I should not have been surprised, I told myself. No doubt he had carried and wielded this sword when he was a young Viking, like as not harrying the Christian coasts from Rhine Mouth to Tiber, and I reckoned it had drunk a hogshead of blood. Surely he would no more part with it than an old drake will part with his duck wife in a pond.

He showed me how to grip the hilt and how to stand. Then he challenged me to stick him with my point, provided I could fetch it before he knocked away my blade. This was my first lesson in swordsmanship, yet I came nearer to meeting his challenge than I, and I believe he, had expected. Indeed I came so near to it once—my point falling short a bare inch of stabbing him in the upper arm—that we both fell back. Even so, it seemed my own will rather than his parry had kept my thrust from going home. True, I had sharp, quick vision and of course the agility of a vigorous, outdoor boyhood; yet Thorhall was a wonderfully lively man with longer reach. I reckoned he was out of practice and had played too carefully to avoid cutting me.

We fell to again, and for a third part of an hour made a pleasant clatter with our swords. Then, panting and sweating, we stopped to drink of an ice-cold spring in the pasture. Then we sat down on the soft spring grass. This was rich grass, good belly timber

for sheep and cattle, the main source of our livelihoods, for there
was no other crop worth speaking of in Iceland, the land being
bereft of timber except dwarf willow and birch. Even so, we
could not have lived here except for our harvest from the sea,
such as seals, whales, walrus, and a multitude of fish.

"What is the name of your sword?" I asked, watching him
wipe away a film of mist that had condensed on the blade.

"I was young when I got him, so I gave him a brave name—
White Snake."

"I reckon you couldn't count the foemen that White Snake
has bit."

Thorhall glanced into my face, looked away, swallowed, and
then fixed his close-lidded steel gray eyes on mine.

"Yes, Leif, I can. Three."

"Only three dead?"

"Two were wounded, and their comrades carried them off the
field. That was in a battle on the shores of the River Maas. We
won that battle but dared not sack Rotterdam because of an army
of North Frisians, mainly Danes, moving in on us. In that raid
our little fleet of thirty ships lost eight, and our loot would not
build a tower for the lying spaewomen who sold us winds. I
made one other raid, my ship and forty-four others—forty-five in
all, a lackey number. We struck at Rouen, in Normandy, and we
struck with fury, for the people there were once Norsemen
who've turned French. But we were beaten back."

It took me a long time to speak, and it took courage.

"What does it mean, Thorhall?"

"No one has told you? Well, we speak of it little in Iceland.
What it means is that the Viking tide has turned back for about
seventy years. Don't ask me what caused it. What makes the tides
of the sea turn back? Partly it was the growing strength of the
Christian kings. Partly it was our falling away from Odin, the
God of Warriors, and turning to the God of Farmers. The Northland no longer overflows with what my grandsires called Shore
Virgins, young men, tall, and yellow-haired, aching in every joint
to harry the Christian coasts. Our yards build merchant ships,
not the Long Snakes of battle. But the tides of the sea, when

they've ebbed to the outmost mark, start to flow again. Our tide will flow again, the Northland tide, the horde of Northmen shouting over their shields, shouting the great shout to Odin. And the time has almost come."

Then Thorhall's spirit drew away from mine, and his glittering eyes turned dark, and he was lost in thought. I fingered my sword, but somehow it did not look as bright as at first. At last Thorhall spoke.

"The beginning could be made here, in Iceland. There are twenty great chiefs, three thousand franklins, twenty-five thousand souls in all. Our first boats would be of walrus hide, braced with whalebone. I've seen one stranded on our north coast, big enough for twenty rowers, but what became of the folk who had manned her, or from what land they had been gale-blown, only Odin knows. Such boats would be a wondrous thing for sealing and walrus hunting and even whaling. They would roll with the seas, they'd be swifter than our wooden craft, they'd not crack open if they bumped a berg, and would be easy to haul across strands. With harder work and a greater catch, and a greater harvest of hides, we could import more lumber. Suppose our franklins bound themselves to build three hundred dragon ships in the next five years. We've got good shipbuilders, good men to man the vessels. They'd rendezvous and victual at the Orkneys, closer to the French and Frisian coast than our own Bergen. And why do I tell you this, a boy not quite fifteen? Can you guess?"

"No."

"Because you're the son of Eric the Red, and Eric's the greatest chief in Iceland and the only one with the strength of will and mind to command the fleet. Who would be his right-hand man? Your mind jumps at once to your brother Thorstein, a better sailor, a better harpoonist, winner in every game he plays. Well, I'll tell you why I've picked you instead of him. The men will never follow him through a Hel of storm and battle. His manner is too lofty, his ways too grand. You would think that some lord from Rome, visiting the king's court nineteen years ago, found his way into Thorhild's bed. Vikings won't put up with slights of any kind. They want a great captain, and they'll fight beside him and die to the last man, but they know not how to flatter or how to cringe."

"You say you've chosen me to be Eric's lieutenant. If Eric makes the choice, as I reckon he will, 'twill be Thorstein."

"Eric loves him more, that I grant. He has Eric's weakness, a Hel-hot temper, although he controls it better, and his main strength, the will to win. Maybe Eric looks up to him more, for his lordly ways, but he must know that these would be his downfall as a leader of men. The fact is, the way Eric feels about each of his two sons is a rune hard to read. I know he scorns what he calls the weak side of you that you took from your mother. The side that came out when you put the splint on the old ewe's broken leg instead of slaughtering her as Eric bade you. He has never been able to conquer Thorhild, and maybe he feels he can never conquer you; and that he can't bear. Yet he heard the prophecy of Thorbiorg, Little Witch, sitting on her high seat, that some day you'd be lord of a strand longer than all Norway's. If he can't be such a lord himself, it stands to reason that he would crave such greatness for his son."

I too had heard the prophecy. Thorbiorg had made it at our great feast of the winter solstice, when last year turned back. She had worn her dark blue coat set with little stones, black lambskin cap, and catskin gloves, and in one hand was her knobbed staff and in the other her bag of charms, so she had been fitted out to soothsay, as indeed she had often done, but that night when she finished telling my fortune she had hiccupped loudly from drinking too much heath-honey mead. The mundane sound had seemed to me to gainsay her glorious augury.

"What you say of Eric doesn't stand to my reason," I answered Thorhall. "I think if I ever stood higher than he, he'd try to knock me down. Maybe I misjudge him. I hope so. But of one thing I am sure. That weakness you spoke of, that I sucked in with my mother's milk, would keep me from being a good Viking. I can never lead a mob—no, I'll say an army, for they kept rank and obeyed orders—an army of marauders to sack and burn helpless towns, kill the people, and play jokes on their corpses."

"Both of your grandsires were marauders, as you call them. The towns they sacked and burned were mainly Christian. And for speaking of them the way you did, I'll give you the side of my sword, if it's the last blow I ever give you."

Then he struck me hard in the side and, in a furious trot, made off.

4

The chill but beautiful Icelandic summer was not yet in full flush. I was not even a good tyro yet in the craft of the sword, and the sounds my flute gave forth made Eric plug his ears, when there occurred an event so large in my fate that my fate was revealed as utterly apart from what I had ever dreamed.

It had cast no shadow before. The weather was ordinary for this time of year, with thin mist clouds blowing, so that our great, rough mountains dimmed and brightened in my sight. I was up a small, swiftly tumbling river, spearing salmon which my mother gutted and strung. A band of my father's eaters, one freeman and four thralls, were building a sheep pen at his shouted orders. On the steep mountainside a lone, squat figure of a man, often hidden by mist, was rolling down small boulders for the work crew to pick up and set in the pen's walls. Although I had not seem him assigned the labor, and his distance from me was nearly half a mile, I was almost sure he was an Irish slave Eric had bought from his great friend, Einer, and whose name was Kol. The price had not been high. Kol laughed too loudly at any joke, although Einer swore he had uttered the harsh outcry only rarely before he had passed into Eric's power. His eyes were round and pale and sometimes looked vacant; his short-cut hair appeared bristly. Yet he was immensely strong and a steady worker. In truth he did not know his strength.

Perhaps in trying to unearth a stone of the right size he had dislodged a large stone. Such accidents had happened before. Perhaps a dwarf dwelling in some cave nearby made magic in sport or wickedness for, when the bounding boulder had rolled and bounded to the valley floor, it did not stop rolling, and as though by malicious aim it sped on and struck the new-raised wall. Such was its force, undreamed of, that the strong structure fell in ruin.

Laughing loudly, a dreadful sound in the deep silence that followed the crash, the very wind ceasing to whine, Kol ran down the mountain. My father, Eric the Red, ran to meet him, and in his hand was a long bar of iron that he had been using to tamp turf into the chinks between the stones. I heard my mother utter a deep gasp, then swiftly turn and look away. My vision must have been the same as hers, for I glanced once more at a salmon I had been watching ascend the shallows in powerful bursts, then I forced my eyes again to the two men drawn swiftly closer to each other by their joined fate.

The word "fey" as used by the old Norse meant death-doomed. Its sign was often high revelry by the soon-to-die, or at least a blitheness of spirit, the face flushed, the eyes holding a drunken shine. Lately many folk applied it to persons with prophetic powers or mere second sight, or even with queerness of varied sort, but my father never did so, nor did Thorhall. And the thought flashed to me now, while Eric and Kol were still a stone's toss from each other, that at last I knew the reason for the thrall's frequent shouted laugh and his wild laughter now. Perhaps deep and close within his soul he, too, had known.

A great gust of wind picked up and hurled away the mist clouds, so that the two comrades of the event, lifted and hurled by some wind stronger and more strange, showed sharply clear and clean cut. Eric wore fine woolen cloth almost as red an his beard, the common attire of great thanes; Kol's garments were of rough friz, a dull gray in color, and since the vividness of both men in the wind-brushed air was like that of swans floating on turquoise blue ice water, they too suggested birds of some rare sort, wingless, long-legged, swift chasers of grasshoppers and butterflies, one of them flamboyant, the other drab-looking but perhaps a more momentous figure at the last counting. They loomed against the deep, rich green of the damp grass.

The great lord came in reach of his thrall. He struck with his iron rod, and the fellow crumpled. What other conclusion

could there have been? So I looked not far off but close by to
the still up-struggling salmon. With narrowed eyes and steady
hand I raised my three-pronged spear. The fish saw me now and
thought to dart past me in a still shallow, so he could gain the
waters of his birthplace and there spawn and prolong his noble
line. Too late he seemed to realize that the time was too reduced,
I stood too close, my arm was already sweeping down, that this
was the moment the minutes of his life had raced toward, minutes sometimes long-drawn, sometimes almost spilled in haste,
but of like goal. So he turned on his side, so that the gay sunlight
gleamed upon his wondrous silvery scales as the cruel prongs
thrust deep. So it came to pass that he died in a silver shining
blaze, and this, too, I thought was a form of laughter.

Lifting him on my spear, and of good weight he was, I carried
him to my mother to be gutted and strung. She looked me in
the eyes. Her face was very white but calm. She stood at her
full height.

"You must go and look at him, Leif."

"Who, my father?"

"I meant to go and look at what is left of Kol."

"I don't want to see it."

"My son, do you think you can go on spearing fish? Sometimes a moment strikes when the work or play must be put aside,
and that moment has struck."

"Very well. I will go."

"We will both go."

We went, and my father glared at me in what seemed deep
hate, but his eyes wavered ere they met Thorhild's eyes, and he
wiped his mouth on his sleeve.

"He broke down our fence with his clumsy bungling, one we've
been a-building all yesterday and since *Midur Morgan* today,"
Eric growled in his red beard. "Even so, I believe I would have
spared him if he had not laughed. He ran down the hill laughing like a loon. Anyhow, he was my slave, for him I had bought
and paid, and could do with him as I pleased."

"He was your slave," my mother answered, "but a hundred
years ago he would have made a good Viking. His thick head

would not have impeded him greatly, since his body was so strong. And, like a great Viking, he laughed at death." She turned quietly to me. "Leif, look now at the head that Kol wore on his corded neck, supported by his broad and manly shoulders."

I did so, at last, and my skin crawled.

"Of what does it remind you?"

"Of the giant clams we sometimes dig in the sand, and which revelers, in haste to get at the meat baked in the strand fire, break open with stones. But the juice of the giant clam is milky, and Kol's juice is more red than Eric's beard."

"'Tis a good description."

"And what else do you say, Leif?" my father asked. "You know something that wants saying. I see it in your face."

"I'm of a mind to go with Kris, and I think I will."

5

The thralls of the building crew stood in a close group, with dull faces, leaning a little forward, their arms dangling, their hands hanging open. The long gust of wind dropped down, and the pale mist drifted in, so that the rough front of the mountain softened and seemed to recede into dim distance. Eric stood erect, still grasping the bloody rod in a powerful grasp, and his whole figure was one of power, for whatever his thoughts might be, whether of remorse or self-justification, but not likely of shame and certainly not of fear, he would not give show of them in his face. At last my mother spoke.

"Eric, I must go to our mead hall," she said quietly.

She had employed the old Norse word for the habitation of a great thane, although scanty and weak was the mead poured in any Icelandic home, even at the feast of the winter solstice.

"Very well," he answered.

"My women and I will make a shroud for him who was Kol. And if you wish to go with the thralls to dig a grave, Leif will remain with the dead one until you return."

"Aye, I do. We'll dig him a deep grave, and over it build a cairn. By Thor's beard, we'll use the very stones that he knocked down, in honor of his strength that sent yon great boulder rolling."

My mother departed mildly, as she did all else. My father strode away, his thralls shuffling after him. I was alone except for the dead, but not for long. Some freemen and other thralls from a nearby field had heard the boulder's crash followed by long silence; and since even small accidents are made much of in the long-drawn uneventful Icelandic days, they trooped in to find out what had happened. At their first glance at a greater ruin their eyes rounded under furrowed brows, and some gazed briefly and some long, and not a man there flinched from the full sight and made not one sound.

Thorhall came soon at his bull-like trot. No doubt he had met my mother on the path and she had told him the news, because his face had changed color in an odd way. Soon I perceived it was only a paleness that glimmered through the weathering. Yet I was shaken that any news told by God or man could make Thorhall blanch.

He gave me a piercing glance, then hastened toward the place of the gravedigging. Across the long meadow I saw my father greet him, I thought with both hands open, and the chieftain and his reeve moved out of hearing of the diggers and squatted on the turf to talk. Other talk was being made in and about our home acre, mainly quiet, but perhaps of great bearing on our lives. It so chanced that half a dozen wenches, eaters of neighbor franklins, were at Ericsholm helping cleanse wool of the spring shearing. No doubt some of them took off for home, flushed with excitement, and had well-nigh run the whole distance, for in three hours after my mother's departure visitors came from farther homesteads, and their number slowly swelled into a crowd.

Kol had met death an hour before *Hadegi* which was three hours before our noon. By *Midur Morgan*, three hours after noon, every franklin dwelling within four leagues had assembled here, some of them summoned by the smoke signals of their neighbors, and among them were three great chieftains, Harafn, Ketil, and Bjorn. At *Nattmal*, three hours before *Midnaetti*, with the sun still high and shining, came Ring Ivarsson, the Law Speaker of the Fifth Court, higher than the Quarter Courts, himself not a great chief but a franklin under Endride, who was second to Eric in power and his close friend.

Ring looked upon the dead and the iron rod that dealt death, and then gave leave for the burial and the erection of the cairn. Thereafter the whole assembly convened before our mead hall, and seal-oil fires were lighted in stone lamps, and bonfires of oil-soaked driftwood, and cooking fires for boiling seal meat and the roasting on great spits of three steers that Eric had ordered slaughtered. At the ensuing funeral feast, Harafn, Ketil, and Bjorn ate the baked beef hearts served them by my mother's hand; she and my father and my brother Thorstein ate the tongue; the Law Speaker and Thorhall and I ate succulent backstrap; the visiting franklins ate of the carcasses as they chose, free folk devoured what remained, and thralls and their families filled up on boiled seal meat and smoked fish.

Such was the order of eating in Iceland, and if Eric had pressed the choice tongues upon neighbor franklins, they would have been ashamed. Still there seemed to me one anomaly in the precedence, however its rightfulness by the rules of rank. The prettiest woman present, second to Thorhild my mother, sat among the thralls with her red-bearded husband, Horkel, and their little daughter, Swanhild. She was Ellen, one of my father's thralls. Her darkly brooding eyes made me think that she, too, sensed some unnatural injustice. Her raven hair, cut short according to the custom imposed upon thralls, was in dramatic contrast to the blond heads about her. Her child, not more than nine or ten, had inherited none of her brunette beauty, nor much of her father's redness either; instead, her tints were like those of our northern sunrise, pink and pale gold.

Unable to keep my eyes from them very long, I noticed that Ellen never dipped her hand into the big pots of boiled seal and made her meal of smoked fish laid out on wooden trays. Her little daughter imitated her in this, although lubberly Horkel stuffed all the edibles he could reach and hold. To please them, and especially to please pretty Ellen, I made a little nest of grass and put in it six eider-duck eggs baked in the ashes, which I set before them.

Coarse-faced Horkel had eyes only for the eggs. I guessed how his mind worked—if he could pick up four of them, there would still be one each for his wife and daughter.

"There are two apiece," I said quickly.

"Thank you, young master," Ellen answered in a very deep and, I thought, lovely voice. "You are still young, but you seem to have grown two inches since I saw you last."

"I am nine inches over five feet, as tall as my father, Eric."

I said it because I could think of nothing more apt to say. Ellen was gazing straight into my eyes, and hers looked shiny black under her bold, black eyebrows slightly raised, and I felt pricklings across my neck and down my spine. She had grown younger since I had looked at her last, or so it seemed. Surely she was no more than twenty-five, having married at fourteen according to the gossip of old Thorey, my mother's loom woman; and her dark face had the cast and freshness of a girl of eighteen.

This was most strange, considering that my father, Eric, never spared her from the hardest labor in the fields, such as cutting hay, raking it, and then pitching it on a flat wagon with sides racked with walrus ribs and hauled by oxen. She had six of our milk cows to care for, all of them far roamers and kickers, which she must milk mornings and evenings, lug the milk and skim its cream, which she churned into butter. Yet always she had a neater appearance than the other thrall women, often wearing wild flowers, and I had never seen her with a dirty face.

"Then you are three inches taller than me," she told me, with the same look in her eyes.

Meanwhile her daughter, Swanhild, had given me no word or glance as she hungrily eyed the eggs. Only when Ellen's hand stole out and gave her leg a sharp pinch did she mind her manners. And these were manners better suited to a franklin's daughter than a thrall's child, her choice of words unsuited to her station, and the free way she spoke them and her lilting voice deserved a sharp rebuke according to Island ways.

"Thank you, Master Leif, for thinking of us and giving us a treat fit for thanes."

I withdrew with some awkwardness, and now and then thereafter I stole glances at Ellen, and always she seemed to catch them and give me a half-smile or a gay little toss of her head.

That it was I, not my brother, Thorstein, who received these attentions so new and flattering from so pretty a young woman, made me yearn to be more worthy of them, so I fell to thinking of Little Witch's strange prophecy. The spaewoman was here tonight, plainly dressed and without her charm-bag staff, showing that she was to be treated merely as an eater at the feast. A small, fair woman with sharp features and enormous pale eyes, she had taken her seat just below the families of franklins but above the lesser free folk. And presently I decided to make her some little offering as several franklins had done.

It happened that I had in my pouch a pretty piece of what we called goldstone, bought cheap in Norway, although rather rare in Iceland and used to make beads and to decorate clasp pins. This I gave her with the bow owed to spaewomen by thanes and thralls alike.

"I will ask for you good gifts from Thor," she told me in her chirping childish voice.

"I know not whether my God is to be Thor, or Odin, or Kris."

"Leif, you cannot hunt with the cat and run with the mice. But when you make your choice, or be chosen, it will be forever."

"Will I journey soon on the gray sea?"

"Soon and late."

"Can you give me a hint of my fortune, even though the spell song has not been sung and you have not your charm bag? I do not mean happenings far off, but soon."

"I will tell you this, but not another word. I dare not speak another word than this tonight, lest my head fall to aching and my belly turn inside out. In due course you will be known as Lucky Leif."

Then her lips curled in a forlorn and touching smile, as though to tell me that this course would be long, steep, and strange.

6

At last the pots and trays were emptied, the bones gnawed and their marrow sucked, and when the pale twilight had appeared to brighten the dying cooking fires, we wiped our chins and cleaned our greasy hands with damp moss. Now the fires were again fed, and I did not know why until all faces turned with a happy look to a youth who was rising at Einer's whispered word. I had seen him only twice before, at Einer's homestead. He had lately come from the Orkney Islands, and through kinship with Einer's wife he had become Einer's eater. A finely bred young man, with large brilliant eyes and a mouth as tender as a lovely woman's, his carriage suggested agility and strength as he moved to the front of our throng. Einer's rugged face beamed with pride.

I had heard too that Ian was a taleteller, but had never dreamed that in our own neighborhood we had one so gifted until he began to recite in his rich voice Half's saga, greatly beloved in Iceland. It was not quite in the same form we had heard before and was more nobly phrased. I thought that his voice could be compared to an instrument of music which he could play as some master, who had studied long in Rome and taken lessons from turban-wearing masters at Granada and at Constantinople, and at Alexandria, could play a wondrous flute. It would be one of no more stops than mine, yet which sang deep and strong as gale-driven surf beating on implacable rock could sing under its roarings, or as strange and wild as intrepid climbers of Hekla hear in the hall of the Mountain King, or as delicate and dreamy as I had heard from a chorus of elves when I had wakened one summer night.

When Half said farewell to his aged dam, our women wept, and when he went forth to his last battle and died by a hurled spear while standing atop a heap of his slain, shouting to Odin, there was hardly a man among us, thane or thrall, whose hand did not ache for a sword hilt and whose heart did not flame and whose soul did not yearn for the Viking's choice, mighty conquest or bloody death.

When Ian had recited the last beauteous lines, and we too could almost hear the chorus of the Valkyries as they bore the hero to Valhalla on their white steeds, most of us were too moved to shout or even clap our hands. But the great lord Bjorn took a silver cup from his pouch and poured into it a purple liquid from a horn he wore on his side and, with his own hands, passed it into Ian's hands.

Thereafter we yawned, and all the company sought the boon of sleep.

The visiting chiefs and franklins made their beds on sheepskins stretched on the hard-packed dirt floor of our hall. Freemen lay on cowhides about the fires, and the bonded folk went to the earthen huts of our thralls for such sleep as they could find. It would not be long. The Law Speaker had announced that his court would convene at *Midur Morgan,* when the sun, giving short shrift to our summer night, would be only three hours high.

Throughout our rest, beacon fires blazed on the headlands and hilltops, and before sunrise franklins and freemen began arriving from distant homesteads, either astraddle Shetland horses or in small sailing craft or longboats rowed by thralls, which had put into our fiord. Of these, our Law Reader made a careful count, revealing fifty-four franklins from our quarter of the island, which number was a majority of the Hundred moot that could hold the Fifth Court, the verdicts of which were above repeal. If fifty-one of these fifty-four agreed on punishment for a breaker of a law, the Law Reader would pass sentence. This did not mean that sentence would be enforced. More than once, thanes of less power than Eric the Red had flouted or defied the rulings; yet always they had paid a high price in lowered name and fame.

The Law Speaker put on a furred cap and a small scarf of white weasel skins with black tails. It seemed to me he stood taller than before, and his bearing became worthy of a prince. The fifty-four members of the moot, sitting at ease on the ground, stopped their murmur of talk. The great chieftains Harafn, Ketil, and Bjorn stood apart, refusing to pass judgment on an even greater fellow chieftain.

"Most of you descend from Vikings," the Law Speaker began in grave, manly tones. "Those sea rovers had their own law, savage and proud, and, in Christian thinking, wicked. Yet they would die before they would break it. This island has good laws, fitted to our ways, and one of them—that no franklin or even a great chieftain may take the life of his thrall unless that thrall threatens his master's life, injures him, his wife, or his children, is caught stealing, or is overtaken in an attempt to escape. It may be that yesterday this law was wantonly broken. To establish the truth I will call witnesses. Those immediately on the scene were the freeman Starkad and the thralls Snorri, Thori, Olaf, and Oddson. The old law that thralls cannot testify against their lord was rescinded by the Althing of Iceland. However, they cannot be forced to testify against their wills."

I thought none would dare testify against a master as violent and revengeful as Eric the Red. I could not have been more wrong. To each in turn, as he stood calm, his head erect, his arms bowed a little with his hands closed, his quiet eyes fixed on the questioner's face, the Law Reader asked three questions.

"Will you speak or be still?"

"Lord, I will speak," was the invariable answer.

"When the thrall Kol had caused a great boulder to roll down the mountainside and strike a sheep pen his master was building, then Kol ran down, did you see Eric the Red run to meet him and strike him on the head with a tamping bar?"

"Lord, I did."

"Do you know whether Kol caused the boulder to roll down by accident, as a rude jest, or in malice? If you have not certain knowledge, or good grounds for your opinion which you will recite in this court, answer that you do not know."

"Lord, I do not know."

"Starkad, Snorri, Thori, Olaf, and Oddson, you may draw back. There remains to be established, beyond reasonable doubt, whether the boulder was rolled by accident or on purpose and, in case of the latter, what was that purpose. Those most likely to know are Eric the Red himself, his reeve Thorhall, his wife, Thorhild, who, as do all good wives of thanes and franklins, knows well the thralls

of the homestead, and his two sons. It is the ancient law of
Iceland that no man charged with a crime of blood need testify
although, before the moot passes judgment, Eric the Red may
ask to speak, in which case his request will be granted. I cannot
summon Thorhild because it is the ancient law of the Althing that
a wife may not testify for or against her husband, regardless of her
desire. I may call his older son, Thorstein, his reeve, Thorhall,
and his younger son, Leif, and these three may speak if they so
desire, but because two sprang from Eric's loins and the third is a
franklin in his own right and is pledged in fealty to Eric, they may
be still if they so desire. I will call them in order of their rank.
Thorstein, stand forth."

Thorstein did so as though he were a prince. Only three years
older than I and newly turned eighteen, he would not be taken for
my brother by a stranger. Hardly three inches taller than I, he
was built as we picture Balder the Beautiful, somewhat slender,
with a wonderful symmetry and grace. I took after Eric in having
a high, hooked nose; Thorstein had the thin, high-bred nose of
our mother. My mouth was long and thin-lipped and turned down
at the corners, with the dim suggestion of a shark's mouth; his
mouth was short and full and fine. My coarse hair was reddish-
brown, what the old Norse called sorrel, which seemed to mean
the color of dry leaves, while Thorstein's hair was a wavy dark
brown and glossy-looking in the sunlight. Our eyes were completely different in color and setting: mine, long-looking and pale
gray with a dark gray segment, the last being called the Witch's
Mark, his were more open and flashing, and a handsome dark blue.
The fact remained that although he excelled in almost every
game and skill and was in the way of being the hero of the island
in this regard, he had a hard time beating me at seeing. When as
little boys we had gone hunting together, at least half the time
I was the first to spy a wild gander on a distant pool, or a heath
hen half-hidden in heather.

"Thorstein, if you desire to testify, tell the moot whether you
believe the boulder that smashed Eric's pen was rolled down by
mischance," the Law Speaker asked.

"No, sir, I do not."

"Do you believe it was a rude joke?"

"No, your honor. Kol was never a jokester. I think it was done in malice."

The moot was already tense and now a stir passed through it as a random gust of wind stirs the trembling leaves of our stunted birch. The downcast posture of Eric's close friends changed to one of strength. The three great lords, Harafn, Ketil, and Bjorn, seated close to Eric, whose positions would be weakened if he fell, exchanged quick, hopeful glances.

"Against whom?" And now the Lawman spoke in a quiet tone, as was his wont when a trial took a surprising turn.

"Against his master, Eric the Red. He hated all masters, and he hated me, as I learned at last. And while a dullard in many ways, he had one uncanny skill. After a close survey of the ground, he could look at a boulder rounded by glaciers and tell me what course it would take if rolled down a steep hillside. Old Vikings could rise from their graves to tell you that King Ordonos' mountaineers had the same powers. One whole afternoon I watched him do it over Gudredsfiord. I had gone there to harpoon bearded seal. Almost always the boulder passed within ten feet of some mark he had picked out; once his missile actually struck the big stone he indicated, dislodging it, and he laughed till he nearly fell down. I think that hate came over him when he saw that big boulder in line to knock down Eric's new pen, or possibly kill Eric or one of the thralls. But when he had made a clean hit, he was sane enough to run down the hill to plead it was an accident and to beg mercy."

After a brief silence, the Speaker spoke very gravely.

"Thorstein, is there anyone here besides yourself who may bear witness to this uncanny skill you speak of?"

"No, there is not. When I was younger my father, Eric, often went with me a-hunting, taking our thrall Hedric who was killed by a white bear. Later I had but one thrall, Kol."

"You may draw back. And to the moot I say that Thorstein's testimony must be ignored, unless supporting evidence is given by other witnesses. I will give the issue immediate precedence before this court. To that end I will call the great franklin Einer, for it is common knowledge that he owned the thrall Kol before he came, by purchase, into the possession of Eric the Red. Einer, stand forth."

This tall, lank man, Eric's close neighbor and friend, honored by all, told that he had never seen Kol in rude or boisterous play, but his nature had changed since Eric bought him, and he knew not what to think. Of one fact he was sure. Although exceedingly strong, Kol had been a clumsy man.

The Law Speaker next called Thorhall, who, as Eric's reeve, had much to do with the handling and working of our thralls. To Thorhall he put the same question.

Usually so quick and blunt of speech, Thorhall did not answer for some ten beats of my heart. In that interval I gazed upon him, and he had changed since the day before, although I could not perceive where all the difference lay. Perhaps his eyes were more dull than their wont. Perhaps his heavy frame appeared to put more weight upon his feet. His skin looked sallow.

"I knew Kol well," he replied at last, and I thanked the Gods that his voice rumbled as ever. "There was no malice in him, no more than in a milk cow, so if he rolled the rock on purpose it was to scare his fellow thralls, in the way of a joke. So doing, he would risk their lives, and take improper liberties with his lord, and since the rock caused destruction, he would be due a hiding, and I would have given it to him. But he would not be due a killing, and that's that. Moreover, I cannot remember him ever joking in this wise, or joking at all, so in my best opinion the boulder was dislodged by accident."

"In saying that, you must know that it makes the act of Eric all the more black."

"Of course I know it. Do you think I'm a half-wit?"

"Thorhall, you may stand back. And now there remains but one witness to call." Then the Speaker paused, because he saw me bend to my mother's ear to speak in desperate need.

"What shall I say?" I whispered. "I might save Eric with one lie that won't hurt a dead man. At least I could raise a doubt in the moot men's minds. What shall I do?"

"You descend from Harald Bluetooth and are the son of Eric

the Red, great although lame. You are almost a man grown. Do
as a full man."

I had hardly time to look into Thorhild's steadfast eyes and to
catch my breath when I heard my name called.

"If you will testify, did you see the death of Kol?"

"Yes, lord, I did."

"Was it as described by the thralls?"

"Yes, it was."

"Do you agree with Thorstein that Kol hated his master?"

When I hesitated, I heard my father's bawling voice that
rang about the pasture.

"Answer him, Leif. Have you lost your tongue?"

"Eric, you are out of order," the Speaker told him with quiet
force. "No man may interrupt or seek to influence a witness
testifying before the moot. Leif, I will reword my question. Speak
or be still, as you will. Do you believe Kol hated his master,
Eric?"

"No, I do not."

"Have you ever seen him commit an act of malice?"

"Not one."

"Was he given to playing loutish and dangerous jokes?"

"He laughed at other men's jokes but never made any."

"Leif Ericsson, stand back."

White in the face, I obeyed. The scene swam before my eyes,
and that saved me from looking at my father, at Thorhall, or
even at Thorstein.

"I, the Law Speaker, will now charge ye of the moot trying
Eric the Red for murder or manslaughter, however you deem it,
of his thrall Kol. Remember in your deliberations that the old
Viking law, whereby a thane holds the power of life and death
over his boughten thralls, has been dead this hundred years. Aye,
you must disregard Eric being a great chieftain, and Kol little
more than a chained slave. In your deliberations you may consider
the fiery fury that comes upon Eric all too often and consider
whether, at such times, he is in his perfect mind; at the same time
recall that he committed manslaughter in Norway, for which he
was banished from his native land. Today you have heard con-

tradictory evidence, but you must not act on that which you wish to believe, but on that which is least open to doubt, and the best supported. I appoint the great franklin Einer your foreman, and when the majority of your number votes to end your deliberations and pass sentence, you will vote on the several courses of action open to you, an upraised right arm as a sign for yes, the arm unlifted meaning no. If fifty-one or more of your number agree on any one course, whether it be that the defendant be hanged, banished for a term of years or for life, or go free, that agreement becomes the finding of this moot, irrevocable and beyond repeal. If fifty of your number so agree, I will cast a vote by right of Icelandic law. If only a number less than fifty can so agree, the defendant must stand trial again before the Althing at moot hall. And your foreman, Einer, will tally the votes by marks of his knife on the blade of an oar in our ancient custom."

He turned and walked out of hearing of the moot with my father and the three great lords at his heels, my mother and we witnesses and all the spectators hard after. This was not a matter of law, but of good custom, of good manners one might say, and we did not watch the lifting of arms being counted. In a third part of an hour we heard Einer's voice bawling through a birch-bark horn.

"My lord, the Law Speaker! We have reached a verdict."

So we returned to our places, and to judge by his look and carriage Eric the Red was the least concerned of us, but this I took to be his proud show.

"Will the moot rise, in affirmation of the verdict which your foreman will now pronounce?" the Speaker asked. And fifty-four franklins heaved themselves to their feet, grave of demeanor, men to make me proud of the Nordic race. "Einer Lothbrok, speak."

"By a vote of fifty-two to two, we have found Eric the Red guilty of manslaughter and we give him until the autumn equinox to collect his goods and chattels and ready his ship; then he shall go into exile from Iceland for the remainder of his days, with his thralls and such of his freemen and franklins that choose to follow him. Howbeit, it is the verdict of this moot that he may not be barred from trade with Icelandic dwellers, his ship may come and go, and he himself may set foot upon our strands but not pass beyond them; and these decisions we have reached in solemn conclave, our heads ruling our hearts, and may they be pleasing to our Gods, to our great chieftains, and to the folk."

A great silence fell. It was the time of year and the time of day for grass beetles to make their strumming sound, but they were mute, and so were the winds arrested in their murmurous flow. I gazed at my father's face, set like flint, and at his short but massive form that an ox could not knock down, and suddenly realized how slightly I knew him, for I could not surmise whether he would submit to the moot's verdict or flout it in imperious defiance as other great thanes had done. Then Thorhall took a step toward me and bent a little so that his lips were close to my ear. And why he had chosen me for the first confiding of some great secret of his soul I could not dream, but of the momentousness of the tidings I had no glimmer of doubt.

"Thus dies my dream," he muttered, "and I must find one new."

7

The movement of event could not rest. I had a vision of its never resting again as long as I lived.

White in the face, the Law Speaker drew a deep breath, stood at his full height, and fixed his eyes on my father's eyes.

"Eric the Red, I hearby sentence you to the punishment as decreed by the moot in lawful session. Have you anything to say?"

"My lord, I have much to say." Then Eric paused, no doubt to assemble his thoughts, and it came to me that none of his hearers, even Thorhild, my mother, could safely wager a bucket of seal fat what saying would come forth, the meat of it, let alone its skin of words; and the best spaewoman on the island, called Little Witch, would finger her charms in vain to prophesy it.

"Then speak."

"You, my lord, and all of you in sound of my voice, bear witness. Of this island I am sick and tired. It is not a hard life that we live, and I would wish it ten times as hard, if it were even twice as lively. What Norseman fears hardship if his blood can bound? Is this not true?"

And to what might have been the wonder of some alien here, beholding the solemn court that had just sat, the fair-haired, rugged men with long mustaches shouted in one voice, "Aye! Aye!" And it reminded me of an old grandsire's tale of Vikings mourning one of their number slain in battle, then drinking horns of ale to his soul departed to Valhalla, then of the drink going to their heads, and then the whole band beginning to whoop and jig and play leapfrog.

"There is nothing to do here but watch sheep and cattle and spear seals," Eric the Red rumbled on. "Sometimes we find the long-toothed sea hogs on the floes, and we have a good fight, and sometimes they hook their tusks over our gunwales and well-nigh sink us, and more than once our longboats have been smashed and our thralls killed, and again the blood sparkles in our veins. But soon we have naught to do but return to our dull halls, and we had as well sleep and call it being alive. Sometimes we spy a white bear on his white ship, and a few are lucky, while many watch from the shore, and the most had as well go on cutting grass for cattle fodder. And best of all, for the few of the very fortunate spared the humdrum tasks, there's the chase of a white whale. But in Norway there were wild cattle of wide horn, of temper worse than mine, that attack men on sight. There were elk, with flaring antlers and black bells, and their meat was for a man and a hunter, not like the watery grass-fed beef that we eat here. There were ground bears of great fierceness and red deer of prime venison and lean gray wolves. Gods, but I am sick of mutton! By the Thunder Gods of the Red Beard, I am sick of seal blubber. Our butter and milk and cheese taste like fish; some of our dried fish tastes like sandy driftwood. I hate the dirty dusty winds that blow from the tableland, those deserts which with the snow-fields hold nine-tenths of the island. But men say this is the westernmost land, that beyond the Poison Sea forever raves, and beyond that the oceans pour into Hel. Think you there may be other islands?"

And again the great cry was raised, "Aye! Aye!"

"We Norse have giant strength and want to use it," Eric went on, shouting. "We Norse know the lure of distant, undiscovered lands and I want to follow that lure. Ye remember how my cousin Thorker was blown off his course by an east gale, and nearly three hundred leagues west of our shores he caught sight of what he thought was land. All night he flew before the wind, instead of heaving to with a sea anchor, for a wildness rose in his soul. Aye, he had found the Berserk's Way not in fighting Christians but defying the fury of the storm, and when the dawn broke he could still see what he thought was land, a land greater than Iceland. Some say it was a vast icefield covered with dirt and gravel of moraine. But Thorker died believing he had seen the true west land, the Ultima Thule, as a Christian bishop called it, and belike the abode of devils. And in my dreams I visited it, and it was a green land, and there were five seals to our one, and a hundred walrus to our ten, and whales sported every day in the fiord mouths, and there were other great beasts I did not know."

"Lead us there, Eric the Red," shouted an old franklin through his white beard.

"Mayhap, those of you who sicken of these shores. By the Nine Runes, if it were not for our mountains spouting fire, and earthquakes, and rivers of boiling lava to keep us awake and lively, we would have all gone daft. So to the moot I say, I submit to the punishment of lifelong exile, if indeed it is punishment and not a boon. And while Thorhall collects my goods and chattels, I and some of my followers will set sail, for my ship needs little readying—she ever pines and pants for the Swan Road—and we will sail westward and we will seek this green land, and if we find it I will return to these strands, and I will not cross them as your judgment decreed, but it may be you will cross them to board your own ships. And if ye do, with your families and thralls, and some bulls and heifers, and rams and ewes, and take leave of Iceland, I will lead you to this green land, and we will settle there, and there we will walk new strands, and fill our lungs with new air, and behold sights no warrior of Odin or worshiper of Thor, let alone no Christian, has ever seen."

Then out roared Einer, his eyes agleam.

"I will go with you, old Viking!"

"And I, and I, and I," cried a score of voices.

"It may be that the bergs will crush our ships. It may be we will be washed down to Hel by gales compared to which our raving winds are summer zephyrs. But it may be we will have lived as greatly as Ring, Sigurd, Harald Bluetooth, Ragnar Lothbrok, and Ogier the Dane. And that is life indeed!"

With that, Eric gave his red beard a tug and Thorhild a great hug; then in his powerful stride, his arms bowed and swinging, he made off to his hall.

CHAPTER TWO

DEATH OF A SEA KING

I

If it so fell that I would be invited to sail with Eric on his voyage of exploration in the unknown West, I might have the memory of a strange and thrilling experience to take with me.

As the throng was leaving the scene of the trial, it seemed that by accident dark Ellen brushed close to me. But instantly I knew it was not by accident and instead by a purposeful and deliberate move. She had picked a time when I was a little apart from the others; also a beautiful dark glow of excitement was in her face. At once she spoke, barely above her breath.

"Leif, tomorrow morning at sunrise I will be by Weland's Cooking Pot where you found your new sword. If you can keep a secret and arrange to be there, too——"

She paused. My heart was pounding and I had trouble finding breath to answer.

"I will be there, Ellen, without fail."

She and her daughter disappeared in the assembly. I walked on in a daze of hope and doubt. It happened that the next day I turned fifteen, and I was fairly certain that Ellen meant to give me a birthday gift, but there was only one in her power to give that I ached for, an ache I had felt running through my dreams all the night before, although then it was not nearly as strong as now, when I had some cause to believe it would be satisfied. I could not remember when I had been completely innocent of such achings. Between twelve and thirteen they had come on me often, and had been in some fashion relieved by blissful dreams, and by those dreams I discovered that in this regard I could be counted a full man. Whether or not she intended what I so greatly hoped, the following day I would come to full manhood by the island reckoning; yet what I yearned to have occur would verify the status in a way I would never forget. Afterward would I be ashamed or proud? I could not consider the former; I would only be lying to myself and preparing an excuse for defeat.

We Norsemen had never been guilty-minded about a need as natural as a hungry man's killing a stray sheep. It was true that I gave some little thought to the difference in our ages, perhaps ten years, but dismissed it quickly, for several young men I knew had had their first passage with young widows, and merely thinking of it heightened my fears that I was hoping in vain. True, Ellen was not a widow. She was wedded to one of the most dull-witted and brutish men on the island, perhaps the fault of the Gods or her own fault, but certainly not his fault. Yet strong men take advantage of what the Gods or the fates provide; I had seen this truth exemplified by Eric, and by Thorstein, too, for that matter, when he never let an opponent win in any game or trial. Horkel would probably trade his wife's favor for a mess of sheep kidneys. This fact did not reflect on him, in the light of what he was; my making such a trade might reflect on me. Still I would do it in the light of what I was, as seen by my inmost soul.

The night passed with many wakenings and wonderings on my part. I got up at three, with the light clearing with great acceleration, and told a sleepy milkmaid that I had to go out awhile to see about a fox trap. Then the errant thought crossed my mind that Ellen had set a trap for me, but the only skin she wanted was unimaginably no more than a somewhat better life that she might have by the will of my great friend and mentor, Thorhall, while Eric and, I hoped, I were searching for the green unknown land.

Weland's Cooking Pot, sometimes giving forth steam and smoke and bursts of ash or a little lava, lay about in the middle of a hollow perhaps one hundred paces in diameter. This had been formed by the same subterranean forces as the vent itself, for its rim, about ten feet high, was volcanic rock. Most of the hollow grew dense, rich grass, with quite a number of dwarf birch and willows, their trunks thick in proportion to their heights. Truly it was a perfect spot for a tryst. It was out of the way, far from a worn path, and any wanderer who would chance to come up to the rim would be visible by the lovers long before he would

discover them in the copse. To think of this seclusion excited
me greatly as I made my way there, but it also raised plaguing
doubts in my mind that Ellen would take second thought and fail
to appear. It was not as though she were meeting Thorstein,
whose way with wenches was either a graceful gallantry or, when
he chose, an almost brutal disregard, either of which seemed to
make them hardly more palpitant than the other. Today Ellen's
tryst was with a gawky youth barely fifteen.

Yet when I reached the rim, I thought I saw someone standing
all but concealed by willow branches in full leaf. If so, the
person had hair as black as a raven's wing. I waved my arm and
went on. I had timed the distance well; the rising sun was turning the vast and distant snowfield of Vatnajokull into glimmering
pearl and in a few seconds it heaved up into view. My companion
of the adventure emerged from her screen and, wondrously
light-limbed, came running toward me. She did not appear in the
least abashed and I hoped and well-nigh prayed that I did not.

"Master Leif!" she exclaimed quietly. "You came at the very
moment you promised! When you are older and are used to women
you will not be so punctual or bother to come at all! I am so happy."

"I am mightily happy too."

"But I cannot stay very long. I am supposed to be looking for
old Sigrid, one of my milk cows, that last twilight I tied out of
sight in a willow thicket."

"Why did you choose me, beautiful Ellen?"

"At the night of the feast you gave me your favor, although I
am a thrall woman. This morn I wanted to give you mine, if you've
a wish for it. Besides, there was another reason which I may tell
you, or may not tell you, depending on what happens here."

If that was not an invitation to come up and put my arms about
her waist and kiss her dark red mouth, I did not know what it
was. In any event, that was what I did, awkwardly I suppose,
although leaving no doubt of my joy.

"That was a sweet kiss, my lord, but scanty. Let me show you
how."

Then she kissed me again and again, with ever increasing ardor,
her face beautifully flushed and holding a new kind of beauty I

had not seen before. Her soft and silky tongue began to search mine. Her black eyes began to look very deep and strange. As for me, I became wildly aroused, with such imperious heat as I had never dreamed, and we pressed our bodies together, our hips thrusting.

"Shall we?" she whispered.

"Oh, yes. Quickly."

"It was for that I came here, as you well know. I too am starving. But when I invited you, I asked if you can keep a secret. From every human soul."

"I swear it, by the old God Weland who may be in sound of my voice."

"Then, master, do not make too great haste. In Ireland the women have a saying—I can give it in Gaelic; it is difficult in Norse, yet I will try. 'The boar with his sow is oft a better lover than the princely bridegroom with his bride.' Too much haste is the enemy of pleasure." Yet her hands plied with flurried haste at my buttons and belt.

Quickly she spread her long cloak of rough friz on the damp grass. There we made our bed, and she took no chance on my tyroship; by her own skill she did not permit me to be clumsy or inept. Also her lithe body knew many little tricks of muscle, sometimes arresting the delicious progress toward our goal, sometimes hastening it. When it could no longer be delayed, her eyes rolled up, showing the gleaming whites, and she uttered a long-stifled cry.

And truly my most lascivious anticipations, visiting my dreams and my daydreams, were excelled tenfold.

For a few seconds she lay motionless, as though half-stunned; then she sprang up with a laugh of utmost joy that had a triumphant ring. We both dressed with dispatch, although not with frightened haste; then she came up to me, in happiness impossible to feign, and took my hands.

"I told you, Master Leif, that there was a second reason why I invited you instead of some other."

"Yes."

"In Ireland there is an ancient cult of love that our women

know. They have heard of it, even if not schooled, when their breasts are no bigger than apples—say at twelve or, at most, thirteen. It was said to have been taught us by the Fairy Queen Titania, but that I doubt. One of its dictums is this, translated the best I can into Norse. 'If you can't lie with a younker with down on chin, take a medium elder, with a few silver hairs in his beard.' Do you know, Master Leif, I believe it's good advice!"

"Do you mean I gave you great pleasure, Ellen?" I asked with intense anxiety. "If so, it was not a tithe of the pleasure you gave me!"

"And the last time for how long! In a few days my great master, Eric, will be sailing in search of the new land, and it stands to reason he will take both you and Master Thorstein with him, while my lord Thorhall remains to gather up his goods. Still—who knows what is waiting up the road, even one of our poor Icelandic cart paths, not to speak of the Swan Road of the ships? Now Master Leif, I wish to ask a question I have no right to ask, yet I will boldly venture. Rebuke me if you see fit. Was this, this golden morning, your maiden passage?"

I did not reply for some seconds. I was struck with her command of the Norse language, indeed the power and beauty with which she used it, worthy of a king's son taught by a venerable reader of runes and the poetic utterances of scalds long dead. Instead, she was born a thrall, belonging to a Norse family long settled in Ireland, and the wife of a thrall. So my father had answered my mother when she had protested the laying of so many heavy labors on her back. And if she presumes above her station, Eric had added, his reeve would lay on the whip as well.

In a way of speaking she had presumed above her station today, I was thinking, but how I rejoiced that she did!

"Ellen, this was my maiden flight," I told her, wording it more fitly than I had thought possible.

"I wish it were mine! I wish I were fourteen instead of twenty-four. How differently I would shape my life, and perhaps help to shape yours. And always remember, Master Leif, that what happened today is our secret—ours alone. I cannot tell what would happen if it becomes shared by others. This much I do know. There is death in the pot."

She spoke these strange words quietly, causing a creeping of my whole skin. Then she walked away in her fine, free stride, pausing only at the rim of the hollow to wave her hand.

2

The shouted commands of Eric the Red frightened the plover and the gulls in and about our strand as he victualed and fitted out his ship, *Narwhale,* for exploration into the unknown West. It was only wind that he blew out of his red-bearded lips; yet as a consequence our home acre became busied as a school of herring in shotting time. Pots of boiling seal tar outsmelled the salmon dryer, sailmakers sat all day with crossed legs and plying hands, the backs of thralls bowed under heavy casks, saws scraped and hammers pounded, ropes of walrus hide were flung and made fast to form rigging, and rich franklins stuffing sirloin a league distant wiped their chins in haste to stow their tribute of butter, cheese, salt mutton, eider-duck eggs in brine, walrus-gut garments against breaking seas and rain, skeepskins, and precious planks in the *Narwhale's* hold.

But the rude laughter of Kol, bursting forth at any mishap, was heard no more; and he reckoned he had gone farther than the brave ship would ever sail. I wondered where. Certainly not to the Christian heaven. Although born and raised in Ireland, now largely a Christian land, I had once seen him sacrifice a lamb to the Thunder God with a muttered prayer for what I could not dream. In Valhalla there was no room for thralls, nor any in Avalon, the abode of heroes. But perhaps he had only turned some kind of corner out of our sight, while he still watched with his strange eyes the lading of the ship.

For five days I waited with hungry ears for Eric to invite me to join the ship's company, meanwhile diligent at my allotted tasks. In the performance of these I often encountered Ellen, and always she lowered her head a little in deference to my rank, while only a small quick crooked smile was for me alone. Then

the thought struck me that if Eric left me out there was someone
here to take me in, in many a triumphant and delectable stolen
hour; still it would be no real consolation for a perilous adventure in unknown seas. I could wait for my turn at making love,
and to a maiden more suited to my own youth. On the other hand
a voyage of discovery of a yet unknown land would not be made
again in the history of mankind.

It did not take me long to learn that my brother, Thorstein,
would join the company. Indeed he had sat long with Eric, helping
him to shape his plans, on the night following the trial. My
father's silence persisted as to my going or being left on shore, and
when I spoke of the matter to Thorhall, he looked glum.

"Maybe Eric's too busy to speak of it, and maybe he wants
you to stay ashore with me to help assemble his goods for moving,
and most likely he thinks you're too green."

"I can do a man's work."

"Then why not speak out like a man, and ask him his bent?"

So when my father sat long at table over a bowl of purple
wine shipped in a wineskin from Norway, and he and I were alone
in the hall, I rallied my courage, the job taking more than I had
thought, and spoke out.

"My father, am I to go on the *Narwhale* in search of the green
land?"

He took a deep draught and wiped his beard. Then he turned
a little on his bench, even this little movement of his thick body
one of power, and his small eyes, green as submerged ice, gazed
into mine.

"Why, I hadn't thought of it," he said.

"Will you think of it now?"

"I am, but most of my thoughts are adverse. You're not a deep-
water sailor, although you handle your little sailing skiff well
enough in the fiord. You are good at harpooning seals, and you've
done well at the walrus hunting, but you've never stood up to a
white bear or sunk your shaft in a whale. In your left iris there's
a segment darker gray than the rest, which we call the Witch's
Mark. A few say it's a sign you were born lucky, but the most

believe that both eyes will be darkened while you're still young. Leif, I can use only lucky men on a sail like this."

"Thorbiorg, Little Witch, told me at the funeral feast that some day I'd be known as Lucky Leif."

"I heard her say so. But did you see her smile? It had a crook in it I'd not seen before." Eric passed his blunt but heavy hand across his brow. "Let that go," he went on hastily. "If you went with us, Leif, what can you offer to earn your passage?"

"Hard work, fair weather or foul."

"That is not enough. Any cattle drover can give that. But I'll give you a chance to supply what's a sore need. My ship is the *Narwhale*, but you'd never know it by the look of her. You've seen a few narwhales; you were hunting seals that day Thorhall narrowly missed harpooning one. Have you ever thought we haven't a narwhale horn stuck in our stem to give her luck to fool the Fog Giant that walks the icefields on calm days? If you'd supply us that, I'd ship you gladly."

Well I remembered the narwhale that had escaped Thorhall's swift harpoon. He was perhaps twenty feet long, seven or eight of this measurement being an ivory horn thrusting from his mouth. What was the use of it was unknown even to old Norse who, trapped by ice while walrus hunting, spent half a year at the North Cape. Certainly the horn was not used to attack boats, as did swordfish that Vikings had met in the great inland sea of Rome. His head was small and lumplike, his body burly.

If a narwhale tusk could thrust from the stem of the good ship *Narwhale* when she ventured forth on the Swan Road it would be a splendid thing. The quest of such a horn would be a noble quest. But fury fired my heart and made hoarse my voice as I answered my great sire, Eric the Red.

"How can I get one? It is too late. You haven't given me enough time."

"To tell the truth, I didn't think of it till this minute. The notion wouldn't have struck me now, save for a report I heard from a sailor about an hour ago. You could rightly ask why I did not buy a narwhale horn—a dozen or more have been brought ashore since I came to Iceland—or dispatch Thorhall Hunter to take one out of the sea. I deemed it that I, or some man of my line, father or son, must himself capture the beast and unroot his horn, or the Sea Gods, Njord and the rest, would not give good fortune to our prow, but evil fortune. The cares of the homestead filled my days; Thorstein never crossed the wake of a narwhale in all his roamings. Until lately you were a strapling, but suddenly you are more of a man than I thought. As for time, where the school of narwhale was seen is two days' sail, there and return. They were on the shallow bank behind Gull Nest Island, I suppose attracted there by devilfish, uncommon thick this year. You can take with you a thrall or even a friend to sail the boat while you're harpooning and bringing your prize alongside. Perhaps I could spare Thorstein long enough to go with you."

"No. He's such a hungry hunter he'd try to snatch the harpoon from my hands."

"Why, I think you're right," Eric answered with a dim, well-satisfied smile.

"Instead I'll ask Ian, the poem speaker. At the feast he told me that he loved to sail and had a boat of his own in the Orkneys. It comes to me that the Gods love him and if he is my companion, they may smile on the enterprise."

My sire looked a little taken aback, although I could not guess why, then gave his hearty assent.

3

I meant to start at *Midur Morgan* the next day. Before the dimness of that same evening I had addressed Ian, whose splendid face lighted at my proposal. Since Einer, Ian's master, held his lands in fief to Eric, there was no doubt of his consent, and happily I tramped homeward. But before I slept, my joy was slaked somewhat by a chance meeting with Thorhall.

I had not intended to tell him of the next day's venture. I had wanted to take him by surprise when my little sailing skiff, *Whistling Swan*, returned to our home strand, riding gunnel-deep from the weight of a mighty tusk. But a sudden worry over the ways that narwhales sounded, and perhaps a boyish impulse, prompted me to speak.

"Did Eric say Gull Nest Island?" Thorhall asked, amazement in his voice, when I had told him my plans.

"Yes. He said that bank teemed with devilfish."

"It teems with toadfish, conger eels, and sea lice. Maybe he meant to say Sea Mist Bay. If he'd said that, there would be sense to it. Besides, it's not half as far and the flowing tide and our coastal current would bring you home, your sail stowed and your oars out, if the wind's contrary. You would never make out and back to Gull Nest Island in two days, with the best winds gold can buy. Does Eric expect a narwhale to turn on his side and cast his soul when the harpoon strikes home? Small as he is, and rarely sounding, and never charging the boat, yet he'll give you an all-night haul unless he spouts blood. Why, Leif, you'd be lucky to get back, empty-handed, in four days."

Then Thorhall's face darkened and his tone changed to a deep rumble.

"Go to Sea Mist Bay," he told me with great force. "Narwhales are often seen there; it is one of their best feeding grounds, although our whalers rarely hunt them there, because they are shy beasts and make out of the bay into that wicked water studded with skerries where the boats daren't follow. But if you come on a school, and they run, and you think you're all gone, sit quietly and sail in the school's wake, and watch like a towering gerfalcon, and soon you may see a swirl, or some other movement in the bay water, then follow the stream of bubbles, and it may be that soon a very old narwhale will breach, one that's too weak to keep pace with his mates, yet lucky enough to miss meeting a killer whale. It will take blind luck for you to win; still there's some hope, and none at all behind Gull Nest Island. By the Nine Runes, I think that Eric had eaten daft fish and was out of his mind!"

He left me, never doubting that I would follow his instructions. Instead, I went to bed with a heavy heart and a mind troubled by indecision. Soon I fell into troubled dreams as though a kobold whom I had offended stood on my forehead. In these dreams I was sailing a vast and lonely sea which the sea gulls had deserted, although sharks followed my craft and swam under my keel, and their teeth flashed in the light from the dismal sky. After an endless voyage I was wakened by myself, talking in my sleep.

"Thorhall, I will go to Sea Mist Bay." And my scattered thoughts rallied strongly and I knew this was how I should have answered him in the first place. And when soon I went back to dreaming it was as though the vexing kobold had gone to supper, draining the stone dish of milk we invariably set out for him and his mates, for my sleep was deep and restful and my visions fair.

When I wakened again, no thought of heeding Eric instead of Thorhall crossed my mind. Before my berserk's breakfast, as we called the heavy *Midur Morgan* meal, I had put aboard my boat a skin bag of dried salmon, oily and tasty and giving such strength as the salmon needs to climb our rushing rivers. Also I shipped a whole sealskin of fresh water, lest Odin of the Gray Cloak, and of old time demanding obedience of his son Thor, should punish me for my disobedience of Eric by blowing me far to sea. The night before I had made fast to my bow the end of a coiled line, fifty fathoms long, made of walrus hide wondrously strong and light. By the time I had eaten, my new friend Ian, his great eyes shining in the sun, waited on our strand.

Just before we loosed our mooring lines, Thorhall came down to the strand at his burly trot to hand me his whaling spear, its blade a full foot longer than mine, sharper edged and pointed, and of better steel. I kept mine also, in the hope of hurling home two spears, that the narwhale's eyes might swiftly darken and his soul more quickly pass into the black seas of Hel. Counting well beforehand, under his left arm Thorhall brought a line of twenty fathoms' length.

" 'Tis as long as you'll need in those shallow waters, so don't cut free too soon and lose me my best harpoon," he said as he turned away.

Our fiord waters were cobalt blue that early morning, with gentle waves. When we had rounded the headland, the brisk but not hard wind was on our stearboard quarter, which puffed our sail full as a woman's belly when six months with child, and made pretty whitecaps on the shallow sea, green as Eric's eyes. The boat

seemed to scamper along in joy, and the bright sun found naught
as good to shine on as my two bright spear points, and Ian's face,
and perhaps the angel-white wings of terns. No gulls followed us.
They seemed to know we would pull no fish guts to throw out,
and by quick darts of their eyes they perceived we were on graver
business, then flew ceremoniously away.

Truly I had never essayed an undertaking of the least small
part as great or as grave as this. My father, the great chieftain,
Eric the Red, had never sent me on more than a mere errand. I
thought that his trust in me, and something more than trust, a
recognition of me as truly his son, of the spirit as well as of the
loins, had increased mightily since I had testified truthfully at his
trial, even if thereby he risked a hanging. Thorstein would have
loved the assignment, and why had Eric given it to me instead
of him? I could think of no reason other than his wishing me a
notable victory, to begin my long climb to equal Thorstein in
repute.

And then, caught up in solemn splendor, the plaguing doubt
struck me whether I should have followed Eric's instructions word
for word instead of being turned aside by Thorhall. Truly I did
not believe that he had heard from some sailor of narwhales behind
Sea Gull Island. No such man had passed by Ericsholm, and
as far as I knew he had not lately left our ground. But there was
another way he might have been informed, by an informant far
more trustworthy than any sailor, and this could be a visitor to his
dreams. Perhaps Njord, the old Norse God of the Sea, had
been that visitor. If so. . . .

At that instant my doubts were not lessened but made greater
by Ian's soft voice.

"Leif, I have never taken part in an enterprise as noble as this,"
he said.

"That I can hardly believe."

"It is quite true. In his coastal journeys and his voyages to
Norway and Ireland, Eric felt no real need of his ship's bearing
some great sign in honor and in verification of her name. Besides,
until now she was only a merchant ship. Otherwise he would
have gone himself to get a narwhale horn to set in her stem, to

precede him on his course, and to honor Odin, God of the Winds, and Njord of the White Feet. Suddenly Eric has seen the need. His vessel will sail seas unknown to any Norseman. She is on a voyage of exploration, not to gather or to sell seal blubber. Perhaps she will meet great perils, such as another Maelstrom that funnels into Hel. And since the Gods know all this better than we, perhaps having read her fate in the Runes of Weird, I cannot help but believe they are watching your little craft and lending you their favor, and you will surely win a narwhale horn of great size and glory."

It came to me to tell him we were on another course than that of Eric's direction, but what would be the good? To the present course we were committed; we could not change it now. So instead I told him something else that might please the Gods.

"If we find narwhales, and the heat of the hunt sets both of us on fire, you must remember, Ian, not to touch either spear, nor the line of either, even if it means losing the prize. If a line catches my foot, and I am in danger of being jerked overboard and lost, still do not touch it. If the quarry sounds in water deeper than our line, only my sword may cut it to save our being hauled down."

"I understand that perfectly well, my Captain Leif. I will mind the tiller oar and the sail. But after we enter Sea Mist Bay, will you call our course?"

"No, steer as your soul bids you. That soul is beloved by the Gods, or you would not have been given the power to stir our souls with wondrous voice and words, and if there are narwhales in my reach, you will take me to them."

4

My heart was assailed with doubt as we were rounding a cape beyond which lay Sea Mist Bay; then it took a deep fall. These waters had lived up to their name, and dim clouds of breeze-torn fog drifted out the wide mouth to be instantly dispelled by the brisk wind of the open gulf. At our first glance, there was nothing to see but mist, as though a thin, gray fold had been laid over our eyes. No man knew why it gathered here when other waters would show a swimming gull at half a mile, and I did not believe, as one Icelandic poet had declaimed, that this was the bed of the Fog Giant. Instead, against my will, I had believed Thorstein when once he said it was the consequence of the water being warmed by a great outpouring from some Hel vent in the bottom.

Yet we sailed in, and sometimes our sight was longer and sometimes shorter, but never a seal, let alone a narwhale, loafed or played or fed in the blue reaches. But we had not sailed far when a force like lightning tingled our backbones. Not far, yet beyond our vision in thin, gray stuff, restricting our young eyes as rheum dims the eyes of the very old, we heard one mighty crashing smash of sea water. There was no hillside from which a big stone could have rolled into the surf. Yet whatever had fallen was of great weight to have made so loud a sound at such a good distance.

Now in the warm current that encircled our island swam fish that we called tunny, sometimes weighing half a ton, and sailors had seen them leap clear of the sea, then fall as though to burst their bones. The leaper that we had heard had been far heavier. No sea we knew was too warm or too cold to hold killer whales, whose ferocious packs tore into pieces the great whales, swallowed whole our playful porpoises, and gulped seals and disgorged their skins. Now it was told that sometimes these monsters, thirty feet long, cleared the water in prodigious bounds. Yet, if a killer whale had leaped, it was a female or a young male.

Ian sailed toward the sound. It seemed to me we sped straight as an arrow, balking the tricks of wind and mist. And then I could not forbear from breaching my intent watch to glance at Ian, to see his face flushed and his eyes gleaming, and doubtless mine were the like, for another sound had become audible, a continuous surging and splashing. And now at the utter butt of vision we made out shapes in motion, pale white against the mist-grayed water, and they seemed from fifteen to twenty feet long, and now and then something, we dared not think what, made a long pale glimmer.

And then the God Odin, rubbing the mist out of his eyes to

see better, or perceiving the glory of our quest and wishing us success, hurled down a wind. It was one big puff such as sometimes fills a sagging sail with a crackling sound, and instantly the fog was torn into scraps and tatters, and these were whisked away like a flock of souls from an inglorious battlefield, and the gray bay turned blue. Sunlight until now dammed up by the fog burst down in a golden flood, and there in the middle distance played a school of narwhales. There were thirty in all, I thought, about half of them boasting one tusk, and two or three with two, and in the immaculate air these shone liked naked blades.

Odin's wind pressed not on our stern but a little forward of our stearboard beam. Quick-handed Ian eased our sail to stearboard, belayed the sheet, then fought his rudder oar until again we made toward the school. And now we ached for time to watch the game, which was most strange. It took a ceremonious form, not unlike an ancient Norse dance of young folk, and at the end of what might be called a measure, two males approached each other with raised horns, and these they crossed like broadswords.

And then a vagrant and daft desire crossed my mind: that I had brought my flute and was myself a master flutist, whereby I could make strange music fit for these strange dancers. Then their stately movements would quicken until the waves rolled and great swirls formed and foam glittered in the sun, and still they would keep time.

But I drove the notion from my heated brain, and instead I clasped Thorhall's harpoon and drew it back, my hand above my shoulder, ready to sweep forward when I would be close enough to trust my aim. Then the Iron Snake would dart, humming and hornetlike, and then arch down; and if the whale's fate moved darkly, and mine most bright, the long fang would plunge deep and put an end to my quarry's merry life.

No such easy victory had been written in the Runes of Weird. When we were still a hundred long yards from the school, a big bull that had seemed to lead the dance sprang clear of the water, and as he struck with a great splash he began to swim at a furious speed. At once the whole band took places in a long line behind him, their flukes in mighty movement, their heads and shoulders

rhythmically rising into sight only to sink again, the water boiling
fiercely in the long wake, and their gait was nigh that of a school
of porpoises scared by a killer whale. Plainly they were making
by the shortest cut for the skerry water, perilous even for
slow rowers in a fresh breeze.

Still my hope did not die. I saw the justice of the setback in
such a quest as this, worthy of the master of dragon ship setting
forth to burn Rome. My faith in Thorhall was greater than ever,
because a very large bull that had not joined in the play, and instead had swum lazily at one side, often sinking from sight, I
could not now make out in the boiling water. My heart seemed to
tell me that he had sounded, and perhaps it only told me of its
ache.

We followed the school as fast as our full-bellied sail could
haul us. We were perhaps two miles from the skerries, where we
must drop canvas and pull on our oars, and that would only
delay our admission of defeat, so I kept my head a-screw and my
eyes falcon-sharp, as Thorhall had bade me. Meanwhile, the quarry
gained at a rate sickening to watch. If any old, decrepit bull,
swimming deep, could follow one quarter as fast, he would still
outrun us. So as the seconds sped, my hopes were sinking fast,
and soon I was hoping against hope.

Great whales have been known to remain submerged three
quarters of an hour. According to the lore of old whalers, a narwhale in his prime could hold his breath for perhaps five minutes.
Fully that many minutes had passed. Now the school was far and
away in the skerry waters; I could dimly see the white, crooked
line of foam. As my gaze wheeled aft in vigilance yet intense, it
never met Ian's gaze, although I knew that his bright face had
darkened. I started to speak. . . .

Then I was struck dumb by a rushing sound close in our wake.
Up burst a little geyser of foam and water drops agleam in the
sunlight. And then, hardly forty feet on our stern, a long
white tusk broke water, gleaming, and then the head and shoulders
of the Old Man Narwhale heaved up into view.

Because I was standing in the bow while Ian sat well aft, and
because he hauled at the sheet to give me room, I could hurl
the javelin safely over his head. Still it sped low to the water on

such a short cast, and the blade glittered in the sunlight so that its passage was a shining streak. And true it kept its course, and deep it plunged into the pale white body a foot behind the blunt head.

The whale made a mighty leap as I belayed the line a little too short. Then as the whale began his run, the boat jerked endwise, shipping water, knocking me to my knees, and well-nigh floundering. I reckoned that few boats had ever reversed their course with such rough dispatch. The beast was death-doomed unless he could sink us, and he knew it. Perhaps too his mates, once his followers ere he had come to honored age, had sensed in their dim mysterious souls his nearing end; and although he was too lame to dance and play, they had feigned being fey in his stead.

Now it seemed his young strength had returned, a last boon from the Ocean Gods, for the torn waters boiled and swirled around him and in his wake, and his head and shoulders and shining tusk alternately rose and fell, and our stem cut the water. If he could live until he reached the skerry waters he could well take us with him into darkness, so I took up my own harpoon and was aiming it as he gave one last thrust of his flukes, then sounded. In great haste I dropped the shaft and began to pay out line.

It never again came tight. The waters heaved, and up rose the brute's pale bulk and lay all but lifeless. When I was about to strike again, Ian told me quietly there was no need. So together we watched the last spark of life pass from him with a little heaving of his chest and a weak rise and fall of his fluke.

Now for the first time I perceived his great size, a total length not of twenty feet, but nearer thirty, his horn too long to stand upright in Eric's hall of nine-foot walls. And beholding his bulk, the thought struck me to sail to a nearby village and let the boats bring it in to render his oil. Instantly I forsook the notion and decided to take only what I had come for, then let the carcass drift, to be eaten by sharks and monsters of the deep and by a horde of shrieking gulls, its disposition if he had died of old age.

And I named him the King of the Narwhales, and the king was dead, but I deemed that I had grown an inch in height and by a modicum of wisdom in the understanding of this wondrous North of which I was the son.

CHAPTER THREE

WESTWARD SAIL

I

The tusk was a vast extension of what would be the dogtooth in the human jaw. To cut it out we had to moor the boat to the carcass and stand on it; and a heavier labor was to put it aboard without dropping it in the sea or capsizing. Sweating and puffing, we finally succeeded, and then as though to commend us the wind puffed from another quarter. It was not a following wind for our homeward course, but it blew only forward of our beam, and thus we could tack with good way on.

Both of us tired by excitement more than labor, Ian and I spoke little on the homeward sail. I could not resist yielding to daydreams of a boyish sort, mainly of what Eric, my mother, Thorstein, and Thorhall would say when they saw the mighty tusk, and of how all our people would run down to the strand, and most of all the modest manner I would assume. The horn looked bigger every time I glanced at it. If shipped to Norway, it would buy a whole flock of sheep, sixty or seventy, or a drove of twenty cattle. And what I dwelt on most fondly, not a surety, but a great likelihood, would be Eric's acknowledgment before the crowd of his pride in me and of my worthiness to sail with him on any sea, or touch any strange, far-off, and perilous strand to which he ventured.

These dreams dissolved, like hoarfrost on a dark, cold day when the sun bursts through the clouds, at my first sight of our home acre. A crowd larger than I pictured coming to view my trophy was already assembled on our strand. Could Little Witch have seen a vision of my triumphant return and these folk have gathered to test its truth? Instantly the thought perished in starvation and shame. The mooring lines of the *Narwhale* had been loosed, her sail furled and ready, and the ship anchored a hundred yards from shore where she could catch the wind. About a dozen hands stood like sticks on her deck. Bow foremost, and her utmost stern grounded, as though readied to be pushed off, lay the longboat. Close by stood a barrel-chested man, gesticulating and waving, and the sun shone on his beard, and I knew it was red.

I turned and looked Ian in the face.

"Do you think Eric the Red has made ready to sail and is waiting for me?"

"Leif, I do not think he is waiting for you. It would be half a day's work to set a narwhale tusk in the stem. I think he took your failure for granted and meant to stand to sea on this high tide. Anyway, he could hardly have expected you this soon."

"No, he would not have expected me this soon." Then I tried to say a brave thing, but my breath failed.

Someone in the crowd had seen us now, and most likely exclaimed and pointed, for every face was turned toward us. Still my father might go aboard and order his anchor hoisted before we could touch the strand, for no more willful man breathes Icelandic air; and in that dark moment I cared not if he did. Instead, at his shouted orders which carried to us like a low rumble of far-off thunder, the men aboard the vessel weighed her anchor, then rowed her back to her mooring place. We gave no sign, we did not wave an arm, only sailed on.

When our canvas sagged in the shelter, I, too, bowed to oars. Not a sound rose from the staring crowd as we drew nigh the strand, and my father stood with his feet far apart, and what was in his face I did not see, for I would not look. I got out and with one strong fierce tug grounded the bow of my boat. Then at last I turned to my sire, looked into his green eyes, and spoke.

"There's your narwhale horn."

"So I see," he answered in a great voice. "You've won the prize you sailed for. I told you there were narwhale behind Gull Nest Island. But I never really believed you'd kill one, you so young and green and had never heaved at any creature bigger than a walrus, and since the loading took less time than I thought, and the wind was fair, and the flood tide would bear me safe over the shoals, I thought to sail today. Happily you made a fast trip and got here just in time to stop me."

"I didn't kill the narwhale at Gull Nest Island. I killed him at Sea Mist Bay."

"Why, those were more likely grounds than the other. I didn't think of 'em. And I should have known you couldn't make the island and back this soon, unless you were gale-driven both ways. Leif, 'tis a fine horn. I've seen a few as good or a little better, but mighty few."

"It's the biggest narwhale horn I ever saw, and I used to hunt 'em," said Thorhall quietly.

"Leif, we'll set it proudly in our stern—that's why I called in the ship—and 'twill take half a day to do a good job. On the flood tide tomorrow we'll stand to sea, and you'll go with us, and you'll not ship as a boy but a whole hand. And you and Ian too can see that the tusk is set to your liking. But now go to the hall and see your mother. She was in one of her sulky spells and wouldn't come to the beach."

"I'll go at once. And if you should take a notion to sail while I'm talking with her, you needn't wait for me."

2

Never could I come near my mother, Thorhild, without a calming of my upsurged feelings and the onset of quiet happiness. Why, I had never asked myself until that day. I had sometimes felt the same when standing on the shore of one of Iceland's lovely lakes, or when fishing in its great and limpid depths, especially when the rising sun caused its lean fringe of dwarf birch and willow trees to stand forth in every detail against the pale tints of the clouds.

Perhaps both gave the effect of tranquillity that somehow implied great strength. Anyhow, both were beautiful. My boyhood word "pretty" did not fit my mother. Beauty was in her face, especially in her eyes and about her tender mouth, in her form and carriage, and always in her voice. I began to think that Eric had done nothing that he could have kept from doing. Still I wanted to know more about the compulsion and my mother could tell me and she would.

"It's perfectly plain that Eric sent me on a fool's errand, but I don't know what made him do it," I said.

"Neither do I," my mother answered. "I can only guess at it."

"I would like to hear your guess. I have a right to."

"You called it a fool's errand. More than that, he wanted to make you feel a fool for taking his bait. You were to come back empty-handed and find him far at sea. In his ship he would have roared with laughter at the thought of it; yet beneath his laughter will still remain the serpent in his bosom that made him do it. Leif, you are very like Eric in inborn force. But while you both can control others—you, I mean, after the leap of years—he cannot control himself. On the other hand, Thorstein is not at all like him. It is hard to believe that he is Eric's son, as he truly is. Eric senses this also, I think; he treats Thorstein like a visiting chief, careful of his speech, respectful in his manner. Toward you he feels—could it be a kind of jealousy?"

"I don't see how it could be."

"Eric can't abide for any one close to him to transcend him. You are barely a man, yet Little Witch saw something strange that night, even though she was tipsy with mead. There is another thing. He has let Thorhall cane you—Thorhall loves you and his blows are light—but Eric has never laid hand on you. He explains that he fears his furious temper will cause him to break your bones, but I do not think that is the reason; I think he is afraid to do so. You see, Leif, Eric heard another prophecy spoken from the high seat. He had a stick and he was going to beat me, but the room turned dark and very cold from some cause I know not, and the fire on the stones became low and flickering like the fires that ringed the Palace of the Dragon that Sigurd broke through. Without thinking, being driven it seemed by forces I did not know, I climbed to the high seat of prophecy and spoke what was sent to me to speak. 'Eric, if you give me the least blow, you will die at my son's hand!'"

"You spoke truth."

"That I know, but he will never strike me. It was believed by the old Vikings that if a son killed a father, or the father a son, their souls could never find peace, ever wandering, ever harried by the winds, until Götterdämmerung. Yet I fear war between you, in which you will both suffer deep wounds. You have brought it nearer by your taking the narwhale horn in spite of his cruel cowherd joke. Only last moon you were half a boy. Now I count you a full man."

"My mother, do you love Eric?"

Her eyes slowly filled with tears. Then she answered in tones as tender as the voice of the flute when softly played.

"Yes, I loved him when I was young and will love him when I am old. I sometimes think that a woman loves a man not because of what he is, but of what she is, which she cannot change. Ever since he learned he could not master me, he treats me kindly and usually with a boyish reverence. When he does not, I forgive his trespasses as I have been bidden."

He would never master me, either, I vowed within my soul.

We kissed each other and then I went to put in my sea bag garments and tools and trifles that I loved for the next day's journey. Also I took my flute in its wooden box, wrapped it safely, and put it with my gear.

3

Our Irish folk, West Men or West Women, as we called them still, as in the days when Ireland seemed the westernmost land in the northern seas—although now the western copes of our own Iceland jutted a thousand miles nearer the sunset than the mouth of Shannon—these West Folk often used the word "daybreak." It may have aptly fitted the end of night and the rush of morning on their native island. Here in their new home it had no meaning. The light ebbed very slowly then as slowly flowed, and it was hard to say when this tide turned, the thickening or the paling of the darkness being so indistinct. At this time of the year, high summer, the sun slipped out of sight for a little while in the midnight hours, and the gulls rested their busy wings and ever raucous voices, and only the biggest, brighest stars showed themselves palely gleaming, hardly reminiscent of the radiant beacons of our deep purple winter skies. Thorhall, who was forever rising and roaming about while Eric snored, could go down to the strand, look at the weather or at ice or see to the boats or sniff the wind, without the guidance of a seal-oil lantern. A strange keel must sail wide of our headlands to escape his vigilant watch.

Yet on the morning we were to put forth in search of the uttermost western land the dawn did break in a fashion, because at *Midur Morgan* a smothering fog that dimmed all eyes was whisked away by a sudden brisk east wind. A drowsing, damp, dull gray void become chock-full of brilliant light and animation. Sea fowl began to fly and scream, fishing terns flashed everywhere, pelicans skirted the coast in sedate flocks, a big school of porpoises swam at frantic speed across and up and down our harbor. All these signs were fair. We who would soon set forth would have danced and jigged on the strand except that this would have been a bad sign, even that every man-jack of us was fey. Those who would watch us depart wiped the cold mist, and some a few hot tears, from their eyes, because they believed we would find a new land where they could join us in a new life, not as safe, perhaps more harsh, but enriched by new things to see and do, perhaps by mighty wonders, and more lively.

The east wind had piled the waters of long fiord high on our strand, and the *Narwhale* was safely anchored in a stone's toss. All hands had gone aboard except bold Thorstein, Einer, Eric, and I; and very soon we too must push out in our sailing dinghy, and a silence fell over the crowd of farewell-sayers, mainly Eric's eaters, Einer's henchmen and their families, and a few other neighbors. It seemed to me that the same expression stole into every face except those of the children, who turned in question and disquiet to the faces of their elders. I think that all perceived in the same instant, as little lightnings dart and weave and zigzag among clouds, or perhaps by one cloud of thought engulfing us all, what a strange and momentous event was occurring here. How many voyagers had set forth on the wild and inimical seas to journey beyond the mists to a destination unknown to themselves or to any of their fellow creatures?

I had dwelt only casually upon it until now, perhaps not really believing or discounting its greatness, as neighbors will discount the greatness of some man in their midst, because they cannot believe that greatness could touch their ordinary lives. Yet suddenly I knew it was truly great. And great was the man who long had contemplated the journey and, when the hour struck, of fate's bringing more than his own, had made ready to go. Perhaps it was a greater journey in the sight of the Gods than when Bjorn, Halfdan, Ivar the Boneless, and Hastings, all sons of the hero Ragnar, had set forth to cross the North Sea to ravish England. I looked at Eric in fresh wonder. He was my enemy in some strange way and for inexplicable cause, but he was also my great sire. He stood like a rock against which beat ocean waves through interminable years. His eyes were wildly green, his broad brow furrowed and sweat-beaded and I knew he was resolved to brave the unknown at almost any risk, to win at almost any cost. My mother, Thorhild, gazed upon his face and then mine, and for what she was searching I knew not. And it seemed to me that the terns had ceased to cry out, a sound different and of higher pitch than any pipe could blow, and flew in time and measure with their fellows, and that this aerial dance was being danced throughout the sky as far as eye could reach.

And then Eric broke the silence with his deep, low, but ever forceful voice.

"Leif, is that your flute that you've wrapped in a piece of sail and hold under your arm?"

"Yes, my father."

"Will you lend it to your mother that she may give us a fit farewell? And if he does, Thorhild, will you play the Strand Song of the Norse Women to the Departing Fleet?"

"Yes, as well as I can."

"My mother, it is not a Christian song," Thorstein said, no mockery in his voice, but with a glimmer in his bold eyes. "Do you not fear that your God Kris will be angered, and sink our ship, and roll Eric and all of us on the rocks?"

"Thorstein, my forebears were heathen when Odin was a youth, not an old man with a gray beard, ere he hung nine days on the Wolf Tree and made the nine-day journey to Hel to bring back the Nine Runes, and I have been Christian for only fifteen years.

Gentle Kris will not be angered by my playing a song of great meaning to my folk."

"By your leave, after you have played it through once, I will sing the stanzas," Ian said quickly.

"Please do," my mother answered.

"'Twould make me proud," Einer, his master, told him.

I unwrapped the magic horn and Thorhild put her tender mouth to the blowhole. Her fingers began to open and close the eight smaller holes, nine in all, the magic number of Odin, and the melody was one that had run through Odin's head, I thought, as he, riding his eight-hoofed steed, chased the north wind. Surely no other than a God of Tempests, not their servants as were sailors, but their master, could have made sound rise and fall, climb high and soar down, come soft and sweet and woeful to the ear, then sing forth full-throated. Perhaps it was the song he had taught the Goddess of the Loom to sing when soon he went to war with Loki the Giant and with Fenris the Giant Wolf.

It might be that Balder heard his mother sing the song, and because he loved the folk, and because, like them, he was doomed to early death, he taught them the divine notes but did not trust to them the spellbinding words. So in time our women made up such words as rose in their hearts and on their tongues, words that any of their number, from a chieftain's wife to a thrall's drudge, could understand, and it was these, in form like our scalds' songs, that Ian sang.

> Sail, Vikings, sail.
> Heed not our wail.
> Will you pause to kiss our lips
> Ere you board your ships?
> Quick kisses, forgotten without thanks
> When you have passed the banks?
> Will you remember us amid your mirth,
> A-frolick on the bloodied earth,
> When you have sacked and burned a Christian town
> And slain the priest in his white gown,
> And the bright-faced maids lay bound,

And the old Jew's treasure's found?
Gods, how you love gold, silver, and bright jewels!
But we thought you loved us, too, we stulty fools!

Blow, winds, blow!
Down the Swan Road go!
Your shields agleam along the prow;
'Neath dragon heads that bob and bow.
Ravage and burn, for gray-beard Odin's sake,
Loot temples, palaces, and distant marts,
But the cruelest theft you've ever made or can ever make
Was to steal our hearts.

The song ended. The scene it had conjured up dimmed in our fancy and no longer could we see the fierce fleet of dragon ships as they set forth, with swollen yellow sails, from Stavanger strand. Instead we gazed upon the *Narwhale,* until lately a broad-beamed merchant, stubby and sturdy, but she had changed in some poetic way since the gleaming tusk of her namesake had been set in her stem. Eric, Thorstein, Einer, and I would go aboard her now. Nothing more of note would happen before we pushed off in the ship's sailing skiff, clambered aboard, and set sail for the lost green land.

But a singular thing did happen, although it would be hard to count as of any note. When I had taken my seat on the stern thwart ready to push off, a young maid between childhood and womanhood, perhaps nine or at most ten, broke out of the ringed throng and ran toward me. Her name was Swanhild and she was the daughter of beautiful Ellen. In the boundless sunlight I saw for the first time that she had inherited her mother's gift from the Goddess Freya, although in bright, not dusky colors.

"My mother wishes you good fortune, but I want to kiss your lips before you board your ship, the same as in the song," she told me in one burst of breath. Her voice was childlike, but her kiss was secretly and strangely ardent as a sweetheart's.

"Go back to your place," Eric muttered with a flushed face. Plainly he was angered that a thrall wench should make so free.

"Swanhild, when we have passed the banks I will still remember and thank you for your kiss," I told the crestfallen girl. And this heightened my father's rage, as I might have known.

Then we pushed off, my back bending to my oars along with Thorstein's and Einer's sturdy backs and the thick back of my father, Eric the Red. And then we clambered aboard, and many hands shipped the skiff, and others weighed our anchors, and we sat sail!

4

All we had to do to begin our journey was to sail out of our fiord and keep on sailing. The wind was straight out of the east, a whistling wind, and our course due west. Eric had chosen this course because it was the shortest to those waters, as well as Eric's cousin Thorker had been able to calculate their position, from where he had seen, or thought he had seen, land. Our own position was about sixty miles south of an imaginary line that we called the Butt of the Sun's Sail. We meant by this it was the place of turning back on his great northern sweep through our skies, always occurring in the month named after the Roman Goddess Juno, at the end of the third week. On that day, at Midfiord on Iceland's northeast coast, the sun hangs above the horizon from cockcrow to cockcrow.

Yet Thorstein, speaking boldly despite the courteous sound of his address, protested this course as unwise.

"Why do you think so?" Eric asked, with amazing mildness.

"Because no few ships, and several whale hunters, have been blown westward on this sea. They could not reckon the distance except by the days of sailing to get home, but it was no small piece. Most of them noted the ascendancy of the North Star over the sea's rim, and since it was this very kind of summer gale that had blown 'em from Borg, straight out of the east and sometimes holding two weeks on end, they found her shining at about the same elevation. None of these craft raised land, only interminable sea. If your cousin Thorker spied land, and not dirty ice, he was either well north of our course or plagued far out."

"So you must reckon that the east coast of the green land bends southwest," Eric remarked after brief thought.

"There's nothing to stop it from doing so, that I know of. We thickheaded Norse are always picturing unknown coasts as straight east and west, or north and south. The earth giants that shaped our shores were not that orderly. 'Tis true that the Norwegian coast from Stadland to Stavanger runs north and south. We forget that from Stadland to North Cape it cuts northeast."

"Or sou'west if you're heading home. The west coast of Iceland does the like, to a sou'ward sailor. Maybe it's the habit of these far-west islands." Eric tossed his red mane. "There's meat in what you say, Thorstein, that I agree. Still, I'll keep this course till I have to change it."

Such was my jealousy of Thorstein that I felt elated by his defeat.

Out of the fiord mouth we stood to sea, and all our hearts leaped up to see our sail jam-packed with wind, every puff that she could take without carrying away, and this a fair wind full on our stern. The stout mast of straight-grained Norway pine, the pick of a hundred in the Stavanger shipyard, bent at the top like an oarsman's back as he spies the smoke of home; and when I touched it I felt a thrill running through it, and the stays thrummed. We pitched with the running waves but did not roll in the least. I reckoned that no round-bellied trader had ever beat her, except when hustled by a hurricane, and the shallow dragon ships, racing one another to a Christian strand on sixty sea legs before a following wind, would be hard put to it to keep pace. And to me the most thrilling sight of all was not our flock of sea gulls, gliding and shrieking and swooping in wild excitement, but instead our rising and falling stem with its glorious forepiece sometimes pointing down toward its chill, dim birthplace, sometimes slanting up to catch the sunlight, but usually thrusting forward toward the new land.

The wind did not vary a point, or increase or flag, for five days. In those days we hands had little to do except ship chores and to stand watch; so I blew many a dinghy sail's fill of air across the blowhole in my flute. My main hope at first was to learn to play the Song of the Norse Women as my mother had played it. This ambition I soon abandoned, such a failure I fetched with squeaks and chirps, making the tune unrecognizable as well as an insult to my own ears. Then I took to our folk tunes, most of them easy, and then to drill myself, and in order to learn the wondrous capabilities of the wooden tube, I sought to imitate the familiar singing sounds of wind and wave.

Happily no one heard my efforts, for my perch was high in the bow where the blast scattered them like skeins of mist. There, my flute and I sheltered from the salt spray, again I learned my incompetence, although meanwhile learning a wonderful thing, which was the variance, multiplicity, and often the perfect beauty of those sea sounds. Listening with utmost attention, I isolated one after another from the medley that often disguised or concealed them. Some were of such low pitch that my ears must strain to hear them, like a chorus of giants singing in Asagard; some were so high and fragile you would have thought a troupe of fairies were playing on tiny harps. The trial might make me a good lookout for a wind-sped ship in thick, drifting fog. Better than most, I would know what the winds and seas were up to.

In all truth we had journeyed far from our crag-ringed coast. Our wake of gulls had long turned back to shore; and their place was taken by four winged companions rather than followers, fowl that we had rarely seen and which Thorhall called albatross. When they soared, their long wings formed a lovely arc; their dizzy swoops took the watcher's breath; in pure sport they missed our rigging by an eyelash; they lazied round and round the ship, then in sudden bursts of speed they shamed a gerfalcon chasing a pochard duck. Surely no more strong or beautiful flyers followed any Swan Road of the high seas.

They showed no sign of quitting us, although the purpose in keeping us company was a mystery that our oldest sea dog could not solve. They paid no attention, other than close scrutiny, to our slops over which gulls had scrabbled and shrieked. Before long I began to find a cozy comfort in their escort, which was only another inkling of how far we had been blown from our home shores, farther indeed than I liked to think, although my soul knew well. Although ravens are Odin's birds, they are not seafarers. I had been told that eagles were sacred to Thor. Swans were servants of Odin, which could change at will into Valkyries, the folk believed, or, laying aside their plumage, could become Swan Maidens who sported on summer evenings in meadow pools. Perhaps our albatross had been sent by some hero turned into a God —such as Ragnar who in life had assayed brave journeys into the unknown—to lend us luck.

Close to the Iceland shores we had seen ice floes in the usual number. Later they had disappeared; and to our surprise we saw few sharks and almost no porpoises. On the fifth day we began to see killer whales as well as a few very large whales, monstrous indeed, which our most far-traveled hands did not recognize. On the morning of the sixth day we again saw ice, in scattered fields, as well as gleaming bergs, and our helmsman's watch became sharp, as did everyone's, and I tootled no more on my flute. Still the blast out of the east sped us spanking.

"You must have paid a spaewife a good sum for this fair wind," Thorstein remarked to Eric.

"I gave Thorbiorg, Little Witch, six walrus tusks, twelve sealskins, and a basket of eider eggs," my father answered, apparently eager to confide what was strictly his own business. "Still, I'm not quite sure she didn't overdo her charm weaving."

"Do you think we might have sailed beyond the waters from where your cousin Thorker spied land?"

"Thorstein, I do think so. I'll tell you why. I'm a fair judge of a vessel's speed in open sea. I have only to twist my head down on one shoulder to count my heart beats—sixty-five per minute according to a fine Italian hourglass of sixty graduations. My method is to pick a swimming tern or gull dead on our course at what I judge a tenth of a sea mile distant, then start counting. I did so several times on the first day out when sea fowl were plentiful, and the figures added up to a sea mile in eight minutes, which is seven and a half per hour. The east wind hasn't abated or veered a point in six days. So at *Midur Morgan* we had sailed one hundred and fifty hours from fiord mouth. Counting loss from unknown causes we're a thousand miles from the Icelandic coast."

"What would be your guess at those causes, Captain? I can't think of any."

Eric dangled his tongue like an urchin learning runes. He pulled it in and spoke with quiet intensity. "Last midnight was wondrous clear. It won't be so clear tonight; clouds are mustering in the west and I think our fair wind will soon blow out. Well, last night I could find the North Star and it was a little higher than when we set sail. That means we've had a southward drift in the last two days, and that could mean we've been picked up by an ocean current. If so, it's no kin to the warm current that sweeps around Iceland. It's out of the north, and if you've washed your face lately, you know it's bitter cold."

I was watching my father's face, a habit I did not like but could not break. Thorstein had glanced southwest, as though to look at weather, and I knew he had heard every word but his thoughts were riveted elsewhere. A faint glow appeared in his lean, weathered face.

"Excuse me for interrupting you, Captain," he said in a well-guarded voice. "But look again at the lowest-lying of those clouds. It has a different appearance from the others. Could it be land?"

A thrill coursed all of our spines as we stood and stared, and at the same instant my heart sank like a plummet. The Gods knew I craved the sight of the merest island, to give proof that we were not sailing an empty sea illimitable until it poured roaring over the brink of the world into Hel. But I had deeply longed to be the first to spy it, and the one of my shipmates whom I hated most to have beat me was Thorstein, my brother.

Still I could not doubt his surmise. It was part of the pattern of his habit of beating me.

"Well, it's not a cloud, that's sure," said Eric the Red in his forceful voice. "Then what is it, if not land?"

"I think it's land," said Einer, who had come up to join our talk. And every man aboard had caught the fever of our excitement and they, too, stared southwest.

"It's brown-colored, like our own shores below the grass, and it's big," Thorstein observed with a faint and knowing smile.

"Make for it," my father called to our steerer. And immediately we were all on the jump, resetting our sail.

Still we clipped along with the wind on our stern quarter and the air remained clear except for distant dimnesses here and there, and our vision stretched far. For half an hour's sail the low-lying brown smudge looked more and more like land and yet a wild curiosity was seizing my mind, although I did not know why. Then I saw a puzzled expression steal over Eric's face, and his eyes had a different light. When my own throat was bursting, he spoke.

"Thorstein, if it's land, it's not the green land my cousin Thorker saw."

"It may be an outlying island."

"Aye, so it might. About the size of Sotra fronting Bergen. But I doubt if it's either one. I think it's a big pack of glacier ice, dirty with moraine."

And that settled the matter for our whole company. All the comfort I received from Thorstein's discomfiture was a sneering smile, if indeed it did not reflect his serene faith he would beat me yet. Soon we were wondering how we could have remained in doubt as long as we did. The pack of dirty ice had lost every vestige of its deceptiveness, and we had seen its like a score of times in an hour's sail from Borg. And now we began to see other packs and, gleaming in the distance, far-scattered snow-white icebergs.

"I'm not discouraged one whit," Eric's big voice boomed. "Where there's moraine, there are glaciers, and where there are glaciers, there is land."

"Captain, the ice we see could have drifted all the way from our own Icelandic glaciers," Thorstein remarked with great calm. And the whole expression was true to his nature, as I perceived only too well. Instead of clutching at Eric's hopeful words, he saw clearly they did not mitigate in one particle his mistake, and he picked a hole in them besides. This was also the nature of great captains, I was thinking. They painted no rosy pictures or evaded no fact. Thorstein would be a great captain in due course.

"It would be a long drift," grave Einer said.

"Einer, only two weeks ago we had an east gale that lasted half a moon. After being blown out of our warm current, ice would melt very slowly in seas like these."

"In any case," Eric interrupted, glowing, "keep a sharp watch for land!"

The incident seemed to me a sort of interruption of our journey. True, we had never lost way, our course had been changed only briefly, our helmsman had never left his sweep, our escort of albatross had not rested from their lovely flight; yet I felt that we were entering a second phase, more arduous than the first. To find land soon had become of immediate urgency; the carefreeness we had felt at first, along with the sense of high adventure, almost sport instead of a grim business to perform or to bitch in failure, sped from our hearts. I had ached to be the first to spy the unknown shore. Now I resolved to do so, with an iron of intent that was new to me, which was no part of my dying boyhood and was hitched to the whole man I must now become.

Our crew of twenty-four stood three watches, of eight hours each. The watch I wanted especially to stand was from five hours before midnight until three hours after, under the command of our boatswain, a freeman named Starkad. It was the coldest watch of all, and it seemed the longest, for most of my shipmates were busy only at catching up with sleep. At its end, the hands were almost invariably drowsy, with eyes tired from straining into the dimness. Yet the light was clearing fast at this hour, and I thought it would be the best time to discover secrets that the midnight gloom had concealed. Vidda, one of Eric's thralls, agreed to change places with me for a woolen shirt I did not need, and Einer hardly bothered to listen to my excuse of sleeping better in the early morning hours.

Eric had been right, as usual, as to the weather. The half gale out of the east began to flag before sundown; then it veered to our stearboard stern. It was still a fair wind, although our clipping gait was sharply cut. Meanwhile, the mists lying westward thickened into low-lying clouds, with which I found no fault, for the moment would come when these would lift, or at least permit long vision through their ragged holes, and at that moment, especially likely to occur just before sunrise, I wanted to be wide awake on deck.

Two days passed since Thorstein had seen the "floating land," as the crew termed his aberration. When I came on watch in late afternoon the clouds westward remained an unbroken bank and the cold sea appeared to stretch on forever. Yet as the light began to fail as the hour neared midnight, the dimness excited me, as though it concealed some mighty wonder. Yet a slight shift of the wind again more easterly was surely a good sign. And I could not make myself believe that a sound I had heard at the outer rim of hearing was not the long sigh of a sounding porpoise, of whose playful clan we had seen none in unestimable square leagues of ocean.

When only a half hour remained of my watch the light tide turned, vision began to lengthen, and I began to catch glimpses of big icebergs of pale blue tint. The clouds to westward were not as dense as before—at least they had a different aspect—and how could I be certain that these were clouds? As my shipmates shook themselves to keep awake, doing only a half job, and stamped their feet and swung their arms to dispel the numbness of bitter cold, I stood in the bow, my eyes questing westward as no eyes of a hungry gerfalcon ever searched the heather for an Arctic hare.

I began to see three layers of color, one brown like our Iceland strands, one above it suggestive of green like that of our lowland grass, and the highest layer, and the most distant, a wan ghostly white. As I watched, the distinctions became more clear. Still I waited until our bell sounded to end our watch, only a moment more. Then, as it struck, I raised my voice in a great shout.

"Land! Land!"

5

It was impossible for me to believe I would ever live again a moment of such glory.

At every upward heave of the sun still deep under the eastern rim of ocean, at every multiplication of the dawn light, the discovery became more certain. This was the green land that Eric's cousin Thorker had seen, although its greenness was only a narrow belt between the brown strands and towering glacier ice. I gazed northward, and southwestward where our sea seemed to widen, still there was no end to the land.

"By the Nine Runes of Odin," cried the freeman Starkad in command of the watch, "you are right."

"Aye, it's land, and there's no doubt of it," another shipmate burst out.

"And a great land, too, or I miss my guess," another shouted.

"Look at it loom out of the morning haze!"

"I'll believe it when I set foot on its strand," protested old, gray, hard-bitten Gorm. "A man's eyes lie to him. You know how the fairy Morgan cheated the hero Roland. Why, she conjured up a whole countryside, hills, rivers, towers, even maidens gathering grapes, the whole piece and parcel, so he'd stand mazed and not seize her by the forelock and make her yield the armor of Achilles. I wouldn't wonder but this too is a trick. It might be played on us by a Norn, so we'd sail on blindly into the Poison Sea, and then pitch over earth's edge into Hel."

Before anyone could answer him, Einer's watch burst out of the hatch, crowding one another, and Einer said not a word when he saw what had riveted our eyes, only stood and gazed, and his men caught his silence and dared not speak. The next to come was Thorstein, who gave me a sideways glance and a small haughty smile. Then, although his coming was no noisier than the others', all of us knew the instant that Eric the Red gained the deck.

He grunted once, then looked low and aloft, to weather and to lee, and to stearboard and to port, and we stopped looking at the land to peer into his face. At last he gave his beard a snatch and then spoke in a voice that seemed too low to hear above the weather, but we caught every word.

"Aye, it's the land my cousin Thorker saw, and he was not one to be fooled by dirty ice. Still, this is a rougher stretch of coast than Thorker raised, mountainous it looks, with monstrous ice and snow not far inland. Who was the first to spy it?"

"Him," answered Starkad, pointing in my direction.

"Who? How can I know the man you mean among that many gawkers? One of you call his name."

I would not call my own name. My mouth would have had to be pried open like a hooked catfish. But Starkad made swift reply.

"Why, your own son Leif."

"Well, I might have guessed it. 'Twas why he moved from Einer's watch to yours, so he could get first look when the light cleared." His muttered tone changed to one of command. "Helmsman, sweep her hard to sou'sou'west. You others set her sail. We'll skirt the coast to look for greener pastures."

Thus began a long sail, during which men snatched food from the galley to eat on deck, and not one of Starkad's heavy-eyed watch turned into his bunk. The sun topped the rim of ocean and shone on the icy mountains and made them gleam, and by the clear, cold light ever we saw more sharply the rugged harshness of the coast. It appeared even less habitable than the reach I had first seen, its mountains higher and more forbidding, with only glimpses of green in the narrow lowlands. Still there was no flagging of hearts in our whole company. By many signs this was a great land, and what infinitesimal part of it we had seen we could not yet dream.

One sign was a wide ocean current sweeping generally south or south by west. To the limit of our vision we could see huge icebergs, and when we got two or three in line not far off our beam we could see that they too were moving not wholly with the wind. Such mighty currents were rarely seen off the shores of islets. We had not sailed an hour from our first landfall when we spied a gigantic whale, the largest Eric had ever seen, larger than the great right whale, with a huge blunt head and with teeth in his jaw instead of bone. He was alone, but within a league we came on a school of very large whales with enormous flukes, and thereafter we were never out of sight of whales of many different kinds, most of them unknown to Icelandic waters. Although killer whales hunted in ferocious packs, we saw few porpoises and no narwhales. For this last I was thankful, I suppose because I did not want my trophy gleaming in our stem to be a common sight in the new land.

In about twenty hours' sail, we passed the mouths of about a dozen fiords. Some appeared filled with bergs or ice floes, but some were enterable, were there any reason to explore this forbidding area of the coast. And just as the daylight failed, Eric beat every man-jack of us in being the first to spy a noble mountain peak, a perfect landfall for ships sailing from Iceland. It looked pale blue in the dimness, the color of a washed-out shirt Eric was wearing, and he promptly dubbed the great mountain Blue Shirt, in his own honor.

"What's the matter with your eyes, you lubbers," Eric shouted to Thorstein and me, "to let an old man beat you?"

At his saying that, I thought with a start how young my father was in truth—no more than forty. He would beat almost everybody a long while yet.

When I went off watch three hours after midnight, the night had only begun to thin, the pre-dawn light perceptibly lagging compared to its rush twenty-four hours before that had brought me my great discovery. I could hardly believe that one day's sail sou'sou'west could make so much difference in the verities of nature, for we were making about six sea miles per hour, according to Eric's calculation, although a school of chubby-looking whales that had fled from us made us appear to stand still. Yet before I turned in I saw the long shadow that was the long shore running endlessly on.

After six hours of intense sleep I rushed to the deck to see no end of land, or any mitigation of its harshness. My heart took a little fall when I looked in vain for our albatross, but it need not have done so, for these were deep-sea fowls, and a crowd of gulls had come from the nearing strand to shriek and clamor in our wake. Sill I wondered where our escorts had gone. It was unimaginable that they had taken up with another ship, because since time out of my mind no ship out of the West had ever touched Europe. I thought of the big walrus-hide boat which Thorhall had found empty and stranded. Perhaps its crew had been blown to sea from this new land. Still I could not believe that our stately companions would pay their courtesies to a craft without a tall and beauteous sail. Perhaps, finding themselves so far west, they had gone to look at the brink of ocean pouring into Hel with a roar compared to which Thor's mightiest clap was a pinprick of sound.

All that day we followed the unknown strand, and all of the next day, and all of the next day. In the morning of the following day Eric sensed a somewhat stronger southward current, but about noon he told us it was dying away, and the water was warmer to the touch than before. The icefields capping all appeared to be receding from the coasts and in the afternoon we could discern them only at a great distance. And now, on both sides of the fiords, well up from the naked strands we could see grass.

Late in the afternoon all of us could take our choice between two guesses: one that the land made a sharp turn westward out of sight ere it ran on southward or that we had come to its southernmost end. But the waters we gazed upon widened instead of narrowed, and soon there was no doubt we had reached a cape which we could round only by sailing straight west. Again the movements of the bergs told us our ship had been picked up by a current faster than we had yet felt, its waters fully as warm as at Borg in Iceland. Countless waterfowl and a scarcity of great whales indicated shoal waters, although our plummet line, twenty fathoms long, never touched bottom.

It was a wondrously clear night, chill but not cold, and at midnight Eric found the North Star. By his reckoning we were nigh three hundred miles south of Ericsholm, due west of Bergen in Norway. If so, we knew nothing to keep rich grass from growing, as well as mighty forests of spruce and northern pine, in some hospitable region of the great land.

That night the hands only snatched at sleep, in their excitement over what the dawn light might disclose. And when the light broke clear we had passed the westernmost peninsula of what Eric named Cape Welcome, beyond which stretched what we did not doubt was the final western sea. In a great voice vibrant with triumph, Eric ordered a northeastward course.

When we had sailed a little way under the lee of the land, the east wind failed. Somehow it had become lost amid the mountains, and we had to make out with an offshore breeze on our stearboard amidships. But although we must tack slowly, we came on something better than the best wind we could buy, which was land suitable to habitation, a land where I thought our tough Norse breed could flourish, the green land we sought.

Its strands remained unutterably empty and barren. Among many of these a crust of rotted ice formed beside still shallows. The only trees we saw were dwarf birch and willows such as we had left in Iceland. But well above the mouths of the countless fiords lay immense meadows, with room for innumerable homesteads and grass for countless flocks and herds. And while the beasts that the settlers would bring increased their number, food for our tables could be found in the sea. Here were seals beyond counting, eider ducks in such flocks as no man of our company had ever seen, and to judge by the busy terns and the fat pelicans and a wondrous kind of falcon, nearly as large as an eagle and handsome beyond compare, that repeatedly dived for underwater prey, there was an abundance of fish.

As we were coming into view of the likeliest-looking country we had seen, Eric ordered only enough sail to maintain headway in the strong current northward. He was gazing at the mouths of what appeared to be narrow, deep-cut fiords, ice-free, exposed only to a west wind in their lower reaches, and quite likely completely sheltered in the upper. In our group was one of Einer's thralls named Ari, well deserving of the epithet Gull Eye. I doubted if a pair of sharper long-range eyes had ever been set in a man's head. He could see detail where normal men perceived only a blur of color and shape. Eric had the captains of the second and third watch often called him to identify some distant unknown thing. Just now he uttered a little grunt of astonishment.

"Cap'n, it looks to me as if this belt o' land is already settled."

"What in the name of Odin do you mean?" Eric demanded as in a fury. But he was not red in the face and instead, because he knew so well Gull Eye's powers of vision, his face looked pallid.

"If those are not cow creatures you can whip me with their tails!"

"Where?"

"Why, don't you see 'em? A long string of 'em. I reckon a hundred, along that dull green hillside above the big gray rock."

At that instant I saw them too. That they were cattle I could

not doubt, but of a sort I had never dreamed. They looked dark
at that distance and oddly square, and the reason for this last
could only be long dark hair, almost sweeping the ground. When
now and then they swung their blunt heads I caught glimpses of
outsweeping, deeply curved horns.

"There are no pens, no barns, no houses," Einer observed. "Eric,
they must be wild oxen of some sort."

"As true as you live, Einer! Beef for our tables while our herds
are too few for slaughter. Dangerous game, I'll warrant, attacking
a man on sight the same as the wild cattle of Norway. The like
of those long-haired brutes has never been seen in Iceland, or in
Norway either."

"My father, I must question the last," Thorstein said in even,
courteous tones. "On my visit to my uncle, three years ago, he
showed me a crude carving in a cave behind Lindenes. It was
of an ox of a sort I'd not seen until now, with sweeping hair and
fine, curved horns. My uncle took it that they were once native to
Norway but had been killed a thousand years ago."

"Well, I name 'em Greenland oxen. And this land, bigger than
all Norway unless I miss my guess, we'll call Greenland. I grant
you, Whiteland would fit it better, on account of that great cap of
snow and ice we can't get shed of, but people will be more eager
to come here if the land has an inviting name."

"Captain, fate dealt you the wrong card or you would have become a greasy merchant," Thorstein ventured with characteristic
boldness.

" 'Tis a good jest from a sharp mind," Eric replied with dignity.
"Still I doubt if any merchant in Iceland will get as much grease
on his hands and face as we walrus skinners, whale hunters, and
seal-oil tar makers. Now we'll return to the matter in hand. The
new land is no Avalon, but in spite of its snowy cap and no doubt
a thousand glaciers, it's a good land, full of game, animals, and
birds we've never seen. There's abundant farmland for as many as
will come. They can burn whale-oil lamps with a three-foot flame.
Life here will be new, life here will be better, and we won't die
of dry rot. And my younger son was the first to spy it. Also he
won the narwhale horn that led us to it. Mayhap he hasn't

Thorstein's brain, and surely he hasn't got his manner grand as King Olaf's, but he's got something more, which is luck. So while we're naming Greenland, I'll name *him*."

"What is my name, Eric, my father?" I asked, my heart bounding.

"Lucky Leif Ericsson."

CHAPTER FOUR

THE ENCHANTED CAVE

I

Two narrow fiords, their mouths separated by a cape and their upper waters by a low ridge flanked by rankly green meadows to a total width of about ten miles, took the eyes of Eric and Einer. We sailed as far as we could into the larger fiord, then reefed our sail, broke out oars, and all hands rowed about two miles. Here we anchored for the night, still in the desolate beach region; and as soon as the light cleared, we launched our longboat. Into it piled the great chief and his elder son, Thorstein, who was born to be a great chief or I missed my guess, I, his younger son, and eight stout oarsmen. Every other member of our company ached to go with us on this first close survey of what was no doubt one of the richest regions of the new land.

On this trip Eric had little to say, but his green eyes were busy and sharp. A delicious feeling which I could not have described began to possess my whole body and brain and I wished I could spend my whole life in exploration of what might be one of the greatest islands in all the seas, surely the most westward of all, and no doubt the last new land that would ever be found by man. The very air I breathed seemed new and different. Every smell was fresh. Countless brooks winding through the meadows poured with delightful gurglings and lovely glimmerings into the sky-blue waters of the wondrous fiord. Colors seemed brighter and somehow different, because they too were virgin in men's sight.

It was a strange thing, hard to realize, that in all probability no mortal man had ever passed this way before in human history. The great Gods knew of the land, lying at the edge of earth, and sometimes took thought of it. Their servants, such as elves and Swan Maidens, and gigantic trolls dwelling in wondrous caves of ice in the lofty sheet now far inland, and dwarf kings in the wild and awesome mountains, called it home and conversed of its affairs. Birds of a feather never seen by man winged over its prodigious silent aloneness, sometimes crying out. Beasts of hair and horn unknown roamed its illimitable wilderness, sometimes making brute sounds to which their utterance was confined. So it must be that the water witches over whom we rowed on the now glassy mere, some old and ugly but many young and beautiful, with jewel-bright eyes and flaxen hair fastened up with jewels, perhaps a whole pack gathered and swimming under us, could hardly believe their ears when now and then one of our company spoke briefly or exclaimed, for here no human voice had ever been heard since the beginning of the world.

If Ian had been among us, speaking in his godly voice, their queen would have fallen in love with him and tried to carry him down to her cavern agleam with jewels. Indeed they were known to be the most lascivious sort of women, often chasing sailors on the strands, and I took pleasure in imagining them aching and burning at sight of our reflections in the water, upsetting our boat and carrying us down, where we would be charmed against drowning, and then their fighting over us in a passionate frenzy. Well I knew that Thorstein would be their main prize of battle; but with gusty, bull-like Eric a close second. Still I would not be ignored, perhaps by the very loveliest although youngest in the band, only a little older than Ellen's daughter, Swanhild. Then suddenly I put the daydream by, pocketing it somehow, for I found myself recalling the child's kiss almost as vividly as her mother's whole embrace, truly my maiden flight, and I could not dwell on one without the other, which I would do in leisure and in warm concentration. For the present my business was with the sea, and new land we had found, its living creatures, and its austere Gods.

We had come to a splendid river and were able to row up its limpid flood for a short distance before the strong current balked us. Dense flocks of fresh-water ducks took wing, many of an unknown sort, and dark darting shapes in the water were obviously salmon, some of them larger than any we had seen or dreamed of, fully of the weight of forty pounds.

"And there," Eric proclaimed, pointing to a little knoll in the meadow clad in stunted birch and spruce trees, "I will build my hall."

Here was a good graveled beach, fronting deep water, for a landing, and thereabouts were league-wide grasslands. Not far was a steep hillside, dotted with stones of a sort fit for sheep pens—and then before I could stop them my thoughts leaped back to Kol lying under a cairn of just such stones. The very next moment I forgot him, because of the rising everywhere from the grass of grouse-like birds, uttering lonely and strange cries, and taking off in steady flight without a whirring sound, then arching their wings and lighting light as a feather.

A few minutes later Gull Eye saw slowly moving specks on a far-distant hill, which he thought were some kind of deer.

On our row back to the fiord Eric was the quietest and calmest member of our company. I knew that his thoughts were busy by his occasional tug at his beard and the short impatient pull of his oars, no longer in rhythm with our steady pulling. At the river mouth he bade us return to the ship. And at half the distance he was ready to tell us his plans—or as much of them as he wanted us to know.

"Sixteen men including Einer and I will man the ship for what exploring we've yet to do," he announced. "We'll stand twelve-hour watches of eight men each, and Starkad's watch, with a little trading of men, will be put ashore at the site I chose, and its first task will be to build a house of turf, say twelve feet long and eight feet wide, with a good dirt floor. I want it standing there when I bring the folk. I want no doubt in their minds that this belt of land is mine, for a few of the number who were great lords in Ireland before the Christians rose and drove 'em out have caught the Irish habit of contention. I hope and believe Einer will find ground to suit him along the very next fiord, the one we scanned, and we can be neighbors still. Our journey should not take longer than a fortnight, giving Starkad's crew plenty of time to erect the building."

Eric fell silent, rowed purposefully awhile, then again idled his oars.

"The truth remains," he went on, "we may have trouble with

ice, or meet with a summer gale. So when we put the men ashore, they must have not only tools but weapons, bows, and seal harpoons, knives, fishing tackle, our big skiff, stores of all needful sort. By Thor of the Red Beard, our ship might run on a skerry and go down, or be crushed in the ice, and then the men would have a long wait before they see another sail or another human face."

"A long wait," Thorstein broke in, "and that's a mild way to put it. In truth we'd wait our lives long, unless some sort of folk dwell in the land, yellow like Laplanders, but savage instead of peaceful. You can be sure that no ship will come to look for us. Thorhild would buy and victual her, and hire the best crew to be found, but they'd only pretend to look, and when the sea began to stretch forever every way they gazed, and they saw all those whales with teeth and all that ice, they'd take it that this is the Poison Sea and spread her sail for home. The fact remains that since I am not in Starkad's watch I ask to be assigned to his watch to stay here while you continue your explorations."

This request took me by wild surprise. Yet instantly I knew it was exactly what I should have expected from my brother, Thorstein.

Eric did not know his own son and was visibly taken aback. He needed some seconds to get his breath.

"It will mean hard work and some hardship, the best you can do. I won't repeat what you said about the risk of being marooned forever. Why in the name of the God Thor—I won't invoke Odin, although this is more in his dominion than the Thunder God's—do you invite the duty instead of waiting to see if you're assigned it?"

"The reasons are very simple. One, that I don't think you'll see much more than I've already seen—abundant marine life, ice, dreary strands, grasslands, and distant snowfields. Two, the adventure attracts me, our aloneness for an indefinite period, and the possibility of exciting happenings. Three, I assume that my brother, Leif, will stay in the watch to which he went out of his way to be assigned, and since I feel he is rather young for duty of this kind, I would like to be with him."

My spirit was proud enough, but my tongue not nimble enough to make a suitable reply, so I kept silent.

"Then, by the Nine Runes, you'll both stay!" Eric burst out.

As it happened—or more truly, as nature had it—the boldest and best men on the ship, including Gull Eye, tried to trade places with Starkad's watchmen, but not one of our fellows would agree. As soon as time and light allowed, we began putting ashore our gear.

2

All hands assisted in the task, and the wonder to me was that our ship had stowed such a great heap of supplies and still contained twice as much more, with cramped but decent eating and sleeping room for twenty-four men. I thought of the startling contrast between Eric's short temper and his long head, because he had failed to furnish nothing that our shore party or the remainder of the ship's company might sorely need. For us there were thirty days' rations, whether we lifted a harpoon or set a trotline, hair-seal garments for wintry weather, walrus-gut capes with hoods for rough days at sea, weapons of every kind known in Iceland, waterproof footgear, skis for snow travel, seal-oil lamps and lanterns, an immense iron kettle for rendering fat, pots and pans, drills for fire making, spare oars for our boat, skins for fresh water, iron axes and steel saws, tools for cutting turf, lines, whetstones, a purse seine, strong needles, skin scrapers and fleshing knives, coarse and fine salt, sheepskin robes, a box of medicines, a measuring stick to align the walls of our turf house, material for making snares, and one of the *Narwhale*'s spare sails to protect our unhoused gear.

Having seen to our needs, Eric made ready to stand to sea. Our shore party of eight lined up on the strand to watch the *Narwhale* weigh, and a short line we made compared to the wondrous, seeming illimitable line of the strand. I confessed to myself a strange feeling. Eight was a small number of humans to be left for an unpredictable period to inhabit this monstrous land, all of us but Thorstein looking like ordinary fellows such as might go forth together to do a day's chore at any homestead in Iceland.

My heart had a pleasant thud, but an awe was in me, too, as my tingling backbone told me, and I took a good look at the *Narwhale* with her wondrous figurehead because only a little accident in a sea, where the least of accidents could have mighty consequences, might prevent me from ever laying eyes on her again.

Some rough Norse jests sped back and forth across these Norse waters. If we became hard up for women we could set snares on the beaches to catch mermaids, although their scaly tails might prove an inconvenience to our intent. If we were caught by a troll, and carried under one arm to his ice palace, and there spitted and roasted over the flame of a hell vent, at least one fellow of our number would upset the monster's stomach, the thrall Gorm being that sour. If we were devoured by white bears, their whole band would hunt down the beasts and devour them in revenge, and thus our whole ship's company would be united. Yet their laughter at their jokes and at our sallies had a raw and nervous ring, for they knew that our gathering here was not a picnic.

All jests ceased and loud mirth gave way to silence when I brought forth my flute, which I had kept wrapped in a piece of sail against the damp. Then I wished mightily that I could play such a noble song as Thorhild had played at our ship's departure from Ericsholm, because the occasion warranted it, as my soul knew well. The best I could do was play a rollicking country tune, the words of which all of us knew, and which all my listeners aboard the ship, including red-bearded Eric, sang with roaring vehemence.

> A country lout to Stavener did go,
> And met a maid whose pretty teat did show.
> What can you do with it? the lass did ask,
> For what a man you are, I'd like to know.
>
> I'll help you out, replied the lout,
> Upon my arms two skillful hands did grow,
> At home I milk ten cows, my daily task,
> And cheese and butter stored me many a cask.

Ensuing verses related other of the lout's adventures, and since my audience appeared delighted, not at all disturbed by my frequent squeaks and off-key notes, I played the tune again and again, the hands singing lustily until the lout's education was completed and the song came to its happy ending.

Then Eric ordered that the oars be run out, and with heavy labor the men rowed until the sail lazily filled from the eastward breeze. We watched her round the bend, until indeed we could see only her top above the dwarf birch trees, and then she was well under way, and a heavy silence fell upon our little band of eight watching from the strand. My brother, Thorstein, broke that silence.

"We've wasted enough time," he said. "Now we must get to work."

"So I reckon," replied the freeman Starkad.

"Starkad, you were put in command of this watch. As far as I know, my father did not appoint anyone in command of the shore party. Ordinarily, you would have first right. But since I am Eric's oldest son, of far higher rank, more used to command, a more experienced hunter—and the time may come when our survival may depend on hunting—the thought comes to me you will choose to assign that right to me."

While Starkad scratched his head, I looked with dread into his face and listened with dread to hear his assent, yet I was not quite sure. His face looked calm as ever, and no dimness appeared in his bright, lively eyes.

"Sir, I am a freeman," he answered quietly at last. "It is quite true that Eric did not appoint anyone in command of the shore party, but it is also true he did not relieve me of my command of the watch. Therefore I'll retain command until I feel I am not competent. Now all hands will take turf-cutting tools for the first chore in building a shelter."

All of his listener's faces, save one, seemed to brighten a little. My brother's face looked cold, his eyes icy, his handsome mouth curled slightly. Only caustic old Gorm made comment.

"Yes, and it had better be as strong a shelter as we can build, for we may have to live in it the rest of our natural lives."

Then, with avidity, the men chose and shouldered their tools.

Thorstein was not remiss, although as soon as our crew fell in behind Starkad, he dropped back to my side.

"Do you know, Leif, I am glad that both you and I are in the shore party?" he told me in low tones.

"You said something the same to Eric."

"I suggested that I wanted to look after you, on account of your lack of experience in wilderness. I really did not mean it. I apologize for saying it. You showed your mettle when you took the narwhale horn. The real reason strikes deeper."

"If you care to tell me what it is, I would like to hear it."

"It will be a fine test as to which of us is the better man."

"I would like to have that settled also."

"Since I am three years older——"

"You can disregard that."

"Good! Your saying so makes me believe that the contest will be closer than I thought, and more enjoyable. And there's sense to it, too, for in the matter of height, weight, and bodily strength there's not much to choose between us. The contest will be between our strengths of mind and of will—which of us was better endowed by our father, Eric. Our mother, Thorhild, gave you certain traits that I do not possess—but I doubt if they will be much use to you in these surroundings."

When he gazed to the distant mountains, so did I. These were of naked rock, rugged and wild and austere beyond description, and beyond these, glimmering, was the ice sheet that had no end.

"It will be a rough life," I remarked.

"It will be a good contest between you and me. I wonder whom Eric would pick as the winner. He has more respect for you than—to be frank—I've ever been quite able to understand. But if the thought has crossed his mind that you can match me—but let that go for now. Time will tell."

3

The building of the turf house went forward not swiftly, but with a steadiness that gave the effect of swiftness. The blocks of turf, interbound with dense grass roots, were hard to cut and unearth but easy to put in place. We built it eight feet wide and twelve feet long, as Eric had bade us. At no great distance we were able to cut stunted birch to support its shedlike roof, and this we covered with thatch, mainly sun-dried reeds from a nearby pond, carefully laid to carry off rain water or melted snow, and securely fastened to the turf with wooden pegs. This last precaution was in remembrance of the fierce and raving winds of Icelandic winter, and in foresight of mightier winds shrieking down from the ice sheet.

We left no vent in the roof for the escape of smoke. Well we knew we had no wood to spare for fires and must depend on seal-oil or whale-oil lamps. In the way of a window we omitted only one block of turf from the tier, and this we could close with skins. In all truth, the inkling had come to us all, although it was rarely mentioned, that the winters at Eric's fiord in Greenland were likely to be a good deal colder than those at Ericsholm in Iceland, although the latter might be one hundred or one hundred and fifty miles farther north. With the swiftly shortening days, we often saw the North Star markedly higher in the sky than at this time of year in Iceland. The sunlit days were fully as warm but the nights and the early mornings decidedly more chill. Winter was advancing faster than at our old home this season, and the winds off the mountains had a sharper bite.

Our single door had wooden posts and frame, and the opening covered with nailed-on sheepskins, flesh side out. I caught myself wishing we had made it smaller—not to admit a man walking tall, but one crawling on his hands and knees. For now the thought of the *Narwhale* returning with warm cabins before the wild outbreak of winter was turning from an expectation to a hope that dimmed and brightened without apparent cause. The two weeks Eric had allowed for his absence had ended, and shorter, colder days filed one by one by one behind us. Already Starkad, Thorstein and his keen and blood-hungry spear, and one oarsman had begun seal and walrus hunting in the fiord. Three men rendered the oil, storing it in what skins we had brought with us and fleshing and drying and sewing the new sealskins to hold more. They passed by several chances to harpoon whales because, until hard and enduring frost, we could not conserve the meat.

Starkad appointed me, much to Thorstein's almost but not perfectly concealed rancor, for the most exciting duty of our party. It was to spear salmon and to hunt any game to be found of use to us. This meant that every day I ventured into some unknown region of our environs, and there was something new and thrilling to see every hour of that day. Once it was a herd of tall-horned deer on which I had never before laid eyes, but which I could not doubt were identical with the white-maned, proud-striding reindeer of Norway. Taken by surprise in level grassland, I did not get in arrow range. I had heard my father tell of the excellence of the venison of reindeer, more succulent than the flesh of the great, black elk.

Again and again I met with the long-haired oxen such as Gull Eye had seen from shipboard. They were even more impressive-looking supporting sturdy bodies, their blunt heads warlike. I could hardly wait for my first battle with one of the big bulls, he with two long, magnificently curved, and sweeping horns, I with my javelin and—if the combat came to such deadly quarters—my shining sword. Still I avoided a brush, because there was as yet no way to preserve the beef. White foxes preyed relentlessly on big, white hares and on the grouse-like birds we had seen and which now seemed to be turning white. Once I caught a distant view of what I could not doubt was the great pale gray wolf that I believed identical with the Demon of the Twilight, of which so many thrilling and bloody tales were told in Norway.

On these expeditions I always went alone. Hands were too few in our shore party to employ four where two would do. And it was of aloneness that I became most solemnly and I cannot say other than nobly aware. Our house of turf had a way of fading from sight as soon as I was a mile from its enclosure and small precincts where human voices were a commonplace and where I had seen sticklike moving objects whom I knew were men. It is said that when our God Thor carries a great sheath of thunder-bolts, and wishes to reduce the heavy load, and when beneath his drapery of black cloud he sees no one whom he hates or wishes to destroy, he will often hurl the bolt at the tallest thing directly beneath him, whether a tall tree, or a shepherd's house on the flat heath, or even a man standing taller than a cow. But he would have to look sharply to see our habitation, its green and yellow and black colors blending with the landscape. In any case, although many a crashing thunderstorm raved across our grass-lands in the days of the dying summer, and one blinding shaft broke into slivers a willow trunk not over four feet high and a hundred paces from our door, we were never hit, and in truth I gave little thought to being hit, opening one eye when a great clap crashed, then closing it and going back to sleep.

Yet when hardly a mile from the homestead, my soul came upon a loneliness too profound for my mind to grasp. I thought it was akin to the lonesomeness that comes upon a human spirit in its wandering dreams, not those dreams in which it beholds faces that it loves or hates, or unrecognizable faces, or hears familiar voices thin and strange, voices without breath, but when it moves alone in an unfamiliar and uninhabited realm. At such a distance I would still be in wild meadow, to which many a late-blooming wild flower brought a touch of pale color; still I felt alone as might a single visitor to his native star.

There were a great many furred and feathered folk. The most common of the latter were the grouse-like birds we had begun to call tarmochans, because old Gorm pronounced them very like, if not identical with, a heath fowl he had seen in the moors of Northern Ireland, and so-called there. They were not a sociable bird, as were Icelandic heath hens, rising not in a roaring flock but silently one by one, winging off in silent flight, save for the strange wail they often uttered, then arching their wings, slowly dropping back into the grass. Every meadow pond had been almost black with wild ducks and geese earlier in the summer; now their numbers had greatly diminished, and I well-nigh feared to flush them because when I did so they separated in small flocks, some of which settled on other ponds, but some invariably winged southward in straight and purposeful flight, as though my startling them was somehow a last straw, or better say a last discomfiture to their late lingering, and they had as well begin their southward journey and be done with Greenland. When all were gone, the loneliness of the land, already sea-deep, might become deeper than the soul could plumb.

I had observed that the tarmochans, the hares, the weasels, and the foxes that I saw every day, and the wolves that I glimpsed occasionally at great distance, seemed to be turning white. Well I could picture their invisibility when the land was robed in snow from its white cap to its blown bleak strands. In a sense the smaller white changelings would leave the sight of men, our little handful, as waterfowl left it now, and we would not know of their comings, goings, and doings, which by one way of thinking were somewhat like our own, being mainly to eat, sleep, avoid enemies, and make some sort of preparation for the winter that their dim souls prompted. Yet the real lords of the land, the wolves, would still make their presence known. The longer the winter, the deeper the snow, the more biting the icy winds, the more bold they would become in their relations with us intruders in their white realm; and since they themselves would be snow-white, their assaults could be made in invisible stealth. True, I had never seen a wolf before coming to Greenland. By some strange accident of nature they had never invaded Iceland—perhaps merely because the land had been set in such broad seas. My knowledge of wolves—and in fact a cold lump of terror in my heart that the sight of them caused to form—was born of Norse lore. The most terrible monster in the Norse imagination was Fenris the Giant Wolf.

Absent in Iceland, why were wolves so numerous in Greenland? This island too appeared to be set in well-nigh illimitable seas. Could there be another land far to the north with only a narrow channel between our coasts and those undreamable coasts? If so, the packs might have crossed on the ice. And if there were lands farther north, could there not be lands farther west? I did not believe it. Greenland lay about eight hundred leagues west of Ireland, the Old West Land, and five hundred leagues west of Iceland, until lately the New West Land. Beyond here, as all wise men knew, raved the Poison Sea, and beyond that the brink of ocean.

Still I could not quite dismiss the possibility of there being land still farther west. The notion raised its head at unexpected times and it was hard to cap and keep down as new-caught eels frying in a pan. Sometimes between sleep and waking, when all my fellows were breathing gently and deeply in restful slumber, I mused upon it with many a wild flight of fancy.

Another vagary of my mind became manifest in my daily jaunts into untrodden regions. It was that this harsh, austere, and often desolate land had a strange sort of beauty. Many of these grasslands were hilly, although perfectly habitable, and spurs of much more rugged hills jutted from the mountains eastward. On these the light was forever changing, even on clear days when no mists dimmed the sun, and as the summer ended they seemed to take on new and stranger color. With many a vale between, the hills appeared to climb slowly until their outlines were lost from sight against the precipitous and rugged mountains, and beyond this was the mysterious and immense crown of ice and snow. If these vast vistas were not beautiful, they mazed the mind and thrilled the spine with the effect of beauty.

Meanwhile no fellow complained at my not putting my hand to the chores of the homestead, such as hunting and killing seals, sewing the skins to make oil-tight bags, rendering and storing the oil, and salting or wind-drying their harvest from the river and the sea. For one reason, the main one perhaps, the game that I brought back from my jaunts gave variety to an otherwise dull diet of seal meat and fish, because by common consent we had stored what remained of the edibles Eric had left for our use. Always I had two or three braces of tarmochans which I had stalked and shot, several big white hares, and frequently ducks and geese. Also I could have gotten swans if I had hunted them resolutely. The main reason I did not, and instead bungled accidentally on purpose, as the old saying goes, was that my boat was named *Whistling Swan*, which made her some sort of fellow with all swans, and thus an arrow through her namesake's breast might bring about a stab in the boat's side by the sharp rock. Also I confessed the eerie belief that the lovely swans, floating in such beauty on a glassy pond, the sunlight glimmering through their half-lifted plumage, might at any moment divest themselves of their feathers and become Swan Maidens, a transformation that living men had seen in Norway, and which would be all the more likely to happen here, in this new wild land on which no Christian shrine had ever been raised. Here the old Gods of the Norse still held absolute sway, and supernatural creatures of all kinds must have their weird dwellings.

4

In the second month after the summer solstice, when in every bitter dawn a thin sheath of ice formed on windless ponds, I came on a reindeer stag lame from a wolf bite in the foreleg, and him I slew with one arrow, and lugged home, a good nine miles, a hundredweight of his good meat.

Even my brother, Thorstein, did not make light of my offerings, perhaps because he too spent his days hunting, on water instead of on land. Using the sailing dinghy that was stowed in our longboat, his lonely ventures yielded a far greater return than mine. Every day he harpooned one or more seals, some of large size and a kind we had not seen. Once he towed to the landing a big shark, whose skin and teeth were useful, and the day came that he brought in an immense bull walrus. It so happened that the hands had watched his battle with the beast, hardly a cable's length from the strand, and had shouted in joy unmitigated except for their yearning to be not spectators but participants in the perilous fight.

Meanwhile the days shortened with frightening swiftness; stars blazed in the long black nights, some of which, low in the west, our mariners had never seen; the bite of the winds was more bitter; and when Thorstein sailed to our fiord-mouth, ever he saw fewer icebergs but more and larger floes. The men's willing husbandry of our ship food already betokened their belief that the *Narwhale* would not come in this year. She might be stranded, or gale-driven so far south that he had thought best to make for Iceland, there to wait for the first blush of spring before again setting forth for Ericsfiord in the New West Land. Perhaps he had become icebound. Casting a shadow pale as yet over all these possibilities was one that no one but sour old Gorm ever mentioned, and which even he did not believe, that the *Narwhale* had run on a reef and broken up. We others would not darken our brains with the thought, at least for a long time yet. In that dire case not only our shipmates were lost but we too were most strangely and utterly lost beyond the inhabited world.

In the moon of the autumnal equinox the ice forming in the dawn on the meadow pools no longer melted in mid-morning, only thinned in early afternoon, and at night thickened. This mattered not to the fresh-water ducks, for they had long sped southward, but this year's hatch of eider ducks often made us laugh by mistaking the blue ice for blue water, skimming down to light, and then skidding, squawking, halfway across the pond. Toward the end of the month Thorstein sighted a school of medium-sized whales hardly a sea mile from our landing. Swiftly he returned, manned the whaleboat with rowers and harpooners— indeed our whole crew with the exception of myself—and set forth for the kill. In common civility, if for no other reason, he was willing I too should go. Instead I asked him to leave me the little sailing dinghy, because I wished to make a middling-long sightseeing sail up the fiord, from which voyage I might not return until the second or third day.

He was speechless for a few seconds, gazing at me with slightly narrowed eyes. Then he spoke in a rough but friendly voice.

"Leif, sometimes I doubted if you were Eric's fitly begotten son because you seemed to love a flute more than a harpoon. I'll not question it any more. I'll only remind you that I am his first-born son."

In all truth I rejoiced that I was the younger because when I scored on Thorstein the victory was that much greater. As for the present venture, I had been contemplating it more than a month, wildly hopeful that the opportunity would come to attempt it. My destination—other than mere distance and new scenes—was a white object, which appeared to project from the main range of mountains into the grassy hill country, and which looked as though it arched down in a long and lovely curve. I took it for an almost inactive glacier lying much lower than the great icecap, and I thought possibly it was the head of our fiord. It could even be the maker of our fiord in some ancient time when it was much greater, carrying huge stones and quantities of rock that had gouged out a valley into which the sea had rushed. Occasionally we had seen in the fiord icebergs which might have broken from the overhanging wall of such a glacier and which, although swiftly melting in the sun-warmed salt water, were still of impressive size.

I judged it to be sixty miles by crow flight from our hut. The brisk wind was fair for an eastward sail, yet almost always the night wind was off the land, and I had little fear of an easy homeward passage by the light of the full moon and without back-breaking labor. Still, I stowed no trifling amount of gear in the bow of my little boat. In the lot was the cold-weather garment of reindeerskin made by Lapp women in northern Norway, with knee-length waterproof boots, a long cloak with belt and hood of walrus gut impervious to rain and snow, an ax, a pick, bow and arrows, a harpoon, and my broadsword, this last of no use that I could think of, yet which I brought in ceremonious respect to my sally into utterly virgin country. I had thought too of bringing my flute. Every night of late I had played it about an hour, before the men grew sleepy, and despite my yet meager skill, they listened with pleasure to old Norse tunes, mixed with a few much livelier Irish melodies, my playing of which was passable. Indeed only Thorstein abjured listening. He did so by intense concentration on various handicraft, for instance the sharpening of harpoons and arrowheads and working his two big walrus tusks into handles for a sled the men were building. Truly I believed that he never heard a note I sounded; but I had thought that dwarfs dwelling in rocky caverns and gigantic trolls in underground palaces of ice might listen, and the former might bring me gifts, and the wrath of the latter over a mortal man setting foor in the wind-swept and awesome wilderness might be assuaged.

But on second thought I left the magic horn in my kit bag, fastened with a knot Thorhall had taught me to tie, all but impervious to untrained prying fingers, but which I could unloose in utter darkness with one hand. And that thought was born of fear that some trifling accident might cause the wondrous instrument to be broken in some slight but irreparable way, whereby it would be silenced forever.

In the way of food I had some boiled seal meat and about a dozen sun-dried and highly aromatic fish, one of then a fair-sized sea trout, the rest smaller fish I could not identify, being caught with hook and line in a pothole at the mouth of our river. On the first day's journey I devoured the trout and a good bait of seal meat. I began to wish I had had more respect for my appetite in this chill, brisk, and invigorating air. Unless I made my trip with fair dispatch, I might suffer some belly pangs before I regained camp.

The first day's sail from early morning until two hours or more after the rising of the miraculous white moon in her perfect round bore me fully fifty miles up the fiord. In the role of my father's scout I kept an eye open for good pasture land, and truly it spread far and wide, the grass being dense, thick, and most wondrously green. And the thought struck me that Greenland would be a suitable name for this new land, if one could overlook its icecap, which was of course impossible, for there was simply no end to it, as far as eye could reach or imagination could attain. There were many small fresh-water rivers, in which fish swirled and darted, and innumerable brooks. There were sweet and silent valleys, sheltered by hills, and one considerable stand of birch, stunted, but yet standing house tall instead of man tall. I saw numerous birds, mainly of the ruffianly sort that weathered out our Iceland winters, playful and magnificently vital otters, many works of industrious beavers, an animal unknown in Iceland, several bands of from fifty to a hundred Greenland oxen stolidly making their way in cattle dignity, and a herd of at least a thousand reindeer. Of beasts unseen until now, I beheld only one, a short-legged and for some unknown reason ugly creature, weighing perhaps forty pounds, that threw me a wicked snarl as I disturbed his stalk of a white hare. I made the wild guess that he was of a species well-known and hated in Norway, commonly called a glutton.

The glacier loomed wanly white in the moonlight, and I was

sure now of my guess that it hung athwart the fiord. By laying a tarpaulin on the damp grass, covered by two sheepskin robes, I thought my good bed looked tempting enough to entice a mermaid from her rocky underwater crypt, but it failed to do so, and my only visitor was a white fox that sniffed deeply and made off. Yet it was a strange feeling to be bedded so far from my kind, in a realm unknown to me and to all men.

When the moon set I arose, barely tasted my boiled seal meat, cold, greasy, and hardly palatable in the bitterly cold dawn, and instead ate most of my dried fish. Still any uneasiness I had felt over a meager larder was relieved when I remembered the good stand of birch I had lately passed, where I could certainly kill small game if not big, and bake it on the coals of a roaring fire. When the sun made its belated rising over the icecap, I was well on my way up the fiord, although at a tardy pace. All night the wind had blown off the mountains. During the morning it had again reversed itself in my favor, but had been reduced to a laggard breeze that lazily puffed my sail. Yet the sun seemed singularly ardent this limpid morning, such a sun as had rarely beamed in misty Iceland, save on occasional days in midsummer.

Now, nearly noon, I could see the glacier in all its shimmering glory. Its front was too steep and dangerous to climb, yet I did not despair of exploration not of its crest but of its mysterious heart. Looming ever larger was a great rent in the overhanging face, which I could not doubt was an ice cave, its bottom almost on a level with the fiord, and out of which flowed a splendid river, grayish white in color from melting ice and finely pulverized rock. To judge from its copious flow at this time of year when most glaciers hung frozen, iron hard, from late afternoon until after sunrise—all the little voices of trickling waters silent as the grave—I thought that in high summer and especially in seasons of heavy rain the river might almost fill the cavern mouth with its roaring flood.

"River, I christen you"—then my tongue tripped over the name I had been about to utter, which was Ellen River. And on second thought I perceived that "christen" too was the wrong word, that it would anger the Gods and their dwarf attendants who reigned thereabouts, and a sleeping troll might waken in colossal wrath, and for that matter the God Kris would rebuke me for using a Christian term in a heathen ceremony. This last was what it was— the naming of a river never before seen by man in this setting of aboriginal grandeur, a world removed from the altar of some hushed and holy little church, such as the one at Borg in Iceland, where my mother went to kneel on the New Moon following the first full moon after the spring equinox, in heart-welling gratitude for Kris' rising from the dead, and where she ate of the Body and drank of the Blood of Kris, miraculously transformed into bread and wine. Neither Thorstein nor I had ever been christened. Instead our forehead had been marked with the blood of a heathen sacrifice, a bullock whose throat had been cut with a Viking sword, and the mark too was heathen since time out of mind, a cross with each arm bent at a right angle, so that somehow it suggested a circle.

Aye, I had closed my lips just in time for I had instantly perceived that Ellen River was not the right name for my first notable discovery in Greenland. Perhaps this was true because her gift to me had been stolen from her brutish husband, and her maidenhead had been long lost to some other lover. Then my thoughts flew to the last gift I had received ere our ship stood to sea on a perilous and mysterious voyage. So the door of my lips opened and I spoke again.

"River, I name you Swanhild River." And this was a fitting appellation, I thought, for I meant to drink of its waters before I left these scenes, as I had drunk with some strange deepness of Swanhild's lips, and both had been virginal to a man's kiss.

5

Then I moored my boat strongly to the rocky shore. Thinking of what gear to take with me into the ice palace, I thought first of my broadsword, and second of a supply of food in case I became wearied climbing over moraine or rough ice. But a better notion was to eat now my midday meal, for its strength would serve me as well in my stomach as in a shoulder bag. So I got out the rest of my dried fish. The first was good enough but small; the second had been dropped in ashes and was gritty to my tongue; the third, considerably larger than either, was of a species I had never seen, a stocky fish with a small, round mouth, and its body tapered to two fingers' breadth ere the deeply cleft tail fanned boldly out. Its taste was a little different than any fish I had ever eaten, although I could not tell why, yet pleasant enough, and I picked its scant bones. It was some sort of shad, I thought.

When I rose from my seat in the grass, my head swam a little, although the dizzy feeling seemed warm and pleasant. As I made up the bank to the cavern mouth, my feet felt numb and I reckoned that they had gone to sleep because I had sat in a cramped position. Yet they were strangely slow to waken to their usual precision and strength of step. And as I neared the cavern mouth my eyes played tricks on me with darting lights and sometimes what seemed a second image superimposed not quite exactly on the first, the difference not quite transparent and a little blurred, as a man's own hand seen with both eyes at half a foot's distance. There came a sensation of a drum beating far off, which I quickly surmised was my own pulse loud in my ears.

I wondered what was causing these effects, although I felt no alarm and I arrived lazily at the notion that a spell was being put on me by a water witch, or by a Mountain King who sat on his throne in a bejeweled chamber in the fastnesses above me. Indeed the flow of thoughts through my brain seemed much slower than usual, nor as well connected, with hazy visions intervening between one and another. I had a feeling of cozy warmth.

Then, suddenly, I felt well. All my confusion passed; I knew myself as Leif Ericsson, even now at the threshold of a wondrous cave of ice. There was good walking on the gravel bank of my side of the river, and its waters were strangely lighted, no doubt from the wide maw and another shining aperture far over my head. The walls appeared almost unearthly beautiful. The lofty ceiling appeared beautifully worked by dwarfs and other servants of some mighty being who was ruler here—with glimmering cornices of noble shape, and arch after arch of ice supporting the vast weight of the main mass of the glacier. At any instant I expected to meet a band of dwarfs with long beards and wearing quaint attire, and I had not the slightest dread of seeing a troll, leaning at ease against the splendid wall, each of his hairy feet bigger than my whole body, his head higher than a Norway pine, and a smile of welcome for the first mortal that had ever passed these portals.

Instead, I came on a deposit of round boulders, perhaps rolled here by the river when it was in freshet. It ran from bank to bank but it did not dam the main of its flow, which found its way in the gaps between the stones. Yet the obstruction was enough to cause a limpid pool, its brim only a little higher than the water swirling through the obstruction. And I had never seen such wondrous lighting, fairylike and unworldly, although natural enough, I thought, since the blazing noonday sun illumined the big aperture of the cavern not a hundred steps behind me and caused manifold reflections on every jut and curvature of the walls and ceiling, and glimmered softly on the pool itself. Indeed the light was as clear as an open ground a few minutes after sundown.

Natural, too, or so I took for granted, was a large school of salmon darting with unexplainable excitement throughout the pool, causing many a swirl or soft splashings. Many of them came to the surface, their heads emerging to get a good view of me. Yet I felt a little start of wonder when a large animal, which had seemed asleep against the cold wall, stirred and raised his head. I recognized it immediately as a large, immense, and very old bearded seal.

In hunching movements he made his way to a formation of ice near the head of the pool, and as he climbed upon it, I saw that it suggested a throne. Then my wonder died away, all was right with me, this was only a realm of life unfamiliar to me until now, as I was unfamiliar to its inmates, but we shared the same world and no doubt made obeisance to the same Gods. When a very large salmon heaved himself up, revealing his head, neck, and a part of his back, and then spoke in somewhat strange-sounding voice but in clearly understandable language, his eyes fixed on the face of the bearded seal, I listened intently to what he said but felt no astonishment.

"O King of Ice," he intoned.

"Aye, Grandfather of Salmon."

"Has this visitor from the outer world come to kill us? He bears a shining sword."

"Why, no, he is a visitor come in peace." Then, looking at me, "How may I address you, our honored guest?"

"My name is Leif. I am the son of Eric the Red. I and my band have raised a little house of turf far down your fiord. I would kneel to you, my lord, but we Norsemen know not how to kneel, and in lieu of that I salute you." And with that I raised my sword and held it upright a little above my head.

"I have seen your kind before, when, in my youth, I journeyed far to sea. Those folk followed the Swan Road in floating houses of wood, with a great cloth catching the wind, and sometimes in small wooden boxes, pointed at one or at both ends. Know that these salmon have been trapped here by that great dumping of rock in a long-ago flood. They are my subjects—I have a myriad of others—and it is given to them to spawn here, although only a few of the fingerlings live. I take as my due in sacrifice only twenty of the grown fish every year, whereby about the same number is maintained, century after century."

"On what do they feed, O King?"

"Many small fishes come up from the fiord and find their way through the barrier of rock."

"Do many birds light on the pool?"

"Only a few swans, whom I make welcome. It may be that one or more will come today because, from their high lookouts, they have watched your advance up the fiord, where none of your kind has ever before ventured, and like all birds, from little wrens to great eagles, they are filled from beak to tail with curiosity."

"O King, will you grant me, in due course, a safe return to my own kind?"

"That I cannot do. But I can promise you safety until you pass the great rock on the left bank—it has weathered to a round pillar, very like the stones that your kind worship in faraway lands. This rock marks the border of my domain."

"You are very old and venerable, O King. It may be that old Mimir, the wise one, has given you the gift of prophecy. If so, will you tell me if I will live to make many more journeys as notable as this?"

"I have not the prophetic gift. I can only feel in my heart that you will. But now comes one that has the godly gift. If she is of the mind to speak——"

A shadow flicked along the wall, changing in shape and brightness, with a dim image of that shadow on the opposite wall, and I heard the soft beat of wings. Before I could look behind me, a swan skimmed down and lighted on the pool. There she floated, her neck beautifully arched, her black bill pointed downward, the soft light glorying her plumage.

6

"May I speak to her, O King?" I asked.

"Truly. She is no common swan. She is a far flyer and she has heard the speech of your kind in what you call Iceland, and in Norway. The great God Odin gave her long ago the gift of turning at will into a Valkyrie, and when she was a young swan she often bore from the bloodied field the corpses of great warriors— bearing them with triumphant song to Valhalla. There is no longer any great call on her services in this matter. The Vikings, shouting above their shields, have turned into farmers and traders, but she knows another art which mayhap she will show you. Her name is Minin, which in your tongue means thought."

"Thought, will you take thought of me and what will come to me, and to what I will come in days to come?"

"Leif, you deserve an affirmative answer. You are the only one of your band of eight with curiosity enough to seek the headwaters of the fiord, and we feathered clan, as the king told you, set much store on curiosity. It may be I could tell you some, but not all. I never drank from the Well of Weird; I was afraid that if I flew down, I would not have enough room to fly up. Much that I see

I cannot tell, because my heart is tender. And before I may speak at all, I must change my aspect."

"I pray you, speak the truth, sparing me not."

Minin lighted at the far end of the pond, then walked with stately but awkward dignity a short distance up the graveled shore. Amid some rocks, half-shielding her, I saw a strange transformation taking place, although I could not say that I wondered at it, for this whole new realm of being into which I had come seemed beyond wonder; yet I was so fascinated by it that I could not, in good manners, look elsewhere. Reaching to her ankles she began to peel back and upward the skin of her forelegs, along with its white plumage. This procedure she continued until her upper legs were bare, then her lower belly, then her protuberant breast, and finally the long and lovely span of her neck and her snowy head. Yet not for an instant did she suggest a skinned fowl. Swiftly behind her hands some spirit was at work, some servant of Frey, God of Fertility, and God of Beauty, too, I weaned, since Balder's death— some such minion changed her disfeathered body faster than the eye could follow. The black webbed feet became the snowy feet of a maiden, her legs filled out from ungainly shanks to the beautiful, rounded, silken pillars that support the curved belly, itself so smooth that it reflected the glimmer of the white walls of ice, yet tinted with a faint glow of pink. Her breast came into view, ineffably lovely, the two perfect rounds with their rose-red points standing forth not grossly but with the promise of Freya's breast to a wailing infant, and then her glimmering shoulders and arms that could not be ungraceful in any action. The most enchanting change of all was the shortening of her neck, yet retaining its glimmering whiteness and a suggestion of its curve, and her black-beaked head into the neck and head of a maiden beautiful beyond description. No such maiden born of woman had ever been seen on our crass earth, unless it was Helen, of a lost and ancient world, of whom our scalds sometimes sang, when she was sixteen and a virgin.

So now I knew that Minin was a Swan Maiden, which except for my thick head I would have surmised long since. Many of these wear the plumage of swans when they wished to go speedily to some distant realm; I could not doubt that some of their forebears had been swans, for it was told of the lost Gods Apollo and Diana that their sire was a swan, although himself a God taking that form.

But my eyes were dazzled by this revelation of utmost beauty, and I asked a cowherd's question.

"My lady Minin, as you stand naked in this ice palace, are you not cold?"

She laughed as musically as falls the song of flying swans.

"Leif, the God who fashioned me put within me an immortal warmth. How else could I and my companions besport ourselves in the icy pools of Norway and Iceland? Sometimes, I confess, it becomes a burning, and I cannot forbear from wooing young shepherd lads with bright faces and hair as gold as Sif's, and often they flee from me, but sometimes they are bold, and we make our bed on the very plumage, soft and warm, that I have shed; and in their drowsy trance that follows such love-making as they had never dreamed, they hardly know what has happened when they find themselves on the chill grass and hear a flutter of pinions, and a white swan wings singing into the distant sky, only to disappear. And ever after there is a white ring on their foreheads, to mark the spot of my farewell kiss of blessing."

"I wish I could be such a shepherd lad when you visit our world."

"In all truth, I would bless you even now, here on this bank, while the loins of the salmon ache in their lust to spawn, and the very king is tempted to seek a virgin seal that swims in the sea like a white flame—aye, so I would do in joy. But it so chances that we have lately passed the autumnal equinox, and continence is enforced by our Goddess upon all Swan Maidens until midnight of All Saints' evening, falling on the night of fullness of the next moon. Mark you, Leif, it is a Christian rite which we observe, not because we wish but because we must, for Kris is a deceptive God, seeming so gentle, even weak, yet stronger than Loki ere he wore chains. Those who are called his saints are likewise of mighty thew. But let us speak of this no more. I will not think of our bodies joined in rhapsody, nor must you, and I will grant your just request, that I tell what comes to me, and of which I may speak, of your life in the days to come."

"Pray, speak plain."

"That, bold Leif, I cannot do. I speak the words that come to my lips, and some of them are wild, and some of disordered meaning, and some seem senseless. With the point of your sword, gently prick my snowy skin nearest my heart, and with this quill from my wing I will prick the skin next to your heart. Then we will both suck until we taste each other's blood, for thus we become bound, and when you have need of me hereafter, only call my name, Minin, and in a few minutes you will see me winging in splendid circles far over your head. And when you press your red lips to my white breast, and feel the suction of my red lips on your white chest, let not lust for me overween your heart, for lust is a momentary thing, like the churning of waters under a swiftly passing whirlwind; and that with which we now will deal concerns long years to come, if not long ages."

So we performed the ceremony, and a few drops of the Swan Maiden's blood were hot in my mouth, and despite her injunction my whole body became heated, although I gave no sign but a heavy breathing. And it tasted unlike that of any beast or bird I knew, and it seemed richer and stronger than my own blood which I had often sucked to cleanse a cut. And the maiden's sweet bosom heaved a little, the best she could do, and the pupils of her strange eyes, blue as her sky realm, immensely enlarged.

"Now take both my hands," Minin instructed me. "Forget that only a few minutes gone they were the first joints of the wings of a swan, but some of the strength that bore me through the heavens presses now into your hands, and this will never leave your hands, as long as you live, yet mine will remain unweakened. Now say, not in entreaty but in command, 'Isis, I invoke you.'"

I had heard of the great Goddess Isis. I think her first temples were in far-off Egypt, but later many were raised in Rome before the coming of Kris, and thus knowledge of her powers had come by ship, brought by our far journeyers, or had crept overland, her name to be spoken under one's breath save at her hidden shrines, to Spain, through the kingdom of the Franks and later through the whole vast empire of Charlemagne, and I did not doubt she had a few devotees within a day's march of Stavanger.

"Isis," I said with firmness, "I invoke you."

I cannot aver that then I laid eyes on divinity. Out of the corner of my eye I glimpsed something, which, as near as I could describe the vision, was that of a tall woman of swarthy skin, her black hair worn at each side of her head and cut evenly across about the line of her chin. But the whole image had a dim and shimmery quality, as though I were looking at its reflection in water brushed by a light breeze.

"Behold, she had heard you and risen from her mossy grave. It was her spirit moving through the spirit of the Woman of Endor who called up Samuel from his mossy grave at the request of a king. Whether Isis will whisper in my ear, or remain silent, I do not know. And Leif, some centuries from now, in the land of Orléans many times ravaged by your Viking forebears, there will be born a maiden whose gaze can penetrate all the dim curtains of time, all that has been and all that will ever be. Although her spirit has not as yet been clothed in the husk of flesh and blood, even now it beholds visions deep and far as those of very Isis, Mistress of all Magic. Invoke her in such speech as rises to your lips."

"Maid of Orléans, I invoke your spirit."

Again a vision flicked to the corner of my eye, in this case the left eye instead of the right. It was of a tall, young, handsome girl, with a bright and smiling face and dark hair cut like a soldier's, as seen in a splendid painting that Harald Bluetooth had looted from a palace in Rouen, and this my own mother had seen and described to me. The maiden's form was womanly, rather than girlish, in a wholly lovely way. But the vision that was given me was even less sharp than the others as though beheld through deep, limpid, but flowing water.

"Leif, she is here," the Swan Maiden told me, her strange voice trembling. "I did not believe she would come. Of all the great prophetesses of all the past and future time she is most loath to make herself manifest, perhaps only because it is more difficult, since it is fated that her body will be burned and her ashes thrown in a great river. Truly your life will be no common life, truly it must be that you will perform some mighty deed marking you forever among men, a deed of import beyond their imaginings for centuries to come, perhaps beyond your own imaginings. Now, Leif, mark me well. About five centuries ago there lived in the west part of Britain a truly great soothsayer. Among his sayings was the prophecy of the birth of the Maid of Orléans who is with you now. In these present days he is spoken of as Merlin. Invoke his spirit."

"Merlin, I invoke your spirit."

Again out of the corner of my right eye I saw a human shape, in this case that of a tall man with a craggy head, white forelocks, snow-white hair, and a long snow-white beard that he combed with his fingers. What seemed his reflection in deep water shimmered a little; still it was the sharpest image I had yet glimpsed of my ghostly visitors.

"Only one remains to call," Minin told me. "You have seen her with your own eyes. She is Thorbiorg, a spaewoman of Iceland, and when you speak her familiar name, she will hear you in her far-off home, and her spindle will drop from her hands, and she will sit mazed, and her spirit, strengthened by the spirits of her great predecessors, will speak to you through my lips."

"Little Witch, I invoke you."

And then, with both eyes, I saw Thorbiorg's wraith, not in the least dimmed, and solid and real-looking as when I had given her a piece of goldstone at the funeral feast of Kol, and this stone now hung from a thong around her neck. Yet as I gazed upon her, her shape began to grow dim; I saw the ice wall through her body, her familiar sharp-featured face became a blur, and she disappeared from sight.

"Now hold my hands close in yours," Minin instructed me. "Their trembling will soon pass. Even now the visions sent to me begin to take shape, yet dimly and far off. A ship none other than that I gazed down upon as she neared these shores, with the horn of the King of the Narwhales thrusting from its stem—this very ship with a yellow wing, under your mastery, sails the darkling sea on an eastward course."

"Minin, did you say eastward? Do you not mean westward?"

"Nay, she sails toward the rising sun, but she will reverse her course when the time ripes. Then there will stand beside you by the rail a maiden whose hair is of spun gold like Sif's, and she is named after a mighty hero of the Vikings. But what now? By my father, Odin, I cannot tell what I see. I will not look at it. Vision, change in my sight so I may know it is not true. Nay, its shape grows clearer instead of dimming. Those who gaze over my shoulder, Isis, Priestess of the Tripod, Witch of Endor, Unborn Spirit of Orléans whose birth will rock the world, Little Witch of Iceland, avert your eyes as I avert mine, believe it not I beg you, rally all your powers against the fate now seen in awful visage, that this prophecy will fail! Let no breath of it pass your lips. The high Gods, Odin, Thor, Njord, Frey, would shudder on their thrones. Yet the monstrous evil pales in the passage of the years. It dims into distance in the passage of illimitable seas. One little ship? Is she the same that bore westward the maiden with the spun-gold hair? Never was a lone swan in the whole bowl of the sky as much alone as this little vessel, with her brave sail, in the gray, murmuring hollow of ocean. Great storms break and pass. Some are of the stuff of wind and waves, some of the airy, secret, haughty stuff of souls. Will the seas roll on forever? Is there no land at last, or at least an end, when the whole ocean rolls over its brink into the black Hel?"

"Will I find a new land?" I asked. "Tell me in plain words."

"You will find strife, heartbreak, ecstasy, defeat, victory; the whole horn that is poured out to men who defy the Gods. Will you find glorious death, or live on in a strange fashion for a thousand years? And if you find the land, who will people it? My vision dims—something is different, something is changing—you were not as you were, Leif; I cannot speak as I did. O King of the Realm, on your throne of ice, I beseech you, I beseech that my tortured breath no longer twist my lips in the agony of speech. Bid the King of the Salmon speak in my place. He was old when the first beaked ships of Tyre touched the Land of the Long Burroughs, that men called Britain, to buy tin. He is the forefather of a thousand thousand salmon; in his loins lie immortal seed, and his myriad posterity will still buffet the rivers when Leif's grave is lost, his name no more than a runic carving on a stone in the New West Land, if in truth he finds it and I am not cozened by a dream, a dream beyond all fantasy. To the King of the Salmon, yesterday and tomorrow are one. Will Leif find the land, and if so, who will people it, the living or the dead? O King of the Ice, bid the King of the Waters make answer."

"My brother," the king on the icy throne responded, "will you speak?"

"Aye," the great salmon answered, lifting his battered head above the glimmering sheen of the pool. "Our visitor will find the land he seeks, but nigh a thousand years will pass before he is given his due as the finder. It is a latecomer there, when the moss of five centuries has greened on Leif's lost grave—one who sailed from a southern land that my hordes do not frequent—it is this latecomer whose name will be trumpeted over the earth as the great discoverer. Still, as Minin hinted, mayhap Leif may live on in strange fashion and form for longer than the ghost of Charlemagne will haunt his palace at the Fort of the Franks. Mayhap it is a greater mead than is won by the latecomer. It is akin to the mead won by the Seven Sisters when they were set to glimmer palely, world without end, in the winter sky."

"There remains one question, O King of Fishes, that Minin broached but did not answer. Who will people this land?"

"My brother, greater than I, you have seen my horde blackening the waters of every river in the Northland when the warming sun marks the season of their spawning."

"Aye, that I have seen."

"You have seen the myriad of Minin's kin folk, some of them swans, the most of them smaller fowl but all with webbed feet, who come out of the south on pulsing pinions when our ice breaks, and once more they may feed in our sky-blue pools, and gobble and quack, and make nests, and the breaking eggs disclose their babes in fuzzy dress?"

"That, too, I have seen, their multitudes darkening the sky."

"Their numbers, and the number of my hordes, when put together, do not add to the number of Leif's kind and kinsmen who will people the new land."

I heard, and marveled, but before I could believe or disbelieve the whole front of my head appeared about to break open from heavy pain. Minin gazed at me wildly, then her hands slipped out of my weakened hands. My knees began to give way. It seemed that some pale ghost of hands, all that remained of the solid vision of the moment gone, upheld me a moment more, then let me slip gently to the icy floor. A few pale dreams, like wind-scattered clouds, drifted across my mind, then I sank into deep sleep.

7

When I wakened, in nigh perfect mind, the ice palace was not quite so brightly lighted as before, no doubt because the sun had passed its zenith, although it still stood high. What had seemed the king's throne was empty now and appeared to be only an odd conformity of congealed blocks of ice. Gazing into the pool, I saw salmon, their numbers much fewer than before and these rapidly dwindling as the creatures fled from my long shadow cast across the water. For Minin with the wild blue eyes I looked about in vain. The only reminder of her visit here, and of our wondrous communion, was a long feather whiter than the ice on which it lay.

I picked it up, fastened it in my fur cap with a loop of sinew, and made my way to the sunlight.

No, I was not quite in my perfect mind. I made great haste to gain my boat but instead of loosening her mooring lines and starting down the fiord I found myself making a frantic search of what had been my food supply, although for the moment I could not steady my mind to know for what I was searching. Then I perceived I was looking for some remains of odd-tasting shadlike fish of which I had eaten before entering the ice cavern. I craved it with a desperate craving, I would give my all for a few mouthfuls, and I could hardly keep from crying out in anguish of body and soul when I saw its backbone from which I had picked every morsel thrown on the bank. Then the wild thought struck me of rigging a fishing line and trying to catch another to eat raw.

Some return of sanity reminded me that I had never seen this fish caught in salt or brackish water, and in all the fresh-water fishing I had ever done, in both Iceland and Greenland, a specimen had never ascended the shallows to meet my spear, and not one had ever taken my hook.

So I composed myself more and tried to eat some of the cold, boiled seal meat. I could not swallow even a bite just then and must spit it out, proof it was not ordinary hunger that had sped my wild search for remnants of the fish. In all truth I still craved it fiercely, but the launching of my boat, and busying myself with the sail and the steering oar, took my mind from it somewhat, and slowly the passion—I know not what else to call it—passed off.

So far I had given little thought to what appeared to have happened in the ice cavern. Then I began to contemplate it in all its strangeness; still I was unable to dismiss it as a fantastic dream of sleep or of semi-consciousness caused by a hard fall on the icy floor. If my head had been bumped, I could not feel it. Greatly beyond this, it did not recur to my mind in the vague way of a dream. Occasionally I had been perplexed on first waking from sleep as to whether an experience was real or a figment of fancy, but always in a matter of seconds I grasped the truth. Also every detail of what seemed to have happened in the ice palace lingered sharp and convincing in my memory. I raised my hand and touched the swan-wing feather I had stuck into the band of my fur cap. Its reality was indisputable, but I had picked it up after my fall, and a case could be made that I had noticed it before I fell and a whole fabric of frantastic dreams had been woven around it.

I reached the bank where I had slept the night before, and that morning had had breakfast, and there I decided to spend a second night. The main reason, or so I told myself, was that the weather was changing fast, already noticeably colder, and the clouds rising with great swiftness over the mountain persuaded me that the morrow's wind might be out of the east, to bear me swiftly homeward, instead of forward of the beam as it gently blew then. But there was another reason why I did not wish to set sail that evening. My head ached, I felt somewhat wearied, my thoughts were in turmoil when I would let them flow, and I craved a night of deep sleep.

This I was given, wakened only once by a herd of reindeer making down the bank, one of which snorted when he smelled me. In the morning a fine, fresh, but biting wind blew off the mountains, and after rotating my sail I had nothing to do but mind the rudder oar all the way to our river. At the strand was moored a middle-sized whale of a species I did not recognize, plain proof that yesterday's hunt by my fellows, led by Thorstein, had been successful. Moreover, the prize was a precious one, because the icy wind and deepening cold promised a hard freeze that night, the first deep freeze of the season, and, remembering Icelandic freezes at this time of year, I reckoned that any thaw would be brief and shallow, and that the great carcass would soon be frozen solid, providing many tons of meat for our winter use.

My companions were finishing their day's chores as I beached my boat. They called to me and waved, their own eyes assuring them I had taken no harm on my venture, and no doubt they told themselves that nothing had happened of consequence. I saw one of them filling our largest oil lamp. Another was tinkering with the leathern hinges of our hut door, for no imaginable reason than to make it a tighter fit. These, my fellows, were seasoned, intelligent, and observing men. They could read weather signs as well or better than I.

"I'm glad you got in tonight, Leif," Starkad told me. "Tomorrow the upper windless reaches of our fiord are likely to be iced over. The sight of yon carcass does my heart good. Little sealing we can do when the bay freezes, and we'll have to drill holes in the ice to fish in."

After our good supper, old Gorm had something to say to me of far greater note.

"Leif, I noticed you took that little bait of dried fish I had left in our pantry, and which I'd caught in the pothole at the river mouth."

"Yes, I did. I thought they would break the monotony of a diet of boiled seal meat."

"One of the fish I'd laid aside, behind a skin of seal oil. The reason I did so I had meant to ask Starkad, who used to fish for a living, to name him for me, because I could not remember ever seeing his like. He was a puffy fish, with a small, round mouth and narrow in front of his tail."

"Yes, I noticed him, and I took him along with the rest."

"Was he good eating?" And the old man's question did not come forth as casually as he had intended.

"Very tasty."

"I reckon he didn't give you a belly ache, or anything like that?"

"Why should he, Gorm?"

"Well, since I've said this much, I'll say the rest. Once my mate pulled in a fish looking a good deal like that one, and after killing him with his knife he threw him back. He said he thought it was of a rare kind he called the daft fish. He thought it was a stray from the Poison Sea, and folk who ate him were likely to go out of their minds for a while—at least they see visions, as do the Danes when they eat a certain kind of toadstool. But there's nothing to the story—or I was misled by appearances."

"I guess you were, Gorm. Still, I remember feeling a little dizzy after my midday meal. If you catch another like it, you'd better use it as trap bait for a glutton. The brutes are crazy already, and maybe a daft fish would restore their sanity."

Then I thought of something, a secret thing, no more than a little test I wished to make, which would probably be inconclusive. As soon as I could, on the excuse that it was a little damp from splashed salt water, I took off my sealskin shirt, my back turned to my mates, but with my breast in the full blaze of the seal lamp. A tiny scab was forming on the skin close to my heart. Below it were small blood stains.

What could I do but dismiss the matter from my mind? Or at least try to do so, to dwell upon it as rarely as possible, and attach no importance to it. Wise Thorhall had once told me that countless numbers of men have experiences that with great wisdom they disregard and never reveal to their hard-headed fellows, and of which they eventually lose sight in those reaches of the rivers of their lives that had dropped behind them. There was a world in which men lived most of their waking moments, in which they could cast sums arriving at an indisputable answer. In this world a planted corn seed produced a plant bearing similar seed. A white heifer tupped by a red bull dropped a calf either white, red, or a mixture of white and red. A manlike shape met at a crossroads who spoke rather oddly, or vanished with mystifying swiftness, was in all probability merely one's fellow man. Queer little happenings, if tracked down, usually had a commonplace explanation. But there was another world to the rim of which a great number of people in the aggregate sometimes brushed close. A few had entered that world and were forever changed, not markedly, almost invisibly, yet in all truth.

We Norse had peopled that world, in our imaginations, with a galaxy of Gods and Goddesses, great and small, also with gigantic trolls who could hold a work crew of elves on the palms of their hands, fairies, dwarfs, witches and warlocks, mermaids, valkyries who sometimes took the form of Swan Maidens, Norns who were the administrators of dread fate, and dead folk who could not rest in their mossy graves. The Irish had told us of supernatural beings haunting their native heaths, and some of them had followed the folk to Iceland, and these might well come to Greenland in due course. We had heard tales of eerie beings when we were toddlers; and enough people had seen them or even had dealings with them that most wise elders never doubted their existence. But that I should have entered one of their secret palaces seemed not incredible, but too strange a thing to muse upon without feelings of disquiet. It might be that the daft fish from the Poison Sea had in its juices a potion of some sort which, in a man's innards, permitted him entry into this mysterious other world. Thorbiorg, Little Witch, so like other women in habit and in doing daily tasks, lived her whole life with one foot in its door.

CHAPTER FIVE

OUT OF THE WEST

I

One fact of my journey was beyond dispute. The day of my return was the last day of what we might call autumn. Dread and dismal winter set in that very night, and one week of it told us it was far more severe than the onset of Icelandic winters, except, perhaps, high and far in the mountains where sometimes our men ventured to trap great speckled falcons, these selling for their weight in silver in English and Northland coastal towns. Thin ice formed on the still backwaters of our fiord, and although often the changing winds demolished it, always it formed again, thicker than before. The cold rains changed to sleet and snow. Wolf-savage winds buffeted our walls, whined and wailed and howled over the sea of grass, and caused a deep-voiced surf to beat on our exposed shores; and when Odin on his Eight-hoofed Horse drove these winds back to the Hall of Winds, a still and awful cold gripped the land, an icy grasp which our whale-oil lamps with a three-foot flame could scarcely break. On such days we stuffed with skins our "window"—the hole that we had left in the tier of blocks of turf.

A worse abettor of the cold was our door. During its most merciless onslaughts no one could pass in and out without chilling the room. At these times we went out only at the resistless call of nature and to do what few chores could not be postponed until more clement weather. So it came to pass that I had abundant time to play my flute, with swiftly increasing skill, and almost always a grateful audience.

Yet at the close of the first fortnight on winter's onset, a wonderful thing came to pass. Astonishing as was the event at its occurrence, the change it wrought upon our thinking was of equal or even greater momentum in the long view. Perhaps this change was more marked in me than in any of my fellows, because a thing that I had thought settled was suddenly shown as at least moot, and almost certainly a misconception.

The day was more mild than most, and I thought to walk down the snowy strand to the first bend, there to see if ice floes had been driven deep into the fiord by a western gale, less icy cold than the winds off the ice-capped mountains, yet which had raved in maniacal fury the whole night long. In one glance I saw the sound still open, with only crusted ice along the shores, but in my second glance I perceived a dark speck far down the green Swan Road, which I could not yet identify but which caused a stirring of my hair under my cap of fur. It could be a half-submerged shark, I told myself, although I knew I lied. What was to prevent its being a very large, odd-shaped piece of driftwood, perhaps the trunk of some noble tree that had drifted all the way from Norway and was being driven into our fiord by the still brisk west wind? There was nothing that I knew of to belie this explanation, except the commanding conviction of my mind and heart to the contrary. The weak sunlight flashed dimly at brief, regular intervals on something about midway the length of the object. Then the stunning thought struck me that these pale flashes were caused by wet oar blades.

I could not embrace the thought, nor yet dismiss it. In the first place, the oarsman, if the part of the object that jutted up amid-ship was indeed an oarsman instead of a bump on a log, was not sitting on a thwart but in the bottom of the boat. In the second place, there was only one upraised part, not two as far as I could tell, yet the flashes that might be sunlight on paddle blades alternated from side to side in perfect rhythm, and what boat paddler who defied the interminable and naked seas would be so lacking in skill, and so wasteful of his strength, that he would dip his blade on one side and then the other, instead of keeping his course by a little edgewise thrust at the end of his stroke. Finally, and the most strong persuasion that I was on the wrong track, the flashes occurred too high in the air, indeed higher than the phantasm's head, instead of a foot or so above the water.

Still I stood on the headland and waved. Then, noticing some driftwood there, well-dried and inlaid with rosin of such sort that firemakers rarely came upon, I got my fire drill from my pouch, along with a little sun-dried moss, and in only a few minutes the resinous wood was smoking and then broke into flame. This fire I fed with great avidity to catch the eye of any far-out boatman, if such existed.

And then a wonderful thing happened. My spine tingled as when Thor's lightning strikes a mountainside, often cleaving the rock only a few feet from the wearied climber, and always a sign, since the bolt had not felled him, that he would live another day. I watched with my eyes popping out of my head to convince myself that I had not been cozened by my fervid wishing, although in all truth I had known the truth almost at the instant of its dawning.

The object was changing its course directly toward my beacon.

There was no doubt now. I was sharing this vast loneliness with another human being. What was his kind I knew naught, nor cared not a particle; but I did perceive, with a great leap of my heart, that regardless of this strange fashion of manning and paddling a boat, it made steady progress against a medium-brisk quartering wind. The boat took the waves as gracefully as a swimming tern. It was of a different shape and sort than I had yet seen. That much I knew; I would wait in wondrous patience to know the rest.

Yet is so happened that I solved the mystery of the stroking on both sides of the boat and the high flashes of the blade when our visitor was yet a mile distant. His paddle was long with a blade on each end. These blades he dipped alternately without loss of energy or motion. Whatever else my visitor might prove to be, he was a boatman before Odin! It must be that the Sea God Njord wiped the salt water from his eyes and gaped.

The boat drew nigh, and from my somewhat higher stand I could see that it was decked over with what I guessed was waterproof hide, and the paddler sat in a hole in the decking, no doubt with some kind of drawstring about his waist to prevent splashing seas from wetting him and his gear. He himself wore a cape or long coat of some sort, shiny with the wet, and an attached hood with a latch under his chin. And the fact was dawning on me that the boat itself, and the use its owner made of it, was one of the wonders of the earth, for swiftly I conceived that it was all but unsinkable and indestructible, that while it must fly before the gale, in good weather it could skirt the shores, lightly riding, and it could be used on long journeys, provided its riders had gear to catch fish or kill seals and could stomach them raw, and endure a much more arduous thing, great loneliness.

The paddler's face was coming into my cognizance almost as do landscapes as the light spreads and brightens just before sunrise. I saw its brown cast, and that it was broad at the cheekbones, that the eyebrows were intensely black, and a small black mustache covered the upper lip. Presently I knew too that his eyes were long and thin, apparently black in hue, and he had what we called a "button" nose, the kind the Old Norse had seen frequently on the faces of Laplanders. But best of all was his smile. As I smiled, it grew wider, and so did my smile, so it happened when he pushed in to land we were both grinning at each other with all our might, our first close communication as fellow humans.

He untied a latch around his waist and then, rather shyly, as though he feared I might rebuff him, he came close to me and touched the end of his nose to mine. It was no doubt a most courteous act in his own country—and where under heaven might that country be?—so in return I pressed his hands with both of mine. Then we began to converse, by words and signs, and although neither of us knew one word of the other's language, it was a wondrous thing how much each of us learned about the other.

Pointing to my own chest, I pronounced my name, Leif.

Instantly he pointed to his own chest and said what sounded like Ugruk. Then he touched my face, evidently puzzled by its paleness. Then he made a remark all of which I did not understand, but which was so natural and sensible under the circumstances that I guessed at its meaning.

"Ugruk," he said, in the tone men use when they give their names in the third person, "Innuit."

"Leif," I answered in the same tone, "Norse."

Then I pointed to his little craft made of seal or walrus hide and in a questioning tone said, "Boat?"

"*Kayak,*" he answered instantly.

Then I pointed to his waterproof garment which was indeed a long hooded robe with, as I had suspected, a latched collar.

"Nor'wester?" I said, employing a very apt word that I believed had come into the Norse language through Ireland. The most dangerous gales that beat the west shore of Ireland came from the northwest.

"*Kamleika,*" he answered promptly.

At my pointing he invited me to look into the hole in the decking of his little boat. There was stowed a harpoon with a wooden shaft and a beautifully worked flint head more than a foot long. Under it was coiled a line that I supposed was hide of some kind. There were lines that seemed to be made of sinew with hooks of flint or shell, and stones for sinkers, also some bowls of soapstone. Also I saw about half of a carcass of a seal he had harpooned in the last few days, half-frozen and butchered with a long knife the hand of which was ivory and the blade, as far as I could see, burnished copper—a supposition I could hardly accept, for although we Norse knew how to mix copper with tin and make bronze, we did not know how to harden the pure metal.

And next I braced myself to ask the most momentous question of all, for I had a strange and eerie inkling that its answer might affect my whole life.

"Ugruk, kayak," I said, pointing to the north and then making a sweeping gesture toward the present scene. For the idea had often struck us exiles that some sort of people, possibly resembling Laplanders, dwelt in the northern part of Greenland. True, we had nothing on which to base the notion except Thorhall's tale of finding a deserted skin boat on a rocky coast of northern Iceland, but this was not weak evidence, because the boat had certainly come from somewhere beyond our bourn.

Ugruk shook his head. Then with a great thrust of his arm he pointed with rigid and eloquent finger straight west, and there was something in the gesture that made me believe that distance was almost unimaginably far.

2

I pointed my finger at him, beckoned with it, and pointed to myself. He understood instantly that I wanted him to come with me and gave me a most charming smile which with the brilliance of his black eyes lighted his pale-brown face. At once I started walking homeward along the strand; he slid into the hole in the decking of his boat, tightened the drawstring, and with his two-bladed paddle stroking alternately he kept pace effortlessly and plainly with great pleasure. When we gained our strand he pulled the boat well upon the land, then went to look at Thorstein's whale. He was made so happy by the sight of it that he laughed aloud, for here was a larder of meat and oil which, short of an unseasonable thaw, could cram our bellies and keep high the flame of our oil lamps for months on end.

At the door of the hut he seemed astonished by something and shot me a quick, questioning glance. Then, shaking his head, he made a remark in his own tongue, not one word of which I understood. Still, I could not doubt that he disapproved of our door for some good reason; and I felt a little glowworm of an idea that his disapproval was based on the same fact that we castaways had begun to perceive—that it did not offer good protection against extreme cold. Still, we had not seen any way to remedy the condition. And perhaps at that instant the idea struck me that Ugruk's coming to our lonely abode, the loneliest house in the wild world, I truly believed, might bring not only happiness to our whole band but help and luck.

We reached the hut just as the men were making ready for a heavy midday meal. Their minds fixed on their bellies, they had not noticed Ugruk and me come up, so when I pushed open the door, the brief, casual glance each intended to give me changed into a fixed, all but unbelieving stare, and I could almost hear the dropping of seven jaws. At once they crowded around us, and most of the men shook Ugruk's hand, although this was a ceremony he did not know, perhaps had never seen before, but his beaming smile instantly indicated his recognition of a gesture of friendship.

Thorstein did not shake hands with the newcomer. I noticed this, as I noticed almost everything Thorstein did or did not do, and his making something of a point of the admission seemed to make no sense. Then suddenly I knew it had to do with the long-standing unspoken conflict between us. At this moment Ugruk was the center of attraction, the great surprise, something new and quite wonderful in the men's lives. The fact remained that I, not Thorstein, had found him and brought him home. For me it was a victory equal if not surpassing Thorstein's victory as harpooner and head of the hunt that had fetched home a whale.

In the hospitable Norse fashion, the men were quick to put food in our guest's reach. I had known by his appearance that he had not suffered from famine on his mysterious but surely prodigious journey out of the west; now I knew it by his manners. He shook his head and by movements of his hands urged the other men to precede him to the big brimming metal dish. Suddenly the idea struck me with great force that weeks and likely months had passed since he had eaten cooked meat. Perhaps he had acquired a taste for raw meat. If so, he concealed the fact and was soon chewing cheerfully away on boiled seal and baked whale.

At their first chance, various of my friends questioned me as to where and how I had found this wonder of creation, a human being, in this wilderness of frostbitten land and sullen gray seas. Always they spoke in low tones, forgetting that Ugruk knew not one word of our Norse speech. Where did I think he had come from? When I told of his eloquent gesture from west to east, all of our band took note, the same, startled, unbelieving expression coming into every face.

"Leif, that's impossible," Starkad told me. "Greenland is the westernmost land."

"How do we know, Starkad?"

"Great Gods, the lands have got to end somewhere. Even the ocean ends somewhere—or so our fathers taught us."

"I think he's from the northern part of this land," Thorstein broke in, in his positive almost always convincing way. "He's not greatly different from the Laplanders we've seen. They always live far and away to the north."

"I asked Ugruk if he came from the north," I told my wide-eyed listeners. "He seemed to understand my sign language, and he said he did not come from the north and instead he came from the west."

"A long way or short?" Starkad asked.

"Very long."

"Well, I reckon we'll find out when we learn to speak his language, or he learns to speak ours."

Actually before the day ended Ugruk was able to communicate with us, not with words but in graphic sign language, about a matter of no small moment. Stepping outside, he beckoned us to join him. Then he pointed to our door, with a long well-acted shiver as if from cold. All the men nodded, their eyes fixed on his face; well they knew what piercing cold stabbed through the room on cold days when the door was opened even briefly. Then Ugruk pointed to one of the turf blocks that composed our walls. He made motions imitating the cutting out of other blocks. These he pretended to lie in order in two rows projecting about twelve feet from our doorway. His adroit hands imitated the laying of other tiers about to the height of a man's waist, then bringing both walls together in an arched ceiling.

One thing's sure," observed cross-grained old Gorm. "This fellow of Leif's comes from a cold country. No doubt all their winter houses have entrance tunnels, probably closed at the outer end with some kind of hide. Well, they would be a protection against bitter wind, and the half-warmed air of the tunnel would stop the worst of the chill when the curtain's opened."

"That I grant," Thorstein replied, and there was something in his voice and authoritative manner that suggested Eric the Red. "The trouble with the scheme is that the land's frozen hard as a rock and we'd ruin our axes trying to cut out blocks."

"Still we could build a windbreak," far-traveled Starkad said. "We've plenty of rocks on yon hill, and we can stuff up the holes with moss. Rocks are cold, but when they are covered with snow, it would hold in the heat, for every Norseman knows that a snow-covered roof is warmer than one that's naked."

It came to pass that we began to build the two jutting walls that very afternoon. In a week we had it finished, the roofing supported by the bones of whales. Less than a week thereafter the snow fell in earnest, all day and all night, dry snow of great coldness; yet it packed well on our tunnel and the roof of our hut, and no one of us wasted breath to prophesy it would not weep away until next spring.

In those two weeks I learned fewer than a dozen words of Ugruk's language. *Mukluks* were the knee-high, waterproof, and wonderfully warm footgear that he wore; *parka* was the name of a long reindeerskin robe he had worn under his kamleika—this garment, too, had a hood which appeared to be lined with glutton fur, and which was raised and fastened closely about the face in dry, cold weather. Our big boat he called *oomiac*; our house was a *barabara*, houses of snow blocks which his people, the Innuits, sometimes made when traveling in cold weather were called *igloos*. The word for food appeared to be *kow-kow*. When a food pot was empty, Ugruk said *"Kow-kow pechuck."* A white weasel was called *chikarik*.

Oddly enough, I learned the Innuit word for woman. Ugruk informed me by very graphic sign language. First, with his closed fists in front of his chest he plainly conveyed the idea of a woman's breast. To clinch it he made a sign at which most of our hale and hearty Norsemen would have laughed: I did not do so, because my friend was so deeply in earnest and, after all, there was nothing funny about his representation. At the crotch of his legs he laid his two forefingers together, both pointing downward and representing a cleft, then said the word *meeluk*.

While I was learning these few Innuit words, Ugruk's quick mind had stored something like fifty Norse words. These were almost altogether nouns and verbs; he did not bother with many conjunctives, prepositions, or, at first, personal pronouns. When he wanted me to play my flute, which was every night and during idle hours of the swiftly shortening days, he would say in a boyish tone of entreaty, "Leif play pretty?" When we were tramping abroad and hunger came upon him he would propose, "Leif, Ugruk, go eat?" Within a month he achieved such linguistic feats as this:

"Okukshak (old) *shaman* (priest) see deer, go hands and

knees, get close, shoot stick with feather, iron point, deer fall dead."

I could imagine no one more removed from a priest, Christian or heathen, then hard-bitten Gorm, but evidently his gray hair was associated in Ugruk's mind with the elders of his tribe who conducted ceremonies to appease the Far West Gods. Ugruk always treated him with profound respect.

There was only one of our number to whom he was more respectful in a somewhat shy but unmistakable way, and oddly enough it was neither Thorstein nor Starkad, but his finder, Leif. I would have thought we would have established an easy fellowship, since I was from five to ten years his junior. This never happened. He often made suggestions, his head cocked to hear my reply. That reply settled the matter.

Unlike the yellow-skinned Lapps of northern Norway, Ugruk had never seen a ski. For a while I feared that this ignorance would prevent our excursions, since Starkad ruled against his use of one of our few pairs, lest he break them. However, there was Innuit footgear, not equal to our snow ships on well-packed snow, yet useful on any snow and especially valuable over new unfrozen fall. First he made light whalebone egg-shaped rings, one for each foot. Boring holes in the bone with a little drill he had, he fastened narrow strips of hide to form a web. When he put his feet into straps attached to the web, together we could cover ground at a good rate. I left him far behind me when descending an icy slick hillside, but after every fresh fall he could beat me.

Meanwhile, the wild winter advanced apace. It was such a winter as we Icelandic-raised men had never seen. What remained of noonday sunlight was a pale dusk, as seen through fog, low in the southern sky; no hour of the day was really bright; we appeared to dwell in a twilight that ebbed and flowed, thickened and thinned, but never really lifted. Well, we had seen the same in Iceland, but had never imagined such brutal cold. The fiord froze, happily with smooth ice close to the sheltered shores, but in an almost uncrossable pack, a wild wilderness of ice, blocks and bergs and floes jammed and welded together, a kind of nightmare scene in those dim days. And then Ugruk's lore, taught him on some yet unimaginable shore, again stood us in good stead.

Our frozen seal meat had begun to taste stale. Our whale meat gave forth an unpleasant smell when being cooked over oil lamps; Starkad thought that the great carcass had become slightly corrupted before it had frozen hard. We longed for fresh seal meat and Ugruk showed us how it might be obtained.

In the smooth ice along the shores the seal had many blow-holes. By building a snow shelter against the wind, and wearing his reindeerhide robe, Ugruk would wait by one of these holes with such patience as a dog might wait in a doorway for a master who could never return, he having gone to the Corpse Strand at the gate of Hel. Yet he never waited alone; two harpoons were better than one in achieving a victorious ending of the long and bitter watch, provided a seal would come up to blow. Always I sat with him, too cold to speak, benumbed with cold the best I could do, yet strangely and vividly waking to full-powered activity at the second of crisis. Only the Gods knew my whole motive; certainly I did not. At times it seemed only a stubborn and perhaps stupid refusal to concede that Ugruk could endure what I could not endure. Partly it stemmed from a sense of fellowship with him, much deeper than our finding each other on an unpeopled shore could explain. Partly perhaps it was a grim defiance of the Frost Giant, here waxing in power and assaulting me with a cold like death's.

One of his onslaughts on the Greenland shore was unknown hitherto to the widest travelers in our band, including Thori, who had once wintered at the North Cape in Norway, which we reckoned was more than three hundred sea miles nearer the North Star than Ericsfiord. Starkad had remarked, after its first occurrence, that he reckoned the Frost Giant had sneezed. Then and there we named it so—the Big Sneeze of the Frost Giant—and the term amused the men, because it was so fitting, although the phenomenon was by no means a laughing matter. It began with a gust of wind, followed in an instant by an enveloping, blinding cloud of what we thought were ice crystals of minute size. It was grimly true that when a man caught out of doors looked to the ground to seek his way to shelter he could not see it or even his own feet. It caused an uncanny feeling within the soul, something worse than fear, indeed a kind of detachment from all reality, as though it had lost touch with his warm and insensate body and was lost and alone in an unknown element. Not only the ground and the sky and all familiar landmarks vanished from sight but his companion walking at his side. There was nothing for him to do but crouch down and draw his hood close about his face and barely breathe, for even to open his lips to speak caused his mouth and throat to fill with this dry and dreadful cold. Except for the brief duration of the attack, the icy, impenetrable cloud disappearing as suddenly as it had come, some of us would have certainly met death in its black void.

Another aspect of the advancing winter was the increased frequency of our seeing wolves. The dimness of no day passed by without one or more of us catching sight of their white, sinister shapes. Many of them were solitary; more often they prowled about our homestead in packs of from four to seven, heads and tails down, dread phantoms of the twilight, somehow indeed the spirit of the northern winter in eerie incarnation. As yet they never approached us or permitted us to approach them in range of our arrows or our harpoons. We could not believe our eyes at the suddenness of their appearance in what seemed an empty snowfield, and of their vanishing.

My mates spoke of them only rarely, then with worried-looking eyes and eyebrows drawn together. I remembered that the expressions on the faces of both Eric the Red and of bold Thorhall used to change in some subtle way when they spoke of wolves. I supposed they were the oldest animate enemy of the human race. Yet Ugruk showed no deep-seated dread of them, although he kept his harpoon ready in his hand when one came nigh. Moreover, he told me, partly in words, partly by graphic signs, that "the old people" had caught and tamed gray wolves, and his own clan still kept the descendants of the beasts to draw sleds.

I found that I could not doubt this strange and startling statement. In the first place, the ability to lie seemed to have been left out of Ugruk. Also I remembered that Eric had told of very large dogs drawing wheeled carts in various lands in Europe.

The hour struck when the menace that had seemed to hang over us, a kind of foreboding troubling our hearts at every glimpse or sound of the snow-white skulkers, became dire reality.

3

We had reckoned the day to be only a few days before the winter solstice. A low, gray overcast had dimmed what little glimmer the weak and distant sun cast upon the snow, and we had worked or ate or loafed in a bleak twilight. Three hours after noon the dusk thickened to black night, a blind night we thought, with not even the shine of a familiar star to comfort us, the only luminescence in that whole wintry world to be the flame from our oil lamp; but we had reckoned wrongly, for a wind with shark teeth rose in late afternoon and swept from the sky every vestige of cloud. At suppertime the moon in its full face, white as though carved of ice, heaved up over the glinting mountains to the east. All but the great stars faded, leaving only glimmering dust. Vision was short, as always in the brightest moonlight, yet it did not seem so, and the landscape in our environs became a wondrous study in different tones of white—our river mouth like a pool of spilled milk, the snowy strand glistening, the shore ice of the fiord of the purest pearl, the ice pack farther out a deathly pale gray, the long grasslands dipping in long swerves into the valleys and climbing up the sides of little hills, their expanses of deep snow bared to the moon, were a wan white that conveyed some sort of sadness to the soul.

We gazed and went back into the warm, lighted room, and I thought of getting out my flute and trying to find expression in music of a deepening sense of the ominous that I could neither explain nor dispel. For a while I did not do so. Starkad told of a similar night he had seen at the North Cape, so cold that his breath had made a crackling sound, and of him and his companions standing on the strand when a streak of fire darted from the high heavens to the frozen sea in the twinkling of an eye. It had illuminated the landscape as never did a lightning bolt in the memory of man. Starkad had felt one brief blast of all but unbearable heat; then he was stunned by a brain-rocking explosion. Instantly there followed a prodigious long-drawn hiss, as from an angry dragon big as a mountain, mingled with a boiling, bubbling sound. Wildly the men guessed at the explanation, only to discover, in the morning light, effects more strange than the phenomenon itself. Less than a mile from the shore, the six or more feet of sea ice had been shattered like a windowpane by a hurled stone; there appeared to be cracks running out in a starlike pattern, and these cracks proved to be great rifts, which the still sea had been prevented from closing and congealing by the great cold. Venturing there with quaking hearts and what might have been Norse courage or insatiable Norse curiosity—for Mimir the Wise could not tell one from the other—they had found a hole roughly circular and about six feet in diameter bored completely through the ice, and around the hole was a raised ring composed of small ice crystals, three feet high and several feet broad.

"We could only guess at the answer," Starkad said in conclusion, "but I'll tell you our most likely guess. I believe that what we saw was a falling star. You can see them almost any winter night, but most of them appear to burn up before they strike the earth— only the Gods know why. Perhaps this one was so small that it escaped its Gods' notice and fell until it struck and broke through the ice, but it was so hot that it made the sea water boil around there, and some of it bubbled up, cooled, and ran back, but the stream that had shot up formed ice crystals that made the ring."

As Starkad had told the story, old Gorm had listened as intently as we others, but I had the feeling there was something else on his mind. I knew it when he did not wait to hear our comments, and instead rose abruptly and headed for the opening to the low, arched passage that led to the bitter night. Yet as he was drawing aside the white bearskin which hung as an inner curtain, he turned to us and spoke. I never knew why, and perhaps he himself did not know. It was not merely to satisfy our curiosity over his sudden departure. Perhaps it was to hide something that he had sensed, and he did not wish to alarm us until his inkling was proved true or false.

"I think I'll go out and look at the northern lights," he said. "There ought to be a magnificent display on such a dry, clear, cold night as this."

In hardly half a minute he reappeared. Apparently he had made the trip out and back as fast as he could crawl. His expression had changed; it was no longer studious, nor did it give the effect of alarm. Rather it was the resolute expression that a brave man wears when a dangerous chance must be taken.

"There are eighteen or twenty wolves eating our whale," he told us quietly. "It must be that three or four packs discovered it about the same time. The cunning devils are breaking out mouthfuls and swallowing them whole, not snarling or fighting over the meat. Well they know that it belongs to us. If I hadn't heard the crack of a bone breaking I'd never gone to look. Now, Starkad, what do you say? If they should attack us, and it isn't impossible, considering their number, we might lose some lives. Still I want to teach the beasts a lesson—that men have come to this land, and we, not they, are its rulers."

"I hope they will give us a fight," Starkad answered instantly. "It's the only way we can kill a few—we could never hit them with arrows if they make off white as the snow in the moonlight. Every man unbend his line from his harpoon. And no matter how much you are tempted, don't heave at one of them. Keep it in your hands as a spear just in case. . . ."

He did not finish the sentence. The men had understood his instructions and were making great but steady haste. I, alone, as far as I knew, disobeyed Starkad's orders, for only that afternoon I had discovered that the iron head of my harpoon was somewhat loose and needed tightening. In its place I took up my broadsword. I did so with reluctance—a harpoon had so much longer reach— yet the hilt was hardly well-grasped in my hand when I felt a swelling of my heart from joy. A broadsword was almost useless for fighting a white bear, as my mother had told me in what seemed the long ago. But there was nothing wrong with it for fighting wolves which did not have long arms with terrible mailed mauls. Indeed I could trust it more quickly and surely than a harpoon. Truly, though, I had no real expectation of any sort of fight. All the wolves I had ever seen had, at most, growled a little, then made off.

Starkad in our van, Thorstein following close, and Ugruk out of my sight in the rear, we crept one by one through the passage. At its entrance we stood for a second or two, immobilized by wonder at the sight. The wolves had not yet perceived our presence. They were biting and tearing with great savagery at a down-hanging side of meat about twenty feet long, from which we had recently stripped the skin and cut away the blubber for other use. Their crouched forms, darting heads, and ferocious jaws were sharp in our vision in this cold flood of light from the serene moon; and its utter strangeness, otherworldliness it seemed, was emphasized by the brutes' silence, the only audible sound being the crackle of frozen meat being broken by their glistening fangs.

Casting off the spell, I beheld the scene not in its dreamlike aspect but in its grim reality. I noticed first that some of the wolves were decidedly taller and longer than those we commonly saw: it struck me that only that day they had crossed the fiord from some bleak region where game was scarce. Until that moment I had been expecting any instant to have them discover us and dart away. Suddenly I was completely and thrillingly unsure of the outcome. I had time to recall Gorm's words. He knew wolves better than I, knowing well how they almost always turned tail, but after looking at these he had spoken of the possibility of battle.

One wolf caught sight of us; instantly all were looking at us. All stood poised, ready to run, many had a forefoot raised. But they did not run. There was a startling division in their ranks: six formed a little band, confronting us, seven another band; five, the biggest and the most bellicose of all, stood in a close pack, a little in front of the others. Gorm had been right that the assembly was composed of three ordinary-sized packs, perhaps each pack representing one litter. The one in front was a litter at least a year older, and a size or two bigger, than the rest. They had lived long enough to learn that existence depended on courage as much as on caution. All were savagely hungry, and we, tall shapes that they did not know, dangerous-looking too, were not as tall as the upper branches of the horns of an old reindeer bull, at whose throat they need tear but once ere he fell with his wildly smelling blood deluging the snow.

Forming a line, we moved at a steady pace toward the marauders. I had the feeling that there were only eight of us when there should have been nine, but I had no time or thought to count, so I let the matter slide. At once the three packs of wolves moved closer to one another to form a pack, united in ferocity to defend their stolen feast. To them, our tall forms were hateful, because we were allies of the belly hunger they had known so well of late, and which, except for our interference, they could now satisfy. Perhaps they hated the smell of us because, aroused as we were, pugnacious, ourselves ferocious, we might give forth a strong smell like that of a polar bear defending his new-slain seal. Perhaps by nature man has a smell hateful to most wild beasts. Thorhall Hunter had told me that reindeer, dwelling in the wildest heaths of northern Norway, will often go into panic at their first sniff of man.

All the wolves had begun to utter a continuous snarl, as do dogs when they worry fallen prey. It became louder and more threatening as we drew nearer. They stood in a thick mass, the hind quarters of each a little lowered, the five very tall lean wolves in their van. I do not know what spark, as from steel on flint, lighted the tinder of their savage hearts. As though some secret signal had flashed from one to the other, inaudible and invisible, every wolf rushed to attack at the same instant. They ran low to the ground and in complete silence except for the rhythmic thud of their feet. White shapes on the white snow under the white moon, they loomed larger at every forward pounce. Instantly the battle was joined.

My brother, Thorstein, dropped on one knee and the foremost of the band flung himself against his spear, only to be impaled and to die with one last defiant snarl cut short. Starkad had drawn back his arm with lifted javelin, and with perfect timing thrust its point full-powered into the top of the wolf's neck, whereby he crumpled and lay kicking. Gorm stabbed in the side the wolf that had leaped at him, and the steel was swifter than the shining fangs, and the beast lived only long enough to knock the old man down. He seemed to shoot to his feet, bellicose as ever, to stab at a wolf that had thought him easy and safe prey, and although he did not deal a mortal wound, the beast yelped and ran off, streaming blood. One of the pack leaders, tall, lean, and terrifying, had made for me, but I was ready, my eyes and my arm keeping wondrous troth with my soul, and my point went home just under the beast's jaw, and his blood spurted in a great arc as he sank down. Stori missed his stab, and the beast sprang up to bite him in the throat, but somehow his fangs missed their aim and when I could look again Stori was stabbing at another wolf while the first lay quivering at his feet. The sleeve of another of our band had been torn off and his naked arm streamed blood; but as we closed ranks we perceived none of our number lying dead or direly wounded.

The remaining wolves had regrouped and drawn back a little, fearful of the gleaming points that dealt death as swiftly as the hammer blow of a giant white bear. Five of their pack, their lean and terrible leaders, lay still on the bloodied snow, and one other wolf had fled the field. Twelve remained, perhaps enough to overwhelm us if they attacked in force and in full ferocity, and certainly they could have torn down several of our number. Although they still stood snarling in fury and defiance, they bethought themselves before again rushing at our points agleam in the moonlight, and to our amazement another wolf, about midway of the dwindled pack, uttered a kind of moan and he, too, ran off.

"Men, give them the steel," Starkad shouted, and to my soul returned, not as a memory but as a command, the runes graven on my blade, which were to "thrust me deep." So I was not a step behind Starkad, but because the wolves, too, bounded forward at the same instant, I did not see how my fellows fared, being busy with a young and very agile wolf that bounded in a half-circle at my fore, keeping clear of my point, which I swung to keep him at bay until a chance came to drive home my blade. Indeed, this second rush was not nearly as resolute as the first, and only one of our band was bitten on the arm before Thorstein saved him from severe injury, or perhaps death, by a sideways thrust of his swift and deadly spear into the brute's belly.

Suddenly another wolf, charging at Gorm, fell on his back, kicking, with his breath rattling in his throat, and across my bestormed brain could flash only the thought that he had been wounded in the first attack.

Of the eighteen massed against us, only eight were left. Eight lay dead or dying, two had run off wounded. The eight seemed minded to make a last stand. They massed, snarling; perhaps their beast souls told them that they must, at any cost, lay low one of us, his blood smell rank on the snow, or they could never go to Wolf Valhalla as their lord Odin had promised them. It came to me they did not mean to choose antagonists, but to attack our leader, Starkad, all leaping on him at once, all fangs rending; then if they died or were routed it would be in honor. But suddenly a wolf in their midst leaped high in the air, uttering a scream strangely human, and landed kicking first rapidly, then very slowly, as his life ebbed.

Now to me this event seemed a miracle. I knew it was not; and my mind was groping for some rational explanation. To the wolves this sudden death caused by some thrust they had not seen and which seemed from a great distance must have seemed like the death from one of Thor's thunderbolts striking a party of travelers in the wild mountains, who scarcely dared to look at their crisp-burned comrade who only a moment before was sharing their hunger, their fatigue, their thirst, or their craving to reach the shelter of their destination. To the wolves it seemed that they must be being picked off and cast down by some uncanny power.

And suddenly the wild notion struck me what that power was. I could tell in one instant if my guess was true by looking at the death leaper's body. There was no time; events had reached their climax; this last stroke was more than the wolves' great hearts could bear; and suddenly one of the seven bolted, and instantly the other six raced away in his wake, all of them uttering a strange cry as of heartbreak.

Of their united army of eighteen, seven remained. It was no comfort to them now, nor any pride, that they were feared by every beast that roamed the fastnesses—even the shaggy Greenland oxen fearing them with good cause, for although he might kill two or even three before his throat was torn and his blood spurted —the rest could tear him down. Aye, I reckoned the white bears, sometimes touching the strand on their ice ships, feared them likewise. But tonight they had been vanquished by half their number of tall, unknown creatures newly come to their wild and wintry realm.

"I don't see how we killed so many," Starkad said, glancing about him with a dazed look.

"You killed two, I two," Thorstein answered. "But to account for all the rest——"

"By the Nine Runes of Odin," cried old Gorm, who had also killed or wounded at least two, although he did not speak of it, "here's a dead wolf with an arrow through his chest."

His words may have startled and mystified my companions; not so, me. I had leaped to a conclusion. In a few seconds it was verified by Ugruk's emergence from a little copse of dwarf willows, my fine bow, not his own weak bow, in his hand. He had made for the retreat, about forty yards from the massed packs, on first emerging from the tunnel. There he had stood, launching arrow after arrow with merciless aim, and his main aim had been not to share in the glory of our battle but to kill wolves. And then and there I understood Ugruk better than ever and perceived how his people had survived, generation after generation, in an environment ineffably hostile.

"How many did you kill, Ugruk?" I cried, my voice ringing with jubilation and my heart surging in ecstasy.

"Urguk no know. He shoot six or seven of Chief Leif's best arrows. Ugruk missed once, twice, maybe three times, for Ugruk's hands tremble at awful sight."

"Not more than twice would be my guess," Starkad remarked, after examining the bodies of the dead wolves and remembering two that had run away wounded. "That was good shooting in this crazy light when your hands were trembling. Now our hands must get to work. There are nine of us and nine carcasses, and all the pelts must be stripped off before they freeze to the flesh.

By Odin, we'll carpet our house with 'em, warm for our feet when we must get up at night, instead of that cold dirt floor. Fasten your parkas well and get your sharpest knives. You, Oddson, with the bloodied arm, cover it up against the cold, and then work with us, or rest, as you see fit."

"I'll work with you," Oddson answered.

Ugruk came and laid his arm for a second or two along both of my shoulders.

"Leif, Ugruk no ask you when me took bow. Everybody big hurry."

"You did right, Ugruk."

"You got mighty good bow, two, three times better than Innuit bow. I make one for Ugruk."

"You'll have good use for it, I don't doubt."

And with that Ugruk drew forth his flint knife, sharper than some of our iron knives, and began to skin a wolf.

4

Oddly enough, the Christians and the heathens celebrated their greatest feast at the same time of year. It was spread about the end of the third week of the last moon of the year, or of the twelfth month of the Roman calendar. According to Eric, who had got it from a Magus, a kind of wise man, who had had to flee from Rome and who could read Latin, the northern peoples had observed the custom for at least five hundred years before Kris was born, not quite a thousand years ago, but since Kris had been born of woman in that very season, now the Christians feasted the same time as the heathens and called it Christmas.

The heathens cared naught for that. What they celebrated was not the birth of a God but the winter solstice, when the sun turned back from its southern journey and the days stopped shortening and began to lengthen, certain proof that the year had turned. No matter how many bitter months would pass before the ice could be broken and the grass would be green and the reindeer cows would drop their calves and the sky would again be darkened by northward flying fowls, all these wondrous things would surely come to pass.

Thorstein had stuck a pole in the ground and at what he reckoned was the same time every morning he measured its shadow. It continued to lengthen a little until one day the sun did not rise high enough to illumine the vast and distant icecap, although the sky was clear of clouds. But on the very next morning we again saw the pearly gleam, and Thorstein thought that the pale shadow of the pole in the light reflected from the eastern sky was a few inches shorter than the last time he had measured it. We waited three more days to make sure, whereupon the shadow was unquestionably shorter, and the rim of the sun itself gave us one golden wink over the ice-topped mountains. So we prepared for a big meal at midday, in remembrance of the great feasts that were spread in Iceland on or about this same day.

Ugruk had gone forth the day before with his weak, clumsy-looking whalebone bow and returned with four brace of tarmochans. In his white parka he had crept up within twenty or so feet, thus making sure of his aim. Not one of us Norse could have done it. We did not have the infinite patience to perform such a feat; we were too regardful of the minutes, the passing of which did not matter in the least to Ugruk, since they must be spent one way or another, and on that jaunt his business had been to shoot tarmochans. These we plucked before the skin was hard-frozen, kept them inside all night, and in the morning put them to boil over a seal lamp in a big pot that Ugruk had made from a block of soapstone in a single day. Over our other oil lamp we fried reindeer venison in its own fat, and Starkad brought from our stores some hard rye bread made in Norway. Our greatest treat came as a wondrous surprise. From an earthen jug which Thorstein had kept hidden behind some oilskins, we were each given three swallows of strong and delicious honey mead, no doubt from Eric's private store; and there was enough for a second round and, when our bellies had been stuffed with food, a third round. Pleasantly dizzy we sang the old Norse song of welcome to the returning sun, a spell song that our women used to sing to make sure the sun did not lag on its northward journey or wander away from its due road on some other business, and that the days would lengthen at a steady, measured pace, and that the grass would start to make udders overflow when newborn calves, colts, fawns, and kids had need of them. Thereafter we walked straight-backed and with great aplomb to our sheepskins and rank-smelling wolfskins, laid ourselves carefully down, and fell into delicious sleep.

Thorstein won great favor with the men by his generous giving of the precious mead. Although they did not come out and say so, everyone but Gorm, myself, and possibly Ugruk felt that spring would be swifter to break, and there would be fewer great storms, and the Frost Giant would withhold some of his terrifying sneezes, because we had taken due note of the holy day and Thorstein had not been stingy with his hidden treasure. Gorm was a man of little faith in any kind of divine benefits. He appeared to believe that life itself was a vast, acrid joke of which people were the special butts. I had a notion, which I did not entirely like, that the powers of nature moved according to laws too complicated and obscure for us to fathom, and the Gods themselves could not change those laws. As far as I could tell, Ugruk knew no Gods. I had never known him to propose propitiation of any God or spirit. He believed in magic—being practices that people who knew the methods could perform—for instance, the burning of a man's clipped toenails to cause his whole foot to become fevered or break out with a painful rash.

As the days passed, I was better acquainted with Ugruk's mental workings in the exact rate at which he could better understand and speak the Norse language. He could already express more complicated ideas, although in dialect, then could some of our men; and indeed the idea was growing on me that Ugruk's mind was one of the keenest with which I had ever dealt. About a month after the winter solstice, with winter still holding the land in an icy grip, the only sign of appeasing being the longer stay of the sun in the sky and what I thought, at times, were somewhat brighter beams and perceptible warmth, the day came that I thought I might broach to Ugruk a matter of the utmost moment to me, although I could have given no good reasons for my deep involvement in it, except intense curiosity. The day was the most mild in the long parade of inclement days since the fiord froze over. Not one flake of snow melted, still the wind blew without biting, the sun shone almost with ardency, and I reckoned that the temperature was only a little under the freezing point. We were sitting over a blowhole and had killed one seal and were hoping to get another. In our long parkas and fur-lined hoods and mukluks we were not even chilly. I had noticed a large falcon taking off westward, a direction that would take him to the frozen sea, where surely he would look in vain for his usual winter prey, white hares.

"Maybe he means to fly to your homeland," I proposed on the spur of the moment.

"He fly all day and, all night, from new moon to full moon, he no make it," Ugruk replied.

It had so happened that my mother, Thorhild, had instructed me fairly well in numbers. Since we believed a falcon in fast flight could wing a little short of a mile a minute—Eric had made a rough verification of this fact by counting his pulse—I took fifty miles an hour as a likely rate and multiplied it by twenty-four, the number of hours in a day. It came to the stunning number of one thousand two hundred miles. Multiplying this by fourteen, the number of days between the new moon and the full moon, I fetched the prodigious sum of over fourteen thousand.

I knew instantly that Ugruk had not meant to propose any such distance. At the same time my respect for his intelligence and truth would not permit denial that the way was very great indeed, more than my imagination could grasp and far greater than travelers believed was the total span of the earth surrounded by untraversable ocean.

"How many days' paddling in a kayak with neither a head wind or a tail wind?" I asked.

"Ugruk not know. He take three suns to come from his igloo to your igloo, but sometimes for a full moon, and sometimes for many moons, Ugruk no could travel, pack ice no give opening, or great gales blow. Then Ugruk come to shore and make snow house. He always follow shore so can make landing when signs say bad weather."

"How did you live at such times? What did you eat? How did you keep warm?"

"Ugruk have stone oil lamp. You saw. It warm snow house well. Ugruk know how hunt seal any day he can leave igloo, and almost always he keep one, two dead seal in kayak. In warm weather he eat good—duck eggs, white geese, sometimes deer, once when he very hungry he harpoon walrus and come close to sinking kayak, journey finished."

"You must have touched not one land, but many lands," I said, my voice shaking.

"I show you."

Ugruk sprang up and began to draw figures in the snow with the point of his spear. The first one was a very long and jagged line. Did it represent a coast line that he had followed? If not, I could not imagine what it did mean or why he had drawn it. I noticed that it slanted roughly northwest. Whether this was accidental or Ugruk's effort at true depiction, I could not dream.

"This land nearest land to Greenland," he told me quietly. His voice was deep, his eyes strangely shining, and suddenly I knew that I was hearing of one of the strangest and longest journeys ever made by man, and that Ugruk too somehow had sensed its magnitude and magnificence, and in speaking of it he had become deeply moved.

"How many days' paddle in a kayak from our shore?"

"Ugruk not know. But it biggest water Ugruk cross, whole way. Sometimes he blown forward, sometimes he blown back. But he have no much trouble with ice and have summer weather and he kill plenty seal, catch plenty fish, eat raw." Ugruk scratched his head, then showed me all ten of his fingers four times. "About that many days," he explained, "from end of long strand to Greenland strand."

Since the spring and summer winds were generally out of the west, I reckoned that with good luck he might have gained twenty-five miles a day. Forty times twenty-five was a thousand—the main part of the distance between the Icelandic shore at Ericsholm and the landfall of Greenland, the mountain Eric had named Blue Shirt. But the luck would not have been that good. On many days he would lose distance, often he would drift with the wind dragging his little sea anchor. Estimating his gain at only fifteen miles a day, still this body of water would be six hundred miles wide—a long voyage for a skin boat, by the God of the Nine Runes.

"This long coast that you skirted," I said, pointing to the jagged line running northwest. "How many days in a kayak?"

"Ugruk not know. I take whole year from far end to near end." And again he drew his harpoon point from what would be the northwest beginning of the land to the southeast end.

"You spent the winter on the shore?"

"Ugruk travel when he could. When he no could travel he go on shore, build snow house."

"Were there any people on that coast?"

"Ugruk not see any, but he saw where people had come and gone away. Plenty seal bones and fish spines. One broken shaft of harpoon. Some whalebones still standing up in ground, where people had barabaras."

"Do you think they were people like you?"

"Ugruk think so. Harpoon handle like mine."

"You were going east. What shore did you follow before you came to the long land?"

Ugruk drew two parallel lines, roughly at right angles to the upper end of the long line.

"Sea come in here," he told me. "No very big broad sea, narrow sea, Ugruk had fair wind, cross in three days. And land he sail from, she lie straight west from long land, have dangerous shore with only two good harbor, Ugruk come close to going on rocks. She run two, three, maybe four hundred miles. And people like me live on that shore."

"Could you speak with them?"

"Speak a little. Many my words they not know. But they good sealers, good hunters, have good dogs and sleds, harpoon heads very sharp—what you call it?—copper very hard."

"Ugruk, did you pay them a long visit?"

"No. Stay only a half a moon. One hunter away, hunt deer

deep in land, his brother say I take his wife while hunter gone, but hunter come back. We make good friends, his name Ugruk like mine, but me, I go on with journey."

Perhaps the time had come to ask Ugruk what was the purpose, the goal of this great journey. But the words stuck in my throat, I did not know quite why. Perhaps it was only the feeling that the journey was more meaningful, perhaps more tragic, certainly of vaster moment in Ugruk's heart and soul than I could divine, and this he would confide in me when he was ready, and until then I would wait.

"It must be there was land even farther west," I said.

"Many great lands. To reach this land Ugruk had crossed inlet. Innuits said it ran south many days' journey in kayak. Before then he had followed coast of some other big land, saw no people, saw plenty deer, plenty seals and walrus. Before then he cross big gulf. Ugruk remember because he saw big school narwhales, but Ugruk forget how many days, nights he paddle kayak. Before then, he followed coast of great big land, found pack ice, drift ice, work his way around, winter catch him, stay four months on shore big inlet, with big village of people who talk my talk. Ugruk take woman, her name Poochie, in that village. Ugruk, Innuit named Ooliet we have her together. She sew good. She chew skins good, make soft. We eat good—seals, dried fish, deer meat. Ugruk think maybe he stay always. But when spring come he tell Poochie, Ooliet he must go now, they feel sad, Ugruk feel sad, but Ugruk get in kayak and go east same as before. Before he come this big, good land, he travel north along coast. But southern shore he go from, she Ugruk's home shore. Ugruk mean, she run and run eastward all the way from Ugruk's village, and Ugruk no have crossed any big water."

Because Ugruk was describing an eastward journey and my mind had to picture it in reverse, I had to stop and clear my head. Yet the account was perfectly clear. His recital was bringing him closer and closer to his starting place. How long was the shore that he had left to journey northward along the coast of the big, good land? When I knew that, I would have the vaguest notion of the

total distance between Ugruks' village and his present where-
abouts, the western shore of Greenland.

"How long had you been traveling, Ugruk, following eastward
what you call your home shore, when you set out northward?"

"From one spring to another spring."

"A whole year!"

"Ugruk travel slow that year. He go to every village. Yet this
coast very long, three, four times ten days by dog sled, from our river
mouth to place Ugruk take off in kayak. From there she run on
east, but my brother no go that way. Innuits who live on little
river see him get in kayak, paddle north along shore so Ugruk he
get in kayak, paddle north along shore: Ugruk stop at every Innuit village, but my brother not there, nobody ever see him.
Maybe he drown in that very water and Ugruk look, look, sail
east, east, when brother already dead. One night I dream he dead.
His spirit, he come to Ugruk, and he say, 'No go any further, I drown in sudden squall, sea lice eat my body, my bones at
bottom of sea.' But Ugruk no would believe dream. Ugruk still
look, look, still paddle east, east. But Ugruk know now, it was
true dream. And he no go look, go east no more. He stay with you,
Leif. He no go home, too long way. He stay with you always if
you want. You take place of my brother, because he young, like
you. What you say?"

"Ugruk, I want you to stay with me always."

"Then I stay. What else can Ugruk do as good? I no go back
to village at great river mouth, where okuksak, old people, still
live. Ugruk, Leif, we hunt, fish, sail boat, fight wolf, take long
trips, have good life."

The need came to me to steel my heart a while yet against an
emotion beginning to master me. It arose from the thought of two
men, brothers who greatly loved each other, starting forth alone
on illimitable journeys in little boats made of skin, with their
cargo a few robes, crude weapons and tools, challenging the
great Gods, the rages of the sea, the fury of the storm, the immeasurable cold, the unutterable loneliness. One, the younger,
may have had a little accident and drowned only a thousand miles
from his starting place. The other, the elder, had made a journey
perhaps unprecedented in length and arduousness in the history

of mankind. I put away the thought for a moment more. Within my soul was a more pressing need than that of knowing what was their lodestar, what human motive, nobler than perhaps any God in the firmament could feel, had driven them to these lengths. When I spoke, I controlled my voice well.

"You speak of a village at the mouth of a great river where your folk dwelt. The strand that you followed from there to the open sea where you took off was a thousand miles long. Tell me, Ugruk, does that strand run on westward far beyond your village?"

"Long and long beyond. Our people say twice as long as way I go until turn north. Old people say it end on cape of a mighty land which the Chuckchi people, who come in big skin boats to trade with Innuits, much like Innuit but not the same, call Alaska."

I might ask from whence came the Chuckchi people. I did not, because my head would burst. Instead I took one of Ugruk's mittened hands in both of mine and took the strain off my own heart.

"Ugruk, what was your brother's name?"

"Nanook. It means white bear."

"Why did he leave your village to make a great journey?"

"He go look for our father, Puissay."

"Where had your father gone?"

Ugruk began to speak rapidly and in barely controlled excitement.

"Puissay's mother die when he was born. One night her spirit come to Puissay and shook him by shoulder, wake him up. 'Go east till you find mountain where sun come up,' her spirit say to Puissay. 'Wait with good flint knife, and when sun start up, cut out little piece quick, and put in soapstone pot but take care no burn hands. Bring pot to our river, and throw piece in river, and then she no freeze over again, Innuit go in kayak, oomiac all winter long up and down river, catch plenty fish, kill plenty reindeer who swim slow across river, not run quick on ice, Innuit never more go hungry in winter, people live long, be happy.' That what spirit say to Puissay. 'I will start tomorrow,' Puissay say, and spirit smile and fade away. Next day Puissay load kayak and start out. When whole year pass, and he no come back, Nanook, Ugruk's brother, start out in kayak to look for Puissay. And before he go, Ugruk say to Nanook, 'What if you, too, get lost, no come back?' Nanook say, 'You know little harpoon you make for Nanook when he little fellow?' Ugruk say, 'Yes.' Nanook say, 'If Nanook no come back in ten and three moons, he no alive any more, so you bury little harpoon, same as Nanook's body if it float to shore all swelled up and you no let tears flow, you no feel bad no more.' So when Nanook gone ten and three moons, Ugruk bury little harpoon as Nanook tell him, but tears still flow, Ugruk's heart ache. So after while Ugruk make kayak ready, and he start out, look for Nanook. And so, after long, long while, Ugruk come here."

His voice died away. In a few minutes Ugruk grasped his harpoon as though to throw at a seal, but no seal had appeared in the blow-hole and I knew Ugruk had only pretended to see one, to take the strain off both of us. But I knew a better way. It was to ask my companion a question to which he must give thought.

"There is a great land lying west of your village on the river," I said, speaking very calmly. "Also there were many lands that you saw when you turned north, then east. Are there great green lands south of your villiage?"

"Great, great lands," Ugruk answered. "Innuits live only on the north coast. South of us is the moss country, with much water, lakes, rivers, ponds, plenty birds in summer, plenty deer, she stretch southward far as a wild swan can fly from dawn to dark in the spring flight. Then come high mountains and thick woods, and people live there, not yellow-colored like Innuits, more brown than Innuits, call themselves Skraellings, talk different talk, no hunt seals, but catch salmon, hunt deer, some like reindeer, some red, some very big, black as charred wood. Old folk say their hunting ground run east and west forever, north and south forever. Maybe storytellers tell big lie, Ugruk not know. But Ugruk do know mighty long way from his village to come here."

"A mighty long way, Ugruk," I answered. "But you and I will go a longer way before we die."

And my spine tingled as I spoke, and my hair rustled up, and a sharp pain came to my belly, and I knew that I had either lied before the Gods or I had foretold the future truly as might Little Witch with her staff and her charm bag.

CHAPTER SIX

DARK WINTER AND BRIGHT SPRING

I

The first day of the New Year—as we had counted and celebrated it—brought on a period of intense cold. We dared not go into the open for our natural needs but had to achieve them in the low passage that borrowed a little warmth from the well-heated room where we lived; otherwise, the flesh would have been frozen and rotted and sluffed off, almost always causing death. Thorhall had told me how sometimes on rare occasions the whole crew of a dragon ship had been confined below the deck for several days, while the vessel drifted backward, bow end dragging a sea anchor. In the case of the sailors, the enemy they could not confront was a raging gale, with the crash and breaking of great seas and the incredible blast and bellow of wind. Because the Vikings usually skirted coasts on their long journeys, with little inlets or sheltering islands where they could swiftly dodge when the old men had read the strange runes of impending weather, no great number of our ships had been thus bestormed and only a few lost, compared to many lost in battle. The enemy we exiles could not confront seemed worlds removed from the widow maker, the sea in tempest. On these coldest of days there was no wind at all. There was no sound whatever except of our own making; the land and the sea appeared frozen to death, and all else had died except us few, and if the spell lasted long enough we too might die, by some minor mishap, or go mad.

Of this last there was little danger. Norsemen go mad in battle, when it is said that they have found the Berserk's Way; and at the battle's end, if they yet live, they cannot remember how they took such wounds as they bear, or how many of the foemen they have slain. Sometimes also we Norse grow first cantankerous, then morose, then silent, and, at last, occasionally, violent, killing whom we love best, or ourselves, if monotony presses too hard and too long upon us.

During this spell of intense cold, all work requiring nimble fingers, such as cutting up meat for the pot, had to be done indoors, because the removal of a fur mitten could cause the hand to freeze in a matter of seconds. Still, at least twice a day every man-jack of us ventured into the great cold for several minutes. Once was at midday, when the sun shone with a debility almost un-believable in the remembrance of its great sweat-starting glow in midsummer. Yet just to see it still low in the southern sky, rising a little higher every day, reminded us that it was on the way back to us after wanderings in the far south. On this sally none of us dared do anything strenuous, lest we draw the poison of the cold too deep into our lungs. Our mustaches or beards became hoary from our frosted breath, and we wondered why the fur of our parka hoods did not do likewise, and could only marvel that the glutton fur with which they were lined had some property absent in other furs and in human hair. So we walked quietly up and down the strand, breathing slowly through our noses, speaking not a word.

Our other sally was made in total darkness except for star-light, because then there was something wonderful to see, heart-thrilling and soul-stirring as well as awesome in the extreme, which our old Norse called the Lights of Weird. They were born, we thought, a little west of true north, but they spread across the whole northern horizon and played and flickered throughout the northern sky and sometimes the whole sky. These shimmering waves of light were multicolored, but sometimes they appeared to run together to form a great arch, like a rainbow of pale green and rose from sky rim to sky rim, and sometimes this stood as though made of glimmering metal for several minutes before it dimmed away.

Still the time was long-drawn between meals and from first wakefulness to sleep. It was an unwritten law that no well man could slumber like a hog through a great part of the day; and yet tasks to busy their hands were hard to find. The main occupation of most of us was shaping bows of birch, a poor kind of wood for this use, but the best obtainable, or bows of walrus ribs, made fast to a centerpiece of wood or whalebone, a much more difficult task although resulting in a finer product, and fleshing and sewing skins for pants, mukluks, and parkas to trade for good things when our ship, of which all of us dreamed and no one spoke, had hove into port. My main occupation was playing the flute. That was what my companions, with the exception of Thorstein, desired. The fact that my brother did not desire it, and disliked and perhaps even hated for cause unknown every note I sounded, did not lessen this desire and indeed, again for cause unknown, increased my own desire. Even so, Thorstein heard very few of the tunes I played. He continued to apply his whole attention to other matters, usually useful and ingenious tasks.

The new moon brought us as cargo in her little, delicate silver boat decidedly warmer weather. There was no snowstorm to cause or even to signify the change, no wind; in every other respect than slowly lengthening days, they were precisely like those that had gone before. Still a man's breath no longer crackled; no man need take haste in dropping the fur curtains at the outer and inner end of the passage; he could stand there several seconds to answer a coarse parting jest from some inmate without all the other inmates yelling doom upon his head. The men tarred with the finest seal tar every little crack in the bottoms of our boats. One of them cut down and sawed into something he called planks, but were really nothing more than rough slats, a dwarf birch with an oversized trunk, and lugged the lot without effort to what we called our lumber pile, proudly bidding us take note of the beads of sweat upon his face.

The men hunted tarmochans, white rabbits, and white foxes, the first two food for our table, the third supplying a rich, very soft fur that we carefully fleshed and stretched and which we reckoned would sell for a high price in Europe, when the time was ripe, these being larger and more beautiful skins than those of white foxes found in Norway. A few made short jaunts after deer, but found no tracks, and the treeless open grasslands endlessly white with snow gave them the headache, and heartache too, I thought, and they soon returned to the tall flames of our oil lamps.

Toward the end of this moon—indeed when she was so wasted that we could never have seen her silver wisp hanging in the sky, her points pointing westward instead of eastward like the points of a new moon, except for the brevity of the days, night lingering long after we waked, falling long before we slept—in the last stage of her decay ere she would be reborn, Ugruk and I went hunting musk ox. He had seen where they had pawed in search of grass before the great onslaught of cold, and he thought some might still be in that vicinity. Both of us were joyful when he spied a herd of about fifty not more than a mile distant, and we knew how our fellows would rejoice if we managed to get one to give them a change of diet.

No heart-stirring adventure came to pass, if by that I meant a fight with one of the bulls. Yet my heart was stirred not by combat, but by wonder at the ways of beasts, how they have a wisdom of survival, given them by whom? Also I beheld a scene which seemed to me unforgettable and magnificent.

The oxen, in their long black hair, were pawing the snow and eating grass. We had come up in the face of a light wind, as Ugruk directed, and apparently they were shortsighted creatures, for they let us approach within long arrow range before any of them noticed us. Then an observant cow lowed, all the others raised their heads, and at once they began to group themselves in a curious way. The bulls and the full-grown cows formed a ring, heads to the front, tails inward, and within that circle, under its guard, was a lame cow and perhaps ten half-grown oxen, no doubt born the preceding spring. This was their fort. Although all the cows were lowing now with an ominous sound, and an old bull bellowed now and then, not one of them left his place to run as we drew nigh.

"See, they no try run away," Ugruk said. "They know, no use, for wolves can fly over snow like this, leap at their throats, while they sink to their hocks. Anyway no ox can outrun Runner-in-the-Night even on hard ground. They no see very good. Ugruk, Leif wear white parkas, they no can smell us because we down wind, so maybe they think we be wolves. Wolves, they think twice before running into ring of horns. If wolf try to dodge horns, ox on each side give his head a big sweep, one horn almost sure to catch him on side. He no live very long then, Ugruk tell you true. He fall on back and yelp until he die. So wolf no kill many ox."

"Deer can run like lightning on snow like this."

"Reindeer got big feet, hoof split, spread out on snow. Wolf run down young deer, he no like grown deer very good, grown deer strike with both front hoofs, sometimes cut wolf open."

"Don't the deer fight with their horns, too? Both the bull reindeer and cow have fine horns."

"But horns fall off early in spring, when cows have calves, need them most."

We moved closer to the herd. The lowing loudened and became more ominous-sounding; the bellows of the bulls were more frequent; the ring with its long curved spikes tightened a little, strengthening itself and giving no sign of breaking. I remembered something my mother, Thorhild, had told me, that had been told her by the old Magus in Stavanger who could read Latin.

Long ago a great conqueror had come out of Macedonia, a land northeast of Rome, and his soldiers had been taught to stand or kneel in such order that they were largely protected by their shields while their spears made a bristling wall. The formation was called a phalanx. That was the fort of the Macedonian soldiery. Now I was seeing the phalanx of the Greenland oxen.

The scene seemed to me one of the utmost grandeur. Far and away stretched the snow, seemingly illimitable; away to the east loomed hills and mountains and at last the gleaming icecap. Gull Eye, at his first glimpse of oxen, had remarked on their square appearance. This was not so marked at close range; but the impression they conveyed of great strength, endurance, and courage thrilled my yet young heart. Their long black hair, almost touching the snow, waved in the light wind. Their legs were short and looked immensely strong; their lowered heads and out-thrusting horns were the very picture of truculence and defiance.

Why then did I nock an arrow on the string of my bow? Could I not turn away, without taking a noble life? The notion could not cross my mind. It would have hardly crossed my mother's mind, were she here; if it did so, she would instantly dismiss it. True, our band could subsist on seal meat, our fare would be good with the addition of venison, hares, and grouse, but the men would revel over the rich, full-bodied beef. The business of our hunt was to get some. And perhaps of all creatures with beating hearts, man is given the hardest lot. For in addition to his body needs and his instinct to survive, his soul has needs that may be gross or may be splendid; yet they must be satisfied, sometimes, or he cannot live.

"Leif, no use bow. Arrow may only wound, not kill, and we get in trouble. I take bow, you take Ugruk's harpoon. Then we come up in easy range, take good aim, and kill first cast."

So we changed weapons and advanced. The fort stood solid. At sixty feet I threw, and the long blade pierced the top of the lowered neck of a big bull ox. Perhaps it severed his spine or cut into a great artery for he toppled on his knees, tried to get up only to fall, uttered one moan and died.

"Now walk backward, still looking at oxen," Ugruk instructed me. "See, they press closer to each other, filling the gap in their ring. But when we get good ways off, they break ring and go away."

As though Ugruk had seen this in a vision, it came to pass. As we retreated, the sullen lowings of the cows and the snorts and bellows of the bulls reduced in volume and ferocity, and presently died away. Then some sort of signal passed and the whole herd except for one member, mysteriously missing or somehow greatly changed, made off in a slow gallop. At a quarter of a mile their pace changed to a powerful walk, an old bull, with patches of gray in his long black cloak, leading the long file.

Ugruk and I made haste to our trophy to butcher the carcass before it stiffened from the cold. His hide alone would be the pride of our rough house, and I thought I would invite Eric to sleep on it his first night on shore, to pay him off somehow for his attempt to send me on a fool's errand long and long ago. We estimated the whole weight of the beast at four hundred pounds. Actually these Greenland oxen were not as heavy as they looked, because of their long hair growing over very dense, dark gray wool. Nature had endowed them well for life in a rugged and inhospitable land. On second thought, she had dealt the same with us Norse.

We cut out and threw away all the offal except the heart and the sweetbread, which we Icelanders considered a great treat. I observed that the heart was rather small as beef hearts go, and no doubt of great power and tough to eat. I intended to bake it and present it to Starkad as a mead of honor. Also we cut out the tongue, both back straps, and we had started to butcher both rear thighs when Ugruk bethought himself and went to get some kind of a strong pole, the nearest obtainable being the trunk of a young birch we had seen sheltered under a hillside about a mile behind us. In his absence I affixed thongs to the two heavy hams, each of them weighing about forty-five pounds. It would be useless to butcher the forequarters or the sides or the neck. Along with the heavy pelt, we had saved all the meat that Ugruk and I could carry on the long tramp home.

We made that tramp, this stocky Innuit and I, and worked up a better sweat than did our fellow when he chopped wood. Occasionally we had to stop to rest, and now and then we exclaimed over the largeness of this land, and Ugruk made one of his jokes—that our companions had moved our house to the other side of the mountains. But the cordiality of our welcome from our bright-eyed mates atoned for our aching shoulders, tired backs, lame legs, and leaden feet. Our offering almost came up to Thorstein's presentation of a jug of mead, if I were to judge by the men's high spirits. We ate a prodigious meal, and as the men grew sleepy I still had wind to play a few of the tunes they liked best.

It was a wondrously happy event. Cross-grained Gorm was incited to make a remark astonishing us all, for when on very rare occasions anyone mentioned the *Narwhale* it was always with the manner, indeed the assumption, that she would sail into port as soon as the ice gave her way. The old sailor spoke with great directness.

"Suppose the old hooker never gets here," he said, breaking what had chanced to be a long silence. "I count the odds only a little better than even. He'll come if he can, that's sure, but even Eric the Red can't sail a ship on the sea bottom. Well, my point is, we could still make out. We have no women, which is no great loss to me, but a mighty deprivation for you younger men, and we have no honey mead unless Thorstein has hidden another jug, but with fair luck we can eat and keep warm and have treats occasionally as we had tonight, and plenty of good hunting and fishing. We would try to see more of this land, and what we find out Thorstein and Leif could put down in runes to be read by those who come after us. The rough time would be after I die and you young men grow old. Maybe then you could all pitch in to a whole army of wolves, ten packs together, and die fighting. In the meanwhile we've got Ugruk to help us to live better. Odin taught men to love their fate if their hearts could stand it, and, if not, to look her in the face. And best of all we have Leif's flute to lift our hearts when they sink too low. Leif, play us another tune."

2

I did so, a lively one that the Irish had taught us Norse, and I was only half through it when all my hearers except Thorstein stood up and jigged.

Perhaps we were too happy, I was thinking. My comrades' eyes did not have a drunken shine to indicate they were fey; yet they were bright and there was nothing that I knew of to stop every man-jack of us, except Thorstein, from being fey. For instance we need only be working a distance down the strand in arrow cast of our shelter, at some task as lowly as skinning walrus, when the Frost Giant sneezed and kept on sneezing. Perhaps only Thorstein, whose eyes did not shine at all and instead were hot and angry, might be lucky enough to blunder blindly into the wall of our turf house, himself too weakened from breathing ice-crystals to guide us home by voice.

I too might reel through the smother, when all the rest but Thorstein had wandered far afield, and bump into the turf house. Had I not been dubbed Leif the Lucky by Eric the Red? In this case, Thorstein and I would have the whole land to ourselves. Because of the drive to survive that is almost frightening in us Norse, although frequently it ebbs away until we seek death at our own hands, he and I would work together that we both might live awhile, dwelling in the same empty echoing hut. We would be bound to each other by a cruel and mocking tie until one or the other of us died. Gods! Gods! I had never asked a favor from you as you sit in your high seats. I had taken what you give, or what I had toiled for, or what you dispensed. But I now prayed to their whole company—spare me this! And gentle Kris, my mother's God, your great sire knew of hate living side by side with need, if you did not. Now I pray to you, although I am yet outside your pale, spare me this!

I did not believe our little band was fey. Instead, I had a dim and haunting sense of some great stroke of fate, for good or ill but forever momentous, being aimed at us. The stories and the faiths handed down by our fathers were greatly confused from too many tellings. Fate was sometimes called a Norn, but Swan Maidens and Valkyries were also Norns. My darting imagination pictured some common thing, at least no immortal being, as fate's envoy already on the march. The fancy died away. In the next few days I forgot all about it. These days were the common run of our days in Greenland. There was more light, less darkness, indeed the beginning of a sharp division between day and night, but no one did anything notable, and the weather was neither very bad nor very good.

On the night that we counted only fifteen nights away from the spring equinox we had made a good supper of whale meat— a fresh-smelling part of the carcass on which no wolf had drooled —and some wind-dried fish. All of us had eaten except Thorstein who had gone deer hunting and was still away on the moonlit snow, almost certain proof that he had killed a big stag and his return had been delayed by the work of butchering. I had got out my flute as usual, and my mates had asked for various tunes, which I had played. Starkad had asked me to play an old Norse song to be sung when young people drank mead and kissed between stanzas. I was well along with it when Thorstein jerked aside the inner curtain and stood in the blaze of lamplight.

"Stop that cursed tootling!" he demanded in a rough and imperious voice.

I missed only one note. Then, continuing the song, I played

softly enough that no man could fail to hear what Starkad was saying in reply.

"Why, Thorstein? I asked for that piece, and Leif obliged me, and I'm in no hurry to have it stop. What great hurry are you in?"

"Stop it, I tell you!" And walking toward me in long strides, he snatched the flute from my hands.

Too late I saw the expression on his face, not merely ill-tempered, but dangerous in the extreme, which I knew without knowing why. It might have been the expression on the face of Eric the Red when he struck in mighty wrath, and at least twice in his life had killed. Thorstein did not strike me in that way. Instead, with one savage twist of his hands, he broke my flute in two pieces.

I was on my feet now and so was every man. I did nothing for a moment, and could do nothing; the wound was too deep. First in a blur and then with intense sharpness I saw the faces of my mates, and on everyone except Thorstein's was a look of unbelieving horror. It was no more mild emotion than horror. Their eyes were round, their mouths rounded, their skins gray. But on Thorstein's face rage fought with fear. He did not know all that he had done, but he knew he had done too much.

He began to speak in tones not now so furious or lordly, but in angry self-justification.

"There are two hundred reindeer within arrow cast of our door. I think we can surround them and drive them over that high bank of the river—you know the place, a sheer drop of thirty feet. Some will break their necks, a good many break their legs, and we might easily get thirty. And yet you wanted to sit and hear Leif tootle. I confess I shouldn't have broken his flute, but a man cannot always control his anger."

"No, you should not have broken Leif's flute as Eric broke Kol's head," Starkad answered quietly. "It was not yours to break and to silence forever in one jealous tantrum." Starkad's eyes had become very calm, as though his thoughts were elsewhere.

"It was not jealousy that moved me," Thorstein said indignantly. "It was the good of our band. Our struggle here is one of life and death. As for the broken flute, I'll buy Leif a new one. I'll send all the way to Italy to get a good one, with furs of my own catch, when the Norse have settled here and established trade with Europe."

"You say for the good of our band. Thorstein, what could we have done with thirty dead reindeer? We could eat a few of them, but the rest would be no good to Eric and his followers, for if they come at all it will be in the full spring, when meat won't keep."

"Thorstein, may you die and rot and Odin send your stinking corpse to Hel gate to be eaten by dogs," Gorm broke in, his eyes likewise calm and very dark, fixed on the eyes of the elder son of Eric the Red, his owner. And he spoke in the quiet way that comes upon a man when his soul stands forth in its pristine godhead and commands his tongue and lips.

And now it was my turn to speak, although I intended to employ very few words. I arose and confronted Thorstein, perfectly certain what I meant to do. The other men looked into my face and stood back. Starkad slid the big soapstone oil lamp nearer to the wall. There was plenty of room.

"Defend yourself, Thorstein," I told him.

His face flushed with renewed fury and he drew his arm back to strike. But he drew it too far back, aiming too great a blow, to be able to drive it forward quickly. My hand shot out and grasped his wrist, and I twisted his arm behind his back, while he tried to strike me with his left arm, only to be made impotent by pain. I heard the bone of his forearm break. Thorstein did not scream, he only uttered a big grunt, and as I released his arm it dropped helpless at his side.

Fate had indeed marched, in the person of a herd of reindeer, and now it had struck, and Thorstein and I looked into one another's eyes not in challenge, only in wonder as to what might be the outcome at long last, and then both of us turned away.

3

In almost every gang of seamen as large as eight there is a journeyman doctor, often astonishingly capable. In our original band there was none, and when someone mentioned the need of a splint, we looked at one another helplessly. However, we had not reckoned on Ugruk.

"I fix it," he announced.

Having Thorstein remove his parka and shirt, Ugruk examined the broken forearm with great care. Then he cut a piece of slat from our lumber pile, whittled it into a shape to suit him with his knife, and pressed where his clever fingers—or perhaps his eyes quick to observe the slightest departure from natural appearance—told him were the broken ends of the bone. When he had pressed these ends together, while sweat dropped from Thorstein's pale face, he held the splint securely while Starkad bound it firmly with strips of deerskin.

"She all right now, I think," Ugruk said.

Starkad now gave Thorstein a melted spoonful of fat, musky-smelling secretion, apparently identical with civet, which was greatly valued in Norway as a medicine and which we had taken from the gland of a tree-climbing rich-furred animal, similar to a ferret in shape but many times larger. Certainly it acted as a stimulant, because the gray went out of Thorstein's cheeks and he resumed what was almost his natural color. Then Starkad spoke solemnly.

"Leif Ericsson will now be tried on the charge of maiming Thorstein Ericsson without due or lawful cause."

Thorstein was the first to speak. His tone was low and it implied great self-control and latent strength.

"If you please, Starkad, I would rather handle this matter myself."

"Your wishes cannot be regarded," the officer of our watch replied. "In injuring one of our number he has reduced, at least temporarily, the strength of our whole band. There are nine of us here. Ugruk may not act as a judgment-giver because the fact is well known he is Leif's man. Leif and Thorstein, as the two principals, may testify if they so desire but may not be a party to the verdict. Gorm also may not vote, because we all heard the curse he laid on Thorstein for breaking Leif's flute—good evidence that he cannot give impartial judgment. This leaves four men other than myself to constitute the moot, and you four may sit against yon wall.

"Common law, as established by the moot in Norway and the Hundred moot in Iceland, shall prevail here," Starkad went on. "Since we all saw what Thorstein did, and what Leif did in retaliation, the only question before you is what punishment shall be dealt Leif if he is found guilty of the charge. If any of you believe that what he did was justified, you must vote for his acquittal. Since I am serving in deep humility as a Law Speaker, I will vote only if your votes are evenly divided. No vote is to be influenced by your personal liking or disliking of either Thorstein or Leif. First, you will vote on whether Leif is guilty as charged. If you find him innocent, that ends the trial. If you find him guilty, you must vote on the degree of that guilt and on due punishment. I will call on you from left to right as you sit. Oddson, give your verdict."

"Innocent," Oddson replied.

"Stori?"

"Innocent."

"Thorson?"

"Innocent."

"Hagen?"

"Innocent."

"Perhaps I should say this. Perhaps I should not. The question is too deep for my mind; I may only speak my heart. If I had sat with you on the jury, my vote, too, would be 'innocent.' Leif, the charge against you for injuring Thorstein without due cause has been dismissed."

Thorstein did not appear to be listening. After Starkad had spoken, one of the men yawned, another stretched a cramped leg, all of them rose. I went to where I had been sitting at Thorstein's entrance and picked up the two mute hollow sticks of wood that had been my flute, wondering idly what disposal to make of them. It was unthinkable that they could be repaired; at the same time I did not want to put them away and keep them, ever forlorn reminders of the days when they had been magically joined and could sing. I stood with them in my hands. I forgot anyone else was in the room. I thought of parents deprived by some sudden and dire stroke of careless fate of a lovely little daughter who could sing, sweet as a swan. Ever nearer edged the moment they must lay her mute remains in a rocky crypt or put them in a box to be hidden in the ground. The wound I had received began to bleed. It seemed to me that the blood would rise up until it drowned my heart. Then I thought that my mates might be gazing at me in the prodigious compassion of our fellow-ship, aching to do something for me even more than for themselves, but helpless to do either. However, they had looked away for the sake of my pride and in some measure their own. Only Ugruk came up and spoke to me.

"Leif, my brother, will you give me the broken horn?"

It seemed to me he spoke in flawless Norse.

"What do you want of it, Ugruk? It is good for nothing."

"Still Ugruk want it. He want look at it. He want keep it. He keep it out of your sight, sight of the men who heard it sing, you nor they never see it again. Believe Ugruk, this best thing."

"Very well, I believe you. Here it is."

Ugruk took the broken ends and went to the corner where he kept his harpoon, his rook sack, and the rest of his belongings, always neatly stowed. I could not see where he put the ruin; his back was turned, and anyway I had tried not to look. Now the men were getting ready to lie down for the night, and some would have the capacity to drift away, out of the world, into dreamless sleep that was more merciful than death, because in death souls must wander, they must be blown by desolate winds, they must realize in the full the loneliness they had sought so des-perately to relieve or to conceal—or so the heathens believed, and even gave names to a few places that the derelict souls might visit, such as Hel Strand, Valhalla, and the Well of Weird be-yond the northern lights. But some of my fellows would dream troubled, aching dreams tonight and Starkad would have night-mares from which we must arouse him. Once or twice he had told us that if we had not wakened him in time the dream monsters would have got him and he would have died.

I was neither heathen nor Christian, perhaps because I had

inherited too much from Eric the Red to follow gentle Kris, and too much from lovely Thorhild to be a whole-souled heathen.

What would I dream? I deeply feared I would dream of music, perhaps the heartbreaking Strand Song of the Norse Women to the Departing Fleet. The thought crossed my mind that I might never again, except in dreams, hear music. The nearest to it might be the lonely outcry of high-flying swans whose several voices make a kind of harmony and are also most lovely on the ear; still they do not whistle strains as do nightingales, such as a shipmate aboard the *Narwhale* had heard in England. When death comes, all music ends. This might be one of the fees that the remorseless Gods exact for the boon of obliteration in decay and finally in dust.

Only one other of our inmates spoke to me before I lay down. As chance had brought me to a lonely end of the room—the men liked to make their beds rather close together—Thorstein approached me in his fine, proud stride. Once more we faced each other, he not quite so tall as I, but wonderfully lithe. He was much the finer-looking, with his large and brilliant eyes, narrow nose, short mouth, and glossy hair. By the nature of things he would take the eye of woman before I did. In how many more ways could he come out ahead? If I tried I could think of so many that I decided not to think of any.

His expression was not now wrathful nor did it reveal any passion. He seemed only deeply thoughtful.

"Leif, you and I are implacable enemies," he said.

"That is true."

"I do not know exactly how it happened. In fact I know of no good reason we should be enemies, instead of very good friends. I can only say it is fate. Leif, are such things written in stars before we are born? Sometimes I look up at the twinkling lights and think that their formations resemble runes. In any case we both accept the fact—and the grim joke of it is, neither of us can kill the other, because we are brothers, and the very earth quakes at fratricide. All we can do is win victories over each other or deal burning defeats to each other. In fact, I don't want you dead. In that case, I would not have much left to live for—or at least to fight for. I take little joy in triumphs except as they reduce you. I care almost nothing about women. My passion for hunting is tied up with you somehow, I think, although I can't trace the connection. What I live for mainly is to checkmate you, to slow your advance, at last perhaps to topple you—and by that I suppose I mean to top you. I hated your flute with the deepest hate. I could stand to have you equal me, or fall only a little short sometimes, and sometimes be more than my equal at what we Norse regard as manly achievement. But I could not stand to have you do well, in all truth make beautiful music, and see the men sitting there thanking the Gods that you are in their number, when I cannot sound a note."

"You may be wrong about the last, Thorstein," I said, after thinking quickly over all he had said. "You have deft hands. Playing music is mainly a matter of their practiced skill."

"No, I have no gift for it although I know good music when I hear it. Sometimes when I am alone I try to sing. I make only a series of discordant sounds that drive marmots into their holes. But that is not what I intended to tell you."

"Yes, sir."

"You scored on me a great score when you broke my arm in punishment for my breaking your flute. It was an act I would call—well, godly—in the sense that we perceive godliness, especially in Odin, in a lesser degree in Thor. Heaven above and Hel below, are you fated to perform some great feat never before accomplished by a hero—greater than the conquest of Britain by Ragnar's sons only a little more than a century ago? No! It may be that fate has considered giving you the great appointment, she plays with the lots, but has not yet cast them; and in my soul I know that she would cast them thus, except for one thing, except for one man. That man is not Eric the Red. It is I. I am the one who will balk you. I have always longed for such an outcome but until tonight I did not have a great enough motive to make me stick to the resolve, as little lemmings stick to their seaward path, as a great, white bitch wolf, her belly squirming with unborn cubs, follows the track of a reindeer stag whose blood she has tasted. This will be my revenge for your breaking my arm. The bones may mend.

they may be as strong as ever, but the shame of it is burned into my soul, and my soul will be scarred forever, and the great shaggy heroes, Ragnar and the rest, will laugh at me when I try to join their company in Valhalla. Yes, I will balk you. Let that pledge burn into your soul because it is true. Now that you know the truth, I can pass into deep sleep."

He turned away. I waited a moment to see if there would be any sign from the Gods of the truth or the untruth of my brother's promise. There was no song of the wolves as sometimes we had heard as they sat in a ring and wailed to the white moon of their hard lot. No tarmochan wakened in her warm bed of snow and uttered her wailing cry. All that came to me was the remembrance of the smile of Little Witch when she had told me I would soon be known as Lucky Leif—such a strange smile, so knowing of what she could not tell. It had said that my way would be steep and lonely and long. Thus I knew that my ultimate victory or final defeat was yet far off.

4

After the equinox, spring tripped in to keep her appointment with grass roots under the snow, which seemed dead but in which life lay dormant, waiting their time to shoot up in splendid greenery. Too, spring had an assignation with countless reindeer who knew well the buff of winter but in whose wombs lay calves, their legs doubled under them, their strong lips useless as yet, but which, when came the appointed hour, would suck noisily the rich milk from the plenteous bags. Too, spring had arranged a meeting with myriad waterfowl, swans, geese, ducks, cranes, loons, grebes, bitterns, coots, and rails, whose hordes now gabbled and fed in the warm waters of marshes in the deepmost south, but when the sea ice was shattered by the sun and the frozen ponds of the mosslands again sparkled in the wind, they would fly northward under the stars, sometimes crying out, to procreate and make nests and lay eggs and in due course behold the fledglings of which even now they dreamed dim dreams. The stunted willows and birch, to be laughed at by their stalwart brethren in lands less harsh, yet had arranged with spring to meet them here, whereby they would bud and come into leafage and look as much like real trees as the Gods would ever grant.

The days lengthened with the same haste as they had shortened before the winter solstice. Now they were as long as nights, and presently they were longer, and in the heat of the day the top of the frozen ground thawed a little, and we heard the sound of trickling waters. In the evenings retreating winter again locked up the land, but her keys were getting worn and rusty, and slush began to form at the edges of the great ice of the fiord, and pools of water on its top wore only a bare sheath of ice after the whole night, and before one moon after the equinox there were countless pools and the snow was weeping off. We heard the far-off rumble of ice breaking and knocking far at sea, and before long what we called leads, which were straits of open water, began to appear between the icefields. The ice of our river began to crack and move, congeal, crack again, pile up behind barriers of ice, and one day the whole mass went out with a prodigious roar.

The spring grass was forcing its way through the melting snow, the silver gulls lighting on our strand. And then spring came to Greenland in a wild and frantic rush, as if she had almost missed her many appointments, and vast flocks of waterfowl arrived every day. Ugruk and I saw a reindeer drop her fawn, lick it, nudge it into trying its thin legs, and before we left it had found its ordained way to her warm sweet teats.

And the thought uppermost in my mind was not now the loss of my flute or what Thorstein said or did, but the patent fact that this coast was indeed fit for human settlement, that the Norse people, used to hardship, could endure the dreadful winters, that they knew how to use and husband the good days between breaking spring and the onslaught of the cold, and they could have farms here and procreant herds of cattle and sheep, and a new life, an adventurous life.

All this—if they would come. Everything depended on whether Eric the Red was dead and sea lice-eaten in some unknown bottom, or whether fate and the gales had forced him to return to Iceland without visiting our strand. If Eric lived, he would return, bringing his goods and chattels, and his franklins and freemen and thralls, and, I thought, many followers. But we did not spend our days watching distant reaches of the fiord. Besides our chores, and fishing and hunting enough to furnish us fresh and tasty food, we started to build a larger turf house and to collect rocks to make pens, and all in all to make as ready as we could for any people who might come.

On what we thought was by Roman counting the twenty-eighth day of April, of the year 986, thirty-six days after the spring equinox, the lot of us were on the strand, cutting up with axes and letting the tide carry off the remains of the whale, in which decay had set in during the warm weather. Stori had walked off a few feet and turned his back upon us, which we Norse had been taught was good manners in such cases, to answer a call of nature; and so he chanced to be gazing up the fiord.

"By the Nine Runes of Odin, what's that?" he burst out.

All of us looked in the direction he pointed. We distinguished a small object, yellow or pale-colored, against the horizon.

"It might be some sea beast," Starkad answered. "But it might be——"

"The top of sail," Thorstein broke in when Starkad hesitated. "And that's what it is," he went on with great calmness. "Our ship is coming in."

We others were not so calm. We watched in aching hunger for Thorstein's word to be made good, at once with breathless fear lest the spot sink from sight, showing it was the arched back of a white whale or some such creature. Instead the sea mark became higher, more visible, more real, more meaningful with every passing moment.

"You are right, Thorstein," Starkad said in his right to speak first on confirmation of what my brother had said. "It's the top of a sail, but unless Eric's spread a new sail since he left here, it's some other ship. In any case, we are not castaways any longer. Iceland has jumped from fifteen hundred sea miles distant to an hour's sail. Greenland has changed from an outlying all but uninhabited wasteland to part of the known world."

In a very few minutes, as we exiles had measured time, her hull began to show. And then Oddson took off his hair-seal cap and waved it.

"Yes, and she's the *Narwhale*. I caught a glimpse of the horn when the sun struck it."

"But what's that behind her?" Gorm demanded, his voice hoarse with excitement. "It looks like the top of another. And there's a third—and a fourth!"

"Before the Gods, you are right, old man," Starkad cried.

We did not dance or shout. Such conduct would be permissible if we were tipsy with mead, not on such a solemn occasion as this. Perhaps we thought it would anger Odin, God of the Winds, or Njord, God of the Sea. But we began to shake hands with one another, and wonderful was the feel of those hard hands in mine, and perhaps mine the like in theirs. Wonderful was the custom of shaking hands—an odd thing when you thought of it, the clasping of another's hand and both pumping up and down—a peculiarly human action, and of prodigious meaning when it was not perfunctory, because it signified each giving to the other his whole self for the brief moment of the ceremony, for no part of a man so signified his being a man as his hand with which he works and eats. Only Thorstein and I avoided touching each other's hand. I saw Thorstein shake hands with Gorm, despite the awful curse the latter had laid upon him for breaking the flute. Ugruk, whose people were not great hand shakers, and instead touched noses, shook joyfully and energetically every hand he could reach, his grin meanwhile wider than seemed humanly possible.

The *Narwhale* was still a good league distant when Stori, eager to distinguish himself again, recognized Einer's ship; and if Ian, the poem speaker and singer was aboard her, which really I did not doubt, my vision of the music being ended forever had been only a bad dream. A very large ship, close in her wake, looked like that of the chieftain Bjorn, who had been fourth in power to Eric the Red. And now we could see the tops of four other vessels, seven in all, and if that many could stay in one

another's sight on the great crossing from Iceland there must be
as many more that had lagged for one reason or another and by
such charts as Eric could supply would surely find us later in the
day or in the next few days.

By that time our band must have been plainly visible from aboard
the *Narwhale,* we looking like little sticks, and I pictured a great
head counting, followed by a great argument, for we would not
be easy to tally correctly, as we moved from here to there, forever changing places, to get a better view. Eric had hoped to see
eight men. He would have been fairly well satisfied, considering
the risks we had surely run as all-winter exiles in an unpeopled
land, with seven, hoping with all his heart that Thorstein would
be one of the number, and, for Thorhild's sake, and in some
odd, complicated, but quite real way for his own sake too, that I,
Leif, would not be the missing man. What if he had been able
to count only six? When the great fleets of the dragon ships had
returned from their summer raids and sea fights, eights ships returning out of every ten that had sailed had been counted a better
score than average. If the ships had returned manned in the proportion of seven out of ten, with the companies setting forth, the
women's song of welcome was joyfully sung except by those
stricken wives or mothers who had crept away to weep.

What if our number had been five? Eric the Red would have
had little say with words, nothing to reveal in his face. What if
all of us had been missing, the turf house hollow or even half-
completed or barely started, with no rank-smelling kitchen midden,
no seal bones strewn about, so spines of big fish, no human litter
of any sort, and wolves and deer following the strand, not lifting
their eyes to the emptiness, let alone pausing to lift one foot ready
to run? Eric would have bowed his head in sorrow, perhaps spoken
briefly to the wives or mothers whose gaze, in searching the
barren strand, had been desperately sharp, and then he would have
turned his attention to the establishment of the colony which was
his business; and no human, even Thorhild, could have looked
into his heart.

But as it was, some of the watchers counted nine men waiting at the strand, and they kept insisting that they were right, and one by one the other watchers had been won over to their belief. So I reckoned there was a great deal of gabbing and wild speculation aboard the *Narwhale*.

5

The full moon tide was at flood, higher than we could account for in the south wind. Eric the Red slid his ship so close to the bank that he could run out a plank to land his passengers and cargo.

He was the first to come ashore, his beard blazing, his skin ruddy, his thick body appearing to emanate power, his eyes as green as the young grass. He shook hands first with Thorstein, which was proper enough, and besides it caused a little jet of evil to open in my heart, because I meant to vanquish both of them at last, and somehow this cleared the way. Eric turned next to Starkad, in command of our party, and this too was proper procedure, but it so happened that when he turned to me I could not give him immediate attention because Thorhild, the second to descend, had her arms about my neck and her lovely soft lips on mine. She looked younger and more beautiful than ever, I thought.

"My flute has been broken," I told her.

"That is no great woe. You are not broken by your long exile in an unknown land, and instead you have leaped up, you stand as tall as Bluetooth stood, half a foot over six feet, and you have filled out, and stripling is no longer a due word for you. Somehow you can get another flute."

"Sooner than Leif think," came a deep-toned voice at one side that could belong to no one else than Ugruk.

"You know better than to interrupt the close speech of my mother, Thorhild, and me," I told him with no great sternness, "and besides you know nothing about flutes, and what you say is empty wind."

"So? You wait and see. Three moons at best, six moons at longest. Leif, you mother, Thorhild, is as beautiful as a silver gull."

"And you are Leif's close friend! I know it without being told. I am glad."

"Ugruk mighty glad. I tell you, some day. Now you, Thorhild, will you touch noses with me, in sign you my friend, too?"

"Gladly."

So they touched noses while the gathering people stared, but this mattered not to Ugruk, who stood by the ways of his people, or to Thorhild, who was never concerned with the impression she made on folk when she had done what was natural for her to do.

"Is he some kind of Lapp from the northern part of Greenland?" came Eric's rough and resonant voice in my ear. Meanwhile, he grasped my hand and shook it.

"No, my father, he is an Innuit from the west."

I had answered in tones into which I had forced calmness, for well I knew the impact of the words on Eric's innermost being. In all truth, I had thrown what I might compare to a bird dart into a tender spot, not going deep enough to wound him deeply, but which would itch and smart and keep him awake, sometimes, at night, because I intended to say no more than this, and at my bidding Ugruk would say no more.

"That is impossible. Greenland is the westernmost land in all the seas. Ever since Thorhall found that abandoned skin boat, I have reckoned that a people somewhat like the Laplanders lived in the northern part. This man was blown to sea and lost his directions."

Truly he had been blown to sea, I thought, by the wind of a great need. But I gave no more thought to it now, because Thorhall stood before me, unchanged in any particle during our long parting, his skin the color of birch bark, the light that was ever in his eyes glinting and dancing.

"Have you bloodied your sword yet?" he asked me in jest.

"Yes, in the side of a white wolf."

"A good place to bloody it. The wolf fang that you wear biting the wolf that bared his teeth against you! Gods, you have grown! What meat have you eaten?"

"Tough meat, but good."

"That much I perceive."

He turned to speak to my mates. Meanwhile the crowd on the strand was thickening fast. Several franklins subject to Eric had come down the plank, the freemen descended behind them, and now came the thralls, among them a brutish-looking man and a beautiful young woman with short-cut raven-black hair and eyebrows. It was Ellen, and she bowed her head to me with great propriety, but meanwhile her hand brushed against mine, and her forefinger found my palm and tickled it quickly. She was unchanged, but the fair-haired, pink-and-gold maiden behind her was greatly changed since I had sailed from Ericsholm. At that time she had been ten or eleven, although looking a year or two older. At most, now, she was twelve, but the buds of her breast had swollen so that she looked fourteen; and her legs and body and her rounded and bold butt were not those of a herring, as we say— meaning a lass of an age to attract the eye but not yet arouse a fever—and indeed were those of a maiden in first flower.

"I kissed you good-by when you went away, and now I want to kiss you in joy of seeing you again," she told me, the words well chosen for one so young and humbly born. "But I have to stretch to reach you now."

I stooped a little and she put her arms around my neck, and I would have been more conscious of their close pressure except for my great awareness of her kiss, full and sweet as the kiss of most Norse women and girls, and in addition signaling more than the crowd perceived, as a young wife might kiss in her husband's presence whom he thought was his best friend but who was really her lover.

Eric had his back turned, talking to Einer, and had not seen the exchange. I was glad, because he would surely have made a gruff comment about a thrall maiden forgetting her place.

"If I am a few inches taller, you are many times prettier," I told her as she passed on, in no way matching the easy grace of her remark, but the best my disordered mind could assay.

The crowd continued to grow, as our long-empty little roadstead appeared to swarm with ships. If there were mermaids hereabouts I could not help but grin to think of their unearthly green eyes rounded with amazement, and of the start given to the seals and dolphins and schools of fish that used our inlet, and the halibuts and flounders lying on their bellies on the bottom, both eyes fixed to gaze upward, needed both to assure themselves that they were in their right minds. On high ground a mile or two distant a small pack of wolves might have forgotten their ever present frenzy of hunger to gaze down at a pack of such living creatures as they had never dreamed of seeing, and it could be that their hearts were troubled by some inkling of great change.

Eric had ordered all the vessels in his wake to put in here. The following day they would take off for various fiords suitable for settlement, some of which—as I soon learned—Eric had charted before a great movement of ice floes out of the north had forced him from his course, blocked his return to Ericsfiord, and caused him to make a great westward sweep to Cape Welcome, where he had seen the necessity of returning to Iceland. The crews and the passengers of the fleet had been glad enough to pay us a call and feel solid ground under their feet before they went home hunting, for our homestead was only a short sail out of their way.

Nine ships in all had put into our strand, all of them riding low. Only sailors are able to believe how many people, cows, sheep, and what a store of tools, farming implements, gear of all sorts, and almost every kind of supplies necessary to life in a new land, a ship not much longer than a bull gray whale can hold and usually bear safely over tempestuous seas. These nine ships did not compose the whole fleet; Eric was almost certain of six more arriving safely in the next two or three days. His plan was that all of them unload as soon as their masters had picked the sites of their future homes, return to Iceland for equally great cargoes, and perhaps make a third voyage before winter locked the shimmering gates of the land, which were its numerous, deep-cut fiords.

Only one kind of stores did the ships lack—enough food for every mouth over several weeks of famine. This would have seemed the prerequisite of the adventure; instead, after his first survey of the land and its waters, Eric had gambled on these supplying enough fish and game for the whole colony throughout the summer months and to put by for winter. Toward this end, very fine longboats had been built in Iceland in the preceding months out of lumber shipped from Norway, under the patronage of King Haakon who dreamed of adding a new, vast province to his domains. These, with masts and sails, had been secured on the decks of the ships and were to be used by hunting parties, made up of the best hunters among all the emigrants, and under direction of Thorhall, to take whales, seals, walruses, and the larger fishes for the colony's use. Also, when the hunters saw reindeer and wild ox near the strands, they would kill what they could stow and keep fresh.

That night the seal-oil lamps burned with a bright flame, and the whole gathering feasted on perishable stores from the ships and what we pioneers could furnish from our larder. At this memorable fete, so strange to contemplate, considering our remoteness from any other habitable land we could imagine, yet so natural-seeming to occur, Ian recited and sang, and then all sang together, and many faces were wet with tears. In the hugging and kissing that followed, to which Norse festivals had so often led, beautiful Ellen passed me a little signal and faded away in the moonlight. I knew there was some risk in following her, but a long-thwarted hunger drove me to do so. It was not difficult to find her retreat. What we intended to have happen there had already possessed our imaginations with a great fierceness, and it did happen. In about ten minutes we found our separate ways back to the throng and I did not believe that either of us had been missed.

After the cooking pots brought from the galleys had been emptied, Eric and his crew and his passengers went aboard for the night, and so did the companies of all the other ships. So once more our band of nine were together and alone, and a silence almost as deep as that to which we had often listened, only our pulses throbbing in our ears, fell again over our home acre, but it was not the same as the other silences, although we could not say why, and indeed nothing would ever be the same again.

Before I lay down, old, rugged, leather-tough Gorm came up to me quietly and confided news I had not heard, and which I did not believe had been commonly mentioned at the feast, although many people there must have known it. It was so like Gorm to tell me before I slept. He did not believe in keeping back bad news because it would disturb someone's sleep. He believed that men should know the truth, good or bad, as soon as possible, and face it like men; before the Gods it was good for the miserable bastards that we all were; and Gorm took a special interest in me, and I felt he was fond of me in his hard-bitten way and had great hopes for me. So I was proud that he told me.

"Nothing's ever as good as we hope, and rarely as bad as we fear," he began. "Tonight's feast was a funeral feast even more than Eric gave to propitiate the Gods after he had killed Kol. That night there was only one to mourn, or at least of whose departure we took note. Tonight there were nearer two hundred."

"I don't believe you." But this was not true, as my soul knew well, so I quickly added, "What in the name of all the torments of Hel do you mean, old man?"

"Nine ships have arrived safely; there's good cause to expect six more. But twenty-five ships sailed from Borg, bound for the new land. The sea was too wide and lonely and the weather too bad, and there was too much ice, for the companies of seven of the ten missing ships and they turned back. But that leaves three that tried to come on but didn't make it. The fate of one of those three remains unknown. Two were seen to be caught in broken pack ice pounding in a high wind, and they broke up, and everybody aboard them was lost. Well, no great venture is free. Nothing is, for that matter. The Gods charge a high price for all their wares. Eric's a great man—and he'll settle Greenland—and as for the poor lubbers on the sea bottom, our fertile women will soon make up the loss, and everyone will forget that lost batch were ever born. And that's the way life is, world without end."

"As for me, I expect to live up a lot of it, regardless of price."

So I answered Gorm, whereupon he walked away, looking satisfied.

CHAPTER SEVEN

REVIVAL OF MUSIC

I

In the months of waiting for Eric's return, I had somehow convinced myself that when he did return—if fate had ordained his
return and the sea were not to stay empty forever—he would feel
toward me in a different way than before. I suppose I had arrived at this from the discovery of Thorstein's active enmity,
whereby Eric's belittling me and even his cowherd joke, as my
mother had called it, had seemed inconsequential in comparison.
To explain his actions, I had seized upon the comforting thought
that he had only been testing me to see what I could stand. Well,
now I had been tested by a more rigorous examiner, the Greenland winter. Starkad had no doubt reported that I had done my
part as a full man. Indeed, Eric could not help but see that my
mates took my full manhood for granted according to their own
strict standards.

I was disillusioned early the following morning. The briskly rising late April sun was barely up. He had summoned our whole
crew and the grown men of every family that had crossed the sea
with him to hear an announcement, or so he put it, but what he
really meant was to hear and heed.

"You all know that the companies of all the ships in the harbor
and those that no doubt will arrive today must lend to the colony
the services of their best hunters, on land and sea, to provide
meat for all while all others, men, women, and children, go ahead
with house building on the land selected. I have set the total
number to be chosen at about sixty, four for each ship, enough to
man and sail the excellent catboats and sailing dories we fetched
from Iceland. One of the four from our ship will be Thorhall
Hunter, of course. In fact he will direct the operations of all the
parties. My son Thorstein is my second choice, for as you know
he is skilled at hunting not only seals and walrus but he was the
harpooner of the whale that stood you all in good stead. My third

choice is Gorm, old but tough and spry, a great hunter with great experience. I gave a good deal of thought to my last choice and finally picked the castaway from some tribe resembling Lapps dwelling on the northern part of the island. Ugruk—I believe that is his name—is native to these regions, knows how to meet situations new to the rest of us, and ways of taking game that we do not know. These four men are to load the gear they'll need in Thorhall's boat and start their hunt today. I don't believe in wasting time."

As always, Eric spoke with great force. When he stopped, the silence conveyed the effect of being deep and portentous. Although tempted to look elsewhere, even at the ground, I forced my eyes to move from one face to another of my eight mates. Every face except Ugruk's was red, its eyes not meeting mine; Ugruk looked straight at me in mute inquiry. But it took old Gorm to break the silence.

"Ugruk won't go unless Leif goes," he said quietly.

"I'll see about that."

"See about it all you like, he still won't go. He is Leif's man. If you don't believe me, ask him. Use simple language and he'll understand."

"Ugruk!" Eric called in his most masterful manner. "I want you to be hunter to help get meat for all the people, with Thorhall, Thorstein, and Gorm. You are to start today. Do you understand me?"

"Red Beard, I no go unless Leif goes."

"Do you understand what I say is a command, not to be disputed?"

"Still I no go."

"Do you dare disobey my orders?"

"Ugruk under Leif's orders, not under yours. If people no want me to stay here, Ugruk go live with Innuits. If Leif want go with Ugruk, my kayak can hold two till we go up coast, kill walrus, build two-man kayak."

"By the Nine Runes——" Eric broke out, his green eyes glittering and his face flushed. But before he could declare his oath, Thorhall interrupted him with plain, calmly spoken words.

"Eric, don't say what you will wish to the Gods you hadn't said and had rather bitten off your tongue. There's plenty of room in my boat for five and their gear and for a ton of game. If Ugruk leaves us, the chances of the colony hanging on and thriving will be seriously reduced. Besides that, you don't seem to have got it through your head that Leif is the best hunter on land of the shore party—he's won that place—the best salmon spearer. If you remember, he made a pretty good showing when you sent him to get a narwhale horn behind Gull Nest Island. With Ugruk, they are a deadly pair of hunters. You saw the hide of the wild ox in the turf house."

Eric did not reply at once and the rise and fall of his barrel chest told that he was breathing hard. Natural leaders such as he have a sixth sense—or can make a swift appraisal of the reports from their natural five senses—as to the sentiments of their followers. I think he perceived that, respecting Thorhall as they did, this was not the moment for an imperious stand. He answered Thorhall rather quietly.

"You say that Ugruk is Leif's man. What if Leif tells him to go with the others while he remains as one of my foremen?"

"Leif may know the answer to that. I do not."

"What about it, Leif? My proposal was for the good of the colony. Will you tell Ugruk you want him to go?"

Suddenly, a position unforeseen and undreamed of until a few minutes before, I found myself confronting a crisis of import too great for my grasp; and the stand I took could change my whole life. It was not easy to take a stand. I was in the habit of obeying Eric, and I had only newly come to manhood. Oddly enough, I thought not of Eric but of Thorhild. I knew which way my heart leaned and almost instantly I knew where Thorhild's heart would lean. I glanced at Ugruk. He was not grinning now; instead his face was impassive except for the intensity of his gaze as he gave me one great glance. Then I knew what to say.

"No, sir," I told Eric the Red, my father. "Ugruk and I are going to stay together. With your permission, we'll go together with the others in Thorhall's boat. If you refuse that, I'll go with Ugruk in his kayak."

Eric the Red gave his beard an angry tug, but his green eyes looked rounder than usual, and I knew that he was shaken to his depths.

"Well, I'll leave it to the men immediately concerned. Perhaps in this case four heads are better than one. I needn't ask Thorhall or Ugruk—I know how they feel about it—on second thought I need not ask Gorm. But I want unanimous agreement, to make for good feeling and good work. Thorstein, you have spent the winter with Leif, and you've had some bad trouble with him. Do you think he's grown enough—matured enough, I mean—that he qualifies for a place in a hunting party such as this?"

"There's no doubt of it," Thorstein replied in a frank and easy tone.

"Lately he has done you a great injury, in my mind out of proportion to the provocation. It would not have happened if you had been on your guard. Do you think you and Leif can ship and hunt together peacefully and successfully?"

"I must correct you, Eric. I *was* on my guard—but it was not strict enough. I was in vile temper and Leif was too quick for me. We will compete against each other on the hunt—my arm isn't yet as good as new, still I'll accept the handicap—and that competition will make for a bigger kill. I would be very sorry not to have Leif with us."

"Well, that settles it. Leif, you're the taller, but you'll have to grow quite a lot in other ways to be as big a man as your brother, Thorstein—and I'm a good judge of men. You'll be hunting mainly in the north—that's where we saw the most seal, walrus, whales, and shore game. All of you in this party and in the other hunting parties are to be called the Nordrseta men—you deserve a name of your own for convenience and as an honor too, and that's the one I've chosen. You'll have it rougher than the rest of us and the success of the colony will depend in no small way on your handiwork and skill."

The whole throng seemed pleased with the name and, in swift reversal of their feelings a moment before, greatly pleased with Eric. Most leaders know how to wear the plumes of victory; perhaps those that can carry off defeat are not nearly so numerous.

And I was thinking too of Eric's gift as a good namer. Our whole crew had been delighted when he had named the finest landmark, perhaps to prove the finest mountain, in Greenland after his own faded blue shirt. The name of Greenland for this rugged region with its prodigious icecap, yet with its redeeming far-flung grass, was the kind of joke beloved by us perverse Norse. What brave ship had a better name than the *Narwhale?* And he had named me Lucky Leif!

I would need all the luck that my blood sister, Minin the Swan Maiden, could bring me on her swift pinions, if I were ever to prevail over great Eric the Red and that formidable adversary, his son by blood and by body and by soul, my smiling brother, Thorstein.

And then the dark remembrance struck me of a fear that Thorhild had expressed—the fear of ruinous war.

2

Stowing our gear as fast as we could, Thorhall taking note of every item and calling our attention to every one forgotten, our crew of the trim, yare-looking catboat hoped to stand to sea before any of the home seekers' ships could weigh. We were beaten by Einer's ship and the very large vessel of the great chieftain Bjorn, both already laden; still we had got away briskly and handily; and I had had time to paint the name *Nordrseta* on our bow. This was to give notice to other hunter craft that ours was the flag boat of the fleet.

Einer's ship had only a short sail to the mouth of the fiord north and west of Ericsfiord; by cutting corners and hugging coasts well known to Thorstein and where Bjorn dared not venture, we soon overtook his lumbering giant and had open, empty seas ahead of us, which was our desire. The brisk wind out of the south was likewise to our liking. All of us wanted to use it to our advantage, not changing our course to harpoon seals, and instead to gain the waters where Eric had seen herds of walrus, our chief quarry, numerous narwhales, and bottle-nosed whales not too large to tow in a fair wind to the northernmost settlements. There also he had seen whales with gigantic heads, which Eric had named the Greenland whale because of their numbers, and an even greater whale than the mighty blunt-headed beast with teeth in his jaws which I had seen, these monsters being bluish gray in color with jet-black whalebone, to which my sire had given a Christian name that Thorhild knew, Leviathan. With these great whales we would not meddle—only a large vessel could make use of them—but we wished to lay eyes on them.

This last wish was granted. When we had sailed we reckoned about three hundred miles generally north by west from Ericsfiord and passed the headland where Eric had erected a big cairn of stones to indicate his northernmost exploration, the number of monstrous-headed Greenland whales became almost unbelievable, the vast blunt-headed whales were common, and we saw at least one Leviathan, a third again as long as any whale that I had seen. Somewhat to my disappointment we saw narwhales every day, although not one had a tusk as long as that which precoursed the vessel *Narwhale*.

The south wind swung round, as though we had paid a spae-woman a handsome fee, and blew steadily and strongly with the bite of the cold north, and we sped homeward with a ton of the best walrus meat stowed aboard, and towing a young bottle-nosed whale, weighing a whole ton, yet giving us astonishingly little trouble, so rhythmically rolling were the seas. The whale we left at a fiord mouth where three ships had rendezvoused, the meat kept perfectly fresh in the icy sea; and we shared half of our walrus catch with two other ships with whom we spoke half a day's sail from Ericsfiord. What remained we divided between Einer's eaters and our own.

We had been absent from our strand a little under two weeks, a considerably longer hunt than any of the other Nordrseta men had attempted. Also our kill had been a good deal greater than that made by any other party, but the others would give us a good race when more at home on these rugged coasts and hostile seas. They would be our rivals and also our fellow members of an elite and dedicated corps. Thorstein was the first to affix an ivory button, cut from a walrus tusk, to his fur cap as a badge of membership; and it was a wonder how quickly all except two Nordrseta men copied him in pride. One was Thorhall, who wore a splinter of whalebone in his cap. I retained the white plume from Minin's wing.

"Will you get one like it for Swanhild?" Ellen asked me when we had met, apparently by chance, at a hot spring, such as were rather common on the island, and which I regularly passed on my way to the shallows of our salmon river into which fish had begun to run. "It would go well with her name."

"I'll see that she gets one. I don't hunt swans, but some of my fellows do. It won't be as long or as fine as mine, I'm afraid. Mine was a gift to me from a Swan Maiden."

Ellen's black eyes, which before looked long and drowsy, appeared to grow round and glinting.

"I don't believe you!" she burst out, evidently in deep agitation.

"Did you ever see a swan feather to equal it?"

"No, it's longer—with richer plumage—and a wonderful soft shine. Still you could have plucked it out of a newly killed Queen of the Swans. I see what looks like dried blood on the point of the quill——"

"I hadn't noticed that." And it must be that my face flushed and that my voice was no longer calm, for Ellen stared at me wildly.

"Is it your blood, Leif? The Irish as well as the Norse have seen Swan Maidens and sometimes—so the old tales tell— they perform a blood rite with heroes such as Chuchillon when he lived on earth. Also they have a preference for very young men—for they themselves are unimaginably old—such as shepherd lads in the meadows where they light down and doff their plumage and swim in the pools. Did you—no, I won't ask that. But I will ask if you have seen her since?"

"No." But I did not tell Ellen that I might have seen her, soaring in circles over my head, merely by calling her name. At least she had told me so, if what seemed a perfect remembrance, as vivid as my memory of that morning's breakfast, was not a figment of a delirious dream. And by thinking of this, suddenly I knew the real reason I had not, when alone in some grassy wilderness, given that call. I had been afraid there would be no answer.

"Then you were only her passing lover. Even so, it might have spoiled you for going with a thrall woman."

"I want to more than ever."

"Today is the second day you have been home from the hunt. How many days before you and your band start out again?"

"We will start the day after tomorrow. The two broken harpoons will be mended then, the boat recalked, our points sharpened, and stores stowed for hunting on land and sea. Eric wants us to bring in beef of the wild oxen to raise the spirits of the people."

"Then I'll tell you what I found. You know the dense willow growth sheltered by a hill about a mile up river. The thickest part—almost impenetrable, where the stalks are too small to be of any use—hides a grotto in the rock under the hill. I found it by— I started to say by accident, but you wouldn't believe it, and I'll tell the truth. I looked for such a place. A good spirit who had tried in vain to prevent me from marrying Horkel led me to it. To find it I had to squeeze between the willows and the rock, which no passer-by would ever do. It comes as near to being an absolute safe hiding place as we—as I—could wish for. Tonight after dark I'll take there two sheepskin robes. Even in midwinter no wind could reach it, and with reindeerskin blankets——"

She stopped because she had no breath to speak on. I touched her hand and it was cold and trembling. I had trouble drawing my own breath.

"At what time shall I come?"

"Horkel will get up when the stars begin to dim. He works more than an hour on our turf hut before he wants breakfast. If I'm not there when he comes in, I'll have a good excuse—that's my part to which you need give no thought. Come to me, Leif! I want you terribly and need you. You won't fail me?"

"No." And I had started to say, "Never," only to perceive this would not be the truth, that years passed beyond recall had raised a barrier against any long-lasting union, and that years to come, their bringings unimaginable in other ways, would surely part us.

I made haste to dismiss the thought, smiled at Ellen and received her smile, strange somehow, more given to herself than to me, at once touching and triumphant. I could not imagine triumph over a love-making tryst with such a young, yearning, grateful swain as I; this was an unsolvable mystery. And thus balked, my fancy took a wild flight in another direction, a propensity of my mind that might indicate a frailty that might lead at last to madness. I pictured Ellen as an elfin queen, seated on her bejeweled throne in a subterranean palace, all her attendants absent on some business, and her lips curled in a dim smile as she contemplated some great design for the expansion of her domain.

Before the stars began to pale, I was up, and up river out of environs of the soon beaver-busy homestead. Out of her sight, I waited not long for Ellen to pass me up the bank, her step light and joyous, and well she knew when I fell in behind her. When I caught up with her at the willow thicket I clasped her in my hungry arms and fed hungrily from her soft mouth; but in a second or two I sensed a slight drawing away that chilled me a little until she explained.

"I told you that in Ireland there is an ancient cult of love, taught our women by lascivious witches hundreds of years ago, and passed down to our rude wenches as well as to the daughters of kings. One of its maxims is for the eager couple not to start love-making until love can be made in full, without interruption. It should start from the beginning and deepen and sweeten with every hard-drawn breath, with never a slacking off because of words or actions, the tide of rapture slowly but steadily rising until it reaches flood tide. False starts are weakening."

She took me by the hand and led me through an almost invisible gap in the thick growth. Only when we crept along behind it, our bodies brushing the rocks of the hill base, did we come to the mouth of the grotto, not large enough to be called a cave, at first glance more fit for a bitch wolf's den than a trysting place for lovers. Yet although the ceiling was almost as low as that of our turf-house tunnel, there had been room for Ellen to spread two sheepskin robes on a fairly level granite floor.

Soon I took it that lecherous witches, instructing the Irish daughters in a kind of witchery, had known their art well. If in contemplation afterward I could find a fault with our wondrous exchange, it would stem from my own tyroism, whereby Ellen was still more the wooer than the wooed. Indeed she took great joy in that part, with caressings surpassing my most lascivious imaginings, and herself intensely aroused, as I knew by the glowings of her smooth flesh against mine, her tormented breath, and her eyes wells of blackness in this dim light. When she knew that the moment had come for the uniting of our bodies, still the tide that I thought full had still a long way to flow, powerfully as before a gale, ere it reached the inmost strand and burst over it, and after the violence of that culmination, we drowsed for a moment or two as though laving in a warm and torpid sea.

"The Goddess Freya was good to us, Leif," were her first words. "You do not know how I had ached for your return from the north. And now I must wait another fortnight until again you return."

A bold question came to my lips, and my attempt to repress it failed.

"Why did a girl of your beauty and gifts marry a clod like Horkel?"

She did not seem in the least troubled or even startled by the question, but her answer gave me a great start.

"Because I was forced to it by your father, Eric the Red."

"How could he force you? And why should he?"

"Both questions are easy to answer. I was his thrall—the command was given through my father, also his thrall—and you know nothing of thralldom, Leif, if you think I could make any strong resistance. Remember, too, that I was hardly fourteen. And the reason for the command—he believed I looked—and acted—and spoke above my station. But of this you must never speak to him or to anyone. No one must ever know of or even suspect our meetings. You promised me that, and I ask you to remember what I said before—of danger, not imagined, but only too real, too great. Believe me, Leif, for I speak the truth."

"Will you tell me whether his charge was true, and you did look above your station?"

"Yes, I did. I was in love with a franklin, who, in spite of my station, wanted to marry me. He knew the story of how my mother and myself had become thralls—a story I will tell you some day, but which there is no time to tell now." As she spoke she was putting on her dress of rough friz, but which, strangely, did not detract from her beauty and perhaps called attention to it. "I'll say only this. When my mother was a little girl, her father took the wrong side in one of the perennial wars between Irish kings. Both were sold into thralldom, their choice being that or death by torture."

"Perhaps you did not look high enough above your station. Eric the Red was in Ireland during his first period of banishment. Did he not——"

"Offer me what I rebuffed? No, he took an aversion to me at first sight. It never changed."

She spoke very simply, casually it seemed. Again I saw her strange little lonesome smile. A moment later she gave me a light but tender kiss, then stooped, went out the low entrance, and was lost to sight.

3

In the two weeks of my absence, you might have thought that Greenland had caught some strange malady and its face had broken out with far-scattered rash. Before then, despite its ruggedness, its appearance had been tranquil, every part was in harmony with every other part, all had remained unblemished just as it had been chiseled and shaped by some great and primordial God, compared to whom old, gray Odin was a younker. Its element was of silence, it was wrapped in silence, against which even the roaring surf in storm and the cataclysm of the breaking ice in spring made no real rift, and when it spoke at all it was through the corded throats and the gaping, fang-studded jaws of wolves wailing under the ice-white moon glimmering on a snowbound universe.

Now, beside and back from the strand at Ericsfiord and at Einersfiord, and I could not doubt the same held true at several

other fiords, the deep silence had disappeared like a chill enfold-
ing mist in the beams of the summer sun. Living creatures of a
strange, new species scrabbled about, here and there, back and
forth, in a disorder never seen in the reindeer herds even when
chased by wolves. They did not rest nor pause to chew the cud
from early sunrise until late dusk, they had no dignity of behavior,
they shouted back and forth, stones clattered, there were thudding
and clumping sounds unlinked by harmony, and ringing sounds
made by stuff harder than any flint as it struck against wood. And
what at first seemed only a little disturbance of the ground, mere
blocks of turf cut out and laid in a hollow square, grew taller hour
by hour, and rocks were stacked upon rocks, the holes stuffed
with turf and moss, closing up little patches of open ground, and
these, unlike the turf house that blended with the grassy ground,
looked utterly alien to the landscape, ugly and disfiguring. By
the day of my return, flocks of swans, wild geese, and ducks flying
up or down the fiord, and accustomed to cutting a corner directly
over our winter hut, swung wide of the whole homestead.

Early in the morning of the day following my meeting with
Ellen in the grotto, Eric's crew of Nordrseta men again set forth
in our trim catboat, amid some cheers and cape waving by the
work crews, for they had licked their chops over our first haul of
fresh whale and walrus meat after the stale and monotonous meals
of their long crossing. We hunters were pleased enough at the
prospect of fresh adventure, still we were a little sobered by the
realization this was our last glimpse of the *Narwhale* until high
summer. Eric meant to stand to sea in a day or two, making for
Iceland, there to stow his hold mainly with other emigrants and
their goods, and between piles of Norwegian lumber on his deck
to hobble some milk cows newly fresh. Indeed the whole fleet of
fifteen vessels would have weighed before the hunting parties returned to the settlements.

With good forethought, Eric had perceived that the spirits of
the colonists would take a fall when the departing sails had sunk
from sight under the sea's rim, the Swan Road to Iceland closed
for weeks and perhaps months, and so had changed his mind as
to game to be gotten by most of the Nordrseta men. The chances

of a big kill were far greater at sea than on land, and rightly Eric decided that an abundance of edibles, some of which could be wind dried and preserved, would be more comfort to the marooned colonists than a scant mead of delicacies such as reindeer venison and the beef of wild cattle. One crew only was to beach its boat and go inland, and Eric's choice was a crew, eaters of the chieftain Bjorn, that contained a famous Icelandic hunter named Hrafn. Thorhall objected to this choice on grounds that thrilled my soul.

"Eric, Hrafn is a great hunter of white hares and waterfowl. But Leif, with Ugruk at his side, knows how to hunt reindeer and Greenland oxen. Let your boat be the one to put into shore."

"Perhaps that would be best. You would be along, hunter of elk and bear and wild cattle in Norway when Leif was in swaddling clothes. And Thorstein will prove Leif's master after a little more practice with spear and arrow on land. He is the best marksman and steadier by nature."

"Leif was steady enough, I hear, when Thorstein broke his flute." It was a bold thing for even Thorhall, born a thane, to say in Eric's teeth. I thought it very possible that my choleric father would fly into fury. Instead he answered mildly.

"Thorstein was sorely tried, that night, still he knew he had done wrong and that put him off guard. And mark you, Leif, I've never said a word in condemnation of what you did in revenge, considering how you loved that tootling stick that your mother gave you. I'll only say that you loved it too much, considering you are a man, the son of Eric the Red. But Thorstein's arm is mending well—his bow will outcast yours in a few weeks more—and your flute is gone forever, and you'll pay more heed to your work, so perhaps it's all for the best."

Somewhat, but not greatly to my surprise, Ugruk, who was standing close to me, his usual position, spoke boldly.

"Chief Red Beard, Leif will be playing another music stick before Thorstein's arm is strong as before." And his careful use of the Norse language, instead of his usual dialect, lent a strange force to the declaration.

"Ugruk, you are a loon! Have you eaten daft fish? Where would he get another flute—would a dwarf in his mountain den make him one and leave it with his gear?"

"Dwarfs in the rocks made him a fine sword and left it leaning by a rock, or so he told me." And then Ugruk's brown face wrinkled and his black eyes sparkled and he laughed aloud.

Then I was frightened by the deepening color in Eric's face and the intense green of his eyes, but all he did was grunt in feigned or real disgust and stride away.

Our pretty catboat set forth, and at the mouth of the fiord west and north of ours she was joined by Einer's sailing dory, likewise sleek and seaworthy. At other fiord mouths similar craft puffed their sails behind us, and for a short space early on the second morning of our sail, ten of our fleet of fifteen hunters were visible on the same reach of sea. But now we were gaining waters teeming with whales and seals, and distant ice floes had black blotches or scattered specks that we knew were walrus. So the crafts parted company, the crew of each burning to outdo the others; and the next day our boat put into a broad bay as wide as the great South Bay of Iceland, and I thought with a little thrill that ours was the first sail ever to enter there since the world was made.

We hugged its coasts because of something Ugruk had told me and which I had confided to Thorhall. Ugruk had said at this time of year, in the first full flush of spring, the wild oxen craved salt and would lick the beach stones that the tides had washed, and sometimes found dried-up beach pools, the bottoms crusted with salt. For seventy or more long sea miles we saw nothing but sea beasts and birds, among these last great numbers of very large birds with white bellies and dark backs, which stood like men. When we wondered why they did not take wing at our close approach, and instead either dived into the surf or stood huddled, Ugruk gave us the startling explanation.

"They no can fly. For wings they got only paddles."

The thought struck me they might save the lives of stranded men, or even be our rescue if a starving time ever overcame the colony.

At present I was more concerned with Ugruk's prediction of seeing salt-seeking oxen having so far failed. Apparently Ugruk did not share my worry, delighting in every new view, laughing loudly at his mates' coarse jokes, which he knew enough Norse to understand, and anyway almost all of them hung on a matter in which there is a world-wide interest and understanding. Nor was he proved a false prophet. Just as the sun threw its last glint on the green bay water, the old hunter Thorhall made out a large herd of oxen filing across the strand about two miles distant.

The light would fail before we could reach them and I greatly feared that in the morning we would look for them in vain. The grasslands were narrow between the bleak strand and the rugged highlands; still, such was hunters' luck. As distant vistas dimmed, I found myself watching the pearly gleam of the ice pack slowly fade. This was my closest view of the vast sheet since I had my memorable excursion up Eric's fiord, and this evening it seemed singularly and unexplainably impressive. Seafowl had ceased to fly and clamor. There was no moon to arrest the rush of darkness, and my visible universe was great far-scattered stars that were first to light their lamps, the pale waters, and still a seeming figment of glimmer on the utmost crest of the icecap. Then I was startled by the silence of our party. The explanation was only that my mates, too, were watching the death of the day, and in this setting of infinite solitude were moved by it. Perhaps we Norse were lovers of wild nature, particularly in its grander and primordial aspects, to a degree rare in more sheltered folk. It was no wonder to me now that hundreds, perhaps thousands of Icelanders living a dull, safe life should follow that green-eyed half-mad chieftain, Eric the Red, to these perilous strands. And it seemed to me then that I sensed something in our Norse souls that dwelt also in the soul of Ugruk the Innuit. Perhaps it was only because we were alike in being sucklings of that sharp-fanged she-wolf mother, the Northland.

In the morning we did not look long to find the wild oxen— about five miles farther up the strand. Some of our tyros thought we should moor the boat here and stalk the herd on foot, but Ugruk assured them that our boat would not frighten them into flight, and we had better save time by sailing; in this I backed him. When we did put into shore, scarcely a quarter of a mile from the big, shaggy beasts, so innocent of our deadliness, we were all caught up in an excitement old as nature itself—the same that the white bear knows when he swims in silence toward a basking seal, the same that the white weasel knows when he stalks a tarmochan, charged with the cruelty neither greater nor less than the cruelty of life itself.

The bulls and full-grown cows made their ring, the newborn sucklings and half-grown bullocks and heifers in the center along with newborn sucklings that bleated in vain for their dams. Then we commenced killing, hurling at close range our lethal harpoons; and one raging rush of their embattled circle would have overwhelmed us, tramping and hooking us to death. But their Gods had not taught them to attack as well as defend, for their age-old war was with wolves, fleeter than they, more agile, and lusting for the chance to leap at an unprotected throat. Nor had their Gods confided that the day would come that tall two-legged wolves could project iron fangs from far beyond the sweep of their massive horns.

When six of the beasts were down, to furnish the butcherers a ton of good beef, Thorhall roared out his command that we cease the slaughter and, according to Ugruk's instructions, back away, facing the living fort of oxen until their wrath subsided. This we did; and soon the beasts broke their circle and made off at the same heavy gallop I had seen before. It seemed that they were not cognizant of their losses. Yet I wondered if a newborn calf, still unsteady on its legs, might sense a dreadful absence, a mighty loss. Perhaps some cow with an unfamiliar smell, but with overflowing udder, would give the orphan suck along with her own. It seemed to me that Nature, heartless and inflexible in enforcing its laws, might have provided for this mercy at the request of Frigga, wife of Odin, who remembered the hungering lips of Balder the Beautiful at her own bountiful teat.

We skinned and butchered our kill, lugging the meat into the cool shade of a big basalt outcropping, still stalwart and steadfast when all softer stone had crumbled to gravel by the age-long beat of the waves. When the bloody work was done, we gathered ice-cold kelp, abundant in this bay, laid in thick in the aft end of the boat, and there we stowed our harvest, each slab or quarter wrapped in kelp, and the whole lot covered by another thick layer, as protection from the genial late spring sun. At once we set for the settlements, before a most obliging and brisk wind. On the afternoon of our second day's sail and again at noon of the third, we distributed succulent beef among various gangs of women and boys who had come to the beach to play a trick, well-learned in Iceland, on eider ducks. It was to set stones in a certain way to make a small shelter, which had an almost irresistible fascination for the fowls as nesting places, there to lay their tasty eggs for the stone setters to steal. Many had walked three miles from homesteads up the fiords, yet not one long-boned, free-striding Norse woman, free or thrall, declined a cutting from our store on the grounds that it was too heavy to lug back for a feast for her family and neighbors.

Quite possibly a number of the thrall families had never tasted beef. Iceland cattle had been kept mainly to give milk to make butter and cheese, and the meat from the rare slaughtering of old and sterile cows was consumed by franklins and by better-off free folk. So it happened that I gloried in our brief, successful hunt, counting the oxen blood well spilled, for the treat would rejoice many a family of poor thralls whose steady diet was seal meat and fish. Briefly, at least, they might rejoice they had come to Greenland and hold brighter hopes for the future.

The meat of one large oxen we brought to Eric for his many eaters, and all the skins at his express command. Plainly he intended to collect skins for a whole bale to sell in Europe, these bringing a high price because of their oddity, their dense wool and sweeping dark hair. We touched our strand about two hours before sunset. At once Eric summoned a crew of thralls for the greasy and tedious jobs of fleshing the pelts, and I was not greatly surprised to see Ellen and her daughter, Swanhild, among the number. I found an opportunity to give Ellen one straight glance, for which I hoped she might be on watch. She answered with a slight nod of her head.

So it was inevitable that as the stars paled to give full sway to the soon-breaking dawn, I would be making toward our trysting place, which Ellen had named Vixen's Den. I had accepted the name without seeing much sense to it. In the first place, the abodes of foxes are well-dug holes in the ground, not grottoes in the rock. Vixens were famed in Iceland for only two traits, one of them cunning, which fame was well earned, and the other of dubious deserving, a viciousness worse than that of she-wolves. There were many folk tales told in Norway and Iceland of their implacable revenge for a hurt.

Had we been away two weeks instead of one, I would have felt no heavy and prolonged achings for Ellen until we were almost in sight of Ericsfiord. Watching for game, the heart-stifling stalk, then the exultation of the kill or the self-disgust over the miss would have used up my heat almost as fast as it was stored. Besides, the mere sailing of the boat along treacherous coasts, conditions changing from peaceful to perilous in a few minutes, provided a sustained excitement, ebbing and flowing, for every man aboard. Heavy labor and not lust had made me pant; off watch I slept from the moment I lay down until I was called, except on a few dark, still midnights amid the murmuring sea when I wakened in an actual pain of yearning which could not be served and from which I fled into renewed slumber. Yet on the eighth morning after our latest tryst, I could scarcely keep from running as I made for Vixen's Den. Anxiety devoured me over whether Ellen had caught my signal and whether her little nod had meant what I wanted it to mean. I could scarcely stand to think of finding the nest empty, then of waiting and watching in vain, and at last trudging homeward defeated and ashamed, not even sure that my wound—for it seemed no less than that—would be healed after a whole day and another night of weary waiting.

Then I came to the willow thicket and saw where the dew had been shaken from the branches screening our secret path, and I knew that my fears had been in vain. Within the grotto I found my partner already lying between the two sheepskin robes, both of them white except when compared with the snow whiteness of Ellen's body, itself in such dramatic contrast to her raven-black hair, heavy eyebrows, and darkly glowing eyes. She gave me her small, strange, crooked smile, somehow deeply touching, and held out her arms to me. This gesture caused a throwing back of part of the cover, whereby I saw her bosom, with its two beautiful projections, slanting slightly away from each other, the shape of some exotic fruit rather than perfect orbs, white with a whiteness that cast spells except for their crimson tips that to my inexperienced eyes looked virginal.

"Unfasten your shirt lacings, don't break them," she told me in a breathless murmur. "I left Horkel snoring—I had told him last night I would leave the hut before dawn to set stones for eider ducks." Then she caught her breath and added, "Break the thongs if you wish. Only make haste."

This last command I obeyed, until she rescinded it to prolong her rapture. When tumultuous nature had finally forced its needs, she lay in my arms awhile in a half-trance. The dimensions of our world, which a few minutes ago had been solely our joined bodies, extended to include first the grotto behind its shield of willow thickets, then what lay beyond, which meant the homeward path that we must shortly take, and the common affairs of earth awaiting us at its end. She sat up and put on a fawnskin vest, such a luxurious undergarment as would be a rarity in the attires of the daughters of thanes, unheard of in the raiment of a thrall woman.

"There was a great red-deer hunt at my master's manor Lough Gill in Ireland," she explained, when I touched the silk-soft leather. "A king and his entourage were to feast in his hall. Some hinds as well as stags were killed, and a few had newborn or unborn fawns. Horkel was one of his butchers, and he stole three skins, which he gave me, and of which my mother, once the daughter of a thane but sold into thralldom, made the vest. I have cherished it and worn it only on feast days. I was thirteen when it was given me but you see it still fits me well. I had it on under my rough friz the night of Kol's funeral feast, undreamed by everyone but myself and Swanhild. If Eric the Red had known of it he would have ripped it from my body and torn it to scraps in his mighty red hands."

"Today is not a feast day!"

"Oh, but it is! It was made so by your unexpected return."

A few seconds before, I had suffered a pang of jealousy at her speaking of the might of Eric's hands, although she had spoken truth. I had wanted her to notice that my hands, too, were strong, and would build better than my sire's when my chance came. Now that coming seemed nearer because of her compliment to me, its wording and its imagery as unsuited to her station as the fawnskin garment, yet so in keeping with the refinement of her beauty. Still I must not forget that the whole Irish race were given to unique flights of fancy.

"You took note of the dirty work he had me do yesterday afternoon," she went on.

"Truly I did."

"I finished first of all the fleshers—two hours after sundown—and did the best job."

"But that wasn't the reason he gave it to you. I can hardly believe it wasn't spite."

"I assure you it was not. He bears me no malice or no dislike. I can make a wild guess. You must know that his grandfather was a slave, his father merely a freeman, and he rose to become a thane because of the great service he did Herald Graycloak at the battle of Fitje, when Eric was barely eighteen. It is a well-known fact that thanes who rose by their own efforts instead of gaining their place by inheritance are the hardest taskmasters. They are especially harsh with thralls who appear and perhaps look above their stations. They themselves went up; their instinct is to keep others down. Compare Eric with your mother, Thorhild, the granddaughter of Harald Bluetooth. She will get out of bed on a winter midnight to go and nurse a sick thrall woman or her child."

"I wonder if you have looked deeper into my father than anyone. Do you suppose that a self-made thane might want to keep down his own son?"

"It is possible, if the son threatens to tower above him."

"Eric the Red would be a hard man to tower above."

"Leif, it may be Eric rides too hard and too high to please the Gods. I feel he is fated for a great fall."

I dwelt on Ellen's prophecy, spoken in such soft tones and mild manner, throughout my brisk walk homeward. While I had always wished to top him, and sometimes to topple him, I perceived now I could not endure the thought of his falling to shame and ruin. I did not know why. I was not conscious of affection for him, only of deep admiration. Perhaps I was remembering what Thorhild had told me—that she had loved Eric when she was young and would love him when he was old.

It was Thorhild who had given me the flute which I had learned to play quite well.

4

If Eric's fall was truly fated as Ellen had felt, wild rigorous Greenland might be its fitting scene. Also it could be the most likely scene, for life here was fraught with danger. More clearly than in midwinter, indeed as spring flushed into high summer, I perceived how the odds for any man's survival here, let alone his eminence, narrowly outweighed the odds adverse. Its deadly winter onslaught was at least foreseeable, whereby defenses could be raised against it. But in summer its man traps were concealed.

It could strike suddenly, without warning, indeed with what seemed treachery against trustful folk put off guard by its genial sun, its offerings of abundant food, its beautiful waters, its seemingly endless belts of richly green grass, its tender-looking flowers, and ever the thrilling whir and whistle of the wings of wild fowl. Most of its beasts and birds, as well as men, walk the rims, or wing across the depths, of the gulf of death. Perhaps the tarmochans told the story in their strange, heartbroken cry. Sudden death stalked the loveliest landscapes, hid under the calm sea. Almost every creature was the prey of some other; even the shaggy oxen, until lately almost impervious to the perils of the land, had now met with the most dangerous beast of prey ever loosed against his fellow creatures. Only the white wolves appeared to have no natural enemies; yet their grisly laughter and their broken wailings amid the white snow under a white moon voiced a dreadful travail of existence breaking their wild hearts.

Yet our luck had held wonderfully thus far. On his first return to Iceland from his new domain, Eric had been absent about nine months. On his second return, accompanied by the ships of his fellows, he made the eastern crossing in nine days. Then, just at the right time, the west wind wheeled around to blow him spanking home again in ten days' sail, his total absence from the settlement being twenty-nine days in all without loss of a single ship. On this voyage the holds were stowed almost chock-full with thick-wooled dairy cattle and sheep. These could be tethered until winter gales raved over the snow; by then stone pens, tamped with turf and moss, would be completed and afford them shelter against the icy knives. No less than seven of the fifteen ships of the Greenland fleet made a third voyage, mainly to stow latecomers and more livestock; the rest were needed to transport building materials and other supplies from strand to strand fronting the homesteads.

All activities of assembling new colonists and their goods, livestock, and lumber had ostensibly been managed from Eric's cabin on the *Narwhale,* along with rare visits to the strand which by the verdict of the hundred moot he was not permitted to cross. At least no one mentioned his violating the terms of his exile. Yet I guessed there had been some winking back and forth, and of law-abiding franklins looking the other way, when there had been contention and confusion, the smoothing out of which required his bull-voiced commands and imposing presence.

The settlements made swift progress. There were two colonies, the larger called Osterbig, occupying the grasslands about Eric's fiord, Einer's fiord, and several other wide and navigable fiords. Its center, where he proposed to build his hall, he had named Ericshall. The other colony, called Vesterbig, was two days' sail west and north, with a somewhat colder climate, longer summer days and winter nights, its waters beset with larger and more numerous floes, but with a far wider belt of grass, hence far more distant from the icecap and not so harried by its icy winds. Of this colony the great thane Bjorn was chief, and it attracted no few rich franklins, partly because of the abundance of fish, sea beasts, and field game, large and small.

We Nordrseta men continued our hunts, always well north of the Vesterbig's hunting grounds, and reveled in many adventures, large and small. All of us were being schooled in seamanship, many new ways to hunt seal and walrus, charting coasts, and, in some measure, exploration. Thorhall's catboat remained the most successful hunter, mainly because of Ugruk's Innuit lore. The fact remained that Bjorn's big sailing dory beat us to a great find, lying only across the bay on the south coast of which we had landed to kill Greenland oxen. It was an island, some fifty miles wide, which the boat's captain promptly named Disco—his own name—and the big bay which we had been the first to enter he called Disco Bight. Along its strands he had found thousands of nests of the big birds that stood like men. These had proved good eating, and his men had run down and killed more than a hundred for the use of the colonies, and gathered three hundred eggs. Another find were seams of a black rock in the sandstone, which an Irish member of the crew identified as gual, which burned better than peat. The most startling discovery was a lump of pure iron, weighing about fifty pounds.

These discoveries would be of little use to the colonists for a good many years. We had no forges for smelting iron, and the gual was too far distant even from the western settlement, Vester-big, to ship for use as fuel. But Bjorn, who claimed the island as part of his domain, intended to establish a sealing and whaling station there, where blubber could be rendered into oil and shipped directly to Europe. Whether there was enough gual to be worth finding and shipping remained to be seen.

The long summer days shortened to the same length as the nights—when, according to old Norse lore, the dwarfs Elling and Billing, who brought embers for the sunset glow and the sunrise flame, had an equal way to go. Less ice clogged the seas than at any time of year, but early morning frost silvered or snarled the grass at narrowing intervals, and the next moon brought the first light snow. We Nordrseta men hunted far and wide, early and late, to cram the colonists' larders and to supply their equal need of oil for high-blazing lamps of winter. All had been provided with some haven from the lethal cold that would soon assail us. These were mainly turf huts, most of them with low-passage entrances. Only the chieftains and Eric, Bjorn, and a few well-off franklins such as Einer had erected what might be called houses of turf, stone, and wood.

There were enough stone pens to shelter our sheep and cattle from the icy blasts.

We hunters stayed in port only one day between arrival and departure, but at the dawn of that day I invariably met Ellen at Vixen's Den. Sometimes I fancied that I was in love with her, and truly I did do a great deal of mooning over her; but almost always my mind's confronting of what must be done, instead of dwelling on what I wished to do, kept my feelings in tight rein. Any match between us was so unthinkable as to become impossible.

"What if I should give you a baby?" I asked her abruptly on one occasion, just before we parted.

"We Irish women know three days in every woman's month when her womb will receive seed. On other days it will not. If I ever shake my head when you throw me the glance I know, you will know those days are upon me, and we must wait."

"Ellen, are you sure?"

"It is the old wives' belief. But if I should conceive in spite of this care, I would tell Horkel that I was chased and vanquished by a merman on the beach, and he would never doubt it. It has happened many times—or so the folk tell—in Ireland. The babe looks like any other, except that it has sea-green eyes; and it listens always to sounds of the sea."

I put the matter from my mind. That day our craft would set out for the north coasts of Disco Island, where many white bears had been seen. Other boats had already taken fourteen, with dense, unyellowed fur, and Eric craved a great kill, ordering us to abandon the tough, unsavory meat and keep only the skins, greatly prized by kings and noblemen in Europe, and bringing a good price. It so happened that the beasts had departed from those shores, only the Gods knew where, and we returned with only one skin, that of a hermit bear on a mile-wide icefield, and which Thorstein killed with one clean throw of his harpoon, as long and true as he had ever made before his forearm met with accident on a winter night. Even so, our boat came in loaded with walrus meat, tusks, and skins of no small value, for we had met a herd amid broken ice floes only a little north of Vesterbig.

The fight had proved one of the best we ever had with the long-toothed sea hogs. The herd had appeared to be made up of old bulls, with heavy ivory, and we had met them at their time of furious activity, swimming under the floes, climbing them often only to slide off with prodigious splashings, bellowing, and, when our harpoons had driven home, bidding fair to pull the boat apart with their mighty rushings. If the Gods had given them mind to make a concerted attack, they could have smashed us to splinters.

This fight bid fair to be our last until our dogged defense against onrushing winter. Our migratory birds had all gone; only falcons and white owls and snowbirds and a few other harsh-voiced tough-grained kinds that we did not know dwelt in the willow thickets, screamed among the leafless dwarf birch trees, and scrabbled for morsels left by retreating waves on the desolate beaches. Soon the bays were locked; we could not sail on the open stretches because the sea's splashings upon our hull turned to a sheath of ice that would swiftly thicken until its weight would well-nigh sink us. Yet our colonists confronted the bitter season with stout hearts. Because of the industry of the whole band, not one need starve or freeze to death in the gray days and the black and utter silences of the long-drawn nights.

Actually the attack of winter was less fierce than that of the preceding one. We did not know whether it was somewhat milder than most, or of common severity, in which case the Frost Giant had taken note, last year, of our intrusion into his icebound king-dom and had put our little band of veterans to rigorous trial. So we laughed at the shivering newcomers, pretended to wipe sweat from our brows, and showed off by going forth into the icy blasts when the neophytes huddled about their high-flamed oil lamps.

The hero of our colony was no longer Eric, Thorhall, or Thor-stein, but Ian, the singer and poem speaker. Cheerfully his fellows did his chores, so he might make more frequent visits to various homesteads to sing and recite from his priceless store of well-loved songs and stirring tales of Gods and heroes. Ugruk and I had a new venture that promised profit and passed time livelily. He knew how to set snares, baited with fish heads, for white foxes, whose pelts were in great demand by rich folk in more genial lands. Often we were buffeted by knife-edged winds or benumbed with the deadly, silent, implacable extremes of cold. Our reward was a good catch almost altogether of dog foxes, the vixens being too cunning to take our baits.

This winter I could never forget because of one event. Eric decided to celebrate the winter solstice not necessarily on the Day of the Longest Shadow but during any spell of milder weather fairly near the day. His plan was for the whole colony of Osterbig to assemble in his house where we would be packed thick as herrings in a school, but what did our rugged emigrants care for that, when they could feast and sing together, hear Ian recite a beloved saga, and drink from a barrel of Norwegian ale which Eric had brought from Iceland?

In the thick of the gathering Ellen whispered in my ear. We had not met at Vixen's Den for nearly a month, but she need only breathe "tonight?" to stir my heart. Not long after midnight all eyes but ours would be closed in sleep because of gorged stomachs, low-burning oil lamps, one another's warmth as they lay thick and close, and the drowsy effect of ale.

For what we both yearned, both of us received. We need not venture out into the tempered cold of night; we had only to steal away to a dark storeroom under the same warmed roof. Still, we had given each other a gift of bliss many times previously; we expected to make the same delightful trade many times in the future; and it was another gift that came to me that night, previous to our assignation, while the feast was at its height, that would make this night beloved as long as I lived.

When the great kettles were nearly empty of baked beef, walrus meat, and sea fowl, and Ian was tuning his Irish harp, Ugruk thrust through the crowd to take his place before a long, plank table from which foaming bowls had been lately passed. In his hand was what appeared to be an empty sack of friz, such as we used in scores of ways. By clapping his hands hard, he attracted everyone's attention.

"Ugruk, he speak," he announced with what seemed to me great dignity.

"Good for you, old hunter," Gorm called in reply.

"Ugruk, he give present to his brother. He no find it, no good spirit leave it by Ugruk's bed, Ugruk make it with his hands and little flint knives, and seal bones with twisted points that can drill hole a little way down before they break. Ugruk work on it when all alone, maybe in hut, maybe on lonesome hill. If wind blow, Ugruk no get cold, Ugruk sweat, for if he know one little jerk of his hand, one little slip of knife, and he must got start over. Sometimes hand shake, no can work at all. Still he keep on, summer and winter, every time he catch. Now Ugruk finish job. Leif, you come, stand before Ugruk, so all can see?"

"Yes." And at once the throng parted to make me an easy path.

"Leif, you my brother," he told me, his eyes glittering.

"Yes," I answered.

"Ugruk your brother?"

"That I swear by the Nine Runes of Odin, and by Kris, my mother's God."

"We stay, hunt, fish, sail boat together long time?"

"As long as we both live, I think." And now the whole assembly seemed to be holding its breath.

"Then I give you this."

Ugruk reached into the sack. I had noticed that one side of it was unwrinkled and stiff. Therefrom he drew a round tube of willow wood, highly polished, about three feet long and two fingers in diameter. Near one end was a hole; in line with this he had drilled eight smaller holes. As I took it in my shaking hands, Ugruk's eyes filled with tears.

"Play it, Leif, if you can," my mother's soft voice floated to my ear in the hushed room.

"I will try."

So I played, as well as I could, the Strand Song of the Norse Women to the Departing Fleet. My fingers seemed stiff, I blew many a false note, yet I could not help but perceive that the tone of the new instrument, although strangely different than my memory of the old, was beautiful and pure. I am not sure that everyone heard every strain. All except Thorstein, whose face was set like flint, were quietly weeping.

CHAPTER EIGHT

VIXEN'S DEN

I

The ensuing spring was one of good and joyous promise. Great strides could be made in the advancement of the colonies, both Osterbig and Vesterbig, because of the good foundation laying the preceding year. The colonists had broken with old Icelandic ways to adopt ways more suitable to Greenland. The Nordrseta men would still cruise north on their hunting trips, meeting many adventures, and this year we could make longer and more exciting excursions because the need of spanking home with seal, walrus, whale, oxen, and deer meat was not so urgent.

Spring was somewhat beforehand with us, or so declared we veterans of two winters, because the pack ice began to break up only ten days after the equinox, the shore ice had already shown great rifts, and in these leads we saw many seals, as they frolicked in their joy of the new season. Fourteen days after the equinox, the broken, groaning, jamming ice of our river went out with a mighty, exuberant roar. In the whole sky of my happy anticipations, there hung only one small cloud.

Twice in the dying winter, Ellen had shaken her head sorrowfully to my glance of inquiry and invitation. These disappointments had occurred in succession, and my heart was heavy with misgivings when I managed to intercept her at the bubbling spring, its water faintly warmed by some subterranean fire, for on the nights of silent, deadly cold, its sheath of ice was never more than an inch thick, easily broken. Ellen's inward fires were not in the least slaked, as I knew by her welcoming glance and the heightening color in her face, but trouble was there too, I felt, and under their sheen her eyes seemed very dark.

"Today we are going to row boats into the leads," I told her, "to look for leopard seals which Thorstein saw there, twice as big as walrus. If we can't find any, we'll kill Greenland seals."

"I am very hungry," she told me, looking deeply into my eyes.

"Tomorrow morning——?"

"I will go to Vixen's Den in the gray of the dawn."

She did not fail the appointment, and she was shaken by her craving, and I could hardly make enough haste to gratify her needs. Yet except for a moment or two, at the very climax of our interbinding, when there seemed no other world, no other being, did I feel that all was well. I sensed in her a greed such as I could imagine in a man starving on a vast and empty snowfield, who had dug a tarmochan out of its snowy den, clutched and killed it and devoured it raw, but had no certainty or hardly any hope of finding another.

"How soon can we meet again?" I asked, when we had breath to speak; and I could hardly keep my voice from trembling with suspense. "Spring is breaking fast and soon we Nordrseta men will be sailing to Disco Island."

"Leif, I do not know. As soon as possible—that is all I can promise."

"Ellen, is there trouble I do not know?"

"Great trouble. Horkel has changed toward me. A few months ago he would have gladly lent my favors to anyone who wanted them, for a mess of venison. But lately he has begun to suspect that I have a lover—once he was wakened from his hog sleep by snow falling from the roof—and rose and dressed and searched for me, of course without finding me. When I had returned to our turf hut he pretended to believe my story, but he told me to remember that I am his wife, that he owned me body and soul, and he wanted me wholly to himself—which means one passage that I despise about every month. But dim-witted though he is, he is also dogged. He will be no longer easy to fool. Leif, when twice in a row I had to deny your call, I was racked with pain I cannot describe, and which I can hardly believe is natural in women, certainly not common, and which may be the curse of an evil spirit. But I had no other choice. The only reason I could come today was that Eric had ordered some of his strongest thralls to come to the sea beach at sunrise to build a new cairn to replace the old marker that was knocked over by gale-driven ice. As for the future—what can I say?"

It was on my tongue to ask if Horkel suspected me of the intrigue, but I bit back the question because it would sound weak. And instantly after that I had no need to ask.

"My husband never suspected you. It could not cross his mind. In the first place he is truly a thrall, and to him, thanes, franklins, even freemen, seem of a different order of being; and he could hardly imagine the son of a great thane in an affair with a thrall woman. You have told me I am beautiful. At times I can almost believe I am. He cannot conceive of such a thing. In a moment of weakness I told him that my grandsire was a thane. He scarcely paid any attention—the past does not concern him, nor the future either; he works from day to day for what he can get to eat, and to keep the lash from his back. He could not even suspect Thorstein, only seven years younger than I. You are ten years younger."

More likely eleven, I was thinking. I did not like to face the fact, of which there was so little sign in our appearances; yet it remained a fact somehow shocking, in this respect quite unlike love-making between a man of twenty-seven and a girl of seventeen. Still I could not account for a feeling not of guilt but of brooding evil I had not felt before and which seemed an emanation of the unseen, of forces over which Ellen or I had no control. I tried to think it through. As long as I could picture Horkel as a clod— willing to sell his wife's favors for a pan of meat—it seemed that Ellen's and my relationship, based on mutual satisfaction of a healthy human need, had no connection with evil. But suddenly I had learned that Horkel was capable of jealousy—at least of enough manhood to want to keep for himself what lawfully was his own. Yet this did not begin to explain what seemed almost a mist of evil darkening still more the deep dusk of the cave. For the first time I caught myself wishing that Ellen and I had never become involved with each other, and in the same instant hoping with utmost fervor that the involvement need not end.

I wanted a moment more of silence between Ellen and me, to try to find my way through a wilderness of feeling. Instead she began to speak again, telling me something that at first I tried to dismiss as trifling, only to perceive swiftly that it was serving to round out a new concept of Horkel coming to life in my brain.

"One thing I will say for him," Ellen said. "He keeps his face and body clean, not an easy thing to do for a man toiling early and late, and where the year-round water is ice cold and for five months every year is covered with ice. As you know, no thrall is permitted to wash his face and hands, let alone clothes and body, in the hot spring near Ericshall, and the next nearest is a whole league away. I suppose the wife of his first owner taught him cleanliness when he was a little boy, so he wouldn't smell bad. He has stuck to it in the way he sticks to everything that once gets through his thick head. In a way it is a blessing to me, who must live with him, but in another it was my undoing. If he had been foul-smelling I would have made a stronger resistance to Eric's command that I marry him. I have since learned that Eric is not adamant to strong resistance—for instance, when he gave in to the others in the matter of your becoming a Nordrseta man. There is something more I should say for Horkel. He has never struck me or made any move to do so."

In this final respect, he differed from Eric the Red. My sire had once brought a stick with which to beat Thorhild, only to have his intention scared out of him by my mother's taking the high seat and uttering a prophecy.

"Horkel is more of a man, less of a beast, than I thought," I answered.

"Leif, I will meet you here if it is at all possible. But if it proves impossible, you will probably not miss me long. There are other thrall women—of the right age for you—who can take my place. The great thane Bjorn has a daughter of Swanhild's age, Johanna, beautiful as a water lily, and the folk believe that you and she will make a match in a year or two. Bjorn has no sons and she will be heiress to twenty square miles of the best grass in Greenland, fifty or more thralls, and dues from a score of franklins and freeholders under his sway."

"Ellen, you are talking a lot but saying very little," I told her, although perhaps without truth. She might be saying a great deal that I did not know women well enough to understand. "Pick a day that you will try to come, and expect to come."

"You will be leaving for the north in a few days. I have still one good trick that can hardly fail, and I expect to meet you here the first morning after your return."

As I was tramping to our home acre, it would have been impossible—even if I had tried, and I did not try—for me to repel the thought that she had become involved with some other man more suited to her age, one of the several bachelors in our colony, or of the young married men who were given to such roaming. The fact remained that I did not believe it. This did not mean I accepted without question her story of Horkel's sudden jealous guard. Rather it seemed our affair was no longer useful to her except to satisfy her voracious appetite, which she could now control or could be satisfied elsewhere.

That feeling made no sense. Although I was the son of her master, she had never asked me for a single favor except the small one of getting the plume of a swan, as a decoration in honor of her name, for Swanhild. Ellen had never asked any kind of reward for her delicious favors, even to do what I could to soften her hard lot under Eric's iron hand—a lack of covetousness rare in concubines and wandering wives if I were to believe salty old Gorm. She had warned me again and again to keep our secret under strong guard. Was she now fearful of its exposure and of consequences dire beyond my imagination? Or had I been a pawn in a game as intricate as chess? If so, it was a far more dangerous game than chess, for far greater stakes, and perhaps as wild and otherworldly as its wildly bleak and beautiful board that we called Greenland.

Perplexed beyond remedy, I turned my attention to the breaking ice of the fiord, driven by the wind and tide, and took comfort in the thought that the hunt of the Nordrseta men would soon be on.

2

Actually in three days, so swift was spring's advance, Thorhall believed we could pick our way, sailing or rowing, to the largely open sea. We did so with little risk and no great trouble, and in three days' sail we gained our hunting ground, the seas teeming with seals of all sorts, walrus blackening the floes, and great and small whales. Our own party chose to go inland, four of us wearing skis and Ugruk snowshoes, over the still well-packed snow. Entirely by mischance, for game was abundant, our kill was small—two wild oxen from a small herd, and five reindeer—but we touched strands and looked at country on which, as far as we knew or could dream, no eyes had ever laid.

We were back to the headland of Ericsfiord on the eighth day, but were balked for two days more by ice jams in its mouth. On the twelfth day, about noon, we were moored at our home landing. While my mates told their stories to a swiftly gathering crowd, I made off to sit beside my mother at her loom and to gaze upon her almost always grave but beautiful face, and to hear her lovely soft voice. Then she heard sound less lovely, but yet such a change from my naturally and habitually harsh voice that the household elves, hiding until nightfall in their caverns dug in the turf walls, could hardly believe their tiny pointed ears. I had left my new flute in my mother's care during the northward journey, and she asked me to play. This I did, choosing a very high, wild-sounding tune, with many wailing notes, that Ugruk was inclined to sing along with unintelligible words when he pulled oars. She responded by playing a song I had never heard before, which I took for a song of love.

Yet soon I became restless, squirming to search for Ellen. Setting out on a flimsy excuse, I soon found her, washing clothes with some other women in the chill, but not bone-piercing cold, waters of the bubbling spring. I spoke to them briefly about the game and the ice, two subjects of passionate and eternal interest to the whole colony, but these were thrall women, who must hurry every task to get at another, and they were soon busy with their wash, asking only occasional questions as I basked in the genial almost ardent, midday sunlight. I saw my chance to meet in question Ellen's brilliant glance. She nodded happily.

My stifled heart resumed its natural drum, but my mind was far from satisfied. Although she had never failed to keep the tryst to which she had agreed, I felt that the change in our relationship was not less than that she had told me, and might be greater than I had feared. If so, she was not in the least saddened. There was high and almost radiant color in her face and a blitheness in every movement. We came near each other often that afternoon as we pursued various tasks, and always I expected some sign from her, if only a quick shake of her head, canceling our appointment. Not until the first clear light of the sun, not yet upheaved above the icecap in the east, revealed the night's mist brushed from the willow branches that screened the secret path did my heart bound in unclouded and jubilant anticipation.

I entered the dim grotto. My first impression, before my eyes could adapt themselves to the sudden change from daylight to heavy twilight, was that Ellen was wearing a pale-colored cloth over her crow-black hair. Then my spine tingled from mystery and excitement as I perceived that the young woman sitting on the deerskin cover of the bed, with her arms clasped about her knees, looked larger than Ellen but, although somewhat of resemblance, was not Ellen. It was Ellen's daughter, Swanhild.

3

By all appearances, Swanhild had been calmly and comfortably waiting for my arrival. Now that it had occurred, she was not in the least abashed, and swift-striking memory told me I had never seen her in that condition, and only once had seen her crestfallen, when Eric had rebuked the good-by kiss she had given me when the *Narwhale* set out from Iceland on her maiden journey to the unknown west. When she had been assigned to menial or disagreeable tasks, she had felt not shame but fury, as I had seen often in the glitter of her usually softly shining eyes. Although of the second generation born into thralldom, she had shown much more resentment than Ellen, of the first generation so born, and had not imitated her mother in determined and painstaking labor. But whatever her assignment today, she appeared to be delighted with it. I was seeing her with increasing clarity: her blue eyes had that strange soft shine and mystery so often seen in nearsighted girls, now enhanced to a mysterious glow. Her posture and her very glance told of her self-confidence and joy.

"Swanhild, I did not expect to find you here," I said with that inanity that folk think almost their duty to employ when silence stretches long.

"Why should you, when you expected to find my mother, Ellen?"

"Yes, I did."

"She sent me to tell you that she couldn't come—said you'd understand why not—and to tell too that she could never come any more."

This report, so plainly and squarely put by Swanhild's full-throated young voice, left no room for doubt of its absolute truth. It was not conditional and it did not even express regret, and for this last I was thankful, because such an expression would have been irrelevant to the fact, and its omission was in respect to me as a man, able to confront facts without decoration. I was jarred to my inmost depths. I was not and never had been in love with Ellen; yet I had come to think of her as necessary to my happy and successful being. The fact remained she had gone, and there flitted through my brain a remark stalwart Thorhall had made to me when Eric had been sentenced by the Hundred moot to go into exile *"Thus dies my dream and now I must get one new."*

That death had not weakened Thorhall. I felt an inkling of strength whereby the loss of Ellen, all the sharper because I was yet so young, would not weaken me.

In my brief meditation Swanhild had watched my face with lively curiosity. Perhaps she had been told to do so, but that I doubted; and I doubted too that she had seen very much worth telling.

"Did Ellen use the expression 'come any more'?" I asked with good grip on myself and my brain alert. "If she did, it was the same as saying that she had come several times, perhaps many times, before. But perhaps you knew that already."

"Of course I knew it. I had to help my mother fool my father, Horkel. Many a time she told me just what to say if he asked where she was."

"I suppose you knew too who it was she was meeting in secret?"

"I guessed it. When she was gone, you were gone. But I didn't like it very well, Leif. My mother, Ellen, was too old for you."

"According to custom, yes."

Her eyes changed very subtly, then she said a strange thing.

"You and she hugged and kissed. She told me that much. But if that was all you did, what did you want of this nice bed?"

I could make no immediate answer. My brain was surging in the search for what was behind the question. Certainly it was not innocence. Few ten-year-old children, at least in a settlement like ours, where speech is unguarded and they must share in its labors, failed to know all the uses of the bed. Swanhild was about fourteen and might be nearer fifteen, if her mother had not told with careful truth her own age.

In that search, I gave Swanhild one brief glance, but it was as intent as my eying of the quarry when I raised my harpoon to throw, and no aspect of her appearance escaped me. As I had noticed before, she was a size larger than Ellen, and an inch or two taller. She had Ellen's lovely shaping, too, but here the resemblance ceased. Ellen's vividness, which the half-blind could not miss, was caused partly by the contrast of her intensely black hair and heavy eyebrows with the whiteness of her skin. There were no great contrasts in Swanhild's face; every feature and tint were in harmony with one another. Truly she was fair-haired, but the dense shock, cut off at the line of her jaw, contained too many glints of red in the growing light to be called golden, unless, indeed, the term referred to red Roman gold that I had never seen. Her eyebrows had the same color, arched instead of straight as were Ellen's, more narrow, yet so densely grown that they could not be overlooked, her lashes very long and again dense, which I thought had something to do with the shadowy look of her pure blue eyes. They looked innocent enough to account for the childlike question, but I knew that behind that look a busy brain was working, and prompting that question had been design.

I found no fault with that. It made my prospects for adventure all the brighter. My heart leaped at the inkling that now, this moment, I was entering upon one of the great adventures of my life. An adjunct to that inkling was one of peril. With that, too, I found no fault.

The refinement of her high and narrow nose and of the voluptuous molding of her lips was more marked than in any feature of her mother's face. It could be, I fancied, that she resembled a long-gone Irish queen, her distant ancestor, of a house already ancient and famed in the annals of Eire, a sensuous woman of the most lively, cunning mind, to whom her ministers and her enemies were no match, whereby she had extended and enriched her realm, so the folk had prospered and had blessed her name. But this was a wild fancy to the flight of which I was too much given. Perhaps it had conjured up the image of an unscrupulous, great queen not long in her mossy grave, but one such not yet born! It was possible that prophetic glimpses were sometimes given me, now that I had sucked the blood of Minin, a Swan Maiden and a great prophetess, even though in some kind of spell. I could almost see that queen to come, tall, regal, not beautiful but splendidly impressive, reigning over some green land not far from Ireland.

Then the dim and distant vision faded, for I looked again at Swanhild and remembered that she was a thrall and the daughter of a thrall.

"You didn't answer my question about the bed," she remarked, but now her air of innocence was belied by a small, flickering smile. "And you needn't answer, because I already knew that you and my mother were the same as married."

"You said you didn't like it, because of the difference in our ages."

"I said that to please you. In truth I did not care whom my mother went with, as long as she escaped now and then from Eric's harsh rule to find some happiness. Now I have delivered her message. Do I need stay any longer?"

"Not unless you wish to. But I'd like to have you stay awhile."

"Then I will. I have some skins to flesh but I won't be missed for an hour or two. But if you're only going to stand there and stare at me——"

"Remember that your coming was a great surprise."

"And a great disappointment to you. But perhaps I can make it less."

"I am sure you can, if you will."

"We can kiss each other and hug. There's no harm in that; all folk of our age—and you are only three or four years older than I—do that when they get the chance. Besides, I've already kissed you twice, in spite of Eric the Red standing there, and you liked it as much as I did—I could tell that much—and since he's not here, his green eyes are not looking at us, do you want to sit beside me on the bed?"

I did so, exultation thrilling through me. I did not let myself think of the oddity, perhaps an uncanny strangeness, of having made love to a woman so much older than I, and now making ready to do the same to her daughter. Swanhild's young soft mouth was not as hungry-seeming as Ellen's had been, but it was more sensuous. Without her making bold in any way I perceived, her kisses were passion-rousing in the extreme. After a great many long and lingering kisses she too became aroused, as I saw plainly in the dark red glow on her cheekbones. Yet when I started to unlace the thongs to lay bare her breast, the firm grasp of her strong hand stopped me.

"Today we can only kiss," she told me earnestly. "Maybe never more than that."

"You remember how the young folk made free at the Feast of the Returning Sun?"

"There is no harm in that. It is only a Norse custom, the same as the May Night Feast in Ireland, when my mother was hardly thirteen. Your old folk believe that heat in the blood will give more heat to the sun to melt the ice. In Ireland they have another excuse—I forget what. If I wanted to let you fondle my breasts, kiss them even, I would do so. But I don't want you to, now. I keep remembering that I am a thrall maiden, and you are the son of Eric the Red. We will kiss a little more, if you like, and then I will go."

A few minutes later I saw her wave her hand under the arch of the cave mouth and disappear from sight. I remained where I was awhile, at first dizzy and aching from balked passion, and then

half-stunned by what had happened. On the face of it, it was not
so strange. Parents among our colonists were forever providing op-
portunities for their daughters to dally with swains of equal station.
Nor did the strangeness I sensed so keenly without perceiving its
shape stem from the unequal station of Swanhild and me. I only
knew that Swanhild's mother had been my partner in love-making,
yet had made me a present of her daughter—a fact that common
sense could not deny; and would this wake the wrath of the Gods?
Perhaps it suggested incest, which the folk held in utmost horror.
Yet it was not that, really; it was only strange.

And fully as strange was the maiden herself, truly a maiden,
I believed, of beauty earthly except for her melting eyes, but herself somehow unearthly, as marked by the play of her mind revealed in her frank speech, itself a wonder of excellence in a thrall
girl. She had been bold as a Swan Maiden leading a swain to her
bower, and at the same time never losing her self-possession, never
saying what she had not meant to say. Then I had to leave the
dim cave and go out under the summer sky, and see the snow
weeping, and the grass growing in the wet, and listen to the
squawk and clamor of waterfowl. Only thus could I rid myself of
the feeling of being bewitched.

4

While most of the Nordrseta men were away on their second
hunt of this still half-broken spring, Eric met with the owners of
the fifteen boats, the great chieftain Bjorn, Thorhall, Einer, and
twelve other franklins of wealth and power, all of whom, except
Thorhall, were likewise owners of the ships on which they had
sailed from Iceland. The subject of discussion was a change in the
aim and tactics of the hunting parties. This change was possible
because of the increasing supply of food for the colonists. Butter
and cheese were not yet abundant, and would not become so until
the herds of cattle and flocks of goats were greatly enlarged by
import or by their own fertility; but these edibles had become a
staple of the diet of franklins and free folk and were occasionally
found on the soapstone serving platters of thralls. A great deal of

house and pen building remained to be done on all the farms and this labor would never cease in the two growing, industrious colonies; yet more hands could be spared from the building crews to catch and wind-dry great quantities of salmon that would soon swarm the rivers and even to spear seals in nearby waters. The women and children would care for livestock as well as gather countless eider-duck eggs to be preserved in brine.

Thus we Nordrseta men need no longer give all our time to hunting meat. A good part of every trip we could devote to hunting treasure—sealskins of the kind that brought a good price in Europe, white bearskins greatly prized there, white fox and other fur as long as this was prime, and walrus and narwhale ivory. A share of the catch would go to us hunters, a share to the boat owners, and a very small share to Eric, who would supervise the shipping and the sale of all exports. Supplementing the revenue from these, the big ships could sometimes be used as whalers, taking Leviathan, which we now called sperm whales, white whales, Greenland whales, and even blue whales, the giant of them all. These would furnish oil, whalebone—of increasing use in Europe—and hides that made the strongest cables and ropes used in shipping.

Nor did Eric fail to remind his eager listeners that in the intestines of the sperm whale could sometimes be found a fatty sweet-smelling substance called ambergris, selling for its weight in silver in southern European marts, from where it found its way to the cities of the Moors—Egypt, Turkey, and Arabia—as a precious article of trade. In fact in times past whole troves of this fragrant treasure had been found floating on the sea.

Gods, how you love gold, silver, and bright jewels. So Ian had sung in the Strand Song of the Norse Women to the Departing Fleets. No longer great packs of dragon ships put out from Northland ports to harry and pillage the Christian coasts, but plainly that old love, going hand in hand with the love of adventure, still lived in Northland hearts. Hearing of the new plan a few minutes after our return from our second spring hunt, I was as pleased with it as were my boat mates. It might be the first step toward getting a ship of my own, on which Ugruk, I, and a score or so of selected men might go searching the far westward reaches of the ocean. I had not liked to hear that narwhales would be among the prizes hunted for the market. However, these were such shy beasts, almost always taking off at the first sight of a sail, that I did not think the kill would be large.

It so happened that I did not linger to hear my mates discuss ways and means. Nor, on second thought, did happenstance have anything to do with my swift departure. I wanted my mother's welcoming kiss, and then I meant to look for Swanhild. On the last nights of our cruise I had dreamed of her with utmost vividness, while Ellen remained only a ghostly figure in the background. In my waking moments I was somewhat shocked at this inconstancy, or at least the sudden and abrupt change of the bent of my desires. Deciding at last it was only natural under the circumstances, I had let the matter slide.

It was no trouble to find Swanhild. Indeed it was difficult not to believe that she had been watching for me ever since our boat put in, and at the same time a thing hard to believe for the reason it was such a happy thing, so flattering, and which I so greatly wished to be true. She had been cleaning fish with some other thrall women and as soon as her nearsighted eyes recognized me, she went to wash her hands, scrubbing them with sand, at the bubbling spring of cold but not icy water. There I followed her, not in the least furtively but briskly, as though I had something important to tell her. Actually the only importance of our meeting was what she had to tell me.

As I drew near, both my exultation and my anxiety increased. In idle moments of our hunting I had pictured her as pretty, shapely, and desirable, but without knowing it I had toned down those pictures, in some sort of self-protection against disappointment. In her rough friz dress, the wind blowing her fair hair and the genial sun picking up its red tints, she looked vividly beautiful, startling the eyes, and as vital as a white-maned, high-horned reindeer stag met suddenly in some little dale between green hills —or as my father, Eric the Red, when his green eyes gleamed with some intensity of feeling and his red beard flamed. I noticed for the first time she had a rather short, large neck, not uncommon in people of great vitality. She had not the long lean face of most Norse girls; at the cheekbones it was almost as broad as Ugruk's, with something the same planing, and why this should enhance the tingling shock of her nearness I had no notion. At present her voluptuous mouth—did it look so, or did I remember it so?—was a little twisted, as she scrubbed hard to rid her hands of fish slime. I could hardly believe that my mouth had possessed it, as hers had possessed mine, and it might happen again.

When she looked up at me, I perceived the most exciting feature of her face. It was the dim luminescence of her eyes in a kind of darkly lustrous mist, wonderfully soft-looking eyes, wonderfully innocent-looking.

"Leif, you didn't bring me the swan plume that you promised my mother, Ellen, you would get for me," she said at once, without any polite word of welcome, and with just a trace of ire.

"I haven't seen one fit for you yet."

"You forgot me as soon as you set sail. You thought of nothing but hunting. You didn't deserve for me to count the days until I could expect you to come back. After all, I am only a thrall girl and you are the son of Eric the Red." This last was in no way sarcasm but unmistakable defiance.

"I can stay only a minute. Will you meet me tomorrow morning?"

"Yes, but not quite so early. It's so cold then and there's no one to watch me come or go as my father, Horkel, watched my mother, Ellen. Say two hours after sunrise. I've already won the name of an unsteady worker; I might as well live up to it. I'll go up the river, looking for something my mother lost—I don't know what unless it was a sweetheart too young for her. You take the path through the grass to the new sheep pen, cross to the river, and come down. I think I'll get there first—has it been twelve months since we met, or only twelve days?—but if I keep you waiting more than half an hour, you can leave, for I'm not worth waiting for."

All this came forth boldly, and I could well wonder whether this free speech or the misty, somehow touching beauty of her eyes reflected her true self. I did not wonder about it then; I was too exultant over the assignation.

"Two hours after sunrise I'll be there," I told her, meanwhile rallying my courage for a more daring remark. "It will be quite warm by then, and your jacket needn't be laced so tight and you needn't wear heavy clothes."

"I'm not sure. The weather may change." She went on scrubbing her hands.

The early hours of daylight dragged, and I feared that Swanhild's estimate of the sun's height might be faulty, and she would come to the trysting place and go before I arrived. So I was relieved to see the dew palely gleaming on the willow branches screening the path to the grotto. Then when I had waited not more than five minutes, I began to be plagued with doubt whether she would come at all for any one of a dozen reasons, one being that her mother, Ellen, had come to her senses and had decided against exposing Swanhild to a highborn swain who in no likelihood would ever marry her. But the most likely reason that returned again and again to my mind was that Swanhild herself would not want to come. Actually I knew nothing about the young wench except what was visible to the eye and what was sentient to my body when we had kissed. I did not know what was in her mind or in her heart. I had no notion of her aims or ambitions, although these, I believed, she would somehow achieve, by some power in her that I could sense but not identify. She was not half-starved for body linkage with a male as Ellen had been. Any one of a score of young men in the colony could have served Ellen's needs as well as I—I had only her own flattering words to the contrary. Her daughter, Swanhild, might be naturally lascivious. Her misty and endearing eyes were no proof of innocence and instead, I believed, merely a common sign of nearsightedness. Gorm, in one of his salty and philosophic moments, had remarked that lascivious behavior in a woman was flattering to her lover only until he began to wonder how many other lovers she had so flattered. I began to wonder if she was a virgin——

Then the whole web of thought was torn from the loom by Swanhild's appearance in the doorway.

She entered and looked about her with an expression of disdain.

"This is a bleak hole to meet in," she said. "Couldn't my mother, Ellen, and you find any better place?"

"It was safe," I answered. "Safety is hard to come by."

"I suppose that's true. My mother warned me to take no risks of any sort—to break the tryst rather than take any. She seemed to think the heavens would fall if we were caught, although I don't know why. Some young couple is caught kittling every time it thunders—that's an old Irish saying—and what happens when a thrall girl can no longer fasten her belt? Some talk, some guessing, sometimes a marriage, sometimes not; in either case there is no great to do. The rocks are rather pretty here—but it will be so cold dressing and undressing if it should ever come to that. Can't you bring an oil lamp some dark night? If you'd hang a deerskin blanket on the willows to shield the cave mouth, no light could get through to attract attention."

"I suppose I can," I replied to her earnest question, hoping that now her speech would become less forthright and more suitable to a tryst.

"I was sorry to keep you waiting," she went on, her voice deepening and her tone softening and her expression far more intimate. "You know that little stand of dwarf birch a hundred paces down river. I was waiting there, and I saw you enter, but I couldn't come as fast as I wished. I had to wait until two men hunting for hares and tarmochans went over the hill. One was your brother, Thorstein, and the other Einer's son, Ring. I thought they would take forever. But here I am!"

I was more disturbed than I wanted Swanhild to know that Thorstein had come nigh our tryst. A stand of dwarf birch yet not in leaf offers very poor cover for a fair-haired girl in a gray friz dress, and my brother had keen eyes; it would be natural for such an avid hunter to scan the copse in hope of seeing a reindeer. But there was nothing I could do with the worry but stuff it away somewhere in my head, to deal with later. Otherwise my meeting with this vital young woman, vivid even in the dusk of the cavern, and enchanting to my sight, would be spoiled.

She had said, "Here I am!" So in answer to that I went and put my arms about her, and she kissed me with a kind of fierce-

ness, rather than tenderness. Then I sat on the bed and had her
lie in my lap, her breast close to mine, but not so close that I
could not reach the thongs at the throat of her jacket and discover that these were fastened with bow knots to be untied with
one pull. Still I did not hasten to the attempt, although I had no
reason to think it would fail. Instead I feasted on kisses at a
banquet of sensuality, her soft mouth so near and available, her
tongue, that was not yet bold and indeed somewhat stealthy in
its touching mine, making quick and furtive probings under my
lips and causing wave after wave of delicious sensation to engulf
my whole body and brain.

Soon I was driven by ever ascending desire to loosen the top-
most thong of her jacket. She made only a token resistance, one
hand clasping mine, but the strength I had sensed in it before,
greater than in the hands of most young women, perhaps far
greater than I knew, was dormant now. When I had kissed the
lovely hollow between her collarbone she did not lift her hand to
stop me from unfastening all the knots, and the only sign she
made of her feelings was a long, deep sigh, a sign unreadable to
my senses, although I thought it was of relief from tension that
often occurs at wildly wished surrender.

Even old Gorm, who, from his talk, might be mistaken for a
misogynist, had admitted the beauty of the breast of a well-
developed young woman. It was a beauty that struck deep within
natural men, and it had overtones and significance beyond the
visible and sensual. I had observed that the vulgar term boobies
was largely avoided by all but the coarsest men, as if it were an
insult to a feature of woman not only beautiful but somehow
sacred. Their infant lives had begun at a woman's breasts, these
were the source of its warmth and life, and its first introduction
to love. Perhaps there was some connection with their being a
particular joy to lovers, as our poets and singers constantly attested.

Swanhild's breasts were patterned after her mother's, fruit-
shaped, perhaps slightly more erect because they had never been
heavy with milk, and milk white, not snow white, except for
crimson buds. What a decoration to women, I thought, perhaps a
gift of Frigga, wife of Odin, or of Freya, who was to become our

Goddess-Patroness of lovers. The gift had been made when the assembled deities gazed for the first time upon a roughly carven blocklike image which some God greater than any that we knew had conceived as his servant and ambassador on earth. Swanhild's virginal breast was lovely to touch, bliss-giving to caress, exquisite to kiss. And I did more than that, because I was a natural man, and again Swanhild uttered a long sigh, and when the desire and the moment were both meet, she turned a little in my lap to indicate that these fountains were twins, and they should have equal homage.

But when, aroused almost beyond bearing, I slid my hand down her silken side, she seized it in a grasp strong as a smith's, hammerer and bender of iron, and I knew that she was militant in what she would give and what she would withhold, and I had best not force the issue.

5

Later in the day I was frequently in Thorstein's company, watching and listening to him with foxy sharpness, although hiding any sign of so doing. He made no remark that could hint at his awareness of Swanhild's and my intrigue; when the men's talk reverted to young and pretty women and their "best use on earth," my joining in the coarse jesting brought no knowing smile to his lips or in his dark eyes. It happened that Ring Einersson spent most of the day at our home acre, and I talked with him from time to time. He was a forthright fellow, not subtle like Thorstein, and he could have hardly pretended complete ignorance of the affair. Very naturally, he made casual mention of the morning hunt and of the size of the bag.

"Did you see any big game?" I asked.

"Thorstein thought he caught a glimpse of a deer in that stand of birch about a mile up river, but since we couldn't possibly get in arrow range of the open woods, we went on."

So my mind was put at rest and I could look forward joyously to our starting forth the next day on a fresh hunt, because everyone was fresh as a change of wind at sea on account of the immensity of our hunting ground on land and water and its manifold adventures, no two of which were ever quite alike. And when I came home again there was nothing that I knew of to prevent an adventure of another kind.

But there was something I did not know of, then, that would prevent my participation in the northward venture, although it might not delay, and perhaps it would hasten, my next tryst with Swanhild. Late in the afternoon, as I was making from the hot spring, where I had washed, to our hall, I noticed a rare and shapely catboat skipping handsomely before the southeast wind up our fiord. At once I recognized it as the *Johanna*, belonging to the great chieftain Bjorn, used by him and his family for excursions of pleasure, and named after his flaxen-haired daughter, aged fifteen, whom I knew slightly and with whom I had danced at the feast of the winter solstice. At once I sped to the spinning room and told my mother, Thorhild, what I had seen.

"It is no news to me," she answered. "I had word from Inga, mistress of Bjornhall, that she would come today, if the ice and wind permitted, and visit us for a few days. I didn't tell you because I was afraid the ice would be heavy and the wind wrong, and she would disappoint us."

It was easy to see that my mother was overjoyed by the coming visit. In the first place, there had been almost no visiting of any distance during the winter. Besides, Inga, the wife of Bjorn, of an ancient line of great chieftains, was related to Thorhild by marriage, Inga's brother having married Thorhild's sister and they were lord and lady of a great markland in Norway. Inga and Thorhild were very like sisters in the closeness of their affection, and both were worshipers of Kris.

"Johanna is coming with her mother," Thorhild remarked in an offhand way. "It will be delightful to have them both here a few days. We have room for them in the hall, and the thralls they bring can stay with our thralls."

"I'll be sorry to leave for the hunt tomorrow morning."

"Why should you leave, Leif? I want you to stay and get better acquainted with Johanna. Thorhall, Gorm, and Ugruk can sail the boat and make a good kill even if both you and Thorstein stay. It would be rude for you to go, under the circumstances, and also you would forfeit a great deal of pleasure. For the first time in your grown-up life you would be thrown with a beautiful and charming girl who is equal to you in station. You have been deprived of that in this new and savage land."

"It would be rude of me to go—under *what* circumstances?"

"Don't ask me to play cat and mouse with you, Leif, my tall and—not very handsome, but manly son whom I love so well. In addition to her charm of person, Johanna is the most considerable heiress in the colonies. You are the son of Eric the Red. Both Inga and I would be delighted if you two would match. Eric and Bjorn would both consider it a highly proper alliance of two eminent Norse families."

"You forget that Johanna is a follower of Kris—she has been given a Christian name—and I don't think she would take to a half-heathen—more than half, perhaps—like me."

"I don't think that would be an obstacle," my mother answered with smiling eyes.

I considered quickly, taking what pains I could not to be a fool. Being of marriageable age, I expected to marry before long and have a hall of my own. My mother spoke complete truth when she had said Johanna was the great prize of the colonies. How I would love to beat Thorstein to that prize! Moreover, the procurance of a ship whose prow would head into the sunset would be a simple matter if I were the son-in-law of Bjorn.

As for Swanhild, there could be no lasting bond between her and me, and I could not quite smother a feeling that any entanglement with her held hidden but quite real danger.

"Very well, I'll stay," I told my mother.

"I'm so happy," she answered. And her lovely expression said the same.

One glance down the fiord told me that the boat would not touch our strand for another half-hour. I took from my chest my best shirt, made of reindeerskins of different tint that comprised a handsome plaid. This I put on, along with pants made of leopard seal and hair-seal slippers, and combed my rough hair as smooth as I could manage. As I was making for the door to go to

the strand, I heard the very last of what might have been an en-
lightening conversation between Thorhild and my brother, Thorstein.

"I will be courtly as a Norman mark lord to Johanna until she
goes to bed," Thorstein was saying in his forceful way. "If I see
her at early breakfast, I will mind my manners. But immediately
after breakfast I will set sail for Disco Island with Thorhall,
Gorm, and Ugruk."

To judge from the glint in my mother's eyes, she was as happy
over the pronouncement as was I.

CHAPTER NINE

BJORNHALL

I

Inga, wife of Bjorn, was a tall, fine-looking woman of the highest Norse type, stately without losing the native warmth of our race; yet it was difficult to believe that she had borne a daughter of such striking beauty as Johanna. And this beauty was truly of the Northland—sunny, as was beloved where the fickle sun was well-nigh worshiped, with eyes of that pure sky blue that in the north is so often hidden by cold cloud or bleak fog and hence all the dearer to our eyes. She was as tall as her mother, appearing as tall as Thorstein although she was in truth two or three inches less, and I rejoiced, and felt that she was impressed that I could look over her luminous-looking head.

There was a great deal of grace, and of womanliness, too, in her lithe and slender form. The thought crossed my mind that she might be a poor weaver and seamstress, but she could sail a boat close to the wind with the dash of a man; and I would be hard put to it to beat her in a ski race, and when we came to the crest of a steep hill she could take off like a white tarmochan. Oddly, in spite of her being so fair, her hair of such pale gold, her skin like the water lilies I had seen in Iceland, and her long and slender neck and limbs, I was not reminded of a swan. In truth, I had a feeling about swans that was secretive and unworldly. Deep in my heart I was in love with a swan—one that my common sense insisted was a figment of a dream—whose name was Minin, a Swan Maiden, and we had sucked each other's blood in an ice palace. Her I could not compare with anyone.

Johanna's element was gaiety. She had hardly greeted us before she began to tell of a mishap on the day's sail from Bjornsfiord, in which a stay gave way and the swinging boom had struck a thrall and knocked him overboard within a hundred feet of what he thought was a big shark but which proved to be a leopard seal. Her recounting of his changing his wet, icy-cold clothes for a parka provided by a fellow thrall unshielded except by a sheep-skin robe, maintaining his modesty only with the greatest diffi-culty, was just ribald enough to delight my mother and slightly shock her mother and my brother, Thorstein. Eric bellowed his great laugh.

Johanna's native language was laughter. It was shrill and a little raucous, but to my ear delightful. It presented such a dra-matic contrast with Ellen's intensity and Swanhild's seething soul and often sharp tongue. It rang over our rough board as we supped on the delicacies our pantry afforded, and this soon after a moment in which she was deeply solemn and soft-eyed, as she, Inga, and my mother, Thorhild, prayed together for the blessing of their God Kris upon the food. After supper, as we sat in a ring about a high-flaming whale-oil lamp, Johanna lifted us all out of ourselves by her high spirits.

I could not help but glow over her addressing most of her com-ments and anecdotes to me. Only occasionally she glanced at Thorstein, with what I thought was a narrow and cold look. Ap-parently she had taken a dislike to him, at which I rejoiced.

In the morning she ate a hearty breakfast of eider-duck eggs, thinly cut strips of deer meat spitted over flame, along with fried cakes made from a root Ugruk had taught us to gather from meadow pools and pound into flour, rather tasteless unless swim-ming in butter, still the nearest to the barley cakes of Iceland that I had tasted. On my announcement that I was going fishing for char at the mouth of the river, she declared her intention of going with me.

"I regret my fellow hunters and I will stand to sea before you get back," Thorstein said as Johanna and I were setting forth.

"It's quite proper that you should, Thorstein," Johanna an-swered. "Work must come first!"

This last statement, primly pronounced by a girl who I doubted ever lifted her hand in labor, delighted my heart.

On this jaunt our tackle was very fine. Sullen at first because I and not Thorstein would be keeping company with Johanna, Eric came to some conclusion that pleased him, whereupon he provided us two anglers with steel hooks made in Toledo, each worth an otter skin in trade, and loaned to her his own fishing rod, a freak branch that had grown on a dwarf willow, about twelve feet long and slender all of its length, and so limber that the landing of a half-pound lake trout became, if not a victory, a tingling thrill. We had lead sinkers, lines of tough sinew, and for bait we would use salmon eggs, taken last year from gutted salmon and preserved with salt.

We found a school of migratory char in a pothole at the river mouth. They were waiting for some kind of signal, no doubt a prompting from within that the river water, still colder than the fiord water but soon to be made warmer by the sun's heat piercing its shallows, was the right temperature for their spawn to live and flourish. Gaining strength for the ordeal, they were fiercely hungry, and Johanna pulled in fish, screeching during each struggle, almost as fast as I could string them and bait her hook. Once an oversized fish took her bait, nearly jerked the pole out of her hand, bent it nearly double, and fought a great fight ere he surrendered, throughout which she not only screeched but shouted and yelled, calling mainly upon her God Kris, but once, by a slip of the tongue, invoking Odin.

When the frantic biting stopped, our string was three feet long and weighed more than fifty pounds. Yet we lingered awhile, the sun being so warm and the sounds of the running waters so pleasant, to catch occasional fish that had not had breakfast. At last I had time to wet my line as well as string fish and bait hooks; and I had caught about half a dozen char when a fish bit in a different fashion from the others, with a strong, slow, powerful tug. When I had hooked him, he did stubborn but not violent battle. When I laid eyes on him, my eyes bulged. He was rather short and puffy-looking, with a small round mouth, and his body tapered to narrowness just in front of the flaring tail. I had never before seen this fish when newly caught, but I had seen one that had been sun-dried. Still there was no mistaking the resemblance of one to the other. It was what the old Norse called a daft fish.

Such strange feelings came upon me that I had to take pains to hide them from my companion, and then there was born within me an irrational passion. I wanted to keep this fish separate from the rest, hide it from all eyes but mine, cook it in secret, and devour it. As surely as I breathed I would be poisoned by it, if poisoned was the word, and in the next few hours I would be transported to a different realm than this, but which would seem no less real, and which I could not deny might be real. Somewhere hereabouts, I would have a great and, to normal thinking, uncanny adventure. I would pass some little barrier into a world inhabited by bearded dwarfs, gigantic trolls, talking fish, kingly seals, and, perhaps, Swan Maidens. And then the conviction grew upon me, powerful and imperious, that I had only to do this and again I would be with Minin, my Swan Maiden. I thought with rushing joy that the time had been long since Allhallow's Eve, after which a stern injunction decreed was no longer in force. Suddenly my lust for Minin's beautiful body, joined with mine in divine bliss, while I lay enfolded by her white limbs on a snow-white bed, was almost too great to bear.

"Leif, what's the matter?" Johanna asked, her voice different than before, reaching me it seemed from a long distance.

"Why, nothing. This is a very rare fish and——"

"The color drained out of your cheeks and your eyes—they were glassy-looking and staring into the distance."

Instead, with a feat of will, I turned and looked at her. Slowly, it seemed, her image on my eyes became as I remembered it. I remembered her shrill and rather raucous laughter, her excitement as she landed fish, and I not only saw but felt her blonde and vital beauty, essentially Norse, and in the fullest measure given to Norse women. I was a Norseman. I was a seeker of victory in this world, not of weird transports to a supernatural world. All my natural desires could be gratified if I could win her. My hand crept to my knife and into my mind crept an intention grim and perhaps murderous—at least to murder the door opener to unearthly blissful dreams—that intention being to drive my point into the creature's vitals and then cast it into the sea.

But my stealthy movement was arrested by a sound from the sky. And this a real sound, for Johanna raised her head to listen and then gazed upward. High overhead was passing what seemed to be a flock of swans in their northward flight. These were trumpeter swans, winging singing in the spring-blue sky. Perhaps the effect of song was caused by the resonant outcry of different swans at what seemed chosen intervals. But my scalp crept on my skull when the leader of the V-shaped band, that seemed larger and whiter than the rest, changed from straightforward flight to a splendid curve. With her followers, she began a sweeping circle over our heads.

"They see some water, and I think they're going to light," Johanna remarked.

I thought not. I was sure when the leader took what seemed a headlong dive, forsaking the flock and narrowing the circle of her flight. The others remained aloft, silent now, and only she sounded her trumpet, a clear and pure tone, though strong; and my heart told me that she sang to me alone. Not much higher than a hunting falcon towers, she wheeled round and round, and the sunlight glimmered on her wings, and she was beautiful beyond thought.

I took my eyes from that loveliness and fixed them on Johanna. My lips moved, and I knew the words that they formed but did not speak—"Forgive me, Minin." Then my hand that had grasped the hilt of my knife made a strong movement. In my other hand, held by the gills, was a fish of strange sort, and I felt its life pass as my point pierced its heart. And then the circling swan uttered a long-drawn cry of what seemed heartbreak, the most sorrowful sound I had ever heard and one of the most beautiful, and as I cast the dead fish into the river mouth she began to sweep upward to join her band. A moment later she had taken her place at their head and again led them northward, all of them singing like Valkyries riding from a battlefield on snow-white horses, each with the bloodied corpse of her chosen hero—the dirge that the keepers of Valhalla's gates hear from afar, then open wide the portals.

"Why did you kill and throw back that fish?" Johanna asked, after a long silence.

"It was of a kind that people shouldn't eat, or so I've been told," I answered.

"I didn't know what to think. The look on your face—and that swan swooping down and wailing like a woman for a lost lover. I guess it didn't mean anything, it just happened so. Let's take in our lines, and you carry our catch to the thralls, and I hope Thorhild will give me part of that big char for my dinner. I'll help her and my mother spin."

I would be glad to be alone. I must spin a few dreams before I could go on with the common life of our home acre.

2

The great families of Norway, whether of rival kings or of powerful chieftains of ancient name, had at least two customs in common. One was the worship of Odin. They had not turned from him to address their prayers and sacrifice to Thor, who had become the main God of the common people, indeed the main God in Iceland, yet who only a century before had been the God of serfs, thralls, and slaves. The few great folk who had renounced Odin were usually women, my mother and Bjorn's wife and daughter being in this number, and had gone directly to the worship of Kris. The fact remained that Kris had been long accepted by the mighty lords of Europe, such as the German, French, English, Italian, and Castilian kings, and the Duke of Normandy, the latter descended from Vikings. So it would surprise no one if some Norwegian king, envious of European monarchs, trying to imitate them in other ways, should become a Christian.

Another custom of the great mead halls of Norway was for the young women, wives or daughters of thanes, to take part in lordly hunts conducted in a mark lands. Few of them could hurl spears but almost all were taught to shoot the longbow, somewhat lighter than the bows used by men, but with which they shot fallow deer, wild swine, the beautiful high-antlered red deer, and occasionally a great black elk with flaring horns.

This skill had been largely lost in Iceland, for there we had hunted at sea. Plainly Bjorn had tried to maintain the old ways, for among his daughter's gear was an old strong very beautifully worked bow of yew wood. "It has not been fully drawn since last autumn," she told me at the midday meal, "so this afternoon I want to compare my poor skill with your great skill."

"Shall we shoot at a target or go hunting in the hills?" I asked.

"I want to shoot something we can eat." And when I thought it over, this was a truly characteristic utterance of this vigorous, healthy, young woman with big feet on the ground. I wondered how it fitted in with her being a Christian. When I inquired— politely as possible—she told me that a Christian saint, whose name she had forgotten, had been a great huntress.

Johanna and I made ready to set out, our mothers greatly pleased with the plan. But if they counted on quite a little court- ship between my companion and me in the lonesome, lovely hills, they had missed their guess. I could not have asked for a more gay, buoyant, and delightful companion. The weather was perfect for "making hay," as old Gorm would have put it, or for the "ways of a man with a maid," as was written in the runes of the Christians. It was the warmest day of the yet young spring, the wind balmy, the sun ardent, the buds of the willows swelling swiftly. But Johanna's only aim was to beat me at hunting. She would not sit down even a minute on some grassy hillside by any excuse I could invent. I had intended to let her beat me, but on perceiving her competitive spirit I shot as well as I could. The contest was simple enough. We took turns on targets, letting chance dictate their ease or difficulty. The shooter won if he killed at the opening shot; if he missed, his opponent must then shoot, usually at running or flying quarry; and if he likewise missed, the score remained even. When Johanna won, I owed her an ermine skin; when I won, I was due an immediate kiss.

Game was so plentiful this spring that we would hardly re- trieve our arrows without sighting another target, usually a tar- mochan or a hare. Since these were generally at close range, neither of us usually missed his turn; when one of us did miss, his opponent's shot was almost always a miss, although once I scored on my opponent with a brilliant shot at a very large, run- ning jack fox, still snow white, at which to her brief chagrin she had loosed too soon. In five minutes I had peeled off his beautiful hide and put it with my other kill in my pack sack. Johanna wore a similar sack, in which she insisted on carrying her own kill.

Her laughter was a new sound, I thought, to these silent grassy hills in whose shade lay patches of melting snow. They had heard a sound resembling laughter, eerie and demonic, between wailings and sobbings when the wolves bayed at the moon, but not these shrill, somewhat harsh, yet wonderfully merry peals of genuine laughter. Also, in the part of the huntress, Johanna had never been more pleasing to my sight. As she took her stance, her bow slowly arching from the pull of her hand on the string, her fair hair wind-blown, her blue eyes brilliant with excitement, her tall form supple but strong, she could counterfeit Diana, the Roman Goddess of the Chase, known by hearsay in Ireland and even in our wintry Northland. The least satisfaction I took in the hunt was with the kisses that were my mead of victory. They were good-natured enough, indeed gay, but all too brisk.

Her mettle was best shown near the end of the hunt, about two miles from our mead hall, when we had come upon a magnificent lone reindeer stag, one of his antlers already dropped in the spring fall and his white mane flashing at a distance of ninety paces. He had seen us but was not yet in flight, and instead made short, excited bounds; and I saw the intense determination in Johanna's face and the greed for victory in her eyes. She drew her bow to an almost perfect round before she loosed, the arrow humming and describing a beautiful arc. But although the cast did not fall short, a little sideways prance of the quarry caused it to miss. At once he began to make off in long bounds.

But hard behind him sped another shaft, faster than he, gaining with deadly swiftness, and as it arched down it struck him just back of the shoulder blades and thrust deep. As though its weight were ten stone instead of a few ounces, he crumpled beneath the blow, and his snowy mane became incarnadine.

Johanna turned to me, her eyes wide. "That was the best shot I've ever seen," she told me. "Thorstein could not have matched it before his arm was broken. You deserve your prize, and much more." For the first time she gave me a full, sweet kiss, of warmth and duration.

I proposed that I tie my neckcloth, permeated by the human smell, on a stick and erect it near the carcass to give it some degree of protection from the meat hunters of the night. Johanna protested volubly, saying that the cloth, even if it smelled as stoutly as an old mink, would not ward off the fangs of either wolves or gluttons, if any should scent the kill. I was greatly pleased with her thrift as together we cut out the forequarters and fastened them with strips of hide to the tough stalk of a birch sapling. By putting both hams at one end, and the much lighter shoulders at the other, I could distribute the weight so Johanna, some inches shorter than I, need not bear the brunt; even so, her burden was a good fifty pounds.

Not once on the tramp homeward did she complain or even ask to rest, her only respite being at my insistence. At these brief periods she sat close to me, one of her hands on mine, and I had a sense of having made great headway. Still I decided not to force the issue of love-making on my valiant, wearied companion.

We reached our home acre just after sundown, and from among the little throng of thralls that watched our return, greedily eying the meat, the vivid face of Swanhild stood out. I thought that her eyes looked narrow and glistening, and there was a small smile on her lips resembling Ellen's, but her gaze did not meet mine and she said no word.

Johanna and her mother and their servants stayed at Ericshall three days more. A good part of those days she spent with the two dames, at woman talk and doing woman business, but every day she had time for some kind of jaunt with me, once for a little sail in the dinghy in which I had made my way to the ice palace. In the course of those days I showed her the oddities of our region, including a hot spring in a ring of volcanic rock, the bones of some kind of monster we had found in a peat bog, one three-toed foot of which was as long as my body, what was left of a human skeleton in the rocky crypt, and one reach of our river that I thought beautiful almost beyond belief, with glassy waters mirroring the sky, and at sundown its western rim dimmed by long shadows of a stand of birch trees, which seen against the glowing clouds became a wonder of delicate tracery. With none of these, except the gigantic bones, was Johanna particularly impressed. These she thought belonged to the dragon that Sigurd slew.

On the last evening of her stay, as she and I were returning in the dusk from a seashore jaunt, her step lagged slightly as we were approaching the hall. I took the hint and stopped.

"I think we'd better say our good-bys now."

"I suppose so."

"I have greatly enjoyed being with you, Leif."

"I have never enjoyed anything as much as being with you, unless it was the last part of my hunt for the King of the Narwhales and a visit to a glacier when I'm not sure I was in my right mind."

"It was all right for you to enjoy the narwhale hunt more than you enjoyed me. You won a great victory. You and I were only breaking ice. Of course I know nothing of the visit to the glacier."

"It concerned a swan."

"You mean a Swan Maiden? There are no such creatures according to the holy father at Bjord—it is only a heathen superstition. And you thought it was she that circled over your head when we were fishing."

"I don't know what I thought."

"I have this to tell you. Since the winter-solstice feast comes at such a bitter season, my father, Bjorn, will give a feast at harvest home, late in September or early October. I want you to come and I hope you will dance with me."

"I accept proudly."

"Sometimes I wish you wouldn't speak as you do—with a royal manner as if you are set apart. But I don't want that objection to be our farewell."

"A farewell kiss?"

"Yes."

We kissed each other, a long and, to me, an ecstatic kiss, and in it Johanna hinted at the kind of kisses she could give if we were lovers. When, without a word of complaint, no boast, no asking for special consideration because she was a woman, she had borne on her shoulder half the weight of a pole from which hung a hundred pounds of venison, I had decided I wanted her for my wife. I knew of no one who would be such a helpmeet to me on a long and perilous adventure into the west; and, besides that, her merry heart would keep mine merry. Now that she had kissed me in this way I had high hopes that she would accept the office.

3

In concerning myself with Johanna, and by a vigilance of will, I had kept Swanhild out of my mind, in the main at least, and although she had visited my dreams, these had remained dim and confusing, without definite conclusion. It was as though she had slipped in a door where I was, and then slipped out again. Now the time was at hand that we must soon meet, confront each other, and discover our positions in relation to each other.

This occurred late in the afternoon of the day of Johanna's departure. Its occurrence was by Swanhild's design, the device of coming to a drying rack where I was cutting a ham of the newly killed venison to dry in the sunlight and wind. No one was about. Apparently she had paused on her way to the spring, and she had a water jar in her hand. She was perfectly composed, betraying no feeling whatsoever, and the lovely, touching expression of her eyes, so difficult to explain, yet so arresting, was manifest as usual. She stopped in a casual way.

"It was a fine mess of fish that you and the thane's daughter caught at the river mouth," she remarked.

"I didn't know you saw them."

"I didn't when you first brought them in. I was piling stones for the building of the master's goat pen. But I helped clean them that afternoon. I thought that the other thrall women and I would never get through. Meanwhile you had gone hunting with the beautiful girl."

"Yes, then and later she and I saw a good deal of the countryside. But I did not take her to Vixen's Den." And as soon as this last was out of my mouth, I wished I had not said it.

"Why should you? That is where you meet women who are menial to you. You knew better than to show her the bed. She has probably high opinion of you which you want her to keep. In fact the women say that you and she will marry before the year's out. Why not? The mothers of both of you desire it, and although Eric would rather that Thorstein win the prize, he won't be such a fool as to obstruct a match between you and the greatest heiress in the colonies. You will be a fine-looking couple —both of you tall, both highborn, she a true beauty, you not exactly handsome—I don't know why—but manly looking. Haven't you been named Lucky Leif?"

"I'm not sure the name fits me."

"Well, you have in your right eye a segment of the iris that is darker gray than the rest. In Ireland, it is called the Witch's Mark. It can mean wonderful good luck, or it can mean——" she paused.

"I know. Eric told me."

"My eyes are nearsighted. That's their only peculiarity. That stood me in good stead during Johanna's visit. I did not see a good deal that I did not want to see."

"Johanna's gone now. I'll probably not lay eyes on her again all summer."

"Oh, I think you will." Swanhild drew a long breath, causing her beautifully shaped breasts to bulge her tight-fitting jacket. I hoped that she had done it on purpose.

"Swanhild, nothing happened between Johanna and me to prevent our meeting again—many times—at Vixen's Den."

"When?" she asked after a brief pause.

"Why not right now?"

And the saying of "right now" almost stopped my breath, and a tingling wave passed over all my skin, and I gazed at Swanhild's voluptuous mouth with a sudden aching hunger, and it seemed I had never desired anything more, except the great horn of the Narwhale King. Yes, I had so desired the body of a Swan Maiden, lovely beyond thought, the blood of whose breast I had sucked that we might become interbound—but perhaps that was only a figment of a powerful spell. In any case, I had renounced her and now she winged her way through some distant sky. Johanna too was many sea miles distant and would remain in the distance, both in time and space. Swanhild stood near me, almost in arm's reach.

"We can take different paths, as at that first meeting," I murmured, half out of breath and half from an instinct of stealthiness, although no one was even close to being in hearing.

"No, I can't go now. My hands are not fit to fondle you. You see—I can't wash them clean of the slime."

"What slime?"

"Of the fish I cleaned, that you and the thane's daughter caught. Forgive me for not calling her by her given name. I should have said 'the young lady.'" All this Swanhild said in an easy tone, without a trace of spite or jealousy, and without visible change in her countenance. Strangely, I thought of a blue and utterly calm sea, yet in whose abysmal depths monsters fed, wallowed, and made strange and violent love, and volcanoes spouted all undreamed, and unknown currents ebbed and flowed.

"When will you come?" I asked, partly to bring myself back to earth after my wild fancy, partly in irrepressible longing for reassurance.

"Leif, I do not know when, if ever. Understand, I don't blame you for wooing the highborn heiress. You will certainly marry soon, I do not know whom, I only know who it will not be, and that is Swanhild, your father's thrall. Still, for the present I had better save my favors for a swain of my own station. He might be proud that the son of a great chieftain had had me first—that is the way of thralls—but I would take no satisfaction in that pride. Yes, I grant that the coarse-handed, dull-witted fellow would not care in the least whether I was a virgin; he would hardly give it a thought, but I would care about his not caring."

"Why coarse-handed and dull-witted? Many of our thralls, Gorm, for instance——"

"Only a dull-witted thrall would marry a girl like me, a comely girl, one you have called beautiful, as only a dull-witted thrall would have married Ellen, my mother."

"Swanhild, you are too old for your years!" The protest burst up out of me, unrestrainable, angry, and more outraged, not at her but at life, and ashamed.

"Leif, I aged quickly cleaning fish and gutting deer, of which I have tasted only the tripe. But you will be seeing me when you are around home. And if you don't change your mind, perhaps I will change mine. Now I must go to the spring."

She walked away, her head cocked a little as though in satisfaction.

4

Time began to fly, as always in the flush of spring, and although I often glanced into Swanhild's eyes, always she shook her head, or looked away, and gave me some other sign of refusal. She entered my mind as frequently as did Johanna, but always from a different gate to another realm of thought or feeling. Yet of the two girls I daydreamed far more about Johanna, mainly I think because daydreaming about Swanhild made me feverish and uncomfortable. On the other hand daydreams about Johanna were colored by my whole life's desires and hopes—marriage with a beautiful and gifted girl, one with whom I would quickly fall in love, a wife to be proud of, a home of my own, children, high standing in the colony, and the possession of a ship brave enough to stem the mysterious western seas. I had not suffered as much as I had expected at loss of Ellen, and now the same was true of Swanhild's absence. In the first place, my life was one of exciting activity day after day. I went to bed pleasantly tired, and toward morning Nature often relieved balked lust by strangely vivid, delicious dreams that either caused or were the result of a natural physical function. My companion in those dreams was rarely Ellen, more frequently Swanhild, and on a few occasions it was Johanna. More mysterious was an unknown maiden whose beauty I knew without ever quite seeing it clearly—very white, and whose slender neck had a lovely curve.

In high summer a halting of our catboat at Vesterbig afforded me an hour with Johanna. It passed most pleasantly, the maiden seeming greatly pleased to see me, and the distant echoes of her laughter kept me merry company on the long sail home. Meanwhile, the colonies flourished almost beyond belief. Our bulls were virile, the cows fertile, the rams Herculean in endurance, the docile ewes dropped many twins; our folk had richer feeding, except for a great scarcity of corn, than in their whole lives before; and a latecomer from Norway to Osterbig planted vegetables in a little plot, and in July harvested what made the people stare— cabbages and turnips. Another bold franklin planted barley, which rooted well but never came to seed. I knew not why unless the green stalks had been bent down so often by the hard wind that they had lost their pith.

On a night in mid-September the great chieftain Bjorn would celebrate Harvest Home and at the same time show off a new wing of what was, by Greenland standards, his stately hall. All the great thanes of the island and more than a hundred of the more rich and influential franklins were invited, along with their wives and unmarried sons and daughters, and the rumors of its grandeur, the food to be served, the drinks to be downed, and the entertainment to be provided spread far and wide. Even our thralls became excited, which touched me a little because their part in it was, at the most, vicarious—that their master and mistress and the two sons of the latter, whom they saw every day and with whom they held unequal speech, would be among the chosen. If I had been born a thrall, I thought, I would have made offerings to no God, would have cursed all Gods except gentle Kris who somehow lacked power to redeem poor folk from hunger, cold, and humiliation, even if he could save their souls from Hel—all of these I would have cursed; I would have reveled in obscenity and bloody crime, and would have robbed the rich, and never doffed my cap to any, and died young, dangling from a wolf tree.

Another rumor had gotten out, whether true or false I knew not. It was that at midnight Bjorn would revive the ancient custom of the Sweetheart Dance, in which the daughter of the house would invite her favorite suitor to be her partner; and if he accepted, and did not look away as she tendered the invitation, it was tantamount to betrothal. These two would lead the dance, but other maidens who had received proposals from various swains could make known their choice by following the leaders. It was no wonder that when the day arrived my mother, assisted by many clucking thrall women, saw to my thorough scrubbing in hot water, to the dressing of my hair with a little ambergris, and to my attire, which might have suggested, although far from equaled, that of a Scottish laird. On the contrary, Thorstein had declared he would not even attend the function. At the very last, as though to quiet Eric's protests, he consented to make a brief appearance at the banquet, since he would be chasing white bears in the region of Vesterbig that day, but he would wear his hunting clothes, with such blood, slime, and dirt as went therewith.

Our catboat was the most trig, yare, and, except for the *Narwhale* in full sail, the swiftest craft owned by Eric the Red. She was cleaned and scrubbed by the thralls until only a trace, perceptible only to delicate flaring nostrils, remained of her stout reek of fresh hides, butchered meat, seal and walrus blubber, and other and unknown aromatics. Eric, Thorhild, and I wore everyday clothes; in the chest were our fine clothes, along with some jewels for my mother's sunny hair, which sometimes she thought of giving to a Christian shrine, considering that they had been raped from a bishop's robe by Harald Bluetooth on a forgotten raid. Thorstein had preceded us in the sailing dinghy, to come and go when he pleased.

A whole long day we sailed, all of its night, and until midafternoon of the second day, before a brisk wind out of the southeast. At our arrival at Bjornhall, we were made welcome, sharing a room with only three families of great note, given fish cakes to stay our stomachs, and at sundown partook of a feast in the great hall, its floor not of packed dirt but of oaken planks planed to a smoothness suggesting ice. There were baked and broiled beef, boiled and roasted mutton, spitted venison, fried and smoked fish of a dozen sorts, and, the greatest wonder, wheat cakes made from a shipment of flour from Denmark, some to be eaten with butter, others to be dunked in broth, and the rest to be coated with

honey and costly cinnamon for a delicacy after meat. No eider-
duck eggs appeared on the long benches. Those the people had
gathered in the spring and preserved in brine had a rank taste. I
reckoned this was the first feast in the history of the island where
the main dish had not been whale and seal meat.

Along with the edibles, the finest Norway ale flowed as in
freshet, the bowls passed and refilled again and again. Yet these
great folk, chieftains and powerful franklins and their families,
with not even one freeman, were too mindful of their manners
and their dignities to quaff deeply enough to muddle their heads.
When the meal was over and the broken meats taken to Bjorn's
thralls, the people sat about the walls, many of the ladies on
benches, most on sheepskins spread on the floor, to take part in
or to watch the coming entertainment.

For this Bjorn had provided half a dozen harpists of more than
passing skill, two players of the lute, and a skillful drummer on
a drum with two skins, the like of which I had never seen. There
were no flutists, the instruments being rare in both Norway and
Iceland, and no rebec, a three-stringed instrument of which many
of us had heard but none of us had seen, which was played with a
curved bow having strings. Still it was such an assembly of musicians as could hardly be gathered in Iceland, and was a wonder in
yet new Greenland.

They played mainly old Norse country dances, with now and
then a Scottish reel or an Irish jig. Bjorn led forth his dame for
the first dance, Eric the same, and I was a little startled by the
ease and lightness of my sire's barrel-chested step; and next to
the tall flames of the oil lamps his beard was the brightest object
in the hall. At this dance, Johanna's escort was her cousin, but
she took no amorous interest in him and kept scanning the throng
of onlookers, and when her eyes met mine she gaily tossed her
head with a brief smile. When I asked her for the next dance, she
consented quickly and happily, ignoring Einer's son and another
swain who were opportuning her the same instant.

The orchestra struck up a charming tune that we all knew as
"The Hummingbird." This tiny fowl was known to visit the most
northern climes, although it eschewed Greenland and had been

greatly beloved in Norway and Ireland too. In this dance the men played the part of the birds, hovering and darting, and the maidens the flowers from which they sucked. While the girls marched back and forth, arm in arm, we swooped upon them, each choosing the flower of his choice, and instead of honey his prize was a kiss. My lips found the sweet lips of Johanna, and they seemed to me warm and responsive, and my heart leaped high.

Occasionally the dancers rested, some of them drinking ale, and in this interval some children danced with great charm. Later on, Ian sang to the strumming of a lute. As Einer's eater, his station was too low for him to be one of the guests, although the wild and irrational thought struck me that if Johanna knew his real worth, instead of its outward show, she would choose him for the Sweetheart Dance before any swain in the hall.

I danced with Johanna so frequently that it became noticeable to the crowd, and some of them nodded to one another and smiled and looked knowingly. She was the gayest of the gay, her laughter the most ringing, and during sweet passages of the music when we chanced to be dancing face to face with both hands joined, her expression was tender between spells of mirth. If she was aware of Thorstein's absence she gave no sign of it, and truly I thought she had not observed the fact, which delighted my heart.

There occurred an interval in which the musicians rested, and the people sang together. They sang "Wind from the South, Blow Us Home" and "A Maiden Waiting in her Green Bower," both great favorites of the Old Norse, and "My Bridget Standing in the Door," which the Irish loved. Once an old reprobate started a somewhat ribald song, with a lively tune, about merry May when all the houses resounded with the squalls of newborn infants, the point being plainly made that usually the Viking fleets had hove home in the previous October. The ladies did not join in this song, but blushed prettily, and the men bawled it forth.

A certain excitement, other than that of festivity, had spread through the throng during this interval of singing. Well they knew that at its close the musicians would play "Sweetheart's Choice," when Johanna would choose a partner to lead the dance.

And they were resuming their chairs and some were tuning their instruments when a latecomer arrived at the feast. It was Thorstein.

He had not quite kept his oath to wear his grease-smeared hunting clothes. True, he wore hair-seal pants, but these were new and snow white, and black mukluks that Ugruk had taught the people how to make, but his woolen shirt was bright red, such as great chieftains had worn in Norway, and about his neck he had fastened a kind of scarf of ermine skins. A handsome fellow anyway, tonight he surpassed himself. He greeted friends with an air of graceful confidence, his large eyes shone, and he was the mirror of young manliness, suppleness, virility, and prowess. My consolation was that Johanna shot him one glance of hot anger, threw up her head as though in disdain, and then ignored him.

The musicians took longer than usual to get settled, tune their instruments, and put them in position to play. Utter silence held the crowd of onlookers. At last the drummer beat a little roll with his two sticks and the lovely melody began to peal forth. I knew enough music to appreciate its strange structure—each verse having four very short lines, the last ending with a deep sad note, to be followed by a roll of drums. Throughout the first verse, Johanna did not leave her seat. During the second she started toward a little cluster of swains, all of whom had sweethearts in the gathering, and in whose front rank I stood. I thought that her eyes were fixed on mine. She walked slowly, but with not notable grace. Her head was high, her fair hair glimmering in the lamplight, her eyes big.

But she paused and hesitated briefly when about twenty feet from me, then turned sharply to the right. Quickly she made her way to Thorstein, on whose lips was a small smile.

"Thorstein, son of Eric, will you lead this dance with me?" she asked, her clear voice carrying well.

"With great pleasure," he replied, offering her his arm.

They walked to the center of the hall. Other maidens came up to take the arms of their sweethearts and fall in behind the leaders; in only a moment or two I stood alone except for a gawky fellow, well-born but graceless, dim-sighted if not dim-witted, who was often the butt of rude jokes. I felt a deep and powerful longing to draw back and half-hide myself among the onlookers. I ached to bow my head, and I yearned to set my lips in a fixed smile. None of these things did I do, because of forbid-dance decreed by my soul. I kept my position, I held my head high, my face remained grave.

The dance was most charming, I told myself. The men stood in a row, about six feet apart, facing their partners. During every verse the men and maids took three sideways steps, back and forth, and then as the instruments fell silent and the drums rolled, they danced forward to kiss their partners. The rule was that the kisses must last as long as the drumbeat. This period lengthened with the close of each verse, and after the last verse the beat be-came ecstatic, lasting a full minute.

I saw the color rise in Johanna's face, and although her arms hung at her sides her fingers spread, and I believed that these two had exchanged such kisses many times before, and I had served no better than to be Thorstein's foil.

A great cheering followed the close of the dance, and not un-observed, indeed with no few beady-looking eyes watching me closely, I went out into the cool, moist, spring night. A full moon, having climbed to its very zenith, glanced disinterestedly down, for little it made reply to the watchings and dreamings of us earth folk; and that night it looked to be fashioned of ice. Yet the moon was my only company, along with a few stars all but eclipsed by its luminousness, and I made my way to the strand and looked out over the hushed fiord under its sheen of moon-light.

"I will never marry," I told myself. "If I can regain Swanhild, I will keep her as long as she is passionate and beautiful, or until I tire of her. If I cannot regain her, or do not want her, I will be true to my Swan Maiden and fly with a great wing of cloth to her farthermost haunts, and I will eat the daft fish and lie with my beloved on her own white raiment under yon smirking moon, and make divine love with her, and the moon in her high, cold sky will envy me instead of mock me."

But I invoked no Gods, I swore no oath, for well I knew, at last, that no man is master of his destiny, and although he may struggle bravely against his fate, he is forever vanquished.

CHAPTER TEN

A FAREWELL TO TWO LOVES

I

The autumn sped, the last birch leaf fluttered from its lean and empty bough, the winds shrilled, the meadow ponds began to freeze, the waterfowl departed in clamoring flocks, and the cold that was the primal element of Greenland gripped the land.

On the first day of April, before the Nordrseta men took their first stand to sea, when the ice had not yet gone out of our river and the ice of the fiord had only begun to break up, and when only the silver gulls and a few other hardy waterfowl such as coots, loons, and scattered flocks of eider ducks had ventured to our cold shores, I noticed a change in Swanhild's behavior toward me.

For three days it was no more than an increasing civility in the few remarks she made to me. Her eyes still looked hot and angry; there was no sweetness on her lips. But on the fourth day she followed me when I went to air my heavy sheepskin bedrobe on a line of whaleskin.

"You'll need that for many nights to come," she told me in a most forthright way with almost motherly solicitude. "Warm weather's a long way off."

"The sunlight is pleasant and warm," I reminded her.

"Why, the marmots have not yet come out of their holes. If any of them spent the winter in the Vixen's Den, they are still sound asleep. It would have been a good place for them to spend the winter. There was no one to disturb them."

"You are right about that, Swanhild."

"I had no right to be angry about your courting the great Bjorn's daughter. You had your fortune to make, as well as to found a family, and a thrall girl couldn't stand in your way. Anyhow I knew you'd not get her. I knew that Thorstein and she were lovers."

"How could you know?"

"My mother, Ellen, told me. I do not know how she found out, except that she finds out everything. That wasn't what I started to say. I suppose Vixen's Den is as cold as an iceberg. Gluttons have probably got in and torn up the bed——" She paused on a note of interrogation.

"I doubt it. There was no food to attract them there. Would you like to go and see how the bleak little hole is getting along?"

"Yes. Tomorrow I've been told to look for tracks for a lost bullock. If you want to know what I think, he smelled a reindeer hind in heat. There's not as much difference between a bull and a doe as between Eric's son and Horkel's daughter. I'm going to start out about an hour after sunrise. My search will take me past Vixen's Den."

My long-sluggish blood made a great leap.

"Stop and look in, will you, Swanhild?"

"I'd do more than that. I'll wait awhile if need be."

The sun was just topping the eastern highlands when I made my way to Vixen's Den. The willow growth was somewhat thicker across the path, but this would not have halted a wolf, let alone a wolverine, that might have caught a faint whiff of mutton fat from the sheepskins or deer oil from the reindeer robe, so I pushed my way in with deep misgivings of what I would find. To my amazed delight, the crypt was just as I had left it, the bed neatly made, the eider-down pillow in place, the oil lamp still half-full. If I had thought of the seal oil we had left in the lamp I would have been certain of rampage. We could not leave a slaughtered seal on the beach for a single night without the risk of its being torn by the white fangs of the wild hunters. But now, on second thought, the idea struck me that the lamp had repelled night prowlers instead of attracted them, because it had smelled of burned oil as well as fresh, and that smell was one that the beasts associated with human habitation. Man had already made his mark in Greenland. Somehow he had invoked a deep and chilling awe in wild hearts. In any case foxes and, I thought, gluttons hunted mainly by sight and sound rather than smell; the entrance to the silent crypt had been well screened; and in mild winters, when other game was plentiful, keen-nosed wolves were as fearful of human smells as they were reckless of them in starving times of hard winters.

I made a fire with my drill and lighted the lamp. How wonderfully it exuded warmth in the small enclosure! My blood heated as my body warmed and I listened as sharply as any fox for a rustle of branches. When soon I heard it, and the rustle of dead willow leaves under nearing feet, I was sitting on the bed, wearing my heavy jacket, with none of my buckles or buttons hard to undo. Swanhild passed the barrier of thickets and crouched in the low arch. At once the low, bright flame of the oil lamp picked up the strands of red in her bright yellow hair, and itself being yellow it cast a kind of luminousness about her head as though she wore a halo like those worn by my mother's saints.

Nothing else of or about Swanhild was saintly-looking, except possibly the dim luminescence of her eyes. The awkward movements of coming through the low passage she made voluptuous and exciting. Her vivid face would be termed pretty by our common folk; our more discerning would call it beautiful; just now, as she emerged from the gloom of the entrance into the full glimmer of the lamp, it could suggest the face of a sea witch, swimming up from her dim and greenly tinted chambers, and giving a lubber on a codfish boat one clear glimpse of her countenance. My mother sometimes used the word "diabolic" to suggest something or someone belonging to the Devil, as opposed to all good things that belonged to Kris. I felt a fool for having such thoughts about this earthy, open-faced, frank-speaking, shapely thrall girl.

She gave me a faint smile, somehow lascivious, and immediately lay down where she had lain at our last close meeting, her breast against mine, her lips and throat and breast in my easy reach. Then without my invitation, except the parting of my lips, she began to explore my mouth with her warm and silken tongue, a long and detailed and luxurious search, her color meanwhile rising, her breath growing short and her eyes most strangely darkening. Her quest ended with a long tremor of her whole body, during which I could only hold her close.

I spoke at last, under great strain. "Let us both undress and get between the covers."

"I must not do that now. But you can untie all the thongs and loosen all the belts and buttons, yours and mine, and make love to me in any way you wish except the whole way as you did with my mother, Ellen. Leif, do not break my maidenhead. This only I withhold from you now and perhaps always. It is beating the devil around the bush—the holy father at Limerick says so— I may be cheating myself for nothing. Still be satisfied with that for now. I will *make* you satisfied. . . ."

Her words trailed away into a gasp as she slipped her hand under my belt. With her left hand she grasped my hand with great strength and guided it to gratify her craving. I was not so innocent as to think that this kind of dalliance was anything un- usual between young men and women, or even boys and girls. Since the race began, it had served the need of human beings in straitened circumstances. Yet the thought struck me that Swan- hild's skill at arousing me to ever higher fever was either taught her by a witch or by experience for which I could not account; and also that her element was fire. In a few minutes we lay half-swooning in each other's arms.

She rose with her usual briskness, her fingers flying over her raiment. Then she fixed her eyes on mine with a curious in- tensity.

"Was I not a good substitute for my mother, Ellen?" she asked.

"You are not a substitute for anyone. I want you for yourself."

"Are you as sorry as you were that you didn't get the lady Johanna?"

"No. And I never was very sorry, except for Thorstein's beating me."

"I, a thrall girl, making up in some measure not only for Ellen but for a thane's daughter?"

"You were not jealous of either, so why do you ask?"

"I was not jealous of Johanna. I might as well be jealous of Queen Mab. But I was desperately jealous of Ellen. I knew be- fore you did—almost as soon as she knew herself—that she in- tended to get you. I was too young to do anything about it—

except to kiss you in the boat that day, a kiss you wouldn't forget. Also, I knew she couldn't keep you long. She was too old for you."

"Swanhild, you've asked me some intimate questions. I'll ask you one. Do you love your mother, Ellen?"

Her color heightened in the lamplight. "I certainly don't hate her. Have I ever given sign of that?"

"No——"

"I love her, but I haven't much respect for her. She has great desires but no strength of will to carry them out. I'm already stronger than she is. When I took you away from her, she fought no more than a sheep fights a wolf."

"When you——" And I stammered, because although I had heard her plainly I could not believe my ears.

"I told her she was too old for you and if she didn't stop meeting you I'd tell Horkel. She should have dared me to tell him. He wouldn't have done anything. Then at first she wouldn't tell me where you two met—never guessing that I had spied on her and already knew—in fact had found the grotto and went in and saw the bed. But she gave up on this too. She decided it was better that she send me to carry you a message—knowing well what would happen. Well, you can say I didn't do anything about Johanna. In the first place I knew she wanted Thorstein and in the second place I couldn't do anything anyway—my hands are chained by a thrall's chains. Some day——" Then she paused.

"What about some day?"

"I really didn't mean that. A great many things are going to happen—I feel it in my bones—a volcano may erupt and we may all die in the boiling lava. I must go now. If you like, I'll meet you here the day after tomorrow at the same time. You probably won't be going hunting before then."

"Why not tomorrow? It's a three-man crew and they may make a short trip."

"I was hoping you'd say that. You've got more of Eric the Red in you than people would ever guess when you tootle on a flute. You don't know how glad I am."

I had a feeling that there was ambiguity in this last remark, but I could not find it or make any sense of my hazy thoughts; and in a moment I saw her moving jauntily across the grassy meadow as though in search of a lost bullock.

2

The next few years were memorable for countless small events and became impossible to forget because of two great events.

In the early summer of the year following Swanhild's and my reunion, Thorhall had to resign his leadership of our own hunting party to help Eric make records and ship that part of the kill of the whole body of Nordrseta men which was suitable and valuable for export, and to distribute the net returns to the various boats. To round out our crew of five, which we had found a good working number, he as the boat owner appointed the freeman Starkad, who had shown his mettle when eight of the *Narwhale's* crew had been marooned that terrible winter in a turf house at Ericsfiord. However, since Starkad had not had nearly as much experience as the rest of us in hunting and trapping, he did not appoint him master.

"The fact is, I'm going to decide that matter by vote," Thorhall told us. "'Twould not be the way to do it in the old country, and 'twould be a new thing in Iceland, but we're way out westward, where old customs are breaking down and new ones being established, and even the right to rule because of birth rather than ability is being questioned. I own this catboat but Eric is my liege lord. If we were in Norway, I would hold it my duty to appoint Thorstein, Eric's elder son, captain of this boat and leader of this party. As it is, I want a fair vote. This means that Starkad is exempt, because he is a newcomer and has had no experience with us on which to base his judgment. Ugruk too cannot vote because we all know he is Leif's man. That leaves only Thorstein, Leif, and Gorm, not counting me if I want to put in my oar. Gorm, would you accept the appointment if Eric's sons wish to give it to you?"

"No, sir, I am a thrall, not in the habit of command, and also I am too old."

"That last I doubt. Aiming at keeping a happy ship, I'll ask Thorstein and Leif a question. Thorstein, will you yield to Leif?"

Thorstein hesitated briefly. I took it he was thinking of his last great triumph over me, the winning of the prize of the colonies, Johanna, for whom he was building a great hall to rival Eric's, and thought it possible that he would do the generous, lordly, and certainly handsome thing. But I had not reckoned on Thorstein's pride in his prowess in many pursuits more than in the pursuit of woman.

"I am the best hunter at sea and I think the best navigator," he answered in quiet tones. "No, I will not yield."

"What do you say, Leif? Will you yield to Thorstein?"

"I've never yielded anything to Thorstein, without a fight, and do not intend to do so now."

"Gorm, name whom you want for captain."

"I agree with my lord Thorstein that he is the best hunter at sea, but I doubt if he's the best navigator, and Leif is the better hunter on land. I choose Leif."

Thorhall's face was a study. Finally he spoke briskly. "One vote is not enough to settle the issue for the good of all; hence I'll cast my vote. What's good enough for tough old Gorm is good enough for me. Leif, you're the new captain."

"That settles it," Thorstein remarked with evident good nature. And truly it did settle the matter, as far as Thorstein's behavior could reveal. He never questioned my decisions; on the occasional times I need give him direct orders, he obeyed them cheerfully. If he had thought to give me enough rope to hang myself—a terse and useful expression that the Norse had adopted during their stay in England—he had reckoned wrongly. I scratched my head often enough to kill a whole colony of lice, provided I had not been already ridden of the pests by my mother's strict command, in order to choose the best hunting ground on land and sea. By harkening to Ugruk's counsel, and questioning him about Innuit ways of laying snares, our boat kept its leadership of the hunting fleet, not only in taking meat but in harvesting valuables for export, such as ivory and hides and fur.

Some of these goods were traded in English and European ports for lumber, grain, and other staples scarce or unobtainable in Greenland. But with the growth of the colonies, the increase of the herds, the building of better houses, and the giving of feasts at the various halls, rich folk who owned hunting boats, and even big ships fitted out for whale, walrus, and seal hunting, began to import luxuries. Instead of skins, carpets covered the floors of the great halls; on fine occasions all the chieftain families and the richer franklins wore fine raiment; ale was a commonplace at our festivals and French wine not rare at funeral and wedding feasts. Perhaps the surest sign of Greenland's growing importance as a supplier of furs, ivory, seal tar, whale oil, whalebone, and whale rope, and as a market for the good things of Europe, was the interest King Haakon was taking in our affairs. Now and then he sent presents to our great chieftains, and Eric was the recipient of a scroll inscribed in Latin, of which Ian could make sense. Therein the king expressed his high regard for Greenland folk, wished them increased prosperity, and congratulated his "faithful ally," Eric the Red, on his leadership.

Eric immediately had the parchment beautifully framed in ivory to hang in his mead hall. Here it was displayed to all visitors, while Eric pretended to read it aloud, he having learned by heart Ian's rough translation.

An increasing amount of our exports were not traded but sold for silver shillings, a handy monetary unit throughout western Europe. Whenever I could I thus disposed of my share in the catch of our party, about one-twelfth part of its whole; and my hoard grew surely but plagued slowly. Still, it seemed to be nearing the mark whereby the great dream of my life might come true.

One summer night, when he was warmed by ale, and his beard glinted in sun rays pouring through an open window, I made bold to approach Eric on this matter. It was a blunt approach, which I had found to be likelier of success than a meandering one.

"Eric, my father, for what sum in shillings will you rent me the *Narwhale* for a full year?"

He drained his cup and wiped his beard, seemingly intent upon these mundane matters, but I knew by the shine of his green eyes that his utmost attention was caught.

"As she is, you mean? You to victual her, pay the crew, and replace all the gear that you lose or wear out?"

"Yes, although I'd let some of the hands go and mark on others to take their places."

"What if you should sink her?"

"In that case, she'd be sunk with all hands."

"Not necessarily with all hands. If you are close to shore, I reckon most of you could get off in the longboat. Of course if you were far and away on some unknown sea——" And I had seen this expression on his face a hundred times, especially when, fishing at our river mouth, he had felt a fish nibble his bait.

"We would run no risks that we could help."

"Perhaps your whole plan is one big risk. What is it, if you don't mind telling me? I certainly won't rent you my ship for any sum until I know."

"I want to follow in your footsteps, my father, Eric. You sailed westward in search of new lands. I want to do the same."

"I don't think you'll find any. You would find instead the Poison Sea that goes over the brink into Hel. No, I'll not rent my good ship. But if you can raise the money, I'll sell her to you."

"How much money?"

"A modest sum, considering her stoutness. Also, I'd be taking into consideration that you supplied the *Narwhale* horn that brought her luck and honored her name. I'd not sell her at all except I'm of a mind to build a bigger ship, with a great deal more cargo space, for after seven years we're only beginning to perceive the richness of these lands and waters in fur, oil, and ivory. I'll sell you the *Narwhale*, including the tusk, for an even thousand shillings."

"Where in the name of Odin would I get a thousand shillings? That's equivalent to five hundred walrus tusks."

"Oh, you might find them, or their worth in gold, in some dark green sea cave where a mermaid has brought you. If you want her at that price I'll hold her for you a reasonable time."

"I accept. If you give me enough time, I'll bring you the thousand shillings."

It must have been that my voice carried conviction, as I wished, although if Eric could have gazed into my heart he would have seen it cold and fainting except for one small flame of hope. He could not so gaze. He had never been able to do what my mother, Thorhild, did without trying. Hence the expression on my father's face was one of struggle between comforting disbelief and a burning, itching belief. I left him tugging his beard.

3

My little flame of hope was a flickering flame, but its guttering was diminished when I went forth from the sheltered room into the windy night, out of the sight of Eric's green eyes and his barrel chest. Now I could look up to the stars, most of them dim as my dream, but some of them brightly burning as beacon fires, perhaps signaling some great secret. My mind sped easily to Minin, a Swan Maiden. I touched the feather that I wore in my cap, still as beautiful, as snow white, and as luxuriant as when I had picked it up from the floor of the ice palace. If her remote and mysterious world could again merge with my familiar world— if again we could meet, if again we could re-enact the blood rite— if we could do more than that to become interbound—she would tell me to look under a certain rock, or among the roots of an ancient dwarf-birch tree, or in a certain marmot hole on the mountainside, and there I would find a thousand silver shillings as bright as her eyes.

The last I had seen of her she had been winging away with a mournful cry. Perhaps she told me in that cry I would never see her again. Perhaps I never did see her again, but it so happened that she came near me once again, or it so happened that I believed she did so.

The weather that winter day was the kind we dreaded most— no air stirring, the sky gray-looking above an icy haze, no sound out-of-doors, and the cold striking as deep as we eight pioneers could remember from that first and terrible winter. In the warmest rooms of the houses the oil lamps burned at full wick without disseminating heat in the cold corners. When a door was opened to the entrance passage the moisture in the room turned instantly to mystic clouds that darted and danced like ghosts celebrating some great revelry in a churchyard. If water were poured slowly from a jug onto the snow, it turned to slush before it hit, then changed instantly to ice. A bucket of water brought from the hot spring had a sheath of ice before it could reach the kitchen.

In the dark noon I had a hankering to visit the hot spring. I could recite a good enough reason—to pluck the feathers from a long-hung goose frozen so hard that we could not even gut her without chopping her open with an ax, and which Ugruk and I, living together in a warm, well-built house of turf, wanted for our dinner, along with imported barley cakes soaked in her plenteous fat. But I had another reason not so easy to recite nor of which to make sense—I wanted to see with my own eyes and feel through my own skin some other element than cold, that the whole earth had not changed to a block of ice, and at the same time I was wondering how quickly, and with what phenomenon, its steam would turn into ice crystals. Leaving Ugruk shaping a new bow out of a fine piece of imported ewe wood, I put on my most cold-resistant attire—hair-seal pants and long shirt over fawnskin underwear made for me by my mother, Thorhild, and over all this an Innuit-style parka, with a hood lined with glutton fur and thrusting forward from the face to form a pocket of warmed breath to prevent my face from freezing. Long gloves of fox fur protected my hands and wrists.

Still I felt the savage bite of the cold as soon as I emerged from the passage. It was as though it made entrance through the finest seams of my garments—or, more truly, tiny precious puffs of my body heat escaped through these seams. Still by walking as briskly as I dared down the hard-packed snowpath, I became only uncomfortably cool, not chilled through. On arriving at the pool I found that I could not reach its fluid center because the shallow margins were frozen solid, the deeper water was sheathed with ice, and only a ring of about ten feet in diameter, immediately above the bubbling upflow of water usually scalding hot, remained open.

If it gave forth any steam, this was immediately changed to ice crystals invisibly small that disappeared in a kind of dim haze, which we called ice smoke for want of a better word, that over-hung the snow on days of extreme cold.

Some two hundred yards distant I noticed a plank about twelve feet long and a foot wide lying on the snow. It had been brought there to bridge a small bog in which, in warm weather, our thralls, making for the cool but not icy spring to get water or wash cloth-ing, had sunk almost to their knees. The project had been aban-doned just before the freeze-up, the path now encircling the bog; but no one had reclaimed the plank and I thought I could lay it on the thin ice close to the fluid center of the pool and thus cross on it without risk of breaking through and wetting my mukluks. The snow had been wind-packed so solidly that I could traverse it without skis or snowshoes.

Hazy in my head was the inkling that this effort was not worth making. Ugruk and I could boil enough water over our seal-oil cooking lamp to thaw my frozen goose. It might be that I felt a distinct inclination, perhaps even a premonition, against the brief sally away from the spring and the well-trodden path; but if so I ignored it, if for no other reason than a native stubbornness whereby it is difficult for me to abandon even trivial enterprises which I had willed. So I set forth, and I had gone a little more than half the distance to the plank when the Frost Giant sneezed.

The phenomenon began the same as on previous occasions—a gust of wind like massed javelins hurled across the snow. An instant later my eyes were darkened, my whole landscape lost, in a dense cloud of minute ice crystals. I too was instantly and com-pletely lost. Instinctively I had turned my back to the icy blast to protect my face, and now I knew not whether I had turned right or left, hence the pool and the well-trodden path to shelter might be either at my right or my left hand. All I could do was crouch down, my face in my arms, to breathe in as few as possible of the deadly crystals. The blind darkness held a full minute before I thought it began to dim a little and the light from our low, weak sun was coming back.

Then the Frost Giant sneezed again. Then I remembered a

question that Gorm had one day asked in our warm shelter during our first winter of exile—what would happen to a man or a party of men in the frozen wastes if the Giant kept on sneezing? The answer could be made in one word—*death*.

It was a mighty word in any language, in the depths of every soul. The thing itself was exactly as common as birth, but the two did not cancel out each other because of an interval of time between the latter and the former, and in that interval there came into being an awareness of self, perhaps of what men call the soul; and although proud men may laugh at death, or confront it with defiance, or fight it in final fury, still it remained the salient and most solemn fact of life. The blind cloud that enveloped all had not even started to fade when again rushed the bitter blast. My blindness was no greater than before because it was already absolute. But my mind was greatly darkened, looking in vain for any glimmer of hope, only to find none.

I could not backtrack to the spring. My feet on the ice-hard snow had left no distinct prints; the faint impression I could not see or even feel with my mittened hands. There was already a sharp pain in the top of my chest. Well I knew what was happening within: the snow crystals I was breathing were melting, sucking heat from my vitals, and in a matter of minutes I would be unable to breathe at all.

I wanted an enemy that I could fight. If my attacker were a pack of wolves I could fight them in a frenzy of rage and hate, and perhaps win: here there was nothing but deadly darkness. Holding hard to my sense of identity, a wild, strange thought flashed through my mind in a zigzag course as lightning flashes through crowds. There was no enemy here which I could combat, there was only blindness and immobility, but there might be a friend nearby.

Of course I thought first of Ugruk. Then the sickening remembrance hit me that I had gone out the door without telling him my destination. Then and there my mind turned a little corner, and again I stood at the threshold of some other world, what the Old Norse called the Well of Weird, as when flame flickers over valley and hill, and the air is strange in the nostrils, and the dead rise from their mossy graves.

"If you ever need me, call my name, and I will come."

So I shouted, "Minin! Minin!" as loudly as my throat, half-choked with burning ice, could emit sound.

And almost instantly I heard a faint fluttering noise that swiftly loudened, and I thought it was made by the swift, white, beating pinions of a swan.

As though in reply, the winged invisible creature uttered a note as beautiful as low C sounded on a flute, although much stronger, and as clear as the ring of a perfect gong.

"I can't see you, Minin. Light in the open water of the hot spring with a loud splash, and continue to call."

There came a quickening of the beating pinions, then the sound died as my winged visitor began to glide. I knew she was gliding downward in a long slant. A second or two later I heard a loud splash, and then once more the gonglike trumpet sound. I started toward it across the invisible snow. The call grew louder, clearer, more beautiful, more moving. Tears filled my blind eyes, but these did not matter, for these quickly began to freeze and I blinked them away. And soon I was near enough the spring to feel a barely perceptible warmth. Only a moment later I stumbled into the deeply worn path through the snow, a straight path from the spring to the home acre; and I knew that I was saved.

"Minin! Minin!" I called. "Come to me!"

And I heard the first hard beating of her wings, and I thought she was answering my plea, but instead the sound climbed steeply and began to dim. Once more she uttered her deep-throated, far-carrying, lovely cry, ending in a quavering wail. It came to me with great sorrow that this was her farewell forever to her mortal lover.

4

The air had cleared before I gained our turf house; and in the still and awful cold I heard Ugruk shouting my name. I soon caught sight of him, making toward Starkad's house. Then I remembered saying about mid-morning that I intended to go there, to get some lamp wick, of which Starkad's wife was the best weaver in the colony. When he heard my full-throated call, and then turned and saw me standing strong and well, it must be that the sudden riddance of his terrors undermined his spirit in some way, for he threw his arms wide and then toppled in the snow. I hastened toward him as fast as I dared but before I had taken a hundred steps he had revived and was sitting up. When I reached him he looked as usual except for the snow sticking to his garments, his eyes bright slits between the lids, and what I took for an imitation, not the real thing, of his customary wide smile.

"Why you go where you not say you go?" he asked, not with anger but with righteous severity.

"Forgive me, Ugruk. I had forgotten about going to Starkad's and I went to the hot spring."

"How you find your way back? Were you on path?"

"I got on it, in a little while." For I had decided against telling Ugruk or anyone about my winged visitor. He believed a great number of odd things, one being that spirits lived in big stones, and these caused them to move a little or roll when the ground shifted a little in times of heavy rain or deep frost. These spirits were friendly or inimical to man according to whether he had inadvertently pleased or offended them. Every beast, bird, bush, and cloud had its own spirit, and before he killed an animal or cut down a tree he touched an amulet he wore on a cord about his neck, whispering something which I thought was an incantation rather than a prayer. The idea of Gods as we Norse conceived them could not cross his mind. After death there was no reward for good deeds or punishment for evil deeds; all the dead ones departed immediately to some land of ever feasting, where seas and rivers never froze and game was plentiful, although sometimes they returned for brief visits and appeared to living people in dreams. The Innuit language had no word for God, only the names of spirits of various sorts. Occasionally an Innuit had a guardian spirit but this was usually a monstrous being, an eight-legged bear or a two-headed reindeer whom he vaguely glimpsed in the twilight but with which he rarely attempted to communicate. The shamans, who seemed to be a sort of priest, knew spells and magical procedures that could change the weather, bring salmon up a river, or deer to a crossing; but these things were affected directly by charms rather than through the offices of any God. The Innuits seemed to have a moral law against stealing and seemed not to know how to lie. I believed that they strangled old people who were tired of living and that they exposed unwanted babies, but they would divide their last mess of seal meat with a stranger. Apparently they had no rules regarding sexual behavior and I gathered from Ugruk that sexual love played a minor part in Innuit lives compared to family love and love born of companionship. Ugruk seemed possessed by an awed adoration of Thorhild, my mother, but if he ever yearned for a woman of his own he never told me so.

He would have been perfectly agreeable to giving me his share of the fur and ivory catch made by our boat. At my persuasion he arranged for the ship captains to buy him articles in which I thought he would take pleasure, such as knives made of steel wonderfully forged in Toledo, steel needles to replace whalebone needles, iron heads for his harpoons, a copper vessel that cooked meat more quickly than his soapstone pot, and a lute from Granada on which he learned to pluck a series of sounds pleasing to his ear, perhaps because they were reminiscent of Innuit chanting or work chanteys, although I could not call them tunes. Once he placed an order with the captain of Einer's ship, of which I knew nothing, which was more costly than the total of his other foreign spendings. I saw it only when, grinning widely and his long eyes gleaming, he presented my mother with a bulky bundle that disclosed a magnificent cape of ermine skins he had furnished, the black tails interworked with the snow-white pelts, all in all as magnificent and as royal-looking as any robe worn by Hugh Capet's queen.

"But how did Captain Holcar get it out of Rouen?" my mother asked. "Why wasn't he put in jail? Ermine is a royal fur. Only kings and queens and great dukes and duchesses are allowed to wear it."

"Cap'n Holcar tell the cloak maker it was for the Queen of Greenland! He no ask any more questions."

With the most lovely smile my mother approached Ugruk and touched the end of his nose with hers. The Innuit was so deeply moved that he had to straighten his back and march out without another word.

5

This happy event took place in high summer. In the following spring another kind of event came to pass. There were no signs to presage it; I had not been plagued by evil dreams; all was well with the people; I had put by for a time, but never for a moment renounced, my dream of a great voyage westward. Ugruk's spirits seemed a little less buoyant than usual, although he did not know why; and I missed hearing his laughter roaring forth as frequently as before. The spring had broken early, the grass was already thrusting up thick and green; the bags of the cattle almost overflowed. Although I never for a moment divined the fact, I was about to learn one of the most cruel lessons that life teaches.

On warm, bright mornings my mother, Thorhild, liked to make her roundabout way to the top of a considerable cliff that overhung the fiord. Once this had been a rookery for seafowls, probably terns, and a rich deposit of dung still caused wild flowers to blossom there in great number and varied color. Fireweed, geraniums, bluebells, and immense violets were to be seen there, perhaps because the cliff top was sheltered by higher ground behind it from the icy blasts off the ice sheet. Some of these my mother liked to gather; and about a month after the spring solstice she went there, carrying a basket, intending to decorate the table and the rooms of Ericshall in honor of the Christian feast called Easter. It happened that Ugruk saw her set forth. She had waved to him and he had answered by raising both arms, an Aleut salutation the exact meaning of which he had never been able to tell me.

About two hours before noon he had walked up the strand to see to the laying of stones to entice eider ducks into building nests. He had been gone not more than half an hour when I saw him running toward me, as I sat fleshing some foxskins taken on a hunting cruise from which we had both returned the preceding evening. I rose and ran to meet Ugruk, whose pale face was wet with sweat and his dark eyes dimmed by some dreadful vision. He could hardly speak.

"I no can see Thorhild!" he burst out.

"She's probably on her way home——"

"No, she always stay longer than this. She look at flowers, and pick some, and walk around and smell. Sometimes she bend down to touch flower, but no pick. I look up, from where I lay stones, and I saw her, the sunlight on her hair. I lay three more nests, and look again, and I no see her. Ugruk stare and stare, and no see her anywhere. My heart go thump, thump, and I no catch breath. Then Ugruk think, he run across strands and look for her, then remember deep sand and broken rock where he no can run, and he better come here, and Leif, Ugruk go same way as Thorhild go. Maybe we meet her, maybe she all right. But if she slip on wet grass and fall off cliff——"

Ugruk's eyes rounded in horror. In a moment we were both running, as fast as we could, short of quick exhaustion, up the path habitually followed on her morning walks. Occasionally we could see up long reaches, bleakly empty, and often it wound around the bases of hills and crossed valleys, and in these places we might at any moment see her bright head, and the ache in our hearts would be cured.

We came in clear sight of the cliff. I had never taken much notice of its height, fully a hundred feet, and its precipitate side. Indeed it leaned outward a little, and my feeble heart sickened even more that I had never warned my mother of its danger. She would have heeded me, for although she was a confident woman, paying little attention to risks she could not help but run, she would have treasured and remembered my concern for her, for, like all women who deeply loved, she honored and never forgot love given in return.

She was not on the cliff top and we had not met her on the path. I had only one hope left, that she had descended and gone down into some little hollow or glen to look at something that had attracted her attention. That hope was short-lived.

Ugruk grunted and touched my arm.

"Leif! Leif! There is something lying at the foot of the cliff. It looks too small to be a body, yet it is green, and Thorhild wore a green dress. Can you see it? It isn't a body, is it? Speak truth to Ugruk, even if he dies!"

"Yes, it's my mother's body."

It lay perfectly still. Neither Ugruk nor I ran to it; we only walked at a fast pace, and I know not why, except that a certain knowledge in our minds and hearts and souls told us that there was no use to run, and our enfeebled hearts must not be put to this needless strain. In a minute or so we came upon the scene of my mother's death. She bore no visible wound, her clothes were not even torn; very plainly she had fallen clear to the rocky floor of the glen. But her head was twisted on her neck, her eyes were open and sightless, her lips could no longer curl in lovely smiles, and her face no longer reflected her gay, stalwart, compassionate person. Instead it wore the mask of death, strangely like an infinity of others, the curtain that the Gods drop to show that a unique play, performed on the rim of the gulf of death for a shorter or a longer time—a miracle play in a way of speaking, wherein a quantity of clay is breathed upon so that it breathes, toils, loves, hates, laughs, or weeps, and sometimes makes lovely music—has now ended.

I went to Ugruk and threw my arm about his shoulders. He burst into piteous tears and clutched my hand in both of his. How long we stood thus I know not. But a horrid thought was stealing through my brain, slowly but with stubborn insistence, and at last I had no choice but to break our silence.

"Ugruk, are you fit to climb the cliff?"

"Yes, my brother Leif. It is easy to climb by taking up the ridge."

"I will stay with my mother's body. You look at the ground, especially at the place she fell. Sometimes when I play my flute it seems as though no evil has ever come to Greenland, that it could not make its way here over the broad seas, and if it did, it would wither away in the presence of the mighty mountains and the icecap and these unseen and undreamed works of the Gods; but that was a vain illusion. Wherever people go, evil goes with them. It is the nature of evil to hate good—and Thorhild, my mother, was a good woman, whom evil could not reach as long as she lived. Go, and look closely, and then come back and tell me what you see."

He departed at once, and I thought of my mother's spirit, and although I had never prayed to any kind of God—for it is not in the Old Norse heart to ask favors except strength to look their fates in the face—I prayed to that lovely spirit, so lately departed hence that it had not yet gone far, that I had sent Ugruk on a fool's errand.

I saw Ugruk gain the top, then walk about placing his feet with the utmost care, his gaze fixed on the ground. Near the edge of the cliff I saw him get down on his hands and knees, his fingers probing in his fore. Then I saw him rise and begin his descent, carrying a basket such as our women weave of willow withes. When he joined me, I saw that it was half-full of flowers, carefully picked, then laid so they would not be bruised, and among them were wild geraniums, bluebells, big violets, and blazing fireweed.

"I no find any footprints but Thorhild's."

"Thank the Gods!"

"Yet Ugruk see where grass and flowers mashed down, one time a bed of what you call 'em—violets—mashed down and crushed in two places by someone's foot. Maybe Thorhild did it if she was looking at other flowers a little way ahead, but it no like Thorhild to hurt any flower."

"Ugruk, you speak the truth. It would not be like Thorhild to tread down flowers. I have taken a deep chill. My blood is almost too cold and torpid to flow. I dread what you will say next."

"If someone wore fawnskin slippers under mukluks, and took mukluks off, he no make any tracks," Ugruk went on.

"Yes."

"Ugruk find basket about four feet from brink? Why she set it down there, or did Thorhild drop it? From there to edge Ugruk look and look, and he see where Thorhild made one deep track."

"The kind she would make if she was trying to brace herself?"

"That what Ugruk think, but he not know."

"Was the grass wet and slippery?"

"Yes, and she slope a little downhill. If Thorhild lose her balance about four feet from edge, she made track like that to try keep from pitching over. Leif, will you listen to Ugruk? On way down, Ugruk go slow, think, think. Maybe your mother have dizzy spell. Maybe someone push her, someone she know well, she no afraid of. But not enough sign to say for sure. So best thing not to tell Thorstein, Eric, not anyone, that you guess maybe somebody push her. Instead you watch, listen, wait. See what come from Thorhild being killed, what people do they no do before, get what they no have before, and someday maybe somebody say too much, give himself away. But even then you no let on. You tell Ugruk, who lost father, then lost brother, now lose sister, mother, true friend all in one. If Ugruk sure, you sure, that person die. Ugruk kill him, no one ever know. Ugruk help kill his own grandmother after bear claw her face, and the bones rot, and she beg to be killed. Grandmother she was not bad, she good, yet Ugruk help kill her. If someone kill Thorhild, him all bad, no good in him, he bad all through, worse than wolf, and Ugruk laugh when he drop dead in Ugruk's hands."

Ugruk had spoken very quietly. Holding the flower basket in one hand, he had made occasional short jerking movements with the other, and his eyes had burned dim. My mother's face was quiet, and so was her music. It had ended forever, as the music of my flute had ended forever, when Thorstein broke the instrument in his hands. Another flute had been made for me; and I had learned to play it well. Other women whose being and element were music would be born, and in due course they too would become mute.

I thought of this, and somehow it helped me answer Ugruk.

"I think most men would tell you, no, I am Thorhild's son, and it is my place, not yours, to pay any debts incurred by her death. I am not going to say that. Your claim on her is as great as mine because you loved her as much, for when love passes a certain depth, a certain strength, it can no longer be weighed or measured. And it may be that when the time of payment comes, if it ever does come, my hands will be bound."

"Ugruk know that. Now lift up Thorhild so that her head is on my shoulder, and I carry her with one arm. If arm get tired, put her head on my other shoulder. We take her to Ericshall and put on her ermine cloak and put the pearls she brought from Norway in her pretty hair, and lay her on bench like queen."

6

The days of deepest darkness passed. What remained of Thorhild lay in a deep-delved pit beside the fiord. Eric and Thorstein, both numbed by shock and loss, spoke of building a great cairn of stones to mark the spot. But Ugruk and I rose in the night and in secret we took some lumber and erected a stout piece about eight feet high, and about a third of the way from the top we nailed on a cross piece about six feet long. Then we took some white paint, left over from the last painting of our catboat, and painted the edifice so that it could be seen from a long distance. On dim days it could be made out by boatmen rounding a curve in the fiord before they could see the roof of Ericshall.

When my father and my brother saw it in the first light of morning, each gave me a quick glance, but neither said a word.

Watching and listening as Ugruk bade me, I saw or heard nothing that indicated guilt in anyone. True, there were events connected in some degree with my mother's death, but these could naturally follow her loss. One was that Eric decided to take command of the *Narwhale* on her next trading voyage and to spend something like a month in Norway, his exile having been annulled by the king. Out of the wisdom of his years, old Gorm remarked to me that a change of scene would be good for the great chieftain, and I did not doubt this was true. In his absence, Thorstein would act as his viceroy in ruling our whole colony of Osterbig, which now consisted of more than forty homesteads, with their thralls and livestock, owned by franklins and a few freemen, and which of course included the great manorial holdings of Eric the Red.

Another utterly unexpected consequence or aftermath of my mother's death was a change in my relationship with Swanhild. This had undergone almost no change since our first meeting after the dying away of her jealousy aroused by my ill-fated pursuit of Johanna, daughter of Bjorn, who was now Thorstein's devoted wife and mistress of a hall second only to Eric's in the Osterbig colony. Truly I had not suffered greatly from deprivation of a complete union of our bodies. For seven years now I had obtained physical satisfaction by our dalliance, and other needs that I felt but vaguely had been mitigated by a wildly adventurous life with Ugruk and my other mates on sea and land. Often when I would yearn for fulfillment as is natural to men, my lascivious day-dreams would change to revery, and I would be wafted away out of our bleak and strangely beautiful Greenland to some yet un-discovered realm, of which I knew nothing other than that it was real—Ugruk had dwelt on its far-north coast—and that it lay westward. I looked forward with passionate seethings to my meet-ings with Swanhild and back upon them with content and calm.

Perhaps the truth was I did not in my heart desire a closer tie with Swanhild. I felt it could become very strong and at the same time never permanent. Perhaps I did not love her enough; maybe her being the daughter of beautiful Ellen still caused a faint chill within my heart which my common sense could not dispel. De-spite her earthy charms and her vivid prettiness which I had only to see from some other viewpoint to recognize as beauty, I gave more thought to the accumulation of silver coins than to winning her unslaked favor. By such shillings, their number vastly in-creased by some lucky accident, the great dream of my youth and early manhood could come true.

Such an accident seemed not beyond hope. In Norway legend told that walrus, sensing the approach of death, hauled out on some reef or islet, largely underwater at high tide, and cast their strange souls on the ebbing tide. Such islets, we believed, were thickly strewn with ivory turned glossy black by salt water and more precious than white ivory. Some day a very low tide, blown out by a hard wind, might reveal the entrance to a sea king's cave, crammed with gold and jewels.

Since my mother's death, Swanhild's eyes could not meet mine without filling with tears. I supposed that she had looked upon Thorhild as her best if not only protection from the peculiar harshness with which Eric dealt with Ellen and herself. About three weeks after my great loss, I found myself gazing at her with an old and familiar quickening of my pulse and those yearnings that all young men know and old men well remember, more urgent than belly hunger although this last is an urge to acquisition while the other is for riddance. I knew of no reason why I should not yield to it, although yielding and conquering were not exact terms and they became confused in my head.

"Vixen's Den has been silent and forsaken a long time," I told her at the first chance.

"Too long to suit me, Leif," she answered.

"Is your need as great as mine?"

"I think it is immeasurably greater."

"Now?" I asked, half out of breath. One swift appraisal of the immediate situation, my brain wonderfully quick and cunning in aiding my body's intent, told me that the time was eminently suitable, Swanhild's present task being one she could leave and resume without attracting attention, everyone in sight busy at his affairs, and the day warm, bright, and hopeful.

"Start up the river in about half an hour," she told me. "I will not keep you waiting very long, that I promise, for the longer you must wait, the same must I."

And this was another instance of Swanhild's deftness in employing the Norse tongue.

When I arrived at the dim path through the willows that led to the crypt entrance, I had the feeling that Swanhild had not yet kept the tryst. The dew having fallen from the leaves was no encouragement at this late hour; and the maiden was not waiting behind the thickets. I caught no glimpse of her bright head, nor did I hear a blithe voice in reply to the sound of my step.

CHAPTER ELEVEN

MILLS GRINDING SLOWLY

I

But a great start was awaiting me in the shadowy grotto. The tingling thrill did not come on tiptoe stealing through my skin, but took possession of every inch of it at the same instant, every nerve responding most comparably to what happens in sudden, extreme fright except that then the all-embracing sensation chilled and now it was deliciously warm and exultant. On the white sheepskin robe of the bed lay Swanhild, pretending slumber, her hair luminous in the dim light, one bare arm folded under her head for a pillow, and the curve of her naked shoulder, glossy white, visible above the top of the deerskin cover.

So I played the game at once childlike and lascivious that she had begun. The ribald thought crossed my mind that no householder, frightened half out of his wits by smoke and a glimmer of flame in the middle of night, ever got into his clothes as fast as I shed mine. Then I very carefully lifted the edge of the deerskin robe and took the place she had left for me, and in an instant her vital warmth and mine became one, a heathen kind of marriage, and I felt the soft pressure of her breasts against my shoulder blades, her warm and silken belly close against my back, her long and lovely legs, somewhat bent at the knees, coincident with mine. I was blissfully content to lie thus nearly five minutes, wondering which of us would first yield to temptation to reveal awareness of the other's company. At last she stirred a little, sighed in pretended slumber, and removing her arm from under her head she let it softly fall across my chest. The delay was already almost more than flesh and blood could stand, and I felt the wild thudding of her heart at the small of my back, so I turned over and lay my lips upon hers. This she could endure for only a few seconds without making response.

Thus I wakened her from her feigned sleep, but in a broader sense this was the beginning of her wide awakeness to unslaked passion, unrestrained by prior reservations as to how much or how little to give. There was no interruption of our love-making, against which beautiful Ellen at our first flight warned me, a maxim of the lore of love which she said had been taught all Irish girls by their wise elders, but the wise elder who had instructed Ellen might have been Mother Nature, whom the followers of Kris called Mother Eve. There was one great reversal of that long-ago passage. That had been my maiden passage, which was not true of my fellow passenger. Now it was true of my bedmate but not of me. Still as we moved from one delectable exchange unto the next—in that ancient, settled order of events that most discerning and erotic lovers follow—Swanhild was so apt in following where I led, so full and eager in response, that it would be hard for a cynic to believe that she had not traveled this enchanting road before.

Yet before too long, when we had not yet overreached perfection, there could remain no doubt that this was the real surrender of her flower. I had long assumed that she was a virgin in physical fact, despite our love play over several years, and it was attested now by her maiden pain and the sign which horse-breeding chieftains on the steppes of the Tartars far to the southeast of the Baltic Sea are said to exhibit to their fellows when they have celebrated marriage in their tents.

"It is all over now," Swanhild told me cheerfully, when she had wakened from a real but brief nap in my arms. "I'm no longer in danger of losing my treasure to some rude swain who would just as soon have had a mess of fried eels."

"Are you sorry?" I had to ask.

"Not in the least. I am sorry I made you wait so long, and made myself wait. What was the good? If I marry a thrall, it does not matter, and I would have no choice but a thrall. If I never marry, as I intend, only you and I know my secret, and as long as we are together—till next month, next year, maybe several years—we can share the whole loaf instead of half."

It seemed the height of rashness at this time to speak of another aspect of the new relationship, perhaps a boorish act; yet

I had never known Swanhild to flinch from frankness and indeed she was its exponent.

"There might be consequences——"

"Not this time," she assured me before I could finish what I had started to say. "My new moon was seventeen days ago. My mother told me—but I suppose she told you, too—the dangerous days are the twelfth, thirteenth, and fourteenth, according to old Irish wives. On those days we will not meet—unless I lose track of the time."

"And if you should lose track——?"

"The skies will not fall. Countless unwedded thrall girls have found themselves in that fix. If in the first few months I do not marry a thrall, it will be assumed that you or Ring Einersson or perhaps even Thorstein—who may be a sleepwalker for all we know—are the most likely cause of my predicament. At least you three are the most readily available of any young men so high of station that they would not marry thralls. No one need know the truth. Neither my mother, Ellen, or I would be disgraced—being thralls has one advantage. We can go no lower no matter what we do." And then she repeated, with a strange look in her eyes and a guarded but unmistakable intensity, *"We can go no lower no matter what we do."*

For a moment I felt that she meant more than she intended for me to know. But I soon recovered—one of the consequences of a delicious and victorious venture such as I had just made is an almost drunken exultation, and I let it take hold of me as I envisioned another meeting as soon as possible. There remained one little blot upon my happiness, a kind of dark spot in some deep realm of my mind rather than in my heart—and if I had tried to name it in one word, its main component, I would have said guilt. But if it were guilt, what was its cause? Truly I could think of none which a bold man could recognize. A great deal of secret love-making went on among us Norse—Gorm had once said that we lived in a cold climate and hence rarely missed a chance to get warm—perhaps more than among the lordly Franks, but, on the other hand, perhaps less. It was assumed that our Gods punished unfaithful wives, but they rarely did so to our knowledge.

No one had ever hinted that they should punish younkers over-come with passion in a haystack; and the unmarried sons of great chiefs and franklins could be expected to make free as they pleased with pretty thrall girls.

There was something greater than the greatest God in the Norse pantheon, and that was fate, but I did not see what interest she would take in so simple a case of copulation, or what concern she might have with me.

2

Sometimes I wondered if Eric the Red had regretted the naming of his young son Lucky Leif. In Old Norse, as I suppose in many other languages, there is an adage to the effect that a man or a dog will live up to the name given him, as if by some interposition of fate. Truly I had been wonderfully lucky in hunting the King of the Narwhales; again when I had been the first of our ship's company to spy the Greenland coast; again in being the first to spy Ugruk's kayak; perhaps again, although the coiled springs of fury had brought into play my latent powers, when Thorstein had been half a second late in thrusting home the blow he had aimed at me. Unless I wanted to believe in the casting of a spell with uncanny consequences—and I did want to believe it—the lucky landing of a waterfowl, probably a swan, in the hot spring on that brutally cold day the Frost Giant sneezed had saved my life.

The only conspicuous instance of bad luck that I had suffered, other than my mother's untimely death, was losing Johanna to my brother, Thorstein; yet even this was more likely a case of being fairly beaten by a better wooer than I, and perhaps the runes of fate had been so written that if I had won the prize I could not have it and some greater prize as well.

Then there came to me a piece of utterly blind, sheer, un-mitigated luck arising out of another prior piece, the close bond I had made with Ugruk.

The episode had a commonplace beginning. Rising for an early chore, a thrall had sighted a herd of seven sperm whales, most of them feeding or making sport a little way down our fiord. It happened that Einer's sailing dory was moored at our landing, with three of her crew including Ring sleeping aboard her; also this boat was the best equipped of the Nordrseta fleet for taking large whales. She had one very long harpoon attached to a line of two cable lengths, which was deeper than any whale had ever been known to sound in our fiord; and here a harpooned whale lacked the scope of the open sea and was likely to become panic-stricken and wound or even kill himself on deeply submerged rocks jutting out from the precipitate shores. If the spear were well aimed and sped, it would be unlikely that the victim would run with the boat too far for his mighty carcass to be towed by Einer's ship to the settlements.

No wonder our stout fellows rushed for a place at the oars of the sailing dory. All of them loved adventure; a perilous wild ride behind a wounded whale was their notion of complete bliss; all had had some practice at boating. And it was no wonder to me that Thorstein was the first to reach the bow to take hold of the spear; and since Ring was well aware of my brother's greater skill, he made no objection. What puzzled me was Ugruk's behavior. He gave me a little sign not to board the dory and instead to set out with him in our two-man kayak, which he had completed several years before, a source of great joy and sometimes a little profit to both of us. Evidently he had observed something that the others had either ignored or overlooked.

In a moment I saw what had attracted Ugruk's eager notice. Six of the seven whales had moved off about a quarter of a mile; one still remained, motionless except for his slight lift and fall in the gently rolling waves. His flukes were up and visible and occasionally made weak, spasmodic movements; his vast head was submerged except for his blowhole. A flock of sea gulls had lighted on his back and were pecking furiously at some edible they had found in a tangle of seaweed. And now I perceived that Thorstein was no longer making for this whale but had changed his course to approach one of the others.

"That whale, him sick," Ugruk told me. "I think he just about dead. Oil from sick whale smell bad, no good."

Yet we were making straight for the sick whale. As we stroked with our double-bladed paddles he told me why.

"Long time ago my father, Puissay, found sick sperm whale. About a hundred fathoms he found something like wax, dark gray, sweet smell, floating on water. He had big bowl in kayak and he scoop up bowl-full, think maybe he use it to soften skins better than women chew, chew, chew all day. It no good for that, leave bowl in igloo, use a little to flavor old, stale meat. By 'n' by, come boat from way, way west, people call themselves Kuchin, look like Innuit, dress no same, some talk our talk, most talk Kuchin talk. Chief of Kuchins, he say to Puissay, 'Give me bowl of old, no-good sea wax to grease Kamleika.' But Puissay see shine in Kuchin chief's eyes, and he say, 'No, I keep.' By 'n' by, Kuchin chief say, 'Give you new copper pot for old sea wax, grease Kamleika, drive away the smell of rotten fish.' 'No,' Puissay say, 'no trade for copper pot.' By 'n' by, chief offer Puissay three copper pots, six foxskins, ten walrus tusks. Puissay say no, but take six copper pots, ten foxskins, twenty walrus tusks. He no think Kuchin chief pay so much, but he wrong about that, Kuchin chief glad to make bargain, go away laughing."

"The waxy stuff was ambergris?"

"Ugruk never know name till he hear Thorhall say it. But Ugruk hear, long ago, how Kuchin trade with people who come in big boats from way, way south, want ivory, furs, beaver castors, but most want ambergris mighty bad. When I see sick whale at first light I put draw bucket in kayak, then put in three sealskin bags, no leak when necks bound with thongs. Most likely we no find ambergris. Ugruk see three, four sick sperm whales since then, look for ambergris, no find. But this whale same kind Puissay saw, lay same on water, wave flukes slow, weak, same way Puissay saw. Maybe he too vomit up ambergris, or pass out bowels, so we look good."

We came nigh the dying Leviathan. Certainly no waxlike substance floated anywhere near the monstrous ruin. At once Ugruk turned straight into the wind, and we both stroked strongly to make headway, but I found no fault with that, for I perceived that this was the direction from which the mighty sea beast would have drifted before his mates had abandoned him. We had gone a full sea mile, and our hopes were sinking fast, when a dark spot showed for an instant on the lightly rolling waves about half a sea mile farther up wind. As we gazed with greedy eyes, Ugruk caught a glimpse of it, and then we both saw it plainly, but we need not remind each other it could easily be a small, floating bed of kelp.

Actually it was moving faster before the wind than we moved against it, and soon we came alongside. It was not a bed of kelp but a mottled gray substance, and although it was thinly spread over about forty square yards of water, Ugruk skimmed off a draw bucket full without any visible reduction in the total amount. When I had felt and sniffed its sweet, musky smell I must perforce take a swift glance down wind to see how the whale hunt was going, and to wonder whether Ugruk's and my actions would be noticed. About five miles distant I saw the dory, oars in and her sail furled, with what appeared to be about eight slim, upright sticks lining her forward gunwales, and a snow-white curl of foam as her bow fairly cut the water. I could not see the harpoon line at this distance, but I saw, a cable's length ahead, the vast snout and shoulders of a sperm whale alternately rise and fall as he made his death rush, and a great swirling and boiling caused by his threshing flukes.

So Ugruk and I took our time to gather this strange flotsam and put it in our skin bags, filling two of them full, then latching the neck with sinew. The third bag was two-thirds full when the cream became so thin and lay in such scattered patches that we could not skim it without half-filling the draw bucket with salt water. We had taken about nine tenths of the whole treasure, and although it was light as suet, our haul weighed ninety pounds. Now we were in haste to run home and stow our harvest before the whalers touched our strand.

All dwellers in and about the home acre whose hands were not busy at some task, and those who saw a chance to shirk, had gathered around the bend of our shore to watch the whale hunt. When Gorm, who had been left behind, called to ask us what we had in the three sealskins, Ugruk called blandly at my instruction that it was edible kelp, a variety our beachcombers often gathered, although its edibility was not really a fact. However, the slimy stuff could be boiled, strained, and leave a mildly sweet sirup, which was good on the almost tasteless water-root bread on which we relied when our grain bins were empty. The hunt watchers paid us no more attention, and within the hour Ugruk and I had wrapped the three skins in friz and buried them in the dirt floor of our turf house.

3

It was easy enough to look rather crestfallen when about an hour later Einer's sailing dory was moored at the strand. Thorstein, saying very little, and with the calm demeanor of a great thane, was plainly the hero of the occasion. At his first throw the blade had plunged deep into the whale's vitals; she had not sounded even once because of the pressure of the deepening water on her wound; and after a three-mile rush, she had wagged her flukes and died. Einer, who had seen part of the chase from his crow's nest, had already stood to sea with the intention of towing the mighty carcass into his fiord mouth in the wind already veering to the west.

"Is she a full-grown sperm?" I asked Thorstein, in the hoarse voice of envy.

"Oh, I've seen bigger sperm whales, I think. But she's certainly the largest ever to be brought into Osterbig."

It was quickly decided by the boat's company that half the meat and sperm oil would be distributed among the sixty or more homesteads, provided all hands labored at the butchering; a fourth would go to Einer for the use of his dory and for towing in the monster; another fourth would be given to the dwellers of Vesterbig, who would gladly send a ship after their portion.

"You deserve a handsome prize for that beautiful throw," said Ring Einersson, who always walked a little in Thorstein's shadow. "What do you think would be fair?"

"I'll take half the hide, if the rope makers will come for it and pay me the usual price; also if any ambergris is found in the monster's guts, I'd like half of that. The other half of the hide should be divided among my companions of a great hunt, with an extra share for the thrall Stori who first laid eyes on the school. The other half of the ambergris, if any is found, shall be sent to the King of Norway as a token from his loyal liege men of Eric the Red. Leif, I'm sorry you didn't come along to get a share of the prizes. Perhaps you don't like to ride behind harpooned whales."

"It is a rather perilous pastime," I answered.

He was scored upon, however slightly, by this answer. None of the men dared smile but their eyes twinkled.

"When you and Ugruk started off in your kayak, we thought you were going to help us if the whales needed heading off. Instead, we saw no more of you."

"We paddled out to look at the sick whale. We thought his sperm oil might be saved, but he had begun to rot while he was still alive, and we couldn't get near him. Then Ugruk and I gave chase to a fine leopard seal, but he escaped us, and our only bag was some edible kelp."

"The great thane Bjorn imports heather honey from Darstad. It's a fair substitute for kelp sirup."

With this parting shot, not worthy of the wit of a man who could win Johanna, he turned away to speak to Ring. At the first chance I asked Ugruk to find Thorhall and bring him to our turf house on a private and confidential matter. In order to turn ninety pounds of ambergris into ninety pounds of silver shillings, and to store and care for them until I could spend them in a way imaged in myriad dreams, I had to trust someone of experience, intelligence, and, most of all, with that inward law, present in so many more people than most people dare surmise, and especially common in children, of keeping faith and not breaking it. Thorhall filled the description. Unlike Ugruk, who hardly knew how to lie, Thorhall could be a splendid liar when he chose, but he very rarely did so. I knew of no man in Greenland who so exemplified what we liked to think were the native virtues of the Norse race—adventurousness, hardihood, a haughtiness of soul in confronting fate, bravery in speech and action, human warmth, and loyalty to his own.

Presently he came into the turf house where the gleam of a small oil lamp revealed his rangy frame, fair, fine, unruly hair, and forever-alive eyes.

"Ugruk go out?" my companion asked, looking me in the face. "Or he stay?"

"Stay. If I say anything that doesn't make good sense to you, tell me."

Ugruk nodded. Thorhall gazed at me keenly.

"This must be business somewhat bigger than we usually do in Osterbig," he remarked, taking his ease on a bench.

"So big that I need your help, which Ugruk and I will pay for. He and I have got hold of some ambergris."

"I saw the sick sperm whale. I thought of ambergris—the two are connected in sailors' heads. But I've come up to half a dozen in my time, not counting those that I watched die from my deep-plunged harpoon—a dreadful thing to watch, the life going out of sixty tons of brute—and never came on any. Once we found a little in the big gut close to the gall bladder, once we found what seemed to be a piece loose in the lower belly, black, weighing half a pound and with a bad smell. Would you care to tell me how much Ugruk and you found?"

"About ninety pounds."

"Did you say—*ninety pounds?*"

"Maybe eighty would cover it."

"God of the Nine Runes! God of the Norns, who go their own way in spite of him! What have they got up their sleeves for you, Leif, and for you, Leif's brother who came up from the sea? There's glory, and there's grief. All of us Northlanders are a little fey, and that much comes to me. Well, first let me establish your ownership. You are a freeman, Leif, and Ugruk is as free as an albatross. What boat were you using when you found the stuff?"

"Big kayak, two holes," Ugruk broke in, the first sound he had uttered since the talk began.

"You found the ambergris on the open waters of the fiord that belong to no man," Thorhall went on. "It doesn't take a sea lawyer to declare that it belongs to you both, in even shares. But owning it—and keeping it—and disposing of it are three different things. Is that where I put in my oar?"

"Yes, sir. How soon can you borrow a ship for a trading voyage?"

"Not until Eric comes back from Norway. That may be any day, or on any moon. He'll be sick of the sea and only too glad to let me sell the ivory, seal tar, skins of all kinds, seal and whale oil, whalebone, and whale rope that has been accumulating ever since he sailed. My terms are: he furnishes ship and crew, I victual her, I sell all his goods without commission and have the right to sell and keep all the return from my own goods. If there's room enough, he doesn't object to my stowing a limited quantity of trade goods of my friends and neighbors, and I get a commission for handling it, and it's no trick to add ninety pounds. Guarding it from theft and selling it to a Spanish Jew—they're the most honest merchants in Europe—is quite a trick. It means a long sail out of my way. It means risk of getting my throat cut. It means keeping my wits about me every step I take. So instead of ten or fifteen per cent, which I charge my neighbors for selling their wares in Dorstad, I'll charge you and Ugruk twenty-five per cent. I'll make no mark on a parchment, but I'd give you both my hand, and I'll take Starkad as first officer, who'll complete the business for me if I'm lost overside."

"After paying you a quarter of what the ambergris will bring, how much will Ugruk and I have left?" I asked, holding my voice steady.

"The wholesale price of first-grade ambergris, the last I heard, was three English shillings per apothecary's ounce. That is thirty-six shillings a pound. Multiply that by ninety—no, say eighty to play safe—and money in hand will be 2880 shillings. Deduct a quarter of that amount, my share—720 shillings—and you still have just over two thousand. Tell me, Leif, did the ambergris have a sweet, musky smell, and was it black streaked with gray?"

"Exactly."

"Well, it should be prime ambergris. With two thousand shillings you and Ugruk could become rich franklins—but I guess that's not what you want."

"No, we want the *Narwhale* first of all. Eric promised to sell her to me for a thousand shillings, money in hand, provided I did not delay too long. Do you suppose he'll stand by his promise?"

"Yes, you can count on that. You should know that, being his son, and by my accepting service under him when I was born a thane."

"As soon as you return from the voyage, will you buy the ship in my name? He'll take it better if you act for me."

"No, you'll speak with him man to man. He may take it ill, but he'll do what profits him. And you'll need a good part of your extra thousand shillings to victual and equip the *Narwhale* for a long voyage where you won't see many ship chandlers, unless I miss my guess. If you come home with no gain, not even a landfall in the great beyond, you'll need the rest of yours and Ugruk's silver to build a catboat of your own, so you can devote the rest of your lives to hunting in the north. Maybe you should take a different tack to start with. Why not own a good ship, and a hall as fine as Thorstein's, with a wife ruling over it, and little children falling and squalling? What more could a Norseman ask, now that the age of the Vikings is fading into history?"

"No, Ugruk and I are going west, aren't we, Ugruk?"

Ugruk looked at me with some asperity for even bothering him with the question.

"What will I do with my seven hundred shillings?" Thorhall went on, in a thoughtful murmur. "I already own a catboat. I suppose I'll put it with my other savings, more than doubling that amount, and buy from Eric a thousand acres of his best grass, and put up something better than a hut, and again call myself a thane of sorts."

"Why not go with Ugruk and me and our crew to the unknown West? I'd appoint you captain."

"I've got too much sense to consider it." Then, after a long pause, "At least to ship as captain. I'm not going to be responsible when the *Narwhale* goes over the brink of ocean and lands in

Hel. Oh well, I might consider a berth as second mate. I've often wondered what happens to the sun when he sinks in the west, causing him to show up again a number of hours later in the east. The west wind seems to come from a long way off, to judge from the combers. We saw new stars when we came to Greenland; there may be others to be seen way out there. There may be many new sights and strange sights; and I'd like to be among the first to lay eyes on them. I'll think the matter over, for you have a long wait, and an impatient one, until Eric completes his voyage and then I complete mine. And something may come up that you can't go at all."

"That last is quite true," I answered, speaking not for Thorhall's ears but the ears of the Gods and the Norns, in the hearing of whom no wise man will ever boast, or ever assume a certainty of anything coming to pass, or of not coming. These deities could not be called spiteful. They merely want to teach men to remember their place, which is low and small, and to stay in it. Otherwise they might revolt and bring about the Twilight of the Gods before its fated time.

4

My father, Eric the Red, returned from his voyage to Norway in high spirits. His nature did not permit him to grieve long over a loss that could not be retrieved, such as his great loss of Thorhild, and his view was almost always forward, not backward. It struck me as strange that a man who had almost no control over his volcanic temper could so discipline his heart against prolonged grief. The truth was, Eric could usually fight off any feeling that might weaken him.

Very plainly he had made out well with Norway's new king, Olaf Tryggvesson. On a golden chain around his neck he wore a gold medallion, stamped with a likeness of the king's face as seen in profile; and on the opposite side was a representation of the Christian cross. This last astounded me, since Eric had always prided himself on being faithful to Odin; and some deal larger and more profitable than a promised increase of trade between

Greenland and Norway appeared in the making. When plain-talking Thorhall saw the emblem he asked a question which all present had been pondering.

"Eric, have you turned Christian?"

"Not yet. I haven't accepted baptism. But, in all truth, I am thinking of it. Thorhild's spirit in heaven would be pleased and—well, as far as I can judge, Kris is a more powerful God than either Odin or Thor."

"I don't deny the power of Kris," Thorhall said in a low, rumbling voice. "The kings of Europe have flourished mightily under his banners, and no Viking ship of war dares raid the Christian coasts from the Vistula to the Golden Horn. Sweden's lost, except for Queen Sigrid, and so is Denmark—this last by your dead wife's grandsire, Harald Bluetooth—and only in Norway, Iceland, and Greenland does Odin ride his Eight-hoofed Horse, and 'tis said that even there he's begun to yield the path to Thor. Not so, in my heart. Not so in your heart, Eric, or so I thought until to-day; at the very least I thought you'd stick to Thor, God of the Red Beard, God of the Thunder. But now it seems you'll soon be kneeling before an altar with holy vessels on it, dealing with any Christian prince who'll make you a greasy trade, not shouting to the God of Battles. A Christian priest in his white robe is no longer a rare sight in Iceland. I suppose they'll soon be swarming into Greenland. I hope I die fighting a white bear on the ice—my broadsword with its runes against his mailed mauls—before I see that day! At least it would be a heathen death, not one with my hands folded, asking Kris to have mercy on my sins."

Listening to Thorhall's voice, again I thought of pack ice breaking up far away at sea. Looking at him, I thought of a big, gray jack wolf Ugruk and I had caught in a snare, one of his feet entangled by unbreakable thongs, yet fighting and snapping and snarling on three legs, trying to leap at our throats, until I mercifully impaled him on my spear. Yet Thorhall's lean face had remained composed. I knew only by the glitter and gleam of his pale gray eyes how greatly he was aroused.

Eric heard him out with unwonted courtesy and then made civil reply.

"The River of Time flows on, Thorhall, old friend," he said. "The Vikings have been stranded far upstream. Meanwhile the nations of Europe are waxing in strength and wealth and numbers, mainly through what you call greasy trade, but partly through the teachings of the priests of the Christian Church. Olaf's a great king. He too was once a Viking—after the death of his first wife, the daughter of the Wendish King Burislav—until he was converted by a hermit in the Scilly Islands. His second wife, Gyda, sister of the King of Dublin, brought him wealth, as did his first wife, and he'll rule all Scandinavia, under the cross, before he's done. It would be a great thing for Greenland if we'd acknowledge him as our liege lord. We could trade with all other Christian countries and have the protection of Olaf's fleet, and we'd be part of Christendom instead of heathendom, but in any case we've got room in Greenland for Kris, Odin, and Thor, all three. To show you how broad-minded I am, as a worshiper of Odin I married a Christian girl, Thorhild, and was happy with her. If I become a Christian I might marry a heathen princess. We lie the farthest west of any land on earth. I'll do everything I can to bring us closer to the other lands, Christian or heathen. That's the duty of kings and chieftains."

Thorhall appeared to be hardly listening. He spat on the ground and then asked what seemed to be an irrelevant question.

"How soon can the *Narwhale* unload and be put in shape for another voyage?"

"I think in about a fortnight."

"Well, our catch has been good, our harvests are piling up, storing space is limited, and she might as well be turning a profit as lying moored at the strand. I'll take her across on the same terms as before, if you agree."

"I'd be happy to agree. Anyway, Thorhall, you need a sea voyage, and to visit Europe, which you'll find so changed you can hardly believe your eyes. Mary, Mother of God, it's been over ten years since we sailed from Iceland! We're approaching what the priests call the second millennium since the birth of Kris. You'll see thriving towns where before were only a manor house and a palisade—busy cities in the place of sleepy little ports—houses so tall you can hardly believe they were made by human hands. I must go now and look at my new grandson who some day will rule—but let that pass. Bring your accounts to the hall, Thorhall, and we'll cast 'em."

My father strode away, his bowed arms with closed fists swinging back and forth, a figure strong as a bear's but light-footed, graceful one would almost say, certainly far from awkward. Over fifty, he was as resistant to the insidious attack of time as to the blunt blows of fortune. Not one silver hair gleamed in his fiery beard and somehow I got the impression it was brighter red than ever.

The day following, our love-making occurring on this occasion in my own bed in the turf house, I repeated to Swanhild what the great chieftain had said. A lively interest in his doings was natural to his thrall, but the wench showed something more than lively interest, and to judge from her slightly parted lips and rounded, glistening eyes I would take it for a half-hidden but intense excitement. Yet as usual she did not guard her speech. In her eagerness she clasped one of my hands in both of hers.

"Leif, do you know what this means? Eric the Red is going to become Earl of Greenland!"

"He cannot be so appointed unless Greenland becomes a province of Norway. At present we're an independent nation."

"What is there to stop it? There are fifteen great thanes who would have to take the oath of allegiance—and how many of them will oppose Eric if he goes after what he wants like the bull he is? Bjorn has become second in strength to Eric—for a while it looked as if he might overtower him—but now Eric is hand in hand with King Olaf, and Bjorn's daughter is married to Eric's elder son, and they have a son, and that son will wear Eric's crown. The other chieftains, such as Harafn, Ketil, and the rest—without Eric they are like sheep who've lost their bellwether. One thane will oppose him. He'll hold out to the last, but what good will it do him, when he's a landless man, and he laid aside his thanedom to become Eric's reeve. Yes, I mean Thorhall. He's the most true Norseman of them all—unless you beat him at it. How Eric would laugh at my saying that, and Thorstein give his little mocking smile—you who love music better than blood. Still they may laugh out of the wrong sides of their mouths before you're through."

Swanhild fell silent rather abruptly and looked somewhat startled. I had the odd impression that while she had talked about Eric and his fellow chieftains her mind had taken a different bent, involved with an entirely different set of issues, than when she spoke about me. Her attentions to me that day had been especially loving. This was always true when Ugruk's absence and other circumstances permitted us to meet in the warm turf house instead of at Vixen's Den. Her tribute to me just then appeared to be a kind of emotional outburst caused by exultation of a foreign source. I had often found myself wondering whether Swanhild was truly in love with me. Always I had arrived at an opposite conclusion—that the voluptuous girl wanted bodily satisfaction which I could give her, and she would rather that I be the giver instead of some other, since I was the son of her owner, whom she could thus spite in secret. That the affair had gone on several years under Eric's regal, eagle nose gave her great satisfaction.

The fact remained that I was not at all satisfied with my own thinking. It seemed that somehow I was always toning down the truth, belittling it, somehow, making commonplace explanations for little mysteries which, if I could see a little farther, would prove to be great mysteries, and what I deemed ordinary human passions were terrible and blazing passions. One thing I knew— that in spite of a long term of love-making I was not in love with Swanhild; and since she had so many admirable qualities, such as great courage, truly an indomitable spirit, a keen mind, frank ways, an appealing face and form, I could well wonder why.

Just then she was lost in thought. I had thought of a matter I did not like to confront, yet found myself forced to do so. For the first year or so after her complete surrender to me, she had been careful about counting the days of her month and abjured trysts with me on the twelfth, thirteenth, and fourteenth days, as her mother taught her. She still insisted that she did so, but repeatedly I received the impression that her counting had become careless and inaccurate. She had once spoken lightly of the consequences of her conceiving, which I had taken as half-jest. Now it seemed that she felt lightly about it. Actually I could think of no truly serious consequences, for even Eric's fury would in due course pass off. Would he set free from thralldom the bastard son of his own son? It stood to reason; yet I had trouble believing it with force. One fact stood out, large and indisputable: I did not want to be father to a thrall.

"What Thorhall said to Eric was true," Swanhild remarked, after a long studious silence. "All except a few die-hards such as himself, the people of Greenland would go to Kris if Greenland should become a province of Norway ruled by a Christian king. But what did Eric mean when he said that his first wife, Thorhild, had been Christian but his second might be heathen? Was it a slip, or was he just showing off his broad-mindedness, as he said? Could he have meant he might marry Sigrid, the Odin-worshiping Queen of Sweden? No, not even Eric the Red would look that high. All Greenland as his earldom ought to satisfy the grandson of a slave."

"I don't think he meant Queen Sigrid. He's not that big a fool. And if by some miracle he could win her hand—and we must never underrate Eric the Red—he wouldn't trade his chieftainship in Greenland—his earldom, perhaps, if you guessed right—to be the queen's consort in Sweden. He'll never leave here until he dies and goes to Valhalla."

"Who believes in Valhalla any more? Thorhall, perhaps, but not Eric and not you." And then, standing by the doorway, ready to depart, Swanhild said a strange thing. "Yes, he will leave here before he dies. He'll go to Hel."

5

On the twenty-second day after the *Narwhale*'s arrival from Norway, she again stood to sea on an eastward course, this time with Thorhall in command. Unseen among his cargo were two skins the necks of which had been briefly opened, so that he could see, feel, smell, and taste their contents, after which he had given me a great and joyful glance. Eric had been glad to oblige him in giving berths to some of Thorhall's favorite companions, the men taken off being put at other tasks. So it came about that Starkad was first officer, and Gorm and Gull Eye, the latter aging somewhat but still the best man in the colony for standing a dark night watch in berg-strewn waters, were among his crew.

The ship vanished under the horizon in mid-September; and since she would sail all the way to Málaga in southern Spain, the best market both for ambergris and amber west of Constantinople, and she had important and cautious business to transact there, I could not expect her to drop her hook in our fiord until the following spring.

I could wait with patience. Ugruk had taught me how, as we sat behind wind shelters in wicked weather beside the blowholes of seals. That was only for hours that seemed whole days. Now whole days passed as quickly as an ordinary hour, I was so busy with making plans for a mighty voyage, making such preparations as were possible this early, and so busied at times with dreams. What if Eric refused to sell me the *Narwhale* for the agreed price? In that case—if our ambergris turned into its weight in silver—I could buy another vessel fully as seaworthy. True, my heart was set on the *Narwhale* with her shining tusk and I did not believe in vain. Eric wanted and needed a bigger ship to top in prestige his nearest rival, Bjorn.

Until that winter I had seen or heard little evidence that Ellen's and Swanhild's story of direct and recent descent from an Irish thane was really true, and not a wild flight of imagination. Their beauty of face and form lent some credence to it, although both were commonly seen among thrall girls; and Gorm had told me that Kol, himself Irish from the same part of the island, had attested to its truth some years before his death. Of course I was aware of Ellen's ability to speak high-class Norse and teach the same to her daughter, a language learned by Irish girls of good family on account of the long Norse dominance of the island. Swanhild's trysts with me were usually so brief that I had no real chance to explore her mind. To my surprise, one winter afternoon when we were safe from intrusion or disturbance, she told me a tale of ancient Greece which she said Ellen's mother had told her, having heard it from a scholarly Roman priest when she was a little girl. Learned men rarely wasted so much breath on a peasant.

It was a long and involved story of a king named Laius, his wife, Jocasta, and their son, the central figure, named Oedipus. From a great prophetess, Laius heard that he would be killed by his own son, yet unborn, and that this son would later marry Jocasta, his own mother.

When the son, Oedipus, was born, Laius had him exposed on a "mountain cold and steep as Blue Shirt," to die of cold and hunger or in the fangs of wild beasts; thus all three would escape the horrid doom. But the babe, Oedipus, was rescued and raised by another king, Polybus of Corinth, and in time he too went to the great Oracle of Delphi, only to hear the prophecy repeated. And fate so had it that he did kill Laius, neither recognizing the other, and he did marry Jocasta, and had sons and daughters by her. When the truth finally came out, Jocasta hanged herself and Oedipus put out his own eyes.

Caring not a fig for ancient Greece, having rarely heard of it except from a Finnish fisherman in whose country, oddly enough, the old Greek tales were recounted, still I listened with fascination to Swanhild's recital. She put so much spirit in it and used such eloquent and imaginative language. She could not help but laugh a little at Oedipus' desperate attempts to escape his fate, when every trial, every flight from one city to another, every action, brought him closer to the scene and moment of its fulfillment. In the final passages her eyes were round and shining with excitement, her face flushed, and I too was carried away.

"I can understand why Jocasta hanged herself," Swanhild said thoughtfully. "True, she had never dreamed that the king she had married was her own son, but she should have known better than to marry a man so much younger, even though she was very beautiful and young-looking for her years. But it was not right that Oedipus should put out his own eyes. He had not known what he was doing in killing his father and marrying his mother, and I have no doubt she told him she was a good deal younger than she really was in order to get him. And surely it wasn't fair for the Greek Gods to lay a curse on his and Jocasta's children, the sons quarreling and going to war with each other, and meeting unhappy deaths, and one of his daughters being sealed up in a tomb where she hanged herself."

"It's a terrible story," I said. "But I'm surprised that it happened in Greece, which is a beautiful, warm land according to Starkad, who has seen some of its islands and its coasts when he was a young sailor. It's more fitting to Iceland, where the mountains shoot out burning lava, and the earth quakes, and great rifts in the ground swallow people and houses. As for the Greek Gods being fair, I reckon they are as fair as our Gods. Gorm once said they charge a huge price for everything they give, and they certainly inflict terrible punishments on people, more for their mistakes than for their crimes, and sometimes for no reason we can see. Think of poor Kol, getting his skull smashed because Eric the Red lost his temper. But is Eric responsible for that temper? Didn't the Gods give it to him? Are the Gods responsible? Maybe they have to do what the Norns say—and they speak what fate decrees. Beautiful Baldur had every protection that his father, Odin, and his mother, Frigga, could give him to keep the prophecy of his dying young from coming true. But they had forgotten to cast spells against his being killed by a branch of mistletoe. It's over my head, Swanhild. And now you'd better go, for Ugruk and I are going hunting."

Instead of being angered by the dismissal, the wench remained in high, blithe spirits and kissed me blissfully at her departure. For once, I was glad to have her go. My mind could not shed the tragic story that she had told so well, and the dark thoughts that it invoked. I wanted to put on my skis and skim over the snow with my dark-skinned brother, he making good progress on snowshoes. All of Greenland was mantled in white, any way we took, everywhere we looked, and no doubt in vast spaces northward that none of us had ever seen. The marks that men had made upon the land could be identified by close inspection, but the snow upon the roofs and the concealment of all paths caused me to remember my first winter here, ten and more years before, when eight of us dwelt in a turf house, and there we had heat and light from oil lamps, but all else was as the Gods had fashioned it, one vast snowy wilderness, the snow stretching to the brink of the frozen fiord and far spread over the ice, and the very icecap of the island was no longer differentiated by the eye from the snowy wastes of the mountainsides. The weather that day was not severe. Ugruk and I would be warm in our parkas, the wind crust of the packed snow was a little softened, and he and I would take note of every track and sign of wild-folk affairs.

We would see the spayed hoof marks of reindeer, the pawings of Greenland bison, footprints of what seemed one lone wolf but might be a half-dozen wolves running in precise file, gluttons, lynxes, white hares, and the smaller fur bearers such as ferrets and weasels. Sometimes we had come upon the scene of a previous night's killing, betrayed by scraps of fur or spilled feathers and bright red clots of snow. Sometimes we found a track that even Ugruk could not identify, a subject for speculation in many an idle hour.

The wild folk were my folk, in a way of speaking. Except for Ugruk, it seemed that I knew them better than my fellow men.

6

As soon as the ice pack began to break up, Gull Eye's little son Cnute climbed every morning to the top of Tarmochan Hill, an eminence near the home acre, to look down the fiord to see if the *Narwhale* had hove in home. One day in mid-June he fairly tumbled down the slippery hillside. His father's ship, he cried, had come in sight around what we old pioneers called Legbone Bend. When I asked him if the vessel hugged the coast, he replied that she stood well out to sea, persuading me that the home comer must be Bjorn's big merchant ship, of much deeper draught than the *Narwhale*, that had spent the winter among the Danes in Northumberland. But the urchin's report proved true. No doubt he had inherited Gull Eye's notable gift of long and intensely accurate vision.

Soon she showed up plain and real, intensely vivid, her yellow sail splendidly puffed, and her headpiece agleam in the sunlight.

Was she bringing me riches which to my counting were beyond avarice? I would know in another hour, if not less; until then I could stand the strain. My first inkling of good news was Thorhall's jubilant wave in reply to mine as the vessel came into the strand.

When we shook hands, a press of people, rejoicing in his return, prevented any exchange of confidences, but he made a remark that would have startled his hearers if his casual tone had not made it seem so ordinary.

"Leif, I guess you'll be taking off, somewhere, before long."

"I hope so. I've never been any farther than Iceland, where I was born. I'd like to see the great world."

What I meant was, I would like to see a world which no other Norse, no bold Moor, no Phoenician of an age long lost, in fact no human soul on the continent and the islands of Europe, had ever seen.

The dream took one great step out of the hazy realm of dreams to stand clear and real within my reach when my chance came for a few minutes' private talk with Thorhall. He reported that my ambergris had been tested by various merchants in Málaga and was found to be the best and costliest kind. Some Moors and two Greeks had bid for it against a syndicate of Jews, and the bid of the latter for 1104 ounces was nine hundred Castilian piasters, the equivalent of about twenty-eight hundred English shillings. The wharf master's fee for the transaction was only twenty-eight shillings, because the great wealth of Málaga stemmed from her busy wharves, and the Moors made welcome ships from every land. Out of this breathtaking sum, Thorhall would keep seven hundred shillings, becoming again a man of means, and he suggested that I pay Eric one hundred shillings for the transport in his ship of about one hundred pounds of freight, since it had sailed wide of its usual course to Dorstad. Thus a clean two thousand shillings would be left to Ugruk and me because of one lucky find of floating excrement from a sick whale.

My next business was with Eric, and I found myself flinching from it in some degree, but determined to get it over with as soon as possible. My reassurance was that, no matter how he answered me, my voyage of exploration into the unknown west was now perfectly feasible, because there were at least three other brave, stout, and lucky ships that I could readily afford to buy. So when I asked him to receive me alone in his little trading office, an adjunct to his hall, I knew myself to be well-armed. He seemed to sense the fact, because he gave me a quick, searching, suspicious glance before he answered. Then he bade me come at first dark.

The room was well-lighted and warm from a seal-oil lamp. My sire was not as fully at ease as he wished to be, or as he wanted me to believe. He had me sit on a bench across a little plank table on which lay an abacus, a tray with movable counters such as were common in Frisia.

"Are you here on important business?" he asked. "If so, I'll pour you a bowl of the finest Danish ale."

"I would count it of middling importance."

He filled two bowls and when both of us had brushed back our mustaches, mine yellow and his red, we gave each other a deep-throated *skoal* and drank.

"Well, Leif, what's in the wind?" he asked. "Something of mark, I know."

"Only that I wish to make good on a bargain we made several years ago—the purchase of the *Narwhale* for a thousand English shillings."

He stared at me wildly for a second or two, then quickly hid his face in his bowl.

"Well, I don't doubt you've got hands on the sum. I do not know how—I suppose some chieftains and rich franklins are behind you. Isn't that a good guess?"

"No, sir. The money came to me as a gift from the sea!"

"My words in my teeth! Remember what I said about some mermaid leading you to her cave? I know it's not exactly that—I know only that a Goddess of Good Fortune—perhaps a Norn—prompted me that day to dub you Lucky Leif. In the end I hope you'll give me the full account, but I'll not ask for it now."

"Yes, sir, I will tell you the story in due course."

"Thorhall handed me a hundred shillings late this afternoon. He told me it was my due, because he'd had to take the *Narwhale* a long way off her course to do a piece of business in which you and he were partners. I thought he'd lost his wits and overpaid me—now I'm wondering if I shouldn't have asked for more. Now about the ship. I'm not obligated to sell her to you, after so long a wait for you to raise the money. But I confess the price is fair—I want to build a larger vessel—and I will sell her to you if you'll run an errand for me aboard my ship. It's not one to tie your hands in any future ventures. It will only delay your great venture—which you've dreamed of ever since Ugruk came out of nowhere to be your brother—for from three to five months."

"Will you tell me what it is? I'd rather have the *Narwhale* than any ship berthed in Greenland, but of course I can buy some other, if I must."

"I suppose you know—everyone does—that I had some dealings with King Olaf of Norway."

"Everyone knows that."

"If all goes well, every chief, franklin, and thrall in Greenland will benefit. It is our union with, not our subjection to, our mother country. To that end, the king proposed to give me one of his daughters for my wife, provided she herself consented. It happened that despite the gap in our years she was not ill-disposed to the match. I should explain that she, unlike her father, Olaf, clings to the old Norse faith—in fact she should have been born nearly a century ago—and she sees in me a Norseman of the old breed. Also she was fascinated with what I told her about Greenland—you must understand that she's no ordinary princess and her idol is Sigrid, the heathen Queen of Sweden, who's her distant cousin. As for the king, he's eager for her to marry and go to some distant realm, because all his other sons and daughters are converted to Christianity, and her presence in his court, with her blunt speech and sometimes shrewish ways, embarrasses him in front of the Christian princes. But she would not consent to come here with me on the *Narwhale*. She said she would think it over until I had time to return to Greenland and send a ship for her, by which time she'll reach her eighteenth birthday. She told me to provide proper quarters for her aboard the vessel and to send an escort of high rank, a very good indication she intends to come. I am practically certain that she will. She's sick of her father's Christian court and wants adventure."

My father paused, his eyes on mine, to perceive my response to the proposal. But he read very little there. When he had spoken before of a second marriage, I had guessed that it would be with a Norse woman of high position.

"I suppose you've already proposed to Thorstein that he be your ambassador. As your oldest son and heir, he would be your natural choice."

"No, I haven't mentioned it to him, and I won't. Helga is a very beautiful young woman, and Thorstein's word isn't as good as yours, sorry as I am to say so. Now I've given you a summary of the situation. If Helga comes to Greenland and I become the king's son-in-law, I'll be made Earl of Greenland, and in return for that I've promised the king that the great folk of the island will follow me in pledging allegiance to him. He'll add a land of unknown dimensions to his kingdom. There will be a great increase of trade between Greenland and Norway. I told him too that I thought most of our people would go over to Kris—Olaf himself is a fanatical Christian—but I didn't promise it. Well, Leif, what do you say? The western land, if it exists at all, can wait a few months more for discovery—it has already waited thousands of years. As for your sail to Norway, I'll make the *Narwale* shipshape, and victual her, and pay her crew, and replace all lost or worn-out gear. All I'll ask is your word, given with your hand on your sword in Odin's hearing, that you won't lay hand on the girl in love or lust until you deliver her to my strand, and she's either rejected me or plighted her troth. By the same token, you won't try to set her against me. That agreed, I'd be proud to have you my ambassador to her father's court. You're well-grown, Thorhild taught you manners, and you're a true Norseman. True, we haven't been as close as father and son should be—mainly my own fault, since I thought you took after Thorhild instead of me—but if you carry out this mission with the success that I expect, I'll be behind you in your own ventures. And if you should find a new, fertile land—and I no longer deny the possibility—a land that would furnish trade goods of various sort—I'd see that you were made its earl and stand high with the king."

"I can only say I'll consider it and let you know in the morning."

"Leif, what have you got to lose? Helga will have her own maid-in-waiting, and I'd send old Hildegarde, our best sewing wench, to be her attendant too. Of course you'll take Ugruk. On the trip back you'll have Brother Joseph, lately come from Rome to Olaf's court, who is dying to visit Greenland, and who's good company in spite of his cloth. You should see the homeland, my native land, before you go venturing into unknown and perilous seas. You should carry the greetings of King Olaf in case you should find a peopled land, which is not impossible. But think it over tonight. I have little doubt where your thoughts will lead you."

"And you will not sell me the *Narwhale* unless I attempt this mission?"

"Those are my terms, Leif. After your return from Norway, in success or failure, I promise to sell you the ship for the sum agreed."

I too knew where my thoughts were leading. How would I dare venture into the western mists without the good-luck emblem of the great tusk of the King of the Narwhales pointing the way?

7

Often when Swanhild and I first met at our trysting place, she would say that she had something to tell me, but would "wait till afterward." That day, when I was making for Vixen's Den soon after sunrise, as wild foxes barked in an exuberance of spirit caused by the mating season, when tarmochans had ceased to mate and took off in flocks instead of one by one in their steady, brief flight, when what we called snow geese honked overhead, and flocks of eider ducks encircled the half-frozen ponds, I thought about the important news that I must tell Swanhild, but would wisely "wait till afterward." Otherwise, a quarrel might develop, resulting in an angry parting in which I would be left bereft.

The thought struck me that I should be ashamed of such maneuvers, but had a hard time doing so because they seemed so natural and human.

In due course she took a little nap, with her bright head on the thick of my arm. When she wakened, I spoke the words that I had rehearsed, trying not to be casual-sounding nor yet to emphasize their importance.

"Swanhild, it's just possible that this may be our last meeting before I sail for Norway."

She turned her head quickly, glanced into my face, then fixed her eyes on the roof of the grotto dimly lighted by our oil lamp.

"I will miss you, Leif," she answered in what seemed her ordinary voice and manner.

"My father, Eric the Red, is sending me on an errand. I suppose I should feel honored at his choosing me, considering its importance. In fact I am to be his ambassador at Olaf's court, in view of an alliance between Eric and one of Olaf's daughters. In the long run it could mean an alliance between Greenland and Norway. I am taking the *Narwhale* and will be her captain. Of course I'm looking forward to that."

"Of course. It will be your first command of a real ship, but you are the age for it, and you've had so much experience sailing catboats and other small craft that you'll have no trouble. When can we look for you home?"

This she asked politely, even warmly, but I did not fail to take note of the plural pronoun and perceive how much more the question would have meant had she used "I."

"I feel sure he won't have the ship ready for about two weeks more. He has nearly finished building suitable quarters for her and her lady-in-waiting, meanwhile scraping barnacles from her bottom. Now I think he intends to paint her. If so, we can meet at least once, and maybe several times, if you're agreeable."

"Why shouldn't I be agreeable? I am Swanhild, daughter of Horkel. You are Leif, son of Eric the Red. I come and go when you beckon. I have no right to question your comings and goings. I was a fool to be jealous of Johanna—but I was several years younger—and not all my hopes had died."

I could not answer this. I could only finish what I had started to say.

"If I can get away in September I should be back late in March."

"Perhaps—if you have good sailing. I suppose it's not especially important—but I do hope you can return by the middle of March. I have a special reason."

"What is it?"

"Leif, run your hand over my belly."

I did so, and a thought struck me which I tried to dismiss, but could put by only for a moment.

"You've been eating well, that's certain," I said.

"On the contrary, and on my mother Ellen's advice, I've eaten less and worked harder than ever before."

"Then I don't read your riddle!" As though the answer were not as plain as if written in the sky!

"As near as I can tell, it will be born a few days before the spring equinox. My last flowering came on the fifteenth of June, and my mother counted ten moons, two hundred and eighty days, from that date, the way the women count in Ireland. I got mixed up that month and on the thirtieth of June we met in the turf house. You remember that terrible windy day just after the summer solstice. Still it could be a false alarm. If not, I am about two months along, and I haven't felt life, and I haven't been sick in the morning or my nipples haven't itched and I haven't slept heavily, all of which Ellen says are signs. Still, I think it's the real thing. The baby must be very small as yet, for I haven't shown; maybe it's a girl but I hope not, because boys and men make better thralls than girls and women; they can stand up to it better. I would like to have you here when it happens, but of course it's not really important. You won't have anything to do with the baby anyway— it will be in Ellen's and my charge. I doubt if anyone will ask me who is its father. No thrall woman would dream of such a thing; we have to stand up for one another as far as we can. Eric might ask, but I doubt it; Thorhall might from the goodness of his heart, intending to make the man—whoever he is—help us out a little. But if anyone does ask me, I'll say I do not know. That would mean I've gone with quite a number of different men and that settles it. It's a very ladylike answer, don't you think?"

I could not answer or think clearly about anything, partly, perhaps, because of shock, but mainly because I had become conscious of some very strange, even uncanny, contradiction. Very presently I was able to perceive where it lay—between Swanhild's quiet tone, not in the least acrid or sarcastic, although sad-sounding, perhaps heartbroken for all that I knew of women— between this and the expression on her face and especially in her eyes.

I knew her face well. I had gazed down at it as I held it between my hands or when my hands had been cupped over both her breasts. I knew the play of passion in her mouth and eyes and suddenly flaring nostrils; I knew its anguished bliss at the moment of fulfillment; I knew its all but hidden fury when she had spoken of cleaning a string of fish Johanna and I had caught. It was not now the face of Swanhild in despair or in shame or woe. Instead I knew, without being able to identify the signs, that it was the face of a beautiful young woman trying to conceal triumph so great that it was ecstatic. It was the countenance of secret victory, beautified by this and by the glistening of her melting eyes.

CHAPTER TWELVE

A PAGAN PRINCESS

I

Except for telling Swanhild, who, like most thralls, was close-mouthed about the business of the master, I had confided to no one that I had been appointed Eric's ambassador to Olaf's court, and that my main duty might be the escorting of one of the king's daughters to Greenland to become mistress of his hall. The ship-wrights who had built her cabin on the ship knew of course it had provided for some passenger of no ordinary state. Eric had been reticent in regard to the affair, perhaps to stave off gloatings by his fellow thanes, as well as a deal of gossip and speculation by the folk, in case the princess decided to reject the alliance. The people knew that dealings were afoot between the king and their own chieftain but assumed that these were too large for their common understanding; and, as always, they trusted that this, like almost all the other ventures of their red-bearded leader, would turn out well.

Thus the departure of the *Narwhale* caused little more stir in Osterbig than the sailing of any other trading vessel. I felt that the folk would be astonished and perhaps apprehensive to see me in command, since I had never shipped as an officer, let alone as captain, or any large vessel standing to the high seas. However, they did not give the matter a second thought, and plainly I had pictured in their heads only what lingered disquietly in my own. Still, I felt no real lack of confidence. As Swanhild had said, I was of the age to command. Moreover, I had been dunked in salt spray more times than an abacus could count; and there is an astonishing likeness, the contrast almost always a mere matter of size, between tall-masted ship and a catboat.

My first mate was one of the best officers in Greenland, the freeman Starkad. My second mate, to command the third watch, was Gull Eye, the thrall. The vessel, although smaller than some belonging to great thanes, was less stout than none; moreover, she was a good sailer, as had been proved by shifting breezes and great gales. Of course her rigging and tackle were all shipshape because of Eric's unflagging care.

When we had passed Cape Welcome, which deep-water sailors had begun to call Cape Farewell, we took a northerly course until we sighted Blue Shirt, and then turned east by south on a course which, if the stars stood steady and the currents did not shift, would carry us not far south of the southern coast of Iceland. Through the sea mists we saw the pale glimmer of the icecap drop slowly behind us. In the morning it had vanished from sight, the first time it had done so, on a clear, bright day, since I had come to Greenland. Before us lay the vast expanse of the restless, rolling sea.

It was a long way to a landfall on the Norwegian coast, but throughout the twenty-four-day crossing no event occurred worth telling at home before a winter fire. The weather was not always good, but never, in a Greenlander's opinion, became really foul. The wind was variable in the way of winds: we skipped before it when we could, tacked when we must, fled from a brief gale out of the east, and made up the loss in half a gale that hustled us eastward for three days and nights. Ugruk was my chief joy in these long nights and days, largely because he shared with me his own joy in the journey itself, which was the acme of luxury compared with his prodigious journey to Greenland from his village on some vast river vastly westward. To my disappointment, no albatross kept us company, but the glimmering emblem set in our stern rose and fell with the bow in a wondrous sort of rhythm and ever returned to its aim, the distant and inscrutable horizon. The whole company ate and slept well. We had no shirker aboard, no disputants, no half-hidden hates; and we maintained a fellowship regardless of rank that became heart-warming on pleasant days and evenings when only the helmsman had sea duty worth the name, and the rest could lounge on the deck, and I played my flute.

Starkad, who had seen Rome, Málaga, and Rouen, had warned us shore virgins—a term not quite appropriate, since we had all lost our maidenheads in distant and lonesome seas—not to expect too much of Nidaros,* the royal city of King Olaf. But truly my eyes bulged at the great wharves and the seeming-countless roofs of a city only a few years old. In this respect it rivaled Stavanger, which we had touched three hundred and more sea miles to the southeast. And two of its wonders made Starkad gape, these being the royal residence of the king, completed since Starkad's visit there with Eric, and a great church, called a cathedral, half-completed and leaping toward the sky. These were built only partly of wood, the rest being polished stone.

I had half-intended to seek audience with the king in my best Greenland dress of deerskin and hair seal, as a mark of pride in my own country. But I changed my mind when the wharf master came aboard to greet Leif Ericsson, the son and the ambassador of Eric the Red. This official wore the finest Dorstad wool, with a gold chain from which hung the emblem of his office around his neck. So as soon as I could fetch it, I gave ten of my silver shillings to Starkad and sent him forth to buy me two linen shirts, new shoes, suitable headgear, and red coat and breeches fit for a prince. When I put on this attire, all my shipmates beamed with pride and Ugruk was beside himself.

"I am glad you like it," I told my long-tried companion, "because I am going to have you follow me when I call upon the king." I had noticed that the wharf master had a fellow in attendance when he had called on me.

"What Ugruk wear?" he asked. "His deerskin shirt and pants smell like skunk."

"What is a skunk?"

The question took Ugruk by surprise. His startled expression almost made me guffaw. Then he answered in astonished tones.

"Ugruk not know!"

"Well, where did you hear of one?"

"Long time ago, when Ugruk little boy, some Innuits take *oomiak-sook,* very big skin boat, and go up our river. They no go for anything but see country, have good time. They catch plenty fish, shoot deer, river no flow fast, and by 'n' by they cross moss-

* Known now as Trondheim.

lands and come to big lake like sea, where Skraellings live. Innuits too far from home to get back before river freeze, so they spend winter with Skraellings, pretty women, plenty food. One day when Innuits and Skraellings go hunting, Innuits see pretty little animal with stripe down his back. They try to catch; Skraellings no try to catch, no say nothing, wait holding sides to keep from laughing. Then one Innuit pretty near catch animal and he lift up tail and squirt and some get on Innuit. Leif, you believe Ugruk that Innuit smell a mile! He wash clothes, soak all night under ice, clean with fish oil, still no get rid of smell. Skraellings laugh 'til they fall down! Skraellings call animal skunk. When Innuits come back home late next summer, they say every strong bad smell 'like skunk.' Ugruk pick up saying. Now tell Ugruk what he wear when go see king, not smell like skunk."

My first thought was to array him at least as handsomely as the wharf master's attendant. Then the thought struck me that European finery would not become my dark-skinned, narrow-eyed comrade, and instead I borrowed from the chests of various members of my crew, pants, shirt, and moccasins of snow-white hair seal, along with a white ermine cap. So we had no cause to be ashamed when we made our way, Ugruk walking at my right hand and a step behind me, to the palace door, big as a barn door in Greenland, of beautiful worked oak and studded with copper nails. Two minions, wearing identical clothing, threw open the door at our approach. We were shown into a long, low-ceilinged hall, with oaken floors and paneled walls, lighted by whale lamps. I was invited to sit on a cushioned bench, Ugruk was told to sit on a rude board bench close to the outer door.

In a few minutes an officer wearing a leather cloak came to escort me—Ugruk being left on his bench—into the king's presence. On a throne inlaid with silver and gold sat a tall handsome man of about forty, arrayed in a golden crown and an embroidered and bejeweled gown. But he did not need these additions to appear royal. A great-grandson of Harald Fairhair, ruler of the Western Vikings whose fleets harried a thousand miles of Christian coasts, Olaf was himself the archetype of the Norse race. In only one respect did he differ from my picture of a Viking king of a century before. Around his neck on a golden chain he wore a bejeweled cross.

In front of his throne was a small, cushioned stool. It was not intended as a footstool but a kneeling place for couriers and ambassadors from foreign lands, who had well-greased knees. But I reckoned no Norse chieftain had ever knelt there, nor Swedish or Danish for that matter, although Norman lords might have done so, these one-time Vikings having adopted Frankish ways. Greenland was an independent country; and we spoke the Norse Icelandic speech, and followed Norse ways, and were a stiff-kneed people. Even so, my neck was limber enough to permit a fine bow.

"You are Leif Ericsson, son of Eric the Red?" the king asked.

"Yes, sire." Thus I had been told to address him.

"You are a bold man, we see, fit to be the ambassador of a bold father. You are welcome to your mother country. But in all truth your business is with our youngest daughter, Helga, rather than with us. No doubt Eric the Red informed you that we were agreeable and indeed favorable to his suit, which, if successful, would cause us to name him Earl of Greenland, himself and his countrymen owing allegiance to us. The departure of a beloved daughter to a distant land could not weigh against the benefits to both countries, if the alliance were made. Even so, we have sworn with our hand on the Holy Cross that the princess Helga would herself decide whether to become the Countess of Greenland or to remain in our court. Perhaps she has made up her mind by now, perhaps not, but in either case she desires to converse with you, and you will be shown at once into her presence."

From my abrupt dismissal I got the impression that he was an exasperated king in regard to this affair, perhaps because of trouble in getting it settled; and this might be the fault of a vacillating or willful daughter. As for my part in it, I felt no misgivings. Indeed the thought of being closeted with a royal princess did not stir my pulse in the least degree. In my mind, I had already set my course—neither to try to further Eric's suit nor to retard it. In all truth I abhorred the notion of a young girl, however great a princess, becoming mistress of Ericsholm, where my mother,

Thorhild, had held sway, and who now never visited its hall except as a shadowy, flickering ghost all but lost among other shadows. Still I was resolved not to let Helga know this feeling, or any feeling strong in my heart, and be only her escort, as Eric had directed me, until, landed safely on our strand, she either took his hand in marriage or returned on the ship of some great thane to her native land.

2

The chambers of Princess Helga, not half so large as the opulent throne room, were still as large as the whole house of many a well-to-do Greenland franklin. In one lightning-like glance on first entering the door—like a lightning flash in picking out details— I reckoned them at thirty feet by twenty feet. Also they lacked the gilt and ivory, rugs of wondrous weave, gilded lamps, and ancestral swords and shields and bright, beautiful banners fastened to the wall. Yet the furnishings of the maiden's room were far more unique, I reckoned, than those of the daughters of most Christian kings; and I doubted if their like was to be found in all of Europe. No one had to be told that the girl with wheat-straw hair seated in a tall-backed chair at the end of the room had not yet divorced the old Norse Gods to embrace Kris. The heathen chamber proclaimed the fact.

Doubtless the chair was Christian, because my mother had shown me one remotely like it in Kris' little temple in Bjord. At least it was of the same style, even though the latter was the seat of a mere vicar, while Helga's chair had no doubt been occupied by a bishop, or more likely a cardinal, and because of its handsome decoration in inlaid shell, coral, and agate had no doubt been raped from some burning cathedral by one of her Viking ancestors. There were no finely woven rugs on the floor, but instead snow-white bearskins. Instead of handsome carving, two of the walls bore big lifelike paintings, one of Viking ships in battle with Moorish galleys, and the other of a Viking battle field, over which hovered Valkyries on their snow-white horses, choosing slain heroes to bear to Valhalla. The red paint used to represent blood was of such scarlet hue that I could hardly believe it was not blood.

On the other two walls hung weapons and armor, of an older type than commonly seen at the time, tasseled banners bearing the sign of the cross, many of them blood-stained and obviously taken in battle with Christian kings. Hanging there also were the wide flat horns of elk and the tall antlers of red deer, trophies that I thought had been won by Helga's own shafts. I reckoned that Olaf had made a great mistake in naming Helga after the hero Helgi, which was also the name of a great Norse heroine, for she had tried to live up to both.

The room was warm from the lamps and lighted by these and narrow windows of glass, a substance I had never seen before except as beads or goblets. At Helga herself I took a good look. She was of the true Norse type, which is second to none in the world in stature, clean carving, and beauty, and I could fancy her marriage to a Greenland Viking old enough to be her father causing great consternation among pretty young lords and hangers-on of the court. Still she had not been cast in a mold: there was something of startling individuality in her face, although I could not yet name it. Her hair was like that of the Goddess Sif, of a light, soft straw color, paler than any gold, which she wore in long braids hanging in front of her shoulders as did Viking wives and daughters a hundred years before. Her eyes were of intense blue, almost black-looking in this light and in contrast with her heavy flaxen eyebrows. They were not especially large but of deep and peculiar setting, and I caught myself staring at them in loutish curiosity, which I think was natural enough since they gave some subtle clue to her character if I had the wit to discern it. Her nose was somewhat too regal for my liking, high and thin, but her mouth was lovely. It bespoke warmth and intense feeling and stubborn strength, and if I did not take care and keep a firm will, she would have a deeper effect on me than I intended or desired. It would not be as difficult as I first thought for her to deflect me from my steady, sensible, and safe course.

Her chief attraction to me was the way she held her head, not unduly high, indeed bent a little like a flower on a long stem. Then I saw the reason and my neck prickled. Her own neck, long and white, was curved a little, suggestive of a swan's. And into my soul there stole a remembrance of Minin.

This remembrance was immediately expunged by Helga's opening her beautiful mouth and speaking princess-wise from far above me.

"You were announced to me as the ambassador from Eric the Red. Is that true?"

"Yes, Princess. Also I am his son."

"In that case you are entitled to kneel and kiss my hand."

"No doubt that would be a great honor, but I'll not avail myself of it."

Helga's eyes changed expression. Then she said a strange thing.

"Then it must be you have in you at least a drop of the Viking spirit of your father, Eric?"

"Possibly, but I doubt if I am like him in the least degree."

"Do you hate him?" And this seemed to me hardly a courtly question.

"No, I am proud of him in many ways although I know his faults."

"You have every right to be proud. I have known him to do only one weak thing—to wear the emblem of the God Kris to please my father, the king. True, he has not renounced the Norse Gods, but no doubt he will if he can become Earl of Greenland. I blame none of our own chieftains when they turn away from Odin of the Nine Runes, and from Thor with his sword forged by the dwarf Sindri. It is the easy thing to do, the most profitable, the fashion of the day. The strong thing is to stand by our Gods, no matter how many defeats they suffer from the soft, yet mighty hand of Kris. You no doubt will make the switch before very long."

"Perhaps I will. There is only one person who I know will never do so. You too will know him if you come to Greenland. He is Thorhall, born a thane, yet Eric's reeve."

"Eric is a born leader, a great captain. Still, you no doubt wonder that I would consider marrying a widower more than twice my age."

"No, I do not. When Eric the Red undertakes a venture, it

usually succeeds. Of course this is a venture not to capture a whale, or to find a new island, but to win the hand of a young princess. Your own father, the king, told me he had left the decision to you."

"Did that surprise you, Leif?"

"Yes, because it did not fit in with the tale of the kings of Europe told in Greenland. We have heard that they arrange all marriages of their sons and daughters, to their own advantage. It is said that a princess only ten years old was married to a half-mad gaffer of seventy."

"I know of the incident. The child's father gained a province, and the ceremony was performed by a Christian bishop he himself had appointed. But you forget, Leif, that my father, Olaf, is a Norse king. Kings in the Northland are swiftly gaining in might, their thanes have not the independence or the power that they once had, still they cannot easily be brushed aside, and the Norse spirit of defiance is still a living force. The folk would not have taken kindly to his forcing me into a marriage that I did not myself welcome. In all frankness, Leif, although it may be an unseemly thing for a princess to say in regard to her great sire, he could not have done so if he had tried."

As she spoke quietly her eyes gazed into mine steadily and strongly, and I found myself believing her. Moreover, I found pleasure, as well as a mild excitement, in her firm stand. Instead of her vacillation being the cause of the king's exasperation, it might be her steadfastness. I noticed again the beautiful curve of her long neck and it caused me to daydream about Minin. True, Minin was a Swan Maiden, a Valkyrie, perhaps a Norn, but common swans were creatures not only of great beauty but of great strength. They wing for days and nights through vast, empty skies. The full stroke of their wings can break a man's wrist. There was a tale told in Iceland of an underwater swimmer hunting swans in the summer season, intending to seize them by the legs and drown them, but the birds floating in shimmering light on the blue water had perceived his design, and by a sudden and swift attack they had pulled him down and given him the death he had intended to give them. Suddenly I abandoned the

notion that the proposed alliance between the daughter of a king
and the most powerful chief in Greenland would be a mere marriage of state. If Helga herself had not been more than half-
inclined to it, the affair would not have gone this far. Olaf would
be wasting breath if he boasted again of his pious generosity in
letting the princess decide the outcome. He could not have helped
himself. And the thought came to me that imperious Eric the
Red had met his match.

"You spoke of a thane named Thorhall becoming Eric's reeve,"
Helga remarked thoughtfully. "You said that you yourself might
turn Christian but Thorhall never would. Still that does not explain the expression on your face when you spoke of him. The
feeling came to me that he is closer to you than Eric himself."

"Perhaps that is true. I am prouder of him than I am of Eric."

"I do not doubt it, but it is a bold thing to say. You are Eric's
emissary to my father's court, and your duty is to plead Eric's
cause in his pursuit of a royal bride."

"I do not know how to plead. I have made an agreement with
my father, Eric, to fetch you to Greenland, if you choose to come.
That is my whole part." But it might not remain so, I thought,
if the dark blue of Helga's eyes continued to well into mine,
and I kept seeing her beautifully curved neck, and if the warmth
and earnestness of her voice did not stop causing little thrills and
quivers along my spine.

"Pray answer one question, Leif Ericsson. It is of no real importance, I suppose, but I am curious. Are you not hoping that I
will decline Eric's suit, perhaps because you want no woman to
take your mother's place? Eric told me that you and she were very
close."

"I do not believe that you or any woman can take my mother's
place in Eric's life and heart, and certainly not in mine. Still, you
may become his beautiful, young bride and make him Earl of
Greenland—except for our wild mountains and our icecap over
which no earl—and no princess—will ever rule."

"You are no flatterer, Leif. As a woman I am slightly attracted
by it but as a princess I should rebuke you for the lack. Also, you
have not answered my question as to whether you desired Eric's

suit to prosper. You need not answer it now—it would not affect me in the least. No great prophetess has foretold that I would become his bride, but I believe that I will. I consider him the strongest man I have ever met, and every woman wants a strong lover and husband regardless of his age. And in his suit he has two abettors."

"I did not know of them."

"You may as well know. They are the common talk of my father's court, which you will frequent for many weeks and months to come. I have a desire, I may say a longing, to live in Greenland. That has been true ever since I learned of its discovery—that rough, unknown, gigantic far-west land. It must be like Norway was, before the days of Harald Fairhair."

"No, Greenland is more harsh than Norway ever was—colder, less yielding, most of it indomitable to man."

"It will not be too rough for me if I choose to live there. The other abettor is my father, who will be better off—at least more powerful—with me married off and gone. Young as I am, unwedded, I am still an obstacle to his great plans. I was the indirect cause of his meeting the greatest defeat since he became King of Norway. Perhaps you have heard of it—but away in wintry Greenland perhaps you have not. In this city, Nidaros, there stands a temple to the God Frey, the finest in the kingdom. It houses an image of Frey, riding Golden Bristles, his great boar, and the figure is worked in wood, ivory, and with gold harried from the Christian coasts by Olaf's grandsire. Olaf ordered the temple torn down, and the ivory and gold of the image used to make an altar for a church to Kris. The folk refused to obey him. There was nothing he could do but retreat. And who do you suppose he blamed for the people's defiance?"

"You."

"He should have blamed first of all the Norse spirit. They do not take kindly to the decrees of absolute monarchs. But I will confess to you, Leif, that his inability to make his daughter give up what he calls her heathen religion encouraged the people. And when they massed below the king's window, shouting defiance, I stood at my window and cheered them."

"Then it is no wonder that he wants you married and gone."

"And mark you, if I marry Eric the Red—and that is the bent of my mind—my father, the king, will have accomplished a great feat of statesmanship. Greenland, I mean its habitable parts, will in all probability become part of his kingdom. Eric told him so, and I believed it. Wilderness though it may be, he will receive rich tribute in ivory and furs, and our folk will benefit by increased trade for our timber and grain. Rich Greenlanders will buy their luxuries from us instead of from the Franks—such as hourglasses, wine, linen, silk, and fine raiment—which, if we do not ourselves produce, we can buy from the southern marts and sell at a profit. Aye, I am talking like a greasy merchant. But I want you, Leif—for whom I feel an unexplainable respect—to know that my main inclination to marry Eric is my admiration for a great Norseman of a vanishing kind, a great chieftain, a strong man, and—this too I must confess—a Norse yearning for new scenes, new experience, and the thrill of the unknown."

There was an intensity of feeling in Helga's face. In this, it was like Minin's when the Swan Maiden had bade me summon Isis and the other great prophets and prophetesses that I might know my fate. And it seemed to me that now, again, gazing into a face not as beautiful as Minin's, yet on which my eyes feasted, I would know my fate. At least I knew my loneliness, a thing I had never clearly perceived before, a loneliness broken mainly by Ugruk and Thorhall, and it was a strange sort, at once tragic and noble, and it seemed I must endure it all my life long. It was suddenly made sharper by the presence of this brave and beautiful princess, perhaps because my heart told me that it could vanish forever if she were my great companion.

"A few minutes ago I told you a lie," I confessed. "At the time I did not know it was a lie, at least a falling short of the truth, but I know it now. You had asked whether I wanted Eric to win his suit. I had answered it did not matter to me. It does matter a great deal. I will perform my appointed task, but it is one that I hate. I do not doubt that Eric will win you—as my brother, Thorstein, won a prize almost equally great—everything you have told me points toward his victory—but I will no longer pretend to myself or to you that I do not care. The plain truth is, which I declare, I want you for my own, not my father's, bride. But it is also the plain truth that I could not accept you now, even if you were willing, so of that I speak no more, and I will seek strength never to speak of it again."

"Leif, you refused to kneel and kiss my hand. Will you bend to where I sit and kiss me on the lips?"

"I am bound neither to lay hand on you in love or lust. But I am not bound to deny your kiss, if given me for—what I do not know except that it is neither love nor lust. My princess!"

I stooped and bent my head, and the next I knew, Helga's lips were on mine, giving me a warm, sweet kiss. Then I stood straight and strode out of the room, and although bearing the great burden of a heavy heart, I looked my fate in the face.

3

When I came again in the presence of King Olaf, my purpose only to ask his leave to depart, he sent his attendants out of the throne room so he could have privy talk with me.

"Leif—and we will address you so, by right of our place and years—do you feel that the suit you are making on behalf of your father has made progress?" the king asked.

"Sire, the princess Helga said as much," I answered.

"Why, we are glad to hear it. It is within our power and the ancient right of kings to arrange marriages for their daughters, regardless of the wenches' desires, the first consideration being the begetting of posterity—maidens worthy to marry kings and princes, and men fit to wear crowns. The second consideration is the extension and enrichment of the realm. In both of these respects, the great thane Eric the Red is eminently suitable. Aye, it may be a king's duty to bring about such marriages, and harken to no protest, because the God of the Christians imparts to kings, through his priests and by signs and wonders, and even by words spoken in their inward ears, omniscient wisdom. Yet we were a father before we were a king, and our heart ruled our head in

matters affecting our youngest daughter, Helga, and in this matter we lent to her the rein."

"Sire, I am sure she is to be trusted with it."

"Would we could be as sure! Our daughter Helga is impulsive
as well as stubborn. We trust that you painted for her the joys of
life on Greenland, the severe but wholesome climate, the feasts
and festivals, the gathering of the thanes and their families in
joyous concourse, the pleasures of chase and warren in the vast
unpeopled forests, and angling for salmon and great trout."

"No, I have not done so. It was not part of my agreement with
my father, Eric the Red."

"Before Mary, Mother of God, I believe that Eric acted wisely
in not instructing you to do so. The princess might have thought
you were trying to press her to a quick agreement. Let her take
her own time—the outcome will be all the more sure. And now
it comes to me that my decision not to command or to try to persuade my daughter to this course was evidence of the omniscient
wisdom that the God Kris gives to Christian kings."

I needed to smile a little, after such long sobriety, so I smiled
inwardly at what Thorhall would think—and perhaps say, because I had never known him to be frightened into silence—
about Christian or any other kind of kings being given "omniscient
wisdom." I knew enough Norse lore to know quite well how the
Viking chieftains would have received Olaf's boast in the days of
Harald Fairhair—they would have laughed all down their bellies
and be forced to stamp their feet in unexpressible mirth. Also the
king had spoken of Greenland's vast, unpeopled forests. Obviously Eric had not told him that Greenland had not even a spinney, let alone a forest, of full-sized trees. Indeed the king should
have guessed the shortage from the fact that our main import
from Norway had been lumber.

No doubt Eric had had a game to play. I did not penetrate it,
but I thought that at last I had penetrated the real reason for his
choosing me, instead of Thorstein, as his emissary. Eric had said
I kept my word better than did Thorstein—and I knew of scores
of instances of its truth. But knowing I would keep my promise
not to lay hand on Helga in love or lust had put him in a position

to play cat and mouse with me. I could look at Helga, and yearn, and pant, but must not touch her. Picturing this only too truly had given my father, Eric, great pleasure. It was full compensation for his losing the game of sending me on a fool's errand after a narwhale horn, while he stood to sea without me. Truly it seemed to me that this new and greater joke might, from Eric's viewpoint, prove a side-splitting success. I had no reason to believe, despite her warm kiss, that Helga would ever desire to yield to any touch of mine; but I could not be certain of this, and in such case I could well curse the runes that were carved on my heart and soul that I must not break faith.

"The feasts and festivals of which we spoke," the king went on, "are, to my sorrow, heathen and not Christian. Still we are not one to begrudge folk who have not received the blessings of Christian teachings such rude amusements as they can find. In time, sooner than you can believe, this will be changed. The great God Kris, who died for man's salvation, will be the founder of the feast, the celebrant of the festival, not some heathen God or Goddess such as Thor or Frey. Tell us, Leif, if what your great sire told us is true—that you yourself are inclined to follow Kris?"

"Aye, I am, largely because of the teaching and example of my mother, Thorhild, but I am also inclined to shout to Odin and dance before him and make offerings to him in the groves, because of the teaching and the example of great Thorhall, my father's reeve."

"The former is good news, the latter painful. Tomorrow, when we will receive you at the same time as today, you shall meet Novice Joseph. He is not a duly ordained and sanctified priest of the Holy Church. He strives to become a member of an order of monks, known in Italy as the Ambrosians, meaning a brotherhood seeking the blessing of Saint Ambrose. He has been guided from on high to see the world before he withdraws behind the walls of the Ambrosian abbey. Mark you, Leif, priests of the Holy Church may marry—although there is some talk that this may be changed in a few decades—and live lives quite like ordinary folk. But the brethren of the great Christian orders must bind themselves to an austere and celibate life, spent mainly in prayer and in self-castigation. Frankly he confesses to being attracted to earthly pleasures, rich eating, deep drinking, and profane love. On this journey he is testing himself, to discover whether he is worthy to be a friar of St. Ambrose. It is his wish to go to Greenland and do good works there—particularly in assisting Eric the Red to wean the folk away from their heathen Gods to the true Gods, Jehovah and Kris. Tomorrow he will speak unto Helga, and it is our wish that you too be present when he does so, and perhaps obtain much good therefrom."

"Sire, I will surely do so."

But in all truth Novice Joseph would have to tell me something more than I had heard thus far at Olaf's court to increase my inclination to turn Christian. Olaf himself had caused me to veer in the opposite direction. In the first place I did not like his speaking of our Greenland feasts and festivals as crude amusements. No doubt they were of a crude sort compared to those given in the great cities of Europe; but these cities did not stand in a primal wilderness from which they must wrest bare life by brow sweat and the labor of chilled and aching hands. Worse, I suffered from the suspicion that as far as kings were concerned, Christianity was a policy more than a faith. One of its great tenets was meekness, and kings wanted their subjects to be meek, and hence easier to rule and despoil, while they themselves wore ermine and bejeweled robes and boasted of omniscient wisdom. I had already heard of Olaf's overtures of marriage to Sigrid, Queen of Sweden, despite her heathen faith; and I did not believe that his main ambition was her conversion; and I could not help but rejoice that she had stuck to her Gods and refused his hand.

It so chanced that on the morrow, when Ugruk and I were again shown into the waiting room in the palace, we found it occupied by a young, sallow-skinned, nimble-looking fellow who had bright black eyes and wore a white robe and hood. I was almost certain that this was Novice Joseph, and that I could expect a pious discourse of some sort. Instead he gave a great start at sight of Ugruk and startled me too with his first brisk remark in oddly accented but excellent Norse.

"Mary Mother, what manner of man is this!" he cried out.

"What would you take him for, Your Holiness?" I answered.

"My Holiness, fiddle dee dee! I am no more holy than you, which may be a slight exaggeration of speech, considering that I have undergone Christian baptism while you remain a rank heathen; still to judge by appearances I have not missed it far. I am Novice Joseph, far from purged of sins of the flesh, and you, unless I have mistaken your identity, are Leif Ericsson, ambassador from Eric the Red. To answer your question, I know not what to take the fellow for! I have traveled widely—all, of course, in the way of pilgrimage—and I have never seen his like. By complexion he could be a rather dark-skinned Lapp, but Lapps do not have such big white teeth and black slits for eyes. Where in the name of all that is holy and unholy—and a man of the cloth must recognize both conditions—did you get him?"

"He came up out of the sea."

"Like a merman? I have seen mermen—so the sailors said—although they looked to me more like a small variety of sea cow. By heaven, I think he is of a race unknown to the savants of Padua!"

"He might well be. His name is Ugruk and he calls himself an Innuit."

"Yes, I am an Innuit," Ugruk broke in, displaying his perfect command of the Norse-Icelandic language.

"Did you come from the north of Greenland? Your master, Eric, told us that he believed an unknown tribe of savages lived in those parts."

"Shaman—if that is what you are—you have made two mistakes. My master is Leif, not Eric the Red. And I came not from the north, but from the west."

Joseph's eyes rounded. "But that is impossible," he said, turning to me. "Greenland is the most westerly land on earth—or so our geographers maintain."

I opened my hands and shrugged.

"What does he mean by 'shaman'? Do you know?"

"He means a priest or a magician of some sort."

"I am neither one. Your keen Norse eyes have already noticed that the cross attached to my vestments hangs upside down. That is the sign that I am not yet an initiate to the brotherhood to which I aspire. Will you explain this to the aboriginal, as I wish to converse freely with him and do not wish to put him on his guard."

"Of that last there is no danger," I answered. "And I need make no explanations to him because he understood you perfectly."

"Gods in heaven, but I yearn to visit Greenland! The king wishes it, and will you promise me, Leif, to whom I wish to be a friend, you will say or do nothing to oppose it? For instance, at your command I will stay the length of the ship from your young charge. I pledge myself here, and now, by the only God to whom I plight my troth—his name would not interest you, as it is in a foreign tongue—I will never closet myself with her throughout the journey; when I am with her it will always be on the open deck or in your company. I am far from a holy father, far from the meanest saint, even those saints who gained sanctification by helping a favorite cardinal become Pope—still I was born a gentleman, and to another gentleman I keep my word." And Novice Joseph spoke with utmost fire.

"I welcome that declaration," I told him after a little thought. "My bond is only that I myself do not lay hand on Helga in love or lust until she comes to shore at Eric's strand and definitely accepts or rejects his offer of marriage. But since I am making this journey as his ambassador, since my mission is to bring Helga to Greenland in the expectation of her becoming his wife, I am duty-bound, I believe, to prevent if possible any dalliance between her and some other wooer. Joseph, with that agreement I gladly promise to say nothing or to take no step to prevent you from journeying to Greenland on the *Narwhale,* and it is my hope that you will do so, for the way is long, and you are a lively fellow, and I will enjoy your company."

"By Saint Christopher, the patron of travelers, I must make you a confession. When just now I spoke of gentlemen, I regretted using the word the instant it was out of my mouth, thinking that you, born in wintry Iceland, dwelling in Greenland far away and wild, would not know what the term meant, or would resent my using it. It is true you are a rustic. You are also a pagan, which word I believe stems from *paganus,* which used to mean a country lout or peasant. For any man to say he is a gentleman is rather an indication that he is not one; otherwise he should expect gentle folk to know it without being told. Obviously you felt no slight; you understood my motive; and the only answer is that you yourself, Leif, are a gentleman. There is no word harder to define unless we are satisfied with its patent meaning— a gentle man. You are a hunter, a trapper—the tale reached us from one of Eric's sailors that you broke your brother's arm—you fight the elements almost every day of your life, so 'gentle' would not seem to fit you. Yet you remain a gentleman."

"If so, and I doubt it, it came about through the influence of my mother, Thorhild. From her, too, I inherited a love of music and learned to make it. But let us speak now of Ugruk. I would like to have him see Helga, for his great pleasure, and it occurs to me she might like to see him."

"Indeed she will! She has a most lively mind—another way of saying she is devoured by curiosity about everything on earth, and below it and above it. Let me consider a moment as to the best means. King Olaf greatly admires his kinsmen, the Dukes of Normandy, who like many newly great are sticklers for ceremony. . . ."

In the brief pause ensuing I thought again of Minin, my Swan Maiden. The King of the Ice had said that, like most birds, she was eaten up from beak to tail with curiosity. I recalled the lovely downward curve of Helga's neck. I wished she were another manifestation of Minin, to whom I had been led by the hand of fate, finding her in a palace far from my accustomed scenes, and for a few seconds I could almost believe the wild fancy. But even if she were Minin—and her hair was of the same pale gold—still my hands would be bound, and we could not make love beside some haunted water.

"Leif, we will not trouble the king over so slight a matter," Novice Joseph replied with emphasis. "Neither will we ask permission of the princess Helga. When the time comes for us to

enter her chambers, you will bid Ugruk follow you. If either Olaf
or Helga rebukes you, I will take the blame, giving a fine and
pious reason why I wished the two heathens, Helga and Ugruk,
to meet. You see, I am a privileged character at this court, a condition I do not in the least deserve."

Presently a lackey brought word that the princess Helga would
see the ambassador, son of Eric the Red, and Novice Joseph in
her chambers. When at my bidding Ugruk followed us through
the door, the liveried servant started to protest, only to be silenced
by a withering glance from Joseph's black eyes. Helga's dark blue
eyes popped to my satisfaction.

"Leif, is this man a Greenlander?" she demanded.

"By adoption, my lady. He comes from a country without a
name, but it is near a place which certain savages call Alaska, and
through it flows a very great river. His name is Ugruk."

"I have never seen—can he speak Norse?"

"Fluently."

"Ugruk, I am not a wide traveler like your master, Leif. I have
never seen as brilliant black eyes as yours, or as shining teeth, or
a more wide and pleasing smile. Did you know of these gifts?"

"No, beautiful Helga, I did not. I have seen my image in a
pool of clear water——"

"Leif, draw aside the curtain immediately behind you. It is the
entrance to my dressing room. Ask Ugruk to go in and look to the
right, and tell me what he sees."

Ugruk was gone only a moment. When he came forth he
seemed bewildered but by no means frightened. As well I remembered, Ugruk was hard to frighten.

"Well, what did you see?" Helga asked, her eyes shining with
mirth.

"I saw Ugruk. I was standing in the middle of the room, and
there was Ugruk on the wall, not just a picture like those we
Innuits carve of a bear or a reindeer, but Ugruk himself, the
same height, the same width, and the same thick. When Ugruk
stare at himself, himself stare back. When my hand jerk a little,
so did Ugruk's hand." Then in an earnest voice, "Helga, this is
big magic. You believe Ugruk. Suppose some day you stand in

room, and at same time stand on wall. Suppose you go out of room, but the other Helga stay on wall. Suppose some man hate you, because you no marry him. Suppose some woman want to kill you, because you take her lover. One of them go in, take big rock, take stick, take iron kettle, hit you hard. When Helga on wall break into little pieces, Helga in other room fall down and die, pretty bones all broken."

Meanwhile, Helga listened with utmost gravity. Then she carefully collected her thoughts to answer. Joseph had time to murmur in my ear.

"Sympathetic magic. That's what the savants of Padua call it. All primitives believe in it. I think I do too—a little."

"Ugruk, thank you for your concern," Helga said with heart-warming sincerity. "I will never forget it. But I assure you there's no danger. You said you had seen your reflection in water. In a way of speaking that is what you saw today. Imagine a pool being frozen and the ice remaining perfectly clear. Clever artisans in Saxony know how to melt sand, let it harden in a thin transparent sheet, then paint the back with what is called quicksilver. You can see your face in it clearer than in any pool."

"But it makes two people out of one," Ugruk protested. "Ugruk on wall, Ugruk standing in room, no can tell one from the other."

"It is only a looking glass, the finest in Norway. My father, the king, sent for it and paid a purse of silver coins, and the glass was wrapped in many folds of cloth and sent to me on a ship. There will be many such wonders in Eric's hall if I marry him and he becomes Earl of Greenland. Will you come and serve us, and have an easy life with little work, and wear fine clothes and eat fine food?"

Helga's eyes glinted as she asked this question, but I thought that it was prompted by deep-seated curiosity, not self-gain.

"No, Helga, not unless Leif tell me to and then I no do it. I get in kayak, go live with Innuits."

"Leif will never tell you to. I think that master and man are almost as much alike as you and your image in the glass. Joseph! You have just listened to a savage. He may be what you call a pagan but I doubt if he's even that. I wonder if he has any religion except to keep faith with the people and the things that he loves. Well, I will try to follow his example. I am almost persuaded to marry Eric, for he is a great man and Greenland must be a great country, but whether or not I do so I will not turn my coat. Perhaps you should tell my father this—for if his reason for having you attend me was a hope that you could convert me, he is fated for disappointment."

"My princess, do you suppose I shared that hope? Not for one minute. But pray you, do not ask me to tell the king of my recognition of the impossible. He might not let me go with you, Leif, and Ugruk to Greenland, for which journey I would well-nigh trade my journey to heaven in due course, but of course I don't expect to get there anyway."

"I doubt it too, Joseph," Helga answered with a sly smile. "I know not why not—unless you are too fond of anchovies, washed down with Balearic wine."

The thought struck me then that although my companions' conversation had appeared to hold little meat, I would have found a good deal had I the wit to cut away the fat and the gristle. Of one fact I was almost certain. It was that just as my brother, Thorstein, had beaten me to the greatest prize in Greenland, my father, Eric, was going to beat me to the greatest prize in Norway, and perhaps in all Europe. And even to dwell upon it was folly. Very Norne, Queen of the Norns, the Norse personification of fate, had kept me out of the race.

Unless, of course, events most strange would occur in Greenland before the hour of my loss had struck, such as the shattering blow of Thor's hammer on very Blue Shirt—or the wild eruption of a volcano I had thought extinct.

4

The winter passed as one might expect, a period of the year in which frost bit deep, winds blew shrill and biting and sometimes howled, snow fell or changed to sleet or slacked off, spells of pale sunlight took turns, without visible cause, with intervals of intense cold. On the whole the weather was far more severe than that of Iceland, more than two hundred sea miles nearer the North Star, but not equaling in severity that of Osterbig on Greenland, which we knew lay almost due west of Olaf's capital, and not holding a candle, or better say an icicle, to the extreme cold of the first winter spent in Greenland by our eight pioneers. Reason told me that Nidaros and Osterbig should have about the same climate, and that of Iceland a great deal worse. Here reason missed its mark, and I could not account for the discrepancy, unless it was caused by the variation of temperature of adjacent seas.

The nights were long, usually windy, and inclement; the days were short, and often dim and dour. We Greenlanders occupied both with little physical discomfort, even though we did not dig holes, stuff them with dried leaves or dead grass, and curl up and sleep until spring. I played my flute to grateful hearers, I practiced reading and writing the Norse-Icelandic language as enscribed by poem makers, and studied every map in the king's library that even pretended to portray the western ocean only to learn enough reliable lore to stick in the ear of a louse. Even so, Novice Joseph was able to rid me of some perplexities which the geographers of the day did not in the least relieve, because of his having read a Latin translation of an ancient Greek manuscript found in Alexandria and brought to the library at Padua by some learned Roman. It was a sort of summary of the findings and theories of a Greek named Eratosthenes. The meat of it was that our earth was not flat, but a sphere, of 252,000 stadia in circumference, which Joseph said meant 25,000 miles!

"I thought it was a sphere," I answered, to be saying something while my brain stopped rocking. Indeed, no seagoing people like Norsemen could fail to observe the sinking below the horizon of a departing ship, and the slow rising above the horizon of an incoming ship, proof of the curvature of the earth. But this estimation of its size took my breath.

"The Greek fellow had never been around it, so how could he know?" Joseph went on. "My friend, it is astonishing what vast problems our minds can solve with sufficient application. I forget his procedures—they had something to do with measuring shadows—and his argument. I myself have surmised that the earth is spherical, as are the moon and the sun, but that monstrous sum of miles——"

"How far to the eastward of Land's End in Iberia lies Greece?"

"I happen to know that. About two thousand miles. That was the sum arrived at by mariners of Tyre, who taught it to us Romans."

"Are there lands lying east of Greece? My mother told me that Alexander——"

"His little jaunt eastward took him at least three thousand miles."

"The Vikings believed that Land's End in Iberia thrust into the western sea about as far as the western capes of Ireland. The westernmost land in Greenland that we know is two thousand or more miles west of Ireland. The total of those figures is seven thousand. If the Greek was right, that leaves about eighteen thousand miles unaccounted for."

"Leif, my friend, I think I know what you are driving at. There is plenty of room for any lands that we can find. But as a civilized —in these dark times when inquiry is mainly concerned with God, Gods, angels, and various abodes of the dead, I may say an educated man—I wish you otherwise intelligent Norse would forsake the notion of the ocean rolling over a precipice into Hel. I assure you that the steam that would rise up would blot out the sun and the stars. I believe it rolls on and on, sometimes washing shores of islands large and small, until it reaches the eastern coast of Hind, which Alexander visited, and which the Greeks know to be in one piece with Greece, Italy, Gaul, and even your beautiful but somewhat inclement Norway. To venture westward into that ocean as far as Greenland will cause the name of Eric the Red to resound in history. Even I, a churchman of sorts, who should fix his eyes on heaven, was so excited by the discovery that I yearn to go there. And if my guess is correct, that you intend to go much farther, perhaps to the homeland of the delightful savage Ugruk, I can only say it is not impossible that you will succeed. I do not wish to accompany you, you understand. I only advise you, in a friendly detached way, to prepare for a long journey."

This I was doing already—lading the ship with the most necessary and durable stores. In the way of victual I stowed salt meat and fish, rat-proof crates of hard-baked bread, corn, Normandy raisins, dried peas, skins of Spanish wine to raise flagging spirits and expensive sealed casks of imported lime juice, which the Vikings believed freshened stale, stinking water, warding off the dread mariner's disease, which caused a man's teeth to loosen in his gums. The number of water casks I bought astounded the town's coopers. The deal of sail and other spare tackle that I stowed delighted the ship chandlers. And the news of this commerce reached the palace and was remarked upon by Helga as she sat opposite me at a little table, striving with great patience to teach me to play chess.

"I have heard that you are readying your ship for a long stay at sea," she said.

"It may be long and it may be short, depending on the whims of the weather, the will of the Gods, and other variables on which a captain must count when he stands to sea."

"On first hearing the report I assumed that the heavy stowing was for the return voyage to Greenland, with stores ample for our survival in case we were blown far off our course. Since then the notion has crossed my mind that you intend to embark upon another journey shortly after our arrival there, and to save money you are buying stores and tackle here at their source instead of from Greenland merchants."

"That is right in the main."

"Leif, is the journey you intend a soon recrossing to Norway? If so, you must be assuming that I will not take to Greenland, or Eric's hand in marriage?"

"Princess, I make no such assumption. My father, Eric, will capture your fancies more completely on his own strand, which he fits as a white bear fits an icefield, than in your father's court. Indeed, if you do refuse Eric's hand he will have to provide for your return to Norway on some other ship, which of course he will do in his handsome fashion. As soon as we refill our water casks and stow seal and whale oil, I am taking the *Narwhale* on a long voyage into the unknown west."

She made a series of moves on the chessboard, fast as a bird can hop, and won the game. Then she leaned back in her luxurious chair with a faint smile that I thought fixed.

"Leif, have you considered that should I decline an alliance with Eric, your pledge not to touch me in love or lust is no longer binding?"

"Yes, Helga, I have considered it often."

"And you would rather journey into the unknown western ocean than back to Norway with me in your untrammeled charge?"

"I do not know what I would rather do. I know only what I must do. The action is forced upon me by unseen and unknown powers. It is to seek, and to discover if it exists, a land lying far westward of Greenland."

"Your father, Eric the Red, discovered Greenland, and the unseen and unknown powers of which you speak is the ambition, perhaps even the need, to equal or surpass his exploit."

"It happened I was the first of Eric's company to spy the Greenland shore. It was a glory unto my soul. It wants such glory again, and perhaps it will realize a much greater glory, for in this case the venture is mine, not that of my father, Eric, and it is possible that the discovery itself will be of even greater moment than the discovery of Greenland."

"I wish you would not speak in that haughty way. You are not a king, you have no royal blood in your veins of which I know, you are only the younger son of a great chieftain whose grandsire was a slave. Yet on occasions such as this your usage of the language is not that heard upon the street or often within the palace, and indeed it is the Norse spoken by my father, the king, when he addresses the great lords of Europe."

"I cannot help myself, Princess. I say what comes to my tongue. Perhaps I picked it up from my mother, who was the granddaughter of Harald Bluetooth."

"It frightens me a little. It is as though, unknown to yourself, your fate is no common fate, that you have been chosen by Odin to play the main part in some great and perhaps awful drama, such as that which swirled about Tristan or Sigurd. It may be I will have a part in it, whether happy or tragic I know not. I have an inkling of impending events that shake me to the marrow of my bones. Leif! Do you suppose we are both fey?"

"The sign of it, we are told, is a great gaiety of spirit and a strange shine in the eyes. Your eyes look very dark—almost black. Instead of gay, we are both close to tears without knowing why. I know of no immediate danger hanging over us both. In a few more weeks we will take ship together on the perilous sea, but that ship is stout, the crew skilled, and my first officer, Starkad, knows the course like the palm of his own hand. No, I think we will both live—you to become the bride of the Earl of Greenland, I to voyage into the unknown."

"I ask a strange, perhaps an improper question. Whom will you leave in Greenland that you love?"

"There are some that have shipped or hunted with me, and fought wolves and walrus by my side, but my feeling for them is a great fellowship, not love such as you mean. I have a brotherly love for a poem speaker and singer named Ian, and a son's love for an old Viking of whom I told you, Thorhall, Eric's reeve, unless, indeed, he will leave Eric, as his right as a thane, and sail with me. So my answer to your question would be no one unless —and in this case my love is so walled within my heart, or so fenced outside of my heart, that I do not know if it truly is love— so I will answer, no one unless it be my father's bride."

Helga bowed her head a little, her two forefingers pressing down the lids of her eyes. Then she removed them and her dark blue eyes were misty, but not wet, and beautiful as the strange eyes of Minin, my Swan Maiden.

"Leif, you are long past the age that most Norsemen marry," Helga said in a soft and lovely voice. "One score and nearly half a score. I know that you greatly desired Johanna, and perhaps greatly loved her, but you lost her to your brother, Thorstein, many years ago, and that wound is healed by now. Yet you are a true man, loving woman, and surely there must be some young woman in your life of whom you have not spoken."

"Yes, there is a young woman in my life, but I cannot say that I love her in the way of sweethearts, and indeed I must say that I do not. I do not know exactly why this is true. She is good to look upon, keen of mind, resolute, arousing in me deep passion, yet there is some barrier between us that prevents my giving her my love."

"Could the barrier be—*hate?*"

"If so, it is undeserved as far as I know. She makes love with no other man, I with no other woman. At present she is growing great with child."

"Is she far below you in station?"

"Yes, as people count it."

"Do you intend to take her with you on your westward journey?"

"No."

"Do you wish to tell me her name? If I remain in Greenland, and you are far at sea, I will help her in every way I can."

"No, I cannot give her name to anyone."

"What can you give me, Helga, daughter of Olaf the King? Nothing but your close brief guard. So read the Runes of Norne, or my vision fails! Now I will summon Hallfred, my father's scald. I want him to recite one of his great poems."

I had seen Hallfred in the court, or I should say gazed upon him in awe and wonder, for no living poet was his master and hardly any his peer. He had been born in Iceland, of a Norse father and Irish mother and when a very young man attached himself to Olaf Kvaran, King of Dublin, and then to Olaf's brother-in-law, Olaf Tryggvesson. He was an old man now, of gaunt frame and face and wispy white hair, although his voice remained wonderfully youthful and the whites of his very large eyes showed under the brimming, brilliant iris of bluish-gray. At Helga's request he recited a great feat of a still-living hero, Brian Boru. It was the tale of how Brian avenged the murder of his brother Mathgamhain, King of Munster, and how he himself became king. The dreadful story of love and hate, savage cruelty, and remorseless retribution would have been deeply moving in runic writing on a parchment; to hear it recited by its author, himself shaken by its passion, his old eyes blazing and his voice like massed trumpets, caused a tempest of feeling in both Helga and me. I had never seen Ireland but had heard much about its limpid rivers, rolling downs, hills peopled by fairies, and the intense green of its earth; and I wondered to what depths Hallfred would have been moved in telling a story of hate and revenge in the wild wastes of Greenland, under its towering, treeless, and austere mountains capped by everlasting ice.

"I am overwrought," Helga told me, when she had given Hallfred leave to go. "Can't you do anything for me?"

"I can wipe your beauteous eyes of their tears." And I did so, with my silken kerchief.

"Is that all? Can you not hold me, quietly, a little while?"

"I may not lay hand on you in love or lust, and both are sweeping through me as the Lava of Evil Deeds swept the tableland northward of Vatnajokull when the Gods were young. With my hands at my sides, I will play fast and loose with my vow, and like a swindling Law Speaker enforce the letter of its law but not its spirit."

Then I kissed her burning tear-wet mouth, and she replied with a wildly passionate kiss; then with my head bent, I left the chamber.

CHAPTER THIRTEEN

THE DARK POWERS

I

The winter wore away, it seemed as slowly as rock under a trickle of water. In early February, the stern grim season became capricious and inconstant as would be his daughter April, when her time came to be born. One day his winds would howl and shriek like a troop of banshees, and the next day murmur like lovesick doves. On the next day its still cold would freeze a man's ears unless he wore them muffed; and on the very next the sun would break out of the cold clouds, radiant, as though expecting us earth dwellers to forget her sulky spells, and smile up at her, and bask in her lukewarm light, believing her show of having come to stay. Rain and snow took turns; there was a flux of fog, chill, thick and dismal; and if this were Greenland the folk would speak of the Fog Giant striding the shores of the cold but ice-free fiords. Here I had heard his name spoken only once since my coming here. It might be that the people did not believe in him any more, or at least could not see him in the eyes of imagination; and the thought occurred to me that all sorts of wondrous beings such as trolls, dwarfs, elves, and Swan Maidens did not make out well in the countries where the God Kris gained, and Odin and Thor gave ground, and where Christian church bells rang, and small steepled churches were more and more, and the wild and lonely shrines of the Old Ones were visited less and less, and their names sounded ever more rarely on men's lips. Indeed the growth of cities, the cutting of roads through the forest, and the bringing of plows to the wild meadows, and especially the sight of many sails of trading vessels in the harbors were all of ill omen to the Gods of the Vikings.

Yet I must confess that by and large the winter had not been nearly as severe as at home in the same season of the year, despite the fact the nights at Nidaros were somewhat longer and the days shorter. The thought came to me that the slow weakening of our native Northland Gods and the growing strength of Kris improved the weather in some magic way.

"I doubt it," Novice Joseph remarked when I broached the idea to him. "If Kris can keep you from freezing to death, he also ought to be able to bring rain in times of drought, when people starve to death. Yet Toledo, one of the oldest sees of the Holy Church, suffered a calamitous drought only five years ago. Still I like to have you raise such questions, especially to well-educated, less fanatical churchmen, because if Christianity is going to sweep the known world, as our Pope piously believes, it must not be presented as a cure-all. It must appeal to the sober mind as well as the fervent heart."

"It's going to sweep Leif off his feet before he's much older," Helga remarked rather acidly. For we three were together in the palace library, where Joseph had just read to us parts of a great manuscript entitled *The Life of John of Damascus*, lately written by John, patriarch of Jerusalem. Ugruk had taken himself off to shape a bow of an excellent staff of yew wood he had bought at the wharves, and I found myself wishing I had gone with him, because Joseph's translation of the great patriarch's writings from Latin into Norse was mainly over my thick Norse head.

"Perhaps so," Joseph answered Helga. "He hasn't shown much sign of it yet. Leif, when do you expect to make your choice between the pagan Gods and the true God?"

"Perhaps never." And then I said a wild and foolish thing that was out and in the air and in companions' ears before I could stop it. "I may myself become a God of sorts."

"There are periods in Christian history, and such periods will return, when you would be burned at the stake for such a heathen utterance. In all truth, it is worse than heathen—on the face of it it sounds insane. But I am not a good advocate of stake burnings. Tell us, Leif, just what in the Devil—or in the name of the Most Holy—do you mean?"

"I did not mean to say anything. I referred to a sort of waking dream that I have sometimes had in the middle of the night, and which I should have kept secret even from Ugruk. But now I have said this much, I will say the rest. The idea had struck me that if I went to live in Ugruk's country, among the Innuits, who have no Gods whatever, that I might be able to establish myself as their God and have the benefits thereof. I don't know what these benefits would be. I'll just say, have an exciting life and maybe help them to a better life. And Joseph, you yourself have said that a number of our Gods were quite possibly real people, who lived a long time ago, and because of their achievements they were remembered first as heroes and then as demi-gods and then as great gods."

"I did say that. I must keep better guard of tongue. You have a way of remembering and mulling over what you hear. If there is a new West Land, I think you may be the one to find it, topping the feat of Eric the Red. But in the meantime you must take the princess Helga to Greenland, where she will make an important decision. When do you think you can safely sail from Nidaros?"

"Never. There is no safety on the ocean. Still I would like to start on the last days of this moon. We would find open water until we approached Iceland and the floes would be pretty well broken up around Cape Welcome. Helga, would that be too soon to suit you?"

"No, for the sooner this matter is settled—finally and sensibly —the happier I'll be."

"Leif, are you going to take me?" Joseph asked, speaking calmly as he could, yet unable to conceal the craving in his heart.

"With the greatest pleasure, if the king and Helga wish it so. It's only a matter of time until a Christian priest is sent to Greenland to establish a church."

"I am not a priest, you know, or even close to it. Do not take me with any idea that I can convert the heathen—only if you think I would be a good companion at sea. What I seek, Leif, in a small way is what you seek in a large, an extremely large way. The best word for it is adventure."

I glanced at Helga. She nodded and quickly added, "There will be no doubt of my father the king's consent."

From then on the preparations for our journey quickened apace. For instance, I had intended to wait until I reached Greenland to buy a good quantity of spare whaleskin line, thinking it would be cheaper there, but when an Icelandic ship came into Nidaros and found glutted markets for cables and lines made of whaleskin, I obtained an ample supply. Also I bought from a ship chandler of mixed blood—his grandfather had been a Jewish merchant of Cádiz—a wooden stick, graduated, with a movable arm, by which a ship captain could make a rough estimation of the ascendancy above the horizon of the North Star. Also, and finally—the ship fully ladened and most of Helga's chests stowed aboard—I was given a farewell audience with the king.

"Our scribes have written three letters to the great chieftain Eric the Red, all of which will bear our seal, and which you will deliver to him, in case you arrive safely at his mark land," Olaf told me. "One is in Icelandic-Norse, the language of Icelandic poetry, one in the written language of Ireland, one in excellent Latin. Still we are old-fashioned, we do not trust writing as much as plain speech, uttered by a trusty ambassador. You are to tell Eric the following. First, that we offer our prayers that his suit of our daughter's hand may prosper. If it does, we will immediately bestow upon him the title of the Earl of Greenland and grant him a great domain in the region north of Vesterbig, hitherto unclaimed by any settler. When he is made earl we wish him to join with other great chieftains of Greenland in acknowledging us, Olaf the First, their sovereign lord, their tribute to us only when they desire to pay, we may say a token tribute, but for which we will take steps to increase greatly their trade with Norway, Sweden, and Denmark, and give them the protection of our sword. Also, it is our wish that he himself accept Christian baptism, as an example to his people, and to do his utmost to persuade all Greenlanders to do the same, but we urge him not to employ strong measures, indeed we forbid their use, lest the folk rebel and turn more strongly than before to their old Gods.

"These injunctions and proposals comprise the letter. And to you, personally, Leif Ericsson, we make this farewell request. It is that you set an example among my new subjects in accepting baptism. We have taken pleasure in your visit to our court, and if event occurs as we hope, we will see that you are granted a barony—only a little below an earldom—with ample estates for its support. You are aware, as well as ourselves, of the futility at this time of our trying to persuade my daughter Helga to follow Kris. We are quite sure that Eric will presently take this great and saving step, hence we cannot help but hope that Helga will indeed become Countess of Greenland, and follow in the footsteps of her great lord, Eric.

"Now of this I must speak delicately. On the journey pray see that our daughter has opportunity for Christian discourse with Novice Joseph, but perhaps it would be best for you to be present on these occasions, or other officers who can profess interest in the new teachings, our idea being that Joseph has many qualities that young maidens find almost irresistible, and a passionate attachment between our daughter and him would play ducks and drakes—this expression meaning utter disarrangement is one used by the ambassador from England—with our plans. And if Helga and Joseph should go so far as to imitate the conduct of a drake with a duck, and Eric the Red would hear of it, he would be fully justified in refusing the alliance. There will still be many noblemen of high station in Europe who would gladly accept Helga, despite her heathen beliefs, as well as the loss of her virginity, because she is our daughter; still we most fervently pray that the occasion will not arise."

"It will not, my lord, if I can prevent it."

"Understand that we recognize Joseph as a faithful and able servant of our God Kris, but he has not yet taken vows of celibacy and, coming from a warm climate, his blood is no doubt hot. Now you may kneel and kiss my hand, or stand and put your hand in mine if that is more in accord with Greenland custom, and take your leave."

"The latter is more to my liking, sire, since I am a barbarian from Greenland, not a courtier from a more civilized land."

"Courtier or no, you can keep your given word, and this proves you a worthy ambassador from the great chieftain Eric the Red."

I did not know as I left the throne room, although I could easily guess, why the king's farewell remark cast a dark pall over my happy prospects of a month-long journey with beautiful Helga on the still wintry seas, often storm-swept, a world removed from palaces and courts, and my stout ship her sole reliance against a lonely, unseen, and cruel death, with no pagan or Christian rites to ease the casting of her soul, and no arms about her but mine, and these quickly weakening in the icy depths.

2

The king himself, snugly wrapped against a biting east wind, came down to the dank wharf to see the *Narwhale* sail. No trifling number of his great thanes, clad in big fur cloaks, almost all of them wearing swords, likewise attended, and the faces of some expressed satisfaction with Helga's departure to a distant land, and some were sad, and a few old lords looked grief-stricken, for Helga had been their only bulwark against the complete overthrow of the old Viking faith and ways, and the complete conquest of Christianity with new faith and ways. No doubt she had been their heroine when she led the folk to disobey the king's decree that the ancient temple to Frey be torn down. Truly I too would have liked to see her standing at her window that night, encouraging the people to defy her father the king, beautiful as a Valkyrie, her tongue that caressed mine sharp as a sting ray's fang, her voice strident, her language bold and strong as a fishwife's.

Among the most grief-stricken was the great poet Hallfred and the thought came to me that the wondrous lightning of his mind would dim with Helga away, and he would not live long. Yet to stir him a little, and quicken the heartbeats of the wet-eyed gaffers and to make the Christian converts, now the king's favorites, remember the savage glory that they had renounced, I had Ugruk bring my flute and I asked King Olaf's permission to play a farewell song. This he granted grudgingly, for he was in haste to see the fiord waters widen between his wharf and his indomitable daughter; and had he known the melody I had chosen to play, I believe he would have refused his consent. I made what seemed to me the only proper choice. Our ship would in a few minutes stand to sea, wide and awesome and almost empty save for its own spawn, such as huge whales, great sharks, monsters hidden in its depths, and perhaps mermaids and mermen, who still came up from their bejeweled caves to watch the passing of this wondrous thing, a ship.

Helga descended from great Vikings and her spirit was one that they could understand and share, and had she lived in his times, very Ragnar would have made her his bride, and had sons by her who would overrun not only England but all the Christian lands, and one of them would have wrung from Rome a greater booty than had bold Alaric five centuries ago. So I chose the Strand Song of the Norse Women to the Departing Fleet; and it was a sad song always, and now its sadness was greater than ever, for the fleets had long ago departed never to return, and our dragon ships fought other dragon ships on the North Sea and on the Skagerrak and the Baltic, as Christian kings vied for the thrones of the Viking lands, Denmark, Sweden, and Norway; and the Wolf Seats of the Heroes had given way to bejeweled thrones, before which courtiers must kneel.

I played it better than ever before, because my heart was full and throbbing, and its fullness of feeling spilled over into the notes. The farewell sayers stood as if stunned, and the gray faces of a few old men became flushed as if with renewed youth, and the face of the king was sullen, and he gave me a spiteful glance. But more than this was to assail his ears. Once more I played the wailing melody, this time very softly, and a voice rang forth the words—the voice of an old man, a poet of old time whose own songs had wakened glory in countless hearts and had wetted countless eyes. And old age departed from him at this magic moment, and not only his voice was young and strong as well as indescribably sweet but also his bent form sprang erect, and the runes of age were erased from his face and it seemed to give forth light.

There came a strange likeness of expression to every face except the king's, which caused the illusion of resemblance of lineaments to one another, and there was something of the face of Hallfred the poet in everyone. And as the song ceased, he need only to have said the word, and the listeners would have sallied forth, their numbers swelling at every step, and burned down the palace of the king and his new and beautiful cathedral and even little Christian churches where people of the compassionate heart of Thorhild came to kneel. But he remained silent, as was meet, because even in the song he had just sung the evil of the old days, of bloody piracy, pillage, and rapine, had been put plainly; and those days were dead, but with them had passed a savage glory that Northmen might never again know. There would be cruelty and crime in Europe greater than that of the Vikings, and much of it would be committed in the name of gentle Kris; still their day had passed, and some quiet words spoken in Galilee had resounded farther and with greater power than their great shouts unto Odin.

"Hallfred," King Olaf said in the sudden, throbbing silence, "we did not ask you to sing, and our anger rose that you would do so without our bidding, but we have subdued it by thinking of your long years, and the songs you have sung before, and by the teaching that even kings must forgive wrongs against their persons and their place, and show mercy.

"Our daughter, Helga," he went on in a much lower voice, at the same time bending and kissing her forehead, "you too we forgive for your rebellion and your waywardness, and the kiss we gave you was an expression of a father's love for his daughter, abiding regardless of the wrongs you have done us. But heed our decree. If for any reason you do not take in marriage the hand of our loyal subject, Eric the Red, chieftain of Greenland, a cabin will be provided for you on some Norwegian merchant ship returning hence from Greenland, but never again may you enter our royal palace, and instead you will ask sanctuary of Queen Sigrid of Sweden, and I doubt not that she will grant it, and indeed make you her chief lady-in-waiting because you are two of a kind, wrought of the same unblessed clay.

"Leif Ericsson, you will transport our daughter Helga to Ericshall, and woe betide you if any harm comes to her on the journey, or any undue intimacy between you, and between her and any other, for I have promised my liege man Eric the Red her hand and her virgin flower, if she herself be willing. And truly we rue the last condition, born of our generosity and fatherly love; and if we had not given our royal word, we would send Helga to be Eric's bride or his thrall, aye, that would be her only choice, by my implacable decree. And as punishment, Leif Ericsson, for your stirring the hearts of my subjects with unholy passion by the tootling of your flute, no ship that you own or of which you are an officer may ever again enter a Norwegian port.

"We, Olaf the First, Christian King of Norway, have spoken our royal will. Now you and your royal passenger and Novice Joseph, who failed in his duty when he did not protest the playing and singing of a pagan song, but who on the journey may contemplate the lapse, and be fervent in his duty when he comes to Greenland, may board your ship, along with your hands who will take in the plank, and go forth upon the sea. And as a Christian king, heedful of divine instruction, I will pray that if the wrath of God has been aroused by the heathen behavior of you four in sound of my voice, that it be assuaged by our stern rebuke and inviolable decrees, and that no great gales will drive the ship into unknown seas where you will slowly die of hunger and thirst, and no seas nigh mountain high, topped with foam as the mountains are capped with snow, will overwhelm your vessel, and drown you all, and no icefield will clutch her in its cold hands and break her ribs, and no floating berg tear apart her planks, and no sea dragon, mountainlike in size, rise from his dark lair and swallow her whole.

"Our daughter Helga, Novice Joseph, and Leif Ericsson, you have our royal leave to go. Farewell!"

This going was only a matter of our mounting the short plank, its taking in, the loosing of some lines from the snubbing blocks, and the hoisting of our sail. At once the wind filled it with a crackling sound and the ship began to move. And I looked at our good-luck piece, the tusk of the King of the Narwhales, and it pointed staunchly westward, and I sensed a kind of purposefulness in its westward thrust, as though it were reflecting something in my heart. And then I gazed into Helga's eyes, to find them glimmering with tears, but her face was pink, not pale, and she stood staunchly, and I reckoned her as stout a shipmate as I had ever known. My officers and most of my hands were busy obeying my commands, and only Ugruk spoke to me.

"Leif, you play pretty," he said. "You no care if king no let you come to Norway any more. You, Ugruk, maybe some others, we make long, long journey, see new sights, hunt, fish, have good time. You no be sad, my brother. I think we live through big storm that will break soon."

"What kind of storm do you mean?"

"Maybe only wind and wave. Maybe much more, much worse. Still you take load off heart. See how ship skip along. I think her spirit speak to Ugruk's spirit, promise bad things, but good things too. Ugruk not know which will win at last, but if we die, our spirits go see Thorhild's spirit. After while we go below, you and Ugruk, and open Ugruk's fine, new sea chest, and Ugruk show you new bow. We be brothers long time, we brothers still, we stay brothers always. Does Ugruk's mouth tell truth or tell lie?"

"In the name of Kris, Thorhild's God, and in the name of Odin of the Nine Runes, you tell the truth."

"Ugruk glad. For if mouth lie, I take sharp knife, cut mouth clean out, and feed to sharks. Now Ugruk feel weak, hungry, so he go eat."

He left me, and I went and stood beside my helmsman while the roofs of Nidaros dimmed in the distance, and likewise dimmed the palace of the king, and only the sky-leaping tower of the cathedral still loomed in proud victory against the sky.

3

No departure of a ship into the illimitable wastes of ocean is a little thing. Even when potbellied traders put to sea, bound for some foreign port, laden with lumber or grain or hides, or with more rare stuffs, such as beautiful furs for the robes of rich folk, or casks of wine, or marble from Luna, or precious porcelain and glass packed against breakage as carefully as the Earth Mother packs an unborn infant in its mother's womb—even sailings such as these strangely touch the heart and excite the feelings of those who depart in the vessel and those who watch, in troubled silence, her dimming in the distance. As the *Narwhale* took down Trondheim Fiord, I was not surprised by the high color in the faces of the crew, by the brilliance of the men's eyes, and the excited tones of their salty voices.

What puzzled me, and awed me somewhat, was that this upheaval in our hearts did not subside after we had rounded the eastern headland and the fiord's abrupt bend to the northwest hid all sign and sight of the town and of ships in its harbor. Throughout the first watch, which fetched us deep into the lower waters of the fiord, the men remained tense as when a dense fog settles in, blinding the eyes of the watch, and causing a haunting of the imagination by invisible danger. At the end of the watch Starkad came to relieve me if I so desired, and outwardly he seemed his cool and collected self; yet as he stood beside me, and we spoke back and forth in the way of officers, he seemed to be standing on the balls of his feet, and now and then when I said some ordinary thing, he gave a little start.

I took the ship out of fiord mouth in the gloom of night before leaving Starkad to take her by Hitra Island. Even so, I did not immediately go below, and instead stayed on the gently rolling deck, musing upon and watching the throngs of stars. Presently I made out a familiar shape, suggestive of staunch old age, and very dear to me, by the stearboard rail. I came nigh, and the pale starlight showed me the craggy face of Gorm.

"All goes well, think you?" I asked, to be saying something.

"Aye, sir," he answered after a brief pause. "Almost too well."

"I know not what you mean, old man. The journey has just begun. We are not due any ill fortune for a long sail yet."

"Nay, and I think we may meet with none." And then, after a long pause, "But we will meet with something."

"Gorm, you have watched the seas and the skies longer than any man aboard. You have been wetted with spray, and dunked in salt water, and clutched a stay for life or death more times than any three of us put together. With long experience there comes to certain men, especially Norsemen, what could be called a sixth sense. I have long felt that it has been given you."

"It is given to the Irish oftener than to us Norse," he said, avoiding a direct reply.

"Gorm, has a spell of some kind been cast upon the *Narwhale*? Are we journeying to Greenland, or to World's End, or to Corpse Strand?"

"Some of us to all three, belike, or all of us to one. Excuse me, my lord captain. You ask a fair question, and I answer it in riddles, mouthing like a spaewoman over her candles. Now let me speak like the old sea dog I am. For the princess Helga this is a momentous voyage. What she finds, what she feels, at its end, will tell what will betide her. To you, involved with her somewhat, and for Ugruk, bound to you, much can befall; and in a sense this is the beginning of the voyage you propose to make into the unknown oceans of the west. Novice Joseph will see sights as new and as wonderful as Saint Peter's Church in Rome would be to you. But for the rest of us—we are dancing with shadows. There are no omens which old sailors believe either good or evil. Starkad is a great reader of stars; he can find the sun by the shadow of his knife point on his fingernail in a shrouded sky; he knows the landfalls; he has an inborn sense of direction like a wild swan's. Still, when I have said all this, I have not said all. There is something. . . ."

"There is something eerie about this voyage. I can smell it in the air. But I reckon we'll not know, or even come to guessing, what that something is until we pass a certain point in time and space, so I'll put it out of my mind. When we clear Froya, take the ship straight west. When Connelly takes the helm, be sure that he stays awake, for last night he bedded with a wench from his own Ireland, and I doubt if he slept much. Good night, old man."

I waked to a chill sunrise, clear skies, a cleanly rolling sea, and the wind still strong in the east. Gull Eye thought he could still distinguish the dim shadowlike shape of the coast, but for men of ordinary vision this was the open, unbounded sea. Tension had gone out of the men's faces and postures; although no Norwegian was ever stolid, the men went calmly and skillfully about their tasks, and it seemed to me they were uncommonly blithe, which might mean only that the journey back to bleak but beloved Greenland was well-starred and well-begun.

Throughout the crossing to a landfall in Iceland, only ingrates could find fault with the weather. I had crossed the palm of an old Lapp woman on Nidaros' wharf with a silver shilling, and surely these were the best winds ever bought for this modest price. A more than fair part of the time they blew straight out of the east, and their shiftings never brought them forward of amidships. Ice was phenomenally scarce for this time of year, fogs as rare as sleet and snow, and though at times we must crawl we were never becalmed or gale-driven. So it came to pass that Helga, with her swarthy maidservant, Fatima, Novice Joseph, and I passed many an hour together on the deck, seated snugly on a chest containing spare sails and lines. Sometimes Ugruk joined us, but usually he sat in his kayak, his hands working at something above or below the sealskin deck.

The distance from Nidaros to the Icelandic landfall was almost twice as far as from thence to Blue Shirt landfall, but had taken only half as many days. In this homestretch, we had met with contrary winds, and, as we neared the Greenland coast, a great many bergs and scattered, chill, and sometimes blinding mists, the latter combination being a dangerous one, enforcing a cautious advance. Yet, when we had rounded Cape Welcome, which to many a sailor had meant Cape Farewell, the Weather Gods stopped playing scurvy tricks and suddenly showered us with favors.

The day was four days before the spring equinox. Yet an old and enfeebled man, once weatherwise, but now losing track of time as well as of event, would waken from a doze to think this was mid-May. The copious outpouring from the emboldened sun remained a pale yellow, still with more gold in it than in Helga's hair, and as warm to the touch. No cloud was visible on any horizon, no mist or fog lay low on the sea or hung high on the mountains; the southeast wind was brisk but had no bite; you could almost believe it was lukewarm as onion fish chowder too long from the fire.

"This is my first clear view of the icecap," Helga told me, as I paused beside her at the rail. Fatima immediately walked away.

"I wish you could have seen it at close range on the early morning that we raised Blue Shirt. It is close to the coast in that part of Greenland; from here it's sixty or more miles."

"It's near enough to suit me. It's a frightening thing."

"It's a wonderful thing, too. No country known to mariners has anything like its equal. It dwarfs the great snowfield of Vatnajokull in Iceland."

"It makes the glaciers hanging on the mountains of Norway look like icicles. Leif, I suppose you are almost home."

"We should moor an hour before sunrise tomorrow, if this wind holds to the mouth of Ericsfiord, where we'll catch the making tide."

"I wonder if I too am almost home," she mused, her eyes very dark.

"Yes, if what we both expect comes to pass."

"I do not know what to expect. But I'll tell you this—I never have had a home. My father's palace in Ireland was never home to me, perhaps because he was never a real father to me. He was too busy acquiring great manors and riches, and my mother, the daughter of the Wendish King Burislav, had died young. My stepmother, Gyda, sister of Olaf Kvaran, was a kind woman, but had little use for me after, at age eight, I fell under the spell of the Icelandic poet Hallfred and would not accept Christian baptism. After my father, Olaf Tryggvesson, became King of Norway four years ago, I was always a thorn in his side, and his third wife, Thyre, hates me for causes I do not fully understand."

I thought that I understood. I had caught only glimpses of Thyre, the sister of King Sveyn of Denmark, but these had revealed her as an ill-favored woman, shallow despite her pious mien, and I believed her bitterly jealous of beautiful, stubborn, and brave Helga.

"I felt as though I had found a home when I visited Queen Sigrid of Sweden. I was to remain there a year, but after about six months she quarreled with my father, and he ordered me back to Nidaros. One time since then I seemed to find a home—

for a few weeks. Perhaps I shouldn't tell you this. You might
think I mean more than I say."

"Helga, you are a plain speaker and I am not likely to misunderstand you."

"I mean the weeks I have been on this ship. I knew it was
only a temporary home, still I couldn't stifle the feeling. And very
soon, now, we will say our farewells."

"I see no other outcome."

"I suppose you will want to say them on the open deck, in the
presence of Joseph and your followers, so you won't be tempted
to lay hand on me in love or in lust, or for any reason."

"No, I would like for us two to be alone."

"Will you pledge me to keep your hands at your sides? I do not
wish to be a party to your breaking troth."

"Yes."

"Then come to my cabin, three hours after sunset."

She said this very quietly, but the words echoed in my head,
and then began to resound, as the first whish of a snowslide
slowly loudens—while weight of the avalanche increases and its
body grows—to an ear-blasting roar. I almost missed her little gesture of dismissal. Fatima, whose absence had likely not been
marked by my trusty shipmates or by such a good fellow as
Joseph, hurriedly returned to her mistress. I went forward to the
stem, and first I slipped my hand along the base of the great
tusk, to find its silken surface roughened a little by bursting spray
and sometimes breaking waves, but this slow erosion was not apparent to the eye, and I reckoned that the great trophy, the
crown and jewel of the ship, and symbol of her staunchness and
adventurousness, would last as long as she did—perhaps one
month, in case my journey westward was ill-starred, a year at
least if new, bright, and fortunate stars arose, possibly a hundred
years when all of us whom now she proudly bore had gone to
Heaven or Hel Strand, or perhaps only under the ground, or
beneath the dark, unplumbed, forever withholding seas.

For a few minutes I basked in the false warmth of a thought
that struck me often—that in case Helga refused Eric the Red, of
making her my bride and taking her with me into the virgin west.

But the notion glowed without solid fuel in my heart. It was an unwritten law among Norse seamen that if the captain shipped his wife, married members of the crew could ship their wives. And it was a good law, because if some must pine for the strong, white arms of a Norse woman, all should pine. It was born of the fellowship, the brotherhood I could truly say, of men confronting the perils of the sea, wind and wave and ice and reef, and bearing the same hardships, and enduring the same apartness from other humankind. In our ships there were no social barriers between officers and men. An officer could not ask a sailor to run a risk he would not himself run. We ate together and slept in the same close quarters. Yet breaches of discipline aboard Norse ships, let alone shirking and slacking, remained almost unknown.

Truly our first voyage into what Joseph called *mare incognito* would be too dangerous for us to risk our best beloved. There would be danger too of the voyage becoming too safe for us to gain its goals—that the presence of our women would so tame the bold spirits of the mariners that these would quail. But perhaps, if we found a new land, they could go with us on a second voyage, and make homes for us on some distant, undreamed island where none other of our race had set foot. This was a dream by which the Norse mind was peculiarly moved. I knew not why except that we were real heathens—the word meaning the dwellers of the wild heath—and we abjured the settled ways, we loved far horizons, we were lonely and lost in busy cities, we were in love with solitude.

The sun, that had today dealt so kindly with us, was so pleased with herself for her charity that she seemed loath to set. She did so at last, leaving a more than half-grown moon to glimmer on the cold, still sea, and to show us shadows that were land that we might sail in safety. Two long-drawn hours after sunset, when the night chill had set in, and its heat forgot, and late-flying seafowl had sought their roosts, and porpoises had ceased their play under and around the ship and now followed us with a great sedateness, I made my way to the snug cabin Eric had built under the afterdeck for the comfort of his intended bride as she sailed to meet him at Ericshall. And well I knew that my mere coming here alone and knowing well I would find Helga alone would anger the old grim Gods.

But beautiful Baldur, if he had yet lived and had not died an untimely death as do so many other folk and things of beauty, would not be angry. And a poet great as Hallfred could sing of the magic of the meeting place—a small oil lamp blazing under a soapstone shield, casting a rosy light on my beautiful companion. She wore a long white robe of ermine, fastened around the waist with a silken cord, with a collar of sable against which her pale gold hair made striking contrast and held mysterious lights. When she had admitted me, she stood back with a dim and lovely smile while my eyes fed.

"Is not the room very warm?" she asked, and there was a hint of fun-making in her tone.

"I would call it hot." And I thrust my fingers into my throat collar to loosen it a little.

"You promised to keep your hands at your sides. But it need not hold except when you are tempted to disobey the injunction of Eric the Red. The heat of the room is by my provision. I wanted to change cold March into high summer."

"You have done a good job of it," I said, as I removed my winter coat, lined with marmot fur.

"Take off more than that, Leif, in respect to this meeting and perhaps this parting. Under this ermine robe there is nothing but my skin, and no hard sailor's knot fastens the cord." And for the first time I noticed that her lovely feet were bare.

"Before I can obey you, Princess—and by putting it that way I reveal how my mind is playing tricks upon my soul—I must point out one thing. If you refuse to marry Eric, this is still a parting, for how long I know not. Before I can seek your hand in marriage, I am bound to take a long voyage into unknown seas in search of unknown lands. It is against my judgment, all my instincts, and hence against the success of my enterprise, that I or any of my crew bring their wives on this journey of dangerous exploration."

"When I have refused Eric, and if you wish me to do so, I will plight my troth to you before you set sail. Moreover, I will remain in Vesterbig with the wife of my kinsman Bjorn for half a year's waiting for your return. If you do not return in half a year I will take ship for Sweden and dwell with Sigrid the Queen. Look, Leif, but keep your hands to your side, so if you disobey the spirit at least you will obey the letter of the injunction." And very calmly and with lovely, leisurely movements, she removed her ermine robe and stood glossed and aglow in the ruddy light of the oil lamp.

In a thousand daydreams I had seen Helga naked, sometimes as a wraith visiting my bedside, sometimes laving in a crystal-clear pool in a wide green meadow, the little curve of her neck suggestive of a swan. Yet I was shaken by the true coming of the dream, her naked beauty perhaps no greater than I had imagined, but its moving me not only infinitely deeper but in different ways. The dream had stirred me to aching passion, as did its reality; but also there flowed through me and out from me unto her a great wave of tenderness, this of a different sort than I had felt for my mother, Thorhild, and which I had never felt before. The bewitching form of thwarted Ellen had never wakened it; I had felt only its dim semblance for valiant and voluptuous Swanhild, and only for a few minutes after I had caused her maiden pain and she had dropped off to her sleep. What had wakened it now I did not know, unless beauty itself melts the heart of man. Song also melts his heart, the song that the harmoniousness of Helga's beauty sang to me.

As I surveyed her, she stood proudly. She lifted one hand to her breast to call attention to the beauteous snowy hills with scarlet crests, but her hand with fingers spread no less beautiful than these, and only then did I perceive the fact. Then she dropped her hand to her rounded thigh, its whiteness emphasized by the fire glow on her pale, pink nails, and its perfect roundness revealed by its gloss under the lamp. I gazed in a dizzy dream at both of her thighs, tapering to her shapely feet, and at a triangular pale gold region, hardly larger than my hand, between her thighs; and my hand burned and yearned. Lastly she lay her own beautiful hand on her gently curved belly, and it cast a little shadow there; and under the shadow, and at the sides, the white skin had a soft luster which, if I had not already succumbed to what might be called temptation, but which was actually the whole bent of my spirit as well as of my flesh, I would have done so now.

While the revelation had been given me, without knowing it I had unfastened my belts and buckles, and slipped my feet out of my warm reindeer-hide slippers that I wore on deck. Now I tarried no more and bared my whole body to Helga's sight, and perhaps not without pride in my broad chest and long powerful limbs, and certainly not with shame at what else she saw.

"Lie down on the bed, and put your head on the pillow, and keep your arms at your sides, and I too will lie down."

So it came to pass that I lay still, but she did not, and after a few seconds' catching of her breath, she rose on her elbow and began to kiss my mouth. And if kisses were virgin to her soft and humid mouth, as I believed, she had needed no old wives' lore as was passed down in Ireland to instruct her in their giving and their kind; and her Norse inheritance of vitality, aptness for deep passion, and long repressed love of me, at last expressible, were tutor enough. I came into a state of bliss I have never known. Then her hand made one swift pass down my side, touched lightly once, then withdrew, and as I still trembled from the shock, once more she put her head on the pillow, dropped her arms to her sides, and lay still.

"Leif, I have done all I can, with the leave of my soul, to cause you to break both the letter and the spirit of your oath. What now?"

"I will still stand by its letter. That much I must do, although it makes no sense even to me. But to even a long score against my father, Eric the Red, I abjure its spirit. I have not forgotten how he sent me on a fool's errand, I keeping faith and he breaking faith with me. If you do what I ask, you will not be a virgin when you give him your answer to his suit, but he was not one when he pressed his suit, and I think that many maidens lost their virginity to his rough wooing."

"You needn't defend yourself, Leif, and be concerned with me. What is it that you ask? Do not keep me waiting."

"Lie upon me, at full length, your breast against my chest,

and spread wide the outer gates of your virgin door, and leave all the rest to me."

She did so, trembling and almost weeping; so it came to pass that without breaking the letter of my vow, I thrust through her maiden strait, and thereby we were united in a union that could not be wholly severed, no matter what paths we took, as long as we both lived. By gentleness I largely spared her pain, and when the little pain had passed, we came unto each other in the full mystery and glory of the act of procreation, or at least in deep convulsion and illimitable bliss.

Soon after this, she fell to sleep, and I kept vigil over her a full hour and it was my strong intent to keep such vigil all my life long, if my fate consented. At last I arose and dressed and drew a velvet coverlet over my beloved, for the lamp had begun to burn low. When I bowed over her she gave me a drowsy kiss, then I went up to the windy deck and the chill of night.

By the rail I found Ugruk standing watch, partly to await my appearance, but partly, I thought, against forces of danger or of evil that he imagined, or dimly sensed, were on the march.

"A clear, fine night," I remarked to him, "and a favorable wind that we will soon lose, but we can tack up the fiord and we'll have the lift of the rising tide to hasten our passage. Of the storm that you predicted, a mighty and dire storm, I see no sign."

"It is yet to break, my brother, and without giving sign except dim visions behind Ugruk's eyes," he answered.

"Can you describe those visions?"

"No, they are shapes as seen through mist, ebbing and flowing, but never fading away. My heart trembles as it did when the Frost Giant blinded you near the hot spring, and I did not know where to look for you, and my heart trembles as it did when I looked up to cliffs where Thorhild had gathered flowers, and I not see her."

"Ugruk, it is not like you to be afraid of shadows."

"These are not shadows, my brother; these are demons such as the shamans have seen on the piled-up ice. A great storm will break. I think it will come not long after moonset. If Ugruk could run away and cover his eyes and press his fingers into his ears, Ugruk do it. But he cannot launch his kayak and flee to the strand, because he cannot leave his brother, Leif, although he cannot help him in one lifting of his hand. Leif, this storm will break against you, not me, or anyone you love. But if you die, Ugruk he die too; he just fall down and die."

The vision of Ugruk's falling and dying suddenly caused me to share the visions that he saw, out of the corner of my eyes it seemed. They were vague shapes of utmost dread, and I who had rarely prayed did pray.

"Angels of Kris, defend me from these Devils, and ye old Gods of Norse help me too. Ugruk, I believe you every word."

4

At moonset, the *Narwhale* was well up Ericsfiord, past the barren beaches and approaching the grasslands. The milky light had seemed so thin and pale that I did not think we would miss it greatly; but on this score I had missed my guess, for the night turned implacably black, and most of my crew went blind. Immediately I had Gull Eye take the helm. He told me he could still distinguish the stony shore, at this place rising almost sheer, at something like a cable's length, which is six hundred feet. I could not see it this far, at least to take oath that I saw it at all, yet there was a feeling upon my eyes that it was there, and I felt, rather than perceived, that Gull Eye was keeping out about this same distance. Now we had reefed our sail, no longer daring to tack, and were depending on the rising tide with its mysterious currents to bear us home.

In this heavy darkness I perceived Greenland in the eyes of the mind, and some of its aspects became more apparent to me, or at least their effect on me was greater, than in broad daylight. I had seen part of Norway and a great deal of Iceland and their differentiation from Greenland became not one of different terrains, different position in respect to other lands and seas, but of mood. If Greenland were indeed an island, and not an enormous peninsula of a continent, there was none like it; it was the most strange on the broad earth, I thought. Not merely its vast size, its harsh climate, its jagged mountains, not even its prodigious icecap accounted for its alienship forever to common ground where man found suitable abode. A small part of it was habitable, that part comprising many thousand square miles, but the vast remainder, desolate, forsaken by most beasts as well as by men, silent, rough-hewn, its Gods without shape that men could vision or imagine, the home of the winds, perhaps, or of Frost Giants, or the natal place of the primeval forces of wild nature, cast a kind of spell, or induced an atmosphere unlike any other, on the habitable part, those fertile grasslands that men had claimed for homesteads. No human being dwelling here was the same as if he had dwelt in Norway, Iceland, or Ireland, or the chill, dank Hebrides Islands, or the windy Shetlands, or the rainy, far-off, lonely Faeroes, settled by Norse shepherds, the home of stalwart men and bright-faced girls, and where life was good.

These thoughts, in conjunction with those wakened by Ugruk's words, chilled the marrow of my bones.

Now we were opposite our home strand, and men broke out their oars. We made a clean landing on the silent shore, but the news of our arrival would soon be passed, and the house lamps would be lighted, for even now we saw the bobbing spark of an approaching lantern, and presently a pale glimmer that it cast on the snow and on the long, fleet legs of its carrier. A moment later I recognized our first greeter as Thorhall, ever my leader and friend, that great thane who for years had given his allegiance to Eric the Red. And it was a fitting thing that he should be our first welcomer, as well as a natural thing, since he was a night roamer who could not lie long abed, as well as an early riser.

We shook hands and spoke, and I answered his questions as to our crossings, and whether King Olaf's daughter was aboard. And then I had questions to ask him.

"Have you paid Eric the Red the thousand English shillings that I owe him for the ship?"

"Aye, on the first day of the New Year, as you bade me."

"Thorhall, I wish to put to sea again at the first possible hour. The ship is well-nigh readied for a long voyage, victualed except for fresh seal and walrus meat, a few more skins of oil, and some water casks that we have emptied and need refilling. But my great problem concerns the crew. If our married men will go at all—and all of them crave the great adventure—still it would be with reluctance, unless they can bring their wives, leaving their children in the care of kinsmen. Also no less than five of my best hands, including Gull Eye and old Gorm, are thralls belonging to Eric, and they cannot go without his leave, or unless he will sell them to me."

"That last is no problem, Leif. Be sure he would not give them leave, nor would he sell them to you even for a double price, but by the law of the moot, when it convened on the highland between Ericsfiord and Einersfiord, they may buy their own freedom at the price set by the moot, ten silver shillings each, the worth of ten cattle of the common grade."

"By my soul, I had forgotten the passing of that law."

"You were away in the north, hunting. It made no great stir, for how would a thrall go about earning and saving ten shillings? Yet it was a good law, and it showed a trend which I have long observed, that the farther our folk go from Norway, or from anywhere in Europe, to make their homes, the privileges of thanes are more and more curtailed; and while their power wanes, the powers of common men, based on some great dreamer's dream of human rights, wax year by year. You say there are five thralls you wish to buy. Why not give each of them ten shillings, since the chest you left with me is still heavy with silver, and let them buy their freedom from Eric the Red? That business I will myself conduct, if you give me leave."

"Do so, Thorhall, ever my mentor and friend in need, and also give ten shillings to Ellen, and ten to Swanhild, that they may buy their freedom."

"That I will, in great joy, because I have long watched their grinding down by Eric, his putting on them the most arduous or dirty chores. And Swanhild will be especially grateful, for when she is free it may be that the unknown father of her newborn babe will marry her, provided he too is free and not of too high rank. The Gods know she is comely enough to attract a poor franklin or his son."

"Has she told Eric who is the father of the babe?"

"Not that I know of. I think she has told no one, for the babe is not yet a week old, and she has kept to her mother's hut, although not, I think, confined to her bed; and other thrall women who have called there, to offer their kind help in the way of women, have found the door locked, or have been told by Ellen that Swanhild is not yet well enough to receive visitors, or the baby strong enough to be seen and fondled."

While Thorhall and I had talked, four other men and three women had seen the lights of our ship and had come down to the strand to meet the home-comers, or to hear the news. Because we two had stood apart, in confidential talk, with the typically good manners of the Norse none of these had come in sound of our voices. However, one of the women had passed close enough to a lamp that I had a clear view of her face, and I was not surprised to recognize Starkad's worthy wife. Then the thought struck me that I could not go to speak to these welcomers, or wait to greet the throng that would begin to gather when the light cleared and the news of our arrival had made its swift round throughout Osterbig. My first business was with my father, Eric the Red. I must be the first to tell him the princess Helga had indeed made the journey and in due course would give him the answer to his proposal. Also, I felt impelled to visit Swanhild within the hour, indeed before dawn broke to show my coming and going, for if the father of her babe remained unknown except to Ellen and herself, the grave fact was not unknown to me. But for reasons not wholly clear to me, I deeply dreaded the encounter at this time.

"Do you suppose my father, Eric, is awake?" I asked Thorhall.

"I don't doubt he is, because he wants his own hand on the catboat's helm as he passes the mouth of Einersfjord. That's about his location, if he left Disco Island when he intended, and if so he'll arrive at our strand about sundown."

"So he's not here," I said stupidly. Actually my mind was racing to find the answer to a simple question—whether I was glad or sorry that Helga's business with him, and mine, must be postponed the whole day. But my business with Swanhild, the nature of which

I did not know, but which I hoped most fervently would be settled more amicably than my dark fancies foretold, need be postponed only long enough for me to reach the turf hut where she and her mother lived. Moreover, the sooner my visit, the less chance I would run of its becoming known. There was still no glimmer on the icecap, always the precursor of dawn; but in less than an hour the paths to and about Ericshall would be well-traveled.

So I made off, on the excuse of seeing an old beldam of our household whom I deeply loved. But I had not gone more than a furlong when I made out a human form twenty steps ahead of me beside the path. I recognized it as human by its mere shape against the starlit sky, but there was nothing for me to do except keep on, and in a few seconds I heard the warm, deep voice of Ellen that once I had known so well and harkened to with such close attention.

"Wait a minute, Leif," she said. "I have something to say to you before you see Swanhild."

"It must be quite urgent for you to have found me this soon."

"You will remember I am an early riser. I saw the ship's lights, and I thought that you would lose no time in visiting Swanhild. That would be the way of a gentleman, which by and large you follow. Leif, I am going to tell you something—several things in fact—not the whole truth but part of it, and part of what I say may be lies. I have not a strong spirit. I find it easier to lie than to confess. But I do want you to know that for what has happened—and what will happen—I am not wholly to blame."

"I don't know what you mean."

"When I first invited you to an assignation, I had two reasons. One was that my body was starved, and you were a stalwart youth who could satisfy me. But also I took great satisfaction in spiting Eric. I have told you how always he desired to keep me in my place, the place of a thrall, and it would infuriate him beyond words to tell if I gave to you, and you welcomed, my favors. Ultimately I intended to let him know, when our secret became endangered, or you had given me some gift of value. And it was quite true that I am from a noble Irish house. It was my grandmother, not my mother, who was highborn, and who with her father was sold into thralldom. But Swanhild resembles her greatly in appearance, and in all her daydreams she is a highborn lady instead of a thrall brat. And for this, and other reasons I will not now mention, she hated Eric with a blacker hate than my distant cousin, Brian Boru, now King of Muster, had for the murderer of his brother, and there is no hate greater than that, on earth or in heaven or in hell, and there is nothing blacker except cold coals of a fire in which a heretic has burned."

What I could best compare to a cold wind began blowing down my back.

"I am Eric's son. Why did you send her to take your place at Vixen's Den?"

"Send her! Mary, Mother of God, I couldn't stop her. She had guessed our secret, she even knew our meeting place and threatened to tell my husband, Horkel, unless she, not I, could be your mistress. At one time she seemed to weaken. Ring Ivarsson had made her a valuable gift. On the very eve of our last assignation, I thought that everything would be as it had been before. But that night she told me she was going through with it, no matter where the path led. I could not stand against her. She pinned me against the wall with one arm and slapped me twenty times with all her strength. There is no one stronger than she when the spell is on her, an evil spell, a spell cast by a demon whereby she becomes the likeness of its caster. I had lied to you when I said Horkel had become suspicious. The thought of our adultery had never entered his thick head; anyway he would not have cared and would have only tried to beg favors from you. Aye, I lied to you more times than I can remember, but my plan when I had started to go with you, to relieve my passions and to spite my harsh master, did not stop there, once Swanhild thrust me aside and took matters in her own hands. It became a design of unutterable evil. But in her defense I tell you that I believe that for some years she did not push it resolutely. I think that she herself was frightened of its horrible disnature and what would be its monstrous consequences. But when you turned from her to woo Johanna, daughter of the great chieftain Bjorn, what heart remained in her breast changed to stone, and her blood became an evil seepage from organ unto organ, and the powers of darkness reigned within her soul."

"Ellen," I said in a faltering voice, as my hair rustled up on my creeping scalp, "did Swanhild kill my mother, Thorhild?"

"Leif, I think that she did, but I have no proof. After the report of Thorhild's fall, I looked for Swanhild, and I found her walking about our hut with the mien of a queen, naked except for the fawnskin vest I showed you, and for a skirt of satin that came to me through my grandmother, the daughter of Lady O'Connell, the first cousin of Gawain O'Rourke the Black. Aye, you know those names. The O'Connells, the O'Rourkes, the Borus. They stand foremost on the blood-smeared list of Irish feudists, and of seekers of unspeakable revenge. Aye, their blood flows in my veins, and I whispered my own hates into Swanhild's infant ears, and fed her heart with the malice in my heart where it grew monstrously, so when I stand before the judgment seat of God I have much to answer for. Still my spirit was too weak to commit deeds of monstrous evil. Mark you, I say again that I have no proof that Swanhild thrust lovely Thorhild over the cliff edge to her death, but the suspicion steals intermittently into my thoughts, and at night I dream of her doing it, and see the deed from start to finish in my dreams, and the dream ends with Swanhild taking a single red flower, of strange sort, from the basket Thorhild dropped; and when I found Swanhild parading in her finery, a look of wild triumph in her eyes, she was wearing a single red flower of strange sort."

"If I should whisper this to Ugruk—and I will not, because you have only suspicion, not proof—he would seize Swanhild by the throat, and when she dropped from his hands her neck would be broken and the apple of her throat crushed, and life would be done with her, and Ugruk would laugh."

"Look! The dawn light is beginning to break. Make haste to my house, and talk with her, and not be seen coming or going. I will not return there until noon. And there you must do what your dark fate enjoins, but I pray you, a final word, not to kill Swanhild, for despite the awful evil she has done, she was born unto me amid great pain and many wounds, for she was a heavy child, and my passage is narrow as you well know, and for that pain and those wounds, and for her greedy lips on my nipple, I love her still."

Ellen moved, then faded away into the shadows. I looked at a distant glimmer, which was the dawn light on the icecap, and that light was growing swiftly, thinning the darkness of this evil spot, and it was a cold and ominous light; but it would show me the path that I knew well already, and show me, with the impartiality of fate and Gods, much that I did not know.

I strode on, and when I came to Ellen's door, I did not knock, and instead thrust it open. Someone lying on the bed close to a low-burning oil lamp sat up, and the light glimmered on the strands of red in her pale hair; and at sight of me she broke into wild laughter.

5

"We will talk this over like sensible people, as might former sweethearts severed by destiny, but still harboring delicious memories," Swanhild told me, when the wild sound ceased. She had cut it off when she had seen a little stir in a bundle beside her.

"How is the baby?" I demanded. "Why have you put a cloth bandage on its eyes?"

"All babies have tender eyes. I think mine has eyes tenderer than most, because I did so—or so my mother, Ellen, told me— from being born nearsighted. You were born with the Witch's Mark in your right eye—the little segment darker gray than the rest—and I would not wonder but that your mother kept your eyes bandaged for a while, as I will keep my babe's. But you can see, when the light gets better, that he's a fine, strong baby in other ways."

As she was saying this, in a blithe voice, she rose in her shift and put on a reindeer-hide robe, not an uncommon possession for a thrall woman. Then with a queenly gesture, or at least a ceremonious one, she bade me sit on a bench close to the fire, its seat being of wood and its legs of stout bone. She took her seat at the edge of the bed.

"It is too soon after our baby's birth for us to make love," Swanhild remarked, "even if you were so inclined after your journey with a princess of Norway. Otherwise this would be a good opportunity, for my mother, Ellen, said she would be gone several hours."

"Yes, I met her on the path."

"Did not she tell you too that she would be gone a good while? You must grant that she has been very generous to me, and *with* you."

"Still, I must soon be gone. We had planned to sail westward as soon as possible."

"Certainly you will wait to speak to the great chieftain, your father, Eric the Red, and really you should wait for the marriage that will make him Earl of Greenland. It is said that he is planning it for the night of the spring solstice, and there will be a great feast."

"You speak in a strange way, Swanhild. There is a drunken shine in your eyes. It may be you are fey!"

"No, I will live long. I will have one great moment to look back upon, to exult over all my days. I fear you will have stood to sea by then. I know your impatience with delays. But before I tell you of the wondrous moment to come, I must relate a little more of my mother Ellen's history, which I have never told you. But it does not matter if you know it now. My moment of glory is assured."

"Yes, tell me."

"My mother was a young and very beautiful girl, living in Ireland, and in thralldom because of disasters overcoming her noble family. The son of a poor franklin fell in love with her and wanted to marry her. It would have been a good marriage. The father of her lover has since grown rich by trade with Norway, and the son is now one of the greatest franklins in Greenland. All this my mother missed because someone got in the way of their marriage. This is not a guesssing game; I will speak plainly. The interloper was Eric the Red, who in those years was in exile in Ireland."

"What happened? Speak plainly."

"He too fell in love with my mother. He bought her from her then master, an Irish wool grower, intending to set her free. No doubt he had other intentions, for he promised her everything that a rich thane could give his sweetheart. It was no wonder that he swept her off her feet, for he was young then, vital, masterful, his red beard sprouting, his green eyes glistening. No doubt he intended to keep his promise, but my mother, Ellen, made one mistake."

"Will you tell me what it was?"

"I wouldn't have mentioned it, if I had not intended to tell you. She went for a bucket of water to a pool in the woods, and it happened that the day was hot, and great Horkel, Eric's thrall, was swimming there. He waded out before he realized Ellen's presence. And the Irish women are fiery, as you know."

"I know what mistake you mean."

"How can you blame her, if you have any sense of justice? Horkel too was young and powerfully and cleanly built, a massive man truly, and he was stark naked, and she saw his mighty groin worthy of a young bull's. Your thought—your guess—is right. Before Ellen knew what she was doing she had stripped off her dress of friz and was lying in the soft grass with Horkel in the embrace of love. And it was there they were discovered by Eric the Red."

"And that was the real reason why he did not keep his promises to Ellen and instead made her a drudge."

"His rage was red as his beard. He struck Horkel, knocking him down, but it was Ellen who bore the brunt of his wrath, not only then but even to this day. That was her gift from Eric, in which I have shared. He forced Horkel and Ellen to marry—why not, when they were both his thralls? Ever since he has treated Horkel about as well as most thanes threat their thralls—plainly it was Ellen, not Horkel, whom he blamed for the blow to his pride and highness—you and everyone know how he has treated Ellen and me. He has never ceased to vent upon her, and upon me, his fury and spite, he who had not only broken his promise to set her free but had prevented her from making a good marriage, by which now she would be the wife of a rich franklin and I his stepdaughter. Do you wonder that I hate him? Hate is such a weak word!"

"Is that all the story?"

"All except its ending. That will come on the night of his marriage to the princess. You see, I have hidden away ten shillings— they were given to me by your brother, Thorstein, in pity, not expecting or receiving my favors in return, when he saw I was swelling with child. He asked me to keep the gift secret, so pray tell no one. Will you promise that?"

"Yes."

"I think he suspected that you were the babe's sire. It may be he saw me that morning, long ago, when I was on my way to Vixen's Den, and I had to stop and hide in a spinney of stunted birch trees from his keen eyes and the eyes of Ring Einersson, his companion. With those shillings I will buy my freedom from Eric the Red. He cannot refuse to sell it to me, for that is the law of the moot. And I have a wedding present for him too—for him and for his royal bride."

Her eyes had begun to glitter like the eyes of a poison sea snake. I felt my hands growing tense, the cords were iron hard in my neck, icy shivers ran down my spine, and for reasons dimly glimpsed but not yet recognized, I was in great terror. Yet my throat eased enough that I could speak.

"What present?"

"As a free woman, I have the right to come into his hall to witness his wedding. As soon as the pledge is drunk, I will come forward, before all the throng, and give him the gift of which any old man should be proud—a bouncing grandson. 'Here is the son that your son Leif gave to me,' I shall tell him, and my voice will ring clear, so that all will hear. And that is the moment I have lived for, ever since I was old enough to understand."

I hoped to all the heavens of the Christians and to the darkness of Hel Strand that this was all the story, as her silence seemed to imply. But ghosts had been wakened and had walked who would not now return to their mossy graves. The room turned bitter chill. The shadows leaped in grotesque form. I forced myself to speak.

"To understand what, Swanhild?"

She did not like the question. That much I could see in her glittering eyes. Perhaps she realized she had said too much.

"Oh, the reason for his abuse of my mother and me. And he will be paid for it all when I lay his son's son in his arms."

"I want to see my son."

"Look at him, but don't wake him. You can see his face well under his sleeping cap."

"No, I cannot see it well because of the bandage over his eyes."

"Later—in a few days perhaps—I will remove it. It must not be removed now. His eyes might take harm."

"I will remove it, come what may."

Swanhild seized my arm. When I jerked it out of her hands, she ran across the room to seize some kind of weapon, but by now I had broken in my hands the fragile cloth band and looked into my son's eyes. They were white as the eyes of a dead fish and he was stone blind.

But I could not contemplate this, yet. Swanhild was flying at me with an iron poker, her eyes blazing with murderous fury, and I thought of the fury in the eyes of Eric the Red, when he ran with an iron tamper to strike down Kol. That remembrance opened my eyes to the whole hideous truth.

I caught Swanhild's arm and twisted it until she screamed with pain and dropped her weapon. Then I spoke calmly enough.

"Swanhild, who is your father?"

"Horkel, of course. What do you mean?"

"No lies will help you now, Swanhild. When you present your baby to Eric the Red, are you not intending to say more than you told me? If that were all, the vengeance is not equal to your hate. Are you not intending to say, 'Here is your grandson, doubly your grandson, whose father is Leif, your son, and whose mother is Swanhild, your daughter?"

Swanhild gave vent to a piercing scream. I heeded it not, as I bent, picked up the baby in its covering, and held him with my left arm against my shoulder.

"Leif, Leif," she pleaded. "Put down my baby."

"Not yet."

"What are you going to do? Tell me in the name of the Gods."

"I do not yet quite know. I only know I am taking him with me." And with that I started for the door.

Swanhild sprang at me, like a wounded lynx, and I struck her in the face with the full force of my right arm. She pitched to the floor, where I left her lying as I went out into the beautiful spring morning. It was almost time for the sun to rise over the eastern seas. And I would hate it for shining, for I wanted naught but cold, black night.

6

The narrow path through the grass to Ellen's house intercepted a broader path, and when I reached it I knew not whether to turn left, where rowboats lay in a little bay in the bank of the fiord, or to turn right, which would take me through some cattle meadows, past a number of freemen's and thralls' houses, and ultimately to the desolate beach. I would have no trouble getting oars for one of the boats, indeed most of the fishermen left them lying handy on the thwarts, and then raising the stone or some old piece of rusted iron serving as an anchor, and setting forth on the now brimming tide. If I did so, I meant to look for an icefield, common enough at this season, but what I wanted of it I had no real notion, only the sense of its deadly cold, its treacherous crevices, and the absence of all life that causes a strange haunting by most icefields, more desolate than in the wild heart of a desert. True, seals sometimes basked on the ice, and now and then a white bear came voyaging aboard one; and always my heart lifted a little at sight of these sea folk, who made familiar with ice; and then I was half-sorry to hunt them, for their hides or meat or for fuel.

Without any reason that I yet knew, I turned instead to the right. This brought me to slightly higher land, where the east wind bit more sharply, and I pulled up the great shawl in which the baby was wrapped, so that its pink bald head and small red face were protected, and I need not glance now and then to its blind, white eyes; and at the same time it had no lack of air. And then a horrid thought bemazed my mind. I remembered the story that Swanhild had told me, of a Greek who, through no fault of his own, slew his own father and married his own mother; and how, when he knew the truth, he had put out his own eyes. Swanhild had been quick to protest this action, yet as I walked on I felt an understanding of this man and his shutting out of his brain forever the whole visual world. And then I was sorry I had not turned to the left and taken the baby in a boat out on the deep, barely flowing tide, and in the deepest part of the fiord cutting off the anchor and tying it to my leg, and then putting out my eyes with my knife, and then tumbling overboard with the babe clutched in my arms. Both of us would drown in that position, and by some grace it would not change even when we lay on the bottom, until we were devoured by sea lice and other grisly denizens of the utmost deep.

Then there faded out and vanished the dreadful vision before my eyes, because my wild and swirling fancies had been interrupted by sound dropping to me from high in the sky. I looked up and saw a flock of swans moving very slowly through that empty, cold sky, and I wondered at their coming this early in the year, and I listened to their trumpeting, so clear and beautiful and strange.

Suddenly I stopped. Some little landmark had caught my eye without my knowing it, causing me to remember a previous journey, not many years before, down this same path, and Ugruk had been with me, and we sped with all our might, for that path too had been one of dreadful vistas, because of its emptiness of my mother, Thorhild, strolling homeward after gathering flowers on the cliff overhanging the fiord. This was the very path we had taken when we went in search of her, and my heart burned as I realized that it would lead straight to the very spot we had found her body, which at low tide was a graveled beach but which now, at full flood tide, the great tide of the full moon, would be washed by waves five or six feet deep. And now I knew why I had turned right, and I went on knowing that I meant to ascend the cliff to the very spot from which she had been thrust, but what my action would be on my arrival I did not know because the visions constantly changed, and all were confused and half-hidden in cold mist.

I too was cold, body and soul, except for one warm spot, and my dazed mind took a perceptible time to explain this warmth at my left shoulder, which was only from the tiny living body that I carried there, so close that its warmth and mine were mingled and strengthened each other. And now I looked up again, because the swans which I thought had passed by were returning in a great circle, wailing of some woe that I knew not, that was perhaps unknown to everyone except this most beautiful of all winged things, and which perhaps was the price of beauty.

The distance to my mother's death place was short as measured by a rod, but unutterably long to my soul, through which time had ceased to flow, or at least I knew not its passage. Yet the moment came that I could look at the white foam of the tidal waters impounded there until some hand I could not see even in imagination pressed a little lever, or pulled a little cord, or merely turned over, the palm down instead of up, whereby these waters would begin their slow recession. And now I took the course Ugruk had taken when I had bade him look for my mother's footprints or for any sign whether she had been pushed over the edge, or had lost her balance and fallen, a question which had not been answered until last night, although now all doubt had died. And as I turned from the beach to make toward the hills running up toward the brink of the cliff, once more I heard the wild swans, and perceived that again they wheeled, and now were flying much lower than before, and their intermittent cries had become a chorus of terror and unfathomable woe.

As I gained the top of the cliff, only a few steps now from the scene of my mother's fall, the leader of the flock of swans dropped out of their glistening line and began to sail down as if to light in the sea, where I had never in my whole life seen a swimming swan. But she did not, and instead began to circle slowly over my head, these circles ever more narrow, ever closer above me. And now her outcries, pure and deep and beautiful, were almost incessant. But I paid her no heed. Closer I came to the place of my mother's fall, and now I was pressing the baby closer to my shoulder, and with my other hand baring my knife. But

at once I put the knife back in its sheath, for I had seen a vision
of what I could not doubt was my inexorable fate.

It was to kill the babe so it would not know the terror of its
fall, throw it into the sea, and then leap down.

And now the swan dipped level with my head and began to beat
her wings in front of my face and at one side and then the other,
all the time trumpeting in desperate alarm. But when her eyes
gazed into mine, I stopped for a brief space and spoke.

"Are you Minin? If you are, and I do not doubt it, I love you,
Minin, and will love you forever, but I cannot flinch from my
fate for your sake."

And when I had said this, she cried out as though she had
been stabbed to the heart, but her desperate wing beating about
my head had changed to long and powerful strokes as she ascended, and again her cries were intermittent, but of a sadness
otherworldly and eternal.

And then at the very brink I gave the babe a little swing in
my arms, whereby the back of its head struck the stone, and I
had glimpsed only the beginning of a slow seepage of blood into
the scalp when I threw it, past all pain or fright or punishment or
shame, into the sea. Its fall was swift, it caused only a small
splash, a little upfling of water and foam; yet at that instant
I knew that the tide had reached its full, and a mysterious signal
had been given whereby the waters under the cliff would begin
to flow seaward, carrying such freight as the Gods had decreed.
And as I was gathering my strength for a great leap, I saw something green out of the corner of my eyes.

I looked and it was the ghost of Thorhild, wearing a green
dress and carrying a bouquet of multi-colored blossoms, and her
clear and beautiful eyes were fixed on mine. None of her beauty
had faded in dim death, and when she spoke to me, her voice had
the same warmth and sweetness that I so well remembered.

"Leif, do not leap down," she said.

"I have no choice."

"Aye, but you do. There is nothing to be gained by your leaping
down, only chill death in the sea before your rightful time, and
there is much to be gained by your living on. Truly I believe that

gentle Kris wants you to live on, for although you have done a hideous thing, the deed unspeakable of a father slaying his son, yet it was done in mercy, and the powers of darkness took no pleasure in it because your heart was true. Instead of vanishing beneath the waves, of no more use to the world and its people, begin your great voyage as soon as you can stand to sea, and follow the star that leads you, that I think shines within your soul. If there is a great land in the west, sail on and on until you find it, or until death finds you. For when you lay in my womb, in the sixth month, a vision came to me of you, in the strength of your youth, sailing to some unknown strand, and of your carving in the rock the runes of your coming thence, and in the vision that strand seemed *Furder Strande*, the wondrous strand, and my soul besought a vision of your safe return, but it was not given. Yet all my days on earth my heart rejoiced, because it knew that I, Thorhild, had given birth to a son whose name would never die."

Her voice ceased. Her outline became blurred. "Stay with me, Thorhild!" I cried, but she gave her head a little shake, sad but unmistakable, and already she was dimming in my sight; and before I could breathe again, the lovely ghost was gone.

CHAPTER FOURTEEN

THE GREAT PASSAGE

I

As I returned the way I had come, knowing every bend and vista of a path, I knew that the Leif Ericsson who had been was no more, and a new Leif Ericsson had taken his form and brain, although with a different spirit. I knew too that my awful deed would never be forgiven in this world or in any other world to which I might go when done with the present world; yet it was within my power, that of a strong will and a strong body and of hands stronger than any man in Greenland, to make a great measure of atonement. I wondered if I would bear a mark like that borne by Cain, in an old tale told by the Christians, he who had slain his brother. There was already an inch-wide circle on my forehead of skin paler than the rest, where my Swan Maiden, Minin, had pressed her lips ere I had left the ice palace, and now it itched and burned, and I feared it would turn silver, like the mark of leprosy, or have a lazarlike crust. And when I stepped it seemed to me that the lichens that had grown under a blanket of snow now melting away, and which were now revealed, fresh and green and beautiful and youthful, shrank down from under my falling feet; and the stunted trees I passed seemed to shiver as in a blast of bitter wind; and the hares whose white hides were darkening under the returning sun fled from me when still at a long distance, and the ptarmigan that did not huddle in the gorse rose with a cry more desolate and weird than I had ever heard before from their eloquent throats. And even the patches of cloud over my head stirred and moved in what appeared a windless sky, and grouped and parted and darkened despite the outbursting sunlight, as if they were spreading the word of some immeasurable wickedness that one of them had seen in the world over which it commonly loved to hover, and to give sweet rain.

I went straight to the ship and bade Starkad summon Fatima, Helga's serving wench, and he looked wildly into my eyes ere he went on the errand, and Fatima stood pale and quaking at sight of me and sped from me swiftly when I bade her bespeak her mistress and make ready to receive me in her cabin. And while I waited, my brother, Thorstein, came to the foot of the plank and started to ascend, and I stood on the deck at the head of the plank and spoke.

"Do not come in reach of my hands, Thorstein," I told him, "for if you do I will break the bone of your neck as I once broke the bone of your arm, and you will drop dead, and then perhaps my accursed fate will be fulfilled, for I would have slain my brother as well as my son."

"Leif, are you mad! I broke your flute and deserved the punishment you gave me, but since then I have done nothing."

"That is your offense which the Gods will forgive hardly sooner than mine. You did nothing after you had seen Swanhild on the way to a rendezvous with me, except to pretend not to see her; and if you were not sure that I was the waiting lover, you made sure of it before long and did not tell me, Leif, your brother of the womb and of the loins, that she was Eric's daughter and my half sister. Aye, you let the months and then the years pass in silence with your lips still locked. It was a deed of hate, hate of me, of my ascendancy over you, and your keen mind told you that if you waited long enough, the Gods would move against me in awful fury for my innocent breach of their eternal and implacable ban against incest. Now they have moved, but they did not destroy me utterly, and soon I am going forth on the unknown western oceans in search of my soul's peace, and to make such atonement as is in my power; and if you come in reach of me, Thorstein, I will destroy you."

"You will come in reach of me, never doubt," he answered with his lips drawn back in hate and impotent fury, "but not now."

He departed, and in hardly a moment Fatima emerged from the hatch and spoke, wide-eyed, to Starkad, who came and spoke to me. And his face too was pale and his strong voice trembling.

"The princess Helga has sent word that she will receive you at once."

So I went to the room where magic had been made and loveliness had been rife only last night, and tapped on the door, which immediately opened to reveal Helga, fully dressed. Evidently she had been wakened soon after sunrise by an evil dream, or there had come to her a premonition of marching fate. She looked searchingly into my face, and her own beautiful face was wan and strange-looking, but I saw no fear in her wide and radiant eyes.

"Sit down on the bed, Leif, and I will sit beside you, and hold your hand."

"I am not sure you can bear to touch my hand after you learn what it has done."

Yet she slipped her hand between mine and quietly waited. Then I related, falteringly at first, but finally in a rush of words, the whole tragic story—of Eric's revenge on Ellen for her impulsive yielding to her own and to Horkel's lust, and of the vengeance bred by that revenge, whereby Eric's daughter, Swanhild, tempted Eric's son Leif into her incestuous seduction. Still Helga did not withdraw her hand from mine, nor shrink away from me, and only when I told her of my slaying the babe whose blindness was the rotten fruit of incest did her hand tremble and turn icy cold.

"Eric has a fair wind for his return today and may arrive sooner than we thought," I told her at the end. "As soon as possible thereafter I will stand to sea, and it comes to me, a vision such as came to Minin the Swan Maiden as we stood hand in hand, not a foreboding, for that word implies the nearing of some dire stroke of fate or fortune, and what I foresee gladdens my heart and offers hope unto my soul. Nay, I do not see plainly what awaits me, and I think it may be the consequence of another great storm through which I must pass, yet I believe in the vision's truth, and believe it the soothsaying of some spirit unknown. It is that when Greenland drops below the horizon as I sail westward, I will never again lay eyes upon its shore, nor upon the shores of any land known to our mariners, where folk of our kind dwell and have their being."

Helga made no reply for many long-drawn seconds. Her cold

hand lay motionless in mine. My heart leaped, and I knew that this was a moment mighty in my fate. Still, when at last she spoke, she merely asked a question which, to judge from its aspect and the sound of her voice, low and calm, was of no great moment.

"Why wait for Eric's return before you sail? You have no business with him that Thorhall cannot do or has not already done."

"No, I have no business with him, but you have."

Her hand made a little start, perhaps no more than a rush of blood, but I felt it keenly.

"Does the business I have with him concern you or your journey?"

"Aye, it does. And now I will speak plainly, come what may. Helga, I have never had a greater need of courage than at this moment, for I am about to ask you, in case you do not take my father's hand, to take my hand and come with me on my journey."

"But you said you could take no women."

"If you will come, I will ask every member of my crew who has a wife to fetch her aboard to sail with us, and you may bring your servant girl, Fatima."

"You have told me the question you intended to ask, for which you must rally courage. Have you rallied it by now? If so, speak."

"Helga, I love you, I have never loved any other woman as I love you, even Minin the Swan Maiden, who may be a figment of my dreams, and I want you with me always, in danger or safety, in calm or storm. I cannot promise you will ever again lay eyes on familiar shores. It may be I may atone in a measure for my offense against Gods and men and a babe of my own begetting; still I will ever be haunted by it, and if we become one flesh in marriage, you will be haunted by it also as long as you live. Yet if you reject my father, Eric, I ask that you come with me."

"You do not say 'entreat,' or 'beg.'"

"Helga, I cannot say it, except in the locked silences of my heart."

"Leif, I have already decided to reject Eric. I will wait and tell

him so, according to what is meet, and then I will go with you to
the world's end."

And then she toppled weeping against my breast, her arms
around my neck. My own arms remained rigid, with great inward
tremblings, at my sides.

2

While I was in soul-deep speech with Helga, Thorhall had attended to the matter of putting ten silver shillings in the right
hands of five of my father Eric's thralls, so they could buy their
freedom and sail with me if they chose. It had been no mundane
business, if I judged rightly by the flush on Thorhall's face and the
shine of his eyes, which I thought had reflected the luminousness
of sudden freedom in the thralls' faces.

The names of these new freemen were Gorm, Thorvald, Gull
Eye, Connelly, and Freyson. All except the first named were
wedded, but their wives could buy their freedom at seven shillings
each, and all but one would accompany their husbands on the
westward voyage provided—and I thought Thorhall must have
hinted at the possibility—that I would give passage to any woman.
Of these three, one had grown-up children and two could leave
their little ones with loving kinfolk, and only the fourth, Freyson,
had toddlers or babies whose need demanded that their dam remain in Greenland. Of my other seven shipmates, including
Ugruk and Starkad, all free and some of them my fellow veterans
of that first savage winter, Starkad hoped to take his wife and
leave his child with their grandsire, and every man of the four
remaining either had no wife or chose to leave his wife and
children too to conduct his little farm and care for his livestock.

While Thorhall was attending to this business and inquiry,
some oilskins had been put aboard, our empty casks had been
filled, and fresh meat and stale eider-duck eggs preserved in
brine added to our victual. Then the five thralls decided among
themselves to ask Thorhall to pay to Eric the silver shillings I
had given them, the price of their own freedom and the freedom
of four women who were wives to four of their number. And I

did not believe that the cause of their request was fear of Eric's murderous fury that might be waked, and rather that to them it seemed a matter of propriety that a thane should conduct such business with a great thane, if it were possible. Thorhall agreed at once, seeing the sense of it, and perhaps to prevent violence and perhaps murder being committed by his liege lord and old friend. So Thorhall put the seventy-eight coins in a little bag of deerskin and pouched it until the time was ripe to put it in Eric's hand.

Presently a visitor came aboard, Ian the poem speaker, who was in Einer's service, and with him was Novice Joseph, who had disembarked at dawn, leaving his luggage aboard, for a first survey of the settlement. But these two welcome guests had not come yet to take off Joseph's belongings, and instead they had been driven here by some great inward need or desire which I could see reflected in their anxious faces and flurried manner.

Ian was the first to speak when we three had walked together to the bow of the ship, and his voice was raw and nervous.

"Leif, I'll have at my whale in one throw, hit or miss. If you give your leave, Einer will give his leave for me to ship with you, and before you answer, I bid you remember I am no tyro at hoisting sail or at minding rudder."

"That I remember clearly, and you have my leave, and my gratitude as well, for in the first place we are shorthanded for a voyage of great distance, and in the second place you belong in our company, since you were in mine when I took the tusk of the King of the Narwhales, and in the third and main place, I could not ask for a more useful and delightful and brave companion."

Tears stood in Ian's eyes as he shook my hand and then presented me with what he said was a pocket piece over which a great Irish spaewoman, the wife of Olaf the White, had spoken a charm. It was an Irish shamrock carefully worked in green stone.

Then I turned to Novice Joseph, and his eyes met mine in a steadfast glance and he began to speak in his usual blithe tones, which I had begun to realize masked his deeper feelings.

"Leif, my case is different, and my plea not nearly so well-founded," he told me. "In truth, all that I know of sailing is what I picked up on my journey from Rome, via Barcelona and Cádiz, and Limerick in Ireland, to Norway, and from Norway, hence. Yet I am able-bodied, and have no antipathy to hard work. Also my head is better stocked than most, although whether some of its lore would be of use on a journey such as this I cannot say. I know enough astronomy to locate and identify the larger fixed stars. I have invented a crude device for testing the warmth or coldness of water. It is a small copper vessel which is to be filled with sea water and dropped in a much larger uncovered vessel of boiling water. The water in the larger vessel will then cease to boil, and the time required for it to boil again is measured on a graduated hourglass, an experiment I have performed often enough for me to derive a chart revealing whether the water in the smaller vessel is one, two, three, or four fifths warmer than ice water, reckoning boiling water as having a hundred more atoms of heat than does ice water. The device sounds somewhat fantastic, but I can assure you it gives a rough answer to the problem, often an important one to navigators in regions where cold currents in the seas are in juxtaposition with warm currents."

"Joseph, I think I could arrive nearer the truth by sticking my finger in the water in a draw bucket."

"I can cast large sums," Joseph went on, not in the least rebuffed. "Also I can track the planets by a formula invented—or so it is said—by the great Greek mathematician, Eratosthenes, and this too may be of value in calculating a ship's position in an illimitable ocean. As a final recommendation for my good self, I am handy with a falchion. And now for the meat of the matter, which is that I long most fervently to be a member of a company on a small ship braving the fastness of the western ocean in search of a new land."

"Joseph, you can write and speak Latin. Might that be of use to us in dealing with the folk of some such land?"

"It is possible. Often, throughout Europe, are found little islands of people who still speak the language of Rome, although greatly corrupted. Roman ships, Roman legions spread far and wide. But they did not get to Norway, only heard of its existence, and in all truth I have no real hope that they touched any strand far away in the western oceans."

"Why, I'm glad to hear it. It is my hope that the high Gods have ordained that the *Narwhale* will be the first ship to touch such strands. But pray answer one more question, my wise and good friend. Was not your main purpose in coming to Greenland the conversion of the people to the faith of the God Kris?"

"So I told King Olaf. But I had not taken the oath ever to speak truth, and I do not believe I ever will, because even saints must lie sometimes, out of kindness. I made the journey to Greenland in search of adventure. It offered very little compared to the journey you and your fellows are about to make."

"Novice Joseph, I love your company and your discourse. While you may come with us for that reason only, I doubt not that your talents will further our chances of survival and success."

Joseph's great eyes lighted and his sallow face flushed, but before he could answer we must perforce listen to an excited cry from one of the watch.

"Eric's catboat is rounding the bend."

3

Of all the watch crier's hearers, I was most jarred. During my talk with my good friends I had been able to thrust into some dim corner of my brain the greater issues not yet resolved, and which might never be resolved; but now my flight from them was done, and the truth of all that had happened stood forth like a black mountain overhanging a green vale, and looming against a tranquil summer sky. Quickly my eyes sped to Gorm, then to the faces of Thorvald, Gull Eye, Connelly, and Freyson. Gorm's face told me nothing, but the others were pale with fear. All of their lives Eric's word had been immutable law. He had seemed in himself the Thunder God, Thor of the Red Beard. But as my eyes met theirs, the expression on their faces changed, their heads flung up, and their backs straightened. Four of their number were of Norse blood, one of Irish, and all were true men, as I had discovered long ago.

We had nothing to do but watch and wait. The boat neared, I could distinguish Eric's thick body from those of his crew, and before long he was bawling orders for the boat's landing. And then out of her cabin came Helga, wearing a gown of gold cloth, a short cloak of ermine, and a circular band of gleaming gold around her pale gold hair. As she passed me, she nodded her head gravely, and then went down the plank and took her station on the strand.

Eric waited only until the catboat was secured, then leaped to land and made his way toward Helga. He walked with the step of youth, and his arms, bent at the elbows, swung back and forth as his powerful body moved, and truly he was a picture of power that seemed unvanquishable; and the weak sun seemed to strengthen and brighten to set fire to his red beard.

The two met; Eric asked a question. Helga answered it, at the same time shaking her head. Eric asked another question. In answering it, Helga made a little gesture toward our ship. Then she said something more, probably in the way of courteous regret for the pains he had taken in her behalf, and of royal thanks and respect to a great chieftain. Then, after giving him a deep bow, she reboarded her ship and descended the hatch to her chamber.

For a moment Eric appeared stunned; but that state would not last long. In a moment he came in his powerful stride to our plank, and then climbed it, and at its head he found me, and we looked each other in the face.

"By all signs, you are about to put to sea," he said in his strong and resonant voice.

"Yes, sir, we are."

"Well, what are you doing with five of my thralls in your company? Gorm, Connelly, Freyson, Thorvald, and Gull Eye, get your sea bags and disembark at once, and I'll teach you who is your master, and you'll wish to the high Gods——"

"Hold your peace a moment, Eric," Thorhall interrupted him. "I have something for you."

"And what are you doing here, Thorhall?" Eric demanded, his eyes as green as lichens after rain, his beard red as flame above the wick of the winter lamps. "Have you too turned traitor?"

"My only fixed purpose in coming here was to give you this at the request of five thralls," Thorhall answered him, handing him a small deerskin sack of some weight. "In it, you will find seventy-eight silver shillings, fifty of them representing the freedom price of five male thralls, and twenty-eight of four female thralls. Now there is nothing belonging to you on this ship, except what filial debt and respect owed to you by Leif. My pledge of allegiance to you was subject to my withdrawal at my wish. And now that you have stormed aboard, and spoken to me, Thorhall, born a thane, in a voice unfit to use unto a thrall, my purpose holds to sail with Leif, if he gives his consent, and in anticipation of this rift between you, Eric, and me, I have put aboard my gear." And through Thorhall's speech ran a muttering, knocking sound almost too deep to hear, and this I had heard before now and then, and again I remembered of what it reminded me, which was pack ice breaking up before a gale far away at sea.

Thorhall looked at me then in question, and all I could do was yell, "Yes, yes."

"A pack of traitors!" Eric burst out. "Where is my son Thorstein?"

"He came to the foot of the plank but did not come aboard," Starkad answered.

"He is the greater of my two sons. The fact will yet be proved. And someone summon the turncoat Helga. I wish to speak my mind to her."

"Eric, a royal princess is not subject to your summons," Thorhall told him.

"Starkad, you are mate of the vessel. Will you go to Helga's chamber and tell her that I, Leif, entreat her presence?"

All of us stood silent and tense until Helga joined us. But she was not now the regal figure who had come aboard such a brief time before. She still wore her rich gown, but had taken off the golden coronet and her cape of ermine, and her face was no longer serene, but flushed with fury, and I took it that Eric's strong voice had reached her in her cabin.

"My father wishes further word with you," I told her.

"Aye, I do," Eric said. "It comes to me that you would not have made the decision you did, if my son Leif had kept the pledge he made to me, ere I sent him to Norway as my emissary."

"He kept the letter of the pledge, and I remind you, Eric the Red, that you broke the spirit of an implied pledge, made ere you and he came to Greenland, when you sent him on a fool's errand, planning to put to sea in his absence, but the Gods willed that he should succeed in his mission after all, and come to the strand before you set sail. Now the Gods willed that I set sail with him, and become his wife, and that you remain on shore."

"Leif told you about that. Did he tell you that he wooed Johanna, the daughter of Bjorn, but she picked my true son, Thorstein?"

"He told me of that also."

"Treason, treason, thick as the droppings of sea birds on the rock of their roost, and smelling as foul. Leif, you saw me slay the thrall Kol for breaking down my new sheep pen. How should I deal with you, who have broken down all that I built toward true greatness of name and place? I will not now become Earl of Greenland. The country will not now become part of Olaf's kingdom."

"And for that I rejoice," Thorhall said quickly. "Greenland will remain a free and independent nation throughout my lifetime and perhaps a hundred years."

"And Ian! What are you doing on this boat? I take it that treason is catching like the croup, and you have betrayed Einer."

"No, sir, he gave me leave to go."

"And you, Novice Joseph, who in Norway told me of your desire to visit Greenland, and I promised I would urge it to the king, and I kept that promise. Perchance I have misjudged you, and you are aboard only to say good-by to shipmates of your journey hence, but I fear you too have caught the scurvy sickness."

"It is not a sickness, Eric the Red. I am a free man, and I have decided I would rather follow Leif than follow you."

"Leif, it is in my mind to kill you. It is what you deserve."

With a murderous glare in his green eyes Eric glanced about him in search of a lethal weapon.

"Hold your hand, Eric," Joseph said before I, or Thorhall, or any other could speak. "I wear a falchion under my robe and am no novice in its use."

Their eyes met, and Eric bethought himself as to my murder, as all could see in his face. And I waved back Ugruk, who was creeping up behind Eric, his long knife partly concealed under his arm.

"My curse upon you all!" Eric burst out. "May this ship be crushed in the ice, may she strike a reef and break up, may a gale tear her in twain, that you all may go to black bottom of the sea, on the first reach of your road to Corpse Strand. Odin, loose your most terrible winds. Thor, cast your bolts of iron and fire to rend their ship as you split asunder the crags of the mountains. Njorge, raise such seas against them as men have never seen, let alone survived, and hurl them upon the ship, and founder her in one blow. Frey, rider of Golden Bristles, give them no sunshine, and no rain, so their hearts will darken and their casks of water will dry up and crack. And Kris—Kris! You are said to be the son of a wrathful, vengeful God; will you betray him as my son has betrayed me? Put aside your meek mien, and prate no more of forgiveness of sins, but punish him as he deserves; and if there is a darker and more terrible abode of souls than Hel Strand, send there his soul that he may suffer world without end. And now I have done! I leave the ship and go into my hall. But I tell you this, that if the Gods heed me not, or if Thorhild's God defends you from them, think not for one moment you will be spared from my revenge. If you are let to live awhile, still you will find no new land, because Greenland lies at the border of earth, and beyond these seas rolls the Poison Sea, and if you flee them there will be no place for you to go but to some Christian country, and there I will seek you out, and you will die the death!"

Eric wheeled and descended the plank. I was about to give the order to cast off when I saw Ugruk run quickly to his inverted kayak, get something, and put it in my hand.

"Leif play pretty?" he asked.

"I will play a farewell to Greenland," I answered, "and to its sunlit icecap and its tall, grim mountains, and to the woe it has brought to many of its dwellers, but also I will play of the happiness it has brought, ever woe's companion; and also I will play of hope of finding a new land. And as I do so, some of you loose the lines and some hoist the sail, and we will depart from hence with my flute singing, as sings the swan as its soul departs."

I put the flute to my mouth. Music that I had never heard, that even in the instant rose in my soul, came forth, and its distant strains reached Eric's ears as he crossed the strand, and he closed them with his hands. But it seemed to me that the sea birds listened, as did creatures of the deep, and the vast mountains stood mute and magnificent, and some sudden effulgence of the sun made the icecap gleam like pearl.

4

By the time we had skirted the shallows not far below our strand, the sun set in the western oceans, where in due course we might come close to her, beholding her in effulgent glory. However I had observed that she had not so far increased in size, or decreased either, as seen from any land I had visited; and I was inclined to share Joseph's opinion that she was a sphere, about the size of the moon, both perhaps larger than we dreamed, for instance five hundred miles in diameter; and that the Gods had decreed that she encircle the earth forever, making the round trip in what we reckoned was twenty-four hours. But surely she changed her path at least four times a year to account for the different seasons. And then the notion struck me with some force that the passage of a year did not ordain the number of times of her revolving, but the number of times of her revolving ordained the passage of a year. In any case after three hundred and sixty-five journeys, each causing a night and a day, or, in the far north in winter, a dimming or brightening, she fetched up at the same place in the sky.

So I reckoned that a gerfalcon could not keep up with her in his far flights, and no man ever warmed by her rays, and no man she would ever warm, could match her in wide travel.

But she had hardly set when the moon rose, in the fullness of the glory and the beauty of her countenance, and her frail but copious light enabled Gorm, to whom I had assigned the watch, to keep the *Narwhale* on her course. It was the first watch he had ever commanded as a free man, and I thought it might cause a great elation in his soul. Meanwhile some regions of my soul were wildly bright in confronting the future, and some were darker than Hel Strand in contemplating the past. And of this I had sung when I had played my flute, but now it was mute, and I yearned for another kind of music, and truly my need of it was most dire. So I sought Helga, and presently found her by the forward rail, looking not back to the land, but forward to the widening waters of the fiord, under a pale sheen of moonlight as these neared the open sea.

Her servant, Fatima, was not present at this moment, and I took Helga's hand, and my tongue uttered the words that rose of themselves in my throat.

"Helga, will you marry me now? I could wait until tomorrow if you wish, or even longer, but I tell you before the Gods that my need of you tonight, at my side waking and sleeping, and to lie in my arms, and I to lie in your arms, is as deep as the deepmost sea, and beyond my power to tell."

"Yes, I will marry you now, this hour, if Novice Joseph will perform the rite, and if he will not, or has not the authority, we will take our vows before witnesses, the vows of lifelong love and such troth as we may keep, and in any case sleep in each other's arms tonight, for my need of you is likewise beyond my power to tell."

So together we sought out Joseph, and at her bidding both he and I followed Helga to her quarters. And then Helga bade me speak, as was my place and right.

"Joseph, my friend, Helga and I wish to be joined in marriage this very hour. Can you and will you perform the rite?"

"It is not a rite, Leif, my captain, but a sacrament, and a most high one in the creed of Christians. And I tell you now that I have no authority from the Holy Church to perform it, nor do I feel myself worthy to do so, and finally not even a cardinal may marry two pagans to each other unless they first accept the rite of baptism, although a marriage between a Christian and a pagan, for instance that of Clovis, King of the Franks, and Clotilda of Burgundy, was sanctioned, no doubt on the supposition that a Christian wife could convert a heathen husband. The fact remains that we have already passed the grasslands, and the shores of the fiord are here uninhabited, and presently we will venture forth on the open and unknown sea. The Church was created for men, not men for the Church, and our greatest theologians have ever held to the doctrine of reason, which is to do the best one can under the circumstances. It would give me great honor as well as great pleasure to perform a ceremony in lieu of the sacrament of marriage, and anyway I believe that the sacredness of any marriage abides in the hearts of the man and wife; and if it does not abide there the ceremony is proved not a sacrament but empty air. Warning you that I am unfit for the office, that Ugruk is as well-fitted as I except that he is not so fluent of speech, do you still want me to preside at your marriage?"

The expression on my face must have answered his question as to my wishes, for he turned quickly to Helga.

"Joseph, I am perfectly aware that Ugruk is as spiritually fitted as yourself to perform some sort of ceremony of marriage, perhaps better fitted——"

"That I concede."

"Still you will do it more handsomely, and I hope you will grant our petition."

"Truly I will do the best I can. When?"

"As soon as I can change my dress. Leif, do you want me to dress plainly, or to wear my royal gown, my ermine cape, and my coronet?"

"You are a princess and it is your right, and I think your duty, to appear as one on such an occasion as this."

"I had hoped you would see that, Leif."

"I will wear the red raiment of Dorstad wool that I wore at your father's court. Let us meet with Joseph on the deck in half an hour. By then the moon will be higher and in full flood, and we will be close to fiord mouth. And I will ask Gorm to summon the whole ship's company, two or three of whom can at the same time mind the ship, to witness the ceremony."

So we swiftly parted and began our preparations. In a few minutes most of the crew and their wives who were with us were putting on their best clothes and as the time neared Gorm brought fire to a great stone kettle, usually used in rendering oil, now filled with seal tar. It blazed bravely in the big dark, lighting the whole deck, casting a rosy glimmer on our emblem, and no doubt mystifying creatures of the utmost deep, who are said to come to the surface on nights of such effulgent moonlight. Then up from her cabin came Helga, wearing the robe and in the mien and carriage of a princess, and behind her walked her servant, Fatima, dressed in Moorish custom. The latter was no doubt Helga's notion, and one I thought most appropriate, since the girl was a follower of Mohammed, while Helga and most of the onlookers swore by Odin and Thor, and Starkad's wife was a Christian, and Ugruk knew no gods, and I was torn between two faiths; and this mixing seemed to me, and I thought seemed to Helga, a wondrously fitting thing, because in a sense the mixture represented a great part of the known world, while all of us were joined in the search for an unknown world.

Helga and I took our stand before Joseph, Fatima at one side and a little behind the princess, and Ugruk at one side and a little behind me. And then in his rich voice, worthy of a poem speaker, indeed betraying more feeling than in any utterance of his that I had heard, Joseph asked a question.

"Helga, are you in love with Leif?"

"Deeply and passionately."

"Do you love him enough that you can spend your whole life as his wife, and be happy?"

"Joseph, I think that I can. I cannot swear to it, since no one knows what the future will bring, and even the spaewomen catch only dim and hazy visions, yet I have spoken my firm belief."

"It is all the more reliable, in my judgment, because you have qualified it. Leif, are you in love with Helga?"

"Yes, sir."

"Do you want her for your wife all your life long?"

"My mind tells me that I do, and likewise my body, and my soul appears to confide the same."

"If she becomes your wife, will you consider her your chattel?"

"No, sir, I will not."

"You will not demand implicit obedience of her?"

"No, I will not. As my wife, she will be free to do what her heart bids her."

"Suppose that she succumbs to momentary temptation, and lies with some other man, will you take her back to your bed and board?"

"If she wishes to come."

"Suppose that you succumb to momentary temptation, and lie with some other woman, and, worse than that, become enamored with her, will you divorce Helga and marry the interloper?"

"No, I will ask Helga to be patient with my wandering fancy, and give me a little time, and not leave me for such a period as she can bring herself to remain with me; for it is my firm belief that when the storm has passed I will be able to resume my true course, which is at Helga's side, on our journey down the years until one of us dies."

"Helga, can you say the same, even though you are a royal princess, far above Leif in station, of whom a more haughty attitude may properly be expected?"

"Joseph, I can, for it is likewise my firm belief."

"If Leif should turn Christian, will you have done with him?"

"No, unless his love for me, forever a pagan, turns cold."

"All that you have said, Helga, is witnessed and sealed by the fact that you make this journey with him, unto unknown seas, facing undreamed-of perils. I believe you. I believe what Leif has said. I will ask neither of you for oaths, for sometimes oaths become a wall that cramp a human life that should be free, and sometimes their very speaking works against their keeping, the speaker regretting that he has so bound himself, and that binding becomes hateful, and it is better for two who are married to divorce each other, than to live in hate, for hate poisons the human heart, and the human heart is all that we have, the only meaningful manifestation, indeed the only thing we may call proof of the existence of a true God. Not long since, a great prelate of Rome has declared that marriages are made in heaven. In truth, it has become part of the Christian dogma. But surely we should not blame high heaven, if such exists, for the innumerable mismatchings between men and women, and it would be more true to say that marriages are made in a haystack, or in a lonely dell in the forest, or in a borrowed bed, the call not that of soul cleaving unto soul, but of the bodies' imperious desire. Near the close of a proper ceremony of marriage, acknowledged by the Church, the priest states that by the authority in him vested, he declares the twain standing before him man and wife. No such authority has been vested in me. I am no priest. I am only a follower of one who declares all men are brothers, meaning those who follow a straight path and those who wander afield, and who changed water into wine at a marriage feast. I myself am a wanderer far afield. So I ask you, Helga, that after the declarations you and Leif have made, standing before me with your hand in his, whether you now consider yourself his wife?"

"Aye, I do."

"Leif, do you consider yourself Helga's husband?"

"Aye, I do."

"Then, I pray you, kiss each other in the presence of this company, a sign I have done wisely and well, and tonight when you are apart from us give each other little tokens in remembrance of this moment. But now, Leif, broach a small cask of wine that all may drink to your happiness together as long as you both live, and at the same moment drink to something new under the sun, the finding of a great new land across waters which man-bred evil may find hard to cross, and where great wrongs may be righted, and where wonders beyond our dreaming, bringing good unto mankind, may come to pass. And truly the marriage of this beautiful woman and this brave man seems to me a forecasting of beauty and bravery walking hand in hand in centuries unreckoned and undreamed, and it comes to me that whatever Gods there be, they will bless the marriage and this adventure. Tomorrow we will be in seas lonely of man, but also lonely of good and evil, because man has not yet gone thence; and good and evil have no existence except in his heart. And when I have drunk, I will go to my berth, for never before have I bared my heart, and revealed my inmost faith, and caught a distant glimpse of what may be the meaning of the riddle we call life, and hence I am overwrought, and I would have no choice but weep."

Then Novice Joseph did weep, and turned away to hide what he feared was weakness, but I did not hold it so, and instead I knew him for a strong brave man. Then with such stolidness as I could pretend, I called for a small cask of our finest Iberian wine, and this I broached.

5

The sickness in my soul was not cured, and it never would be wholly so, until my soul passed, but it was greatly ameliorated by a deep, sweet sleep with Helga held fast in my arms. In the first moment of wakening I hardly knew where I was, or how I had come to be in bed with this beautiful princess with hair like the Goddess Siff's, her silken and warm body conjoined all its length with mine; and then I remembered what had passed, the good and evil, and then the easy pitching of the ship told me that she rode the rolling waves on the deep sea. I kissed Helga, and she put her moist arms sleepily about my neck, and returned my kiss, and then went back to sleep; and I rose and dressed, and went out on the deck, for the hour was almost at hand when I should relieve Starkad of the watch. He told me that a fresh, strong wind, straight out of the east as well as he could tell by his pilot stars, had puffed our sail throughout the night, and thrust strongly against our stern, and wind-blown waves had sped our advance, and he would not wonder if we were a hundred miles from fiord mouth, and certainly we were on the open and seemingly limitless sea. The harsh, high shores of Greenland had dropped below the horizon, and the weird thought came to me, as an intimation, that I would never again lay eyes on her wondrous icecap as long as I lived.

When I had eaten breakfast, in deep thought bewhile, I sent for Starkad and Novice Joseph, and I would have summoned Gorm also, were he not catching the sleep that his old bones and brain so sorely needed, and I would have summoned Ugruk if I had not found him at my elbow. Then the four of us met in council in the bow, and it was not needful that we speak loudly to be heard by one another, for the moan of the sea, as if in some unknown woe that all things animate and inanimate must share, hardly rose above its soft splashings, and the wind-crammed sail did not crackle and the ship did not creak. And it came to pass that I did most of the talking at this meeting, Joseph the next most, Starkad very little, and Ugruk none at all.

I related what Ugruk had told me, that a great land lay what he believed was due west of Greenland, the coast of which he had surmised was nearly parallel to the coast of Greenland. I told them too that this was the mere beginning of great lands and islands, separated by inlets and deep bays, stretching all the way to the great river of his home, and beyond that river the land ran on and on, a journey of many weeks in a kayak. But also I told them that these lands were inhospitable to men, their climate more severe than Vesterbig's, as well as Ugruk could tell, and although the same kinds of animals were found there, such as reindeer, white bears, and Greenland oxen, the villages of folk were small and far apart, life being so arduous. And then I spoke of what made Starkad's eyes light up, and the color rise in Joseph's sallow cheeks, that Ugruk's great river flowed from the southwest, and even a thousand miles from its mouth it was still a mile wide, as reported by Innuits who had gone thence and there encountered, in an unpleasant fashion, an animal which the inhabitants called a skunk. It was hardly unthinkable, I said, that such a great river did not have enormous tributaries, flowing both from the southwest and the southeast, showing the hugeness of the land.

"In other words," Joseph broke into my discourse, "you think that Ugruk's river was not an island river but a continental river!"

"Aye, I do think so."

"Mary, Mother of God! What else can I say!"

"It comes to me, too, although this is more conjectural than the other, that there may be great lands south and west of the long land Ugruk skirted, and there, as in the Land of Skunk, the winters are not as harsh and the winds not as wild, and that forests grow and spread wide. And it may be there will be other mighty rivers that drain these forests and perhaps wide grasslands, and, amid these, folk of our kind may settle. If we should discover another Greenland, I will have equaled the feat of my father, but what if we should discover a more southerly land, where the sun is more ardent, and grapes can ripen on the vine, and folk need not spend half their strength barely to stay warm, such lands as lie to the south of Norway, held by the Germans, the Franks, and the Iberians, and the Romans, of whom one is among us. So the thought comes to me that we should set the ship on a different course."

"Southwest?" Starkad asked, in the low voice he employed when he scarcely had breath to speak.

"My choice would be south-southwest, or even south by west, making for lands lying south of the land that Ugruk passed, and lands lying south of those lands, perhaps with a climate as temperate as Germany or even Normandy."

"What you are truly saying, Leif, my friend and captain," remarked Joseph, his dark eyes ablaze, "is that while Iceland is an outlying island of the continental mass embracing Europe, Greenland is not merely the westernmost end of that land, but instead is the easternmost island of another continental mass, until now unseen by men of our kind, and undreamed of by the most visionary Greek! Why not? As we once calculated, on the assumption that the theories of great Eratosthenes were well-founded, there are more than fifteen thousand lineal miles of unknown sea or unknown land unaccounted for by known lands or water on this sphere called the world. What if there is no land south-sou'west of us, only the pathless ocean, and we should become lost in its wastes? Well, we would all die, which is by no means an uncommon end to us strange, forked creatures. Yet I ask one favor. Set your course south by west, and before the day is out—and what is one day's sail compared to the vasty distances

of which we dare conjecture and even speak—such daring merit-
ing death in slow fire in certain backward areas of Christendom—
I wish Ugruk to tell of his great journey eastward to Greenland,
and if he will recall the days he traveled by kayak before the wind,
or was blown back by contrary wind, I will make a rough guess,
a wild estimate, of the distance. And with that sum in mind, I
will guess at the size of some new and unknown continent in the
western oceans. Then Leif, by inspiration and common sense,
and what we Romans learned from the Greeks about geometry,
I will venture to guess how far westward you must veer from a
southerly course in order to come upon the land so far southward
of the chill abodes of both you and Ugruk, a land that the sun
blesses the greater part of the year, and gentle zephyrs blow instead of wintry gales, and my friend the grape ripens upon his
vine. And Leif, if you find such a land, the long-locked doors of
Valhalla will be opened unto you when you cast your soul, and
you will spend eternity in the company of heroes, and be honored
by them all!"

If such a thing were true, it might be Minin who would bear
my soul to those adamant doors, for she was a Swan Maiden, and
hence a Norn, and when she so desired she could take shape as a
Valkyrie riding a white steed. But my tender thoughts of Minin
soon slipped out of my head as I thought of my flesh-and-blood
beloved, as mortal as myself, almost as earthy, who only last
night had slept in my arms, and would do so again tonight, if the
Gods were not offended by our bold venturing and let us both
live that long.

6

The boldness of our enterprise must have become more and
more evident to the Gods as we sailed on and over all that water,
under all that sky. Gray-bearded Odin, riding the North Wind on
his Eight-hoofed Horse, could well lean sideways and look down
at our little chip of a ship which sturdily, almost stolidly, poked
her nose into the vasty emptiness of seas over which no human
eyes had ever gazed. Red-bearded Thor was so dumbfounded that

he could not decide whether to hurl one of his thunderbolts, or to smite us with his wondrous sword forged by Sindri the Dwarf, or to wait and see what further follies, if not impudence, we would be guilty of. The God Frey, riding about on Golden Bristles, his great boar, himself bristled with envy and thought upon his little jaunts hither and yon, and they struck him as most trifling, and he cursed in the name of his father, Odin, and his stomach felt sick. But the most startled of all was Njord, God of the Oceans with which we made so free. He knew of and let pass those ships that sailed close to the land, although sometimes he sank them in petulance or wrath, but he had never dreamed, in all the long ages of his life, of seeing a trespasser in these faraway wastes, unvisited by sea birds, where dolphins would not follow us perhaps because of lack of fish in the deep, dark waters, where dwelt whales and great sharks, and perhaps where monsters treading the bottom on their dragon feet had their blind being. Perhaps it caused him to wonder whether he was indeed the omnipotent God of the Oceans. What was little man, that he should come here without godly consent?

I reckoned some very great God, greater than any I could imagine, had sanctioned our journey and told the lesser Gods to hold their protesting tongues and smother their wrath. I wondered if he could be Jehovah, father of Kris. No one had ever told me where his realm began, or where it left off. Could it be worldwide, sky-high, and ocean-deep? As for Kris, I liked to think he meant well by me, despite my not yet following his banner, because of Thorhild's sweet devotion and perhaps prayers in my behalf, but more likely because he was so busy helping the poor and healing the sick he had forgotten all about us. It seemed to me that Eric the Red, and Thorstein, and even Swanhild had almost forgotten us, not because we had been gone so long but because we had gone so far.

Even we ourselves had trouble grasping the fact of our little ship so distant from home and so alone. Sometimes I thought about it for a little while before some mundane matter pushed it from my mind, and on many nights I dreamed about it, and these would have been forlorn and troubled dreams, if it were not for the warmth of Helga's body, and her nearness, and her beauty comforting my soul.

So far, and so very far, we had met with no violence of weather which we had not previously known and survived. Often the winds were high, as likely to be contrary as favorable, although once in a dead calm, only a week out from Greenland, we had perceived by watching a swimming albatross that we were moving southward, carried by an ocean current. In the next four weeks we had met with two great storms, before which we must heave to and drag a sea anchor, and in one case our drift was in the direction we wished to go, and in the other far to the eastward. We had a rough notion of our distance southward of Osterbig by measuring at midnight the height above the horizon of the North Star, but how far west we were only the Gods knew, and as a blind guess, with perhaps some inward prompting true or false, I ventured to Ugruk that we were two thousand sea miles west of Ireland and south or a little southeast of what he called the Long Land, from which he had set forth to the coast of Greenland. Meanwhile we had sailed across a warm current of water, fully a hundred miles wide, which Gorm thought flowed northeast. In this stretch we again saw albatross, dolphins, and great silverfish, as long as a rowboat, that sometimes leaped clear of the waves and glittered in the sunlight ere they fell with a mighty splash. And in this region of the ocean we saw beds of kelp, in which many small, bright-colored fish darted and played.

Our food supply was ample, of greater variety than eaten on most long voyages, and our ship snug. Our greatest trouble was in our minds because, hurried hither and yon by winds of unknown direction, or by great sea currents whose origin and destination we did not know, we could make only the wildest guesses in what direction and how far we were from any known land. Often Joseph, Starkad, Thorhall, and I held widely diverse opinions. Yet it was a dark and rainy day that Starkad could not find the sun by the shadow of his knife point on his thumbnail; and the shifting clouds or the sky blown clear of clouds gave us many a glimpse of the North Star, identified beyond dispute by the pointer stars of the Big Dipper or, as Joseph called the constellation in more classical language, the Great Bear. Its position above the horizon at what we reckoned was midnight enabled this brainy fellow to guess at our position southward of Osterbig. By watching our hourglass and measuring the ascendancy of western stars, he made some kind of estimate, based on a theory which he did not explain because it was over our thick heads, of our east-west position in respect to the east-west position of Ireland.

Still all this was guesswork and all that we really knew was that we were far and away on an unknown ocean, sometimes bright and beautiful, sometimes gray and sullen, but forever mysterious and unplumbable, and we had well-nigh forgotten from where we had come and had only the most foggy of notions, shored up by hope, where we would fetch. No wonder the men off duty liked to hear me play my flute. It took their minds off their perplexities.

And I loved to play it, old and new tunes, and those that I made up, because I either played it better or its sound was more wondrously beautiful rising above the soft swishings of the sea and its eternal murmur.

Five weeks after our departure, in weather fairly warm and sometimes almost hot, and with daylight more and darkness less in every period of twenty-four hours, Thorhall, Starkad, and I met in solemn conclave.

Thorhall had shipped as steward, because my two mates had been appointed, and some of the services of that office had been like those he had given Eric. He reported now that certain of our supplies were running low; and although the most important, the water casks, were plentiful for another fortnight, he knew no answer to the problem that if in the meantime we did not touch land where we could refill them.

"Mind you, Leif, if we turn eastward this very day, and keep to that course every hour that we can run or tack, I think we can reach the shores of Europe more or less alive," Thorhall said. "If we had a favorable wind one third of the time, and a crosswind one third, and a contrary wind only one third, I am sure of it, as far as any man can be sure of anything when he embarks on the great sea. Mark you, this present wind is from the south-west. I have heard a tale, perhaps no more than a legend, that there is a prevailing southwest wind across the ocean at this time of year. To do what I suggest, but against which I protest with all my soul, will mean stinging defeat, although it might mean that we would live instead of die. A straight eastward course is not hard to find and follow. In some moment of every day the sun will show himself."

"You can see the shadow that he casts with my knife point on your thumbnail, six days out of seven," Starkad said quietly. "Do you know where I think we would fetch up? It's only the blindest guess, you mind, yet I'll make it. On the Breton peninsula or per-haps a little south, not far from Gironde Mouth."

"Starkad, if you were captain of this ship, would you give the command to turn back?"

"No, sir, I would not."

"Will you give me your reasons, when to turn back offers us a better chance to live than for us to continue on?"

"I'll give my reasons the best I can, although they're a tangle in my head. There is something more to consider than the best chance for life; and that is the best hope of victory. If we turn back, we accept defeat. We may keep alive, but I doubt if life would be worth much to any of us thereafter. If we keep on, we challenge the Gods but we will be playing our last chance to win. Lately we Norse have met little except defeat. Nation after nation, tribe after tribe, have turned their backs on Odin and Thor and gone over to Kris. No longer the Christians pray—quaking on their knees—*A furore Normannorum libera nos*—that's right because I learned it by heart: 'From the fury of the Norseman, deliver us.' Why, that prayer went up from every city and hamlet on every navigable waterway in England, Ger-many, and France, from the White Sea in the north to the mouth of the Tiber in the south. We were warriors then, that made no truce with death; we conquered or we died. Those days are gone, but even in these days we might beat the Christians to the great-est discovery in the annals of man; we might show them that the Viking spirit is still alive and strong. But it might be, Cap'n, and

Thorhall, I would not speak so boldly, I might even cringe before the wrath of Jehovah, that mighty Christian God—except for one thing."

"What is that thing, Starkad?" I asked.

"Because I've seen more whales, more seals, more dolphins, more sharks, and more fish-eating birds than I have seen since we left the coastal waters of Greenland. It may mean nothing. But it may mean we're getting out of the depthless sea and approaching land."

"Well, why don't you put overside your plummet, on the longest cable we've got aboard, which is two hundred fathoms, and see if you can touch bottom, and if you can—if you can, why, you'll know for certain."

"Not for certain, Leif. 'Twould be only a good sign. But heave to, and stand her into the wind, and I'll try."

In a few minutes, so swiftly we moved, the cable was running out from its great coil. Seamen who had watched the same thing scores of times, only to see the line vanish under the sea to its very end with a dangling plummet, finished their brief chores and stood about to watch. I do not know why their faces had turned pale. They had not heard a word of Thorhall's discourse. And from out of their cabin came Helga and Fatima, and from their bunks rose up sailors wakened from their heavy sleep by what must be a dream, and Ugruk got out of his kayak in which he had busied at some craftsmanship, and old Gorm hastened to join us, spat over the rail, and watched the plummeting line. Last of all came Novice Joseph. He had been sitting in the stern, and the manuscript he had been reading was pinned under his arm. He gave me a smile, half in mockery, half in wild hope.

"If you touch bottom, and we go on and touch land, it must be that the Lord Jehovah did not whisper of its existence into the ears of His Holiness, and has kept it as a surprise," he told me.

At one hundred fathoms, a start ran through Thorhall's body and he looked me in the eyes, and his eyes were burning.

"Leif, we've hit something. It may be a tangle of driftwood, water-soaked, and yet not enough to sink it wholly, and it may be the back of a sea monster, in water just deep enough to buoy him and sleeping off his last meal of a blue whale. Take in twenty fathoms, and I'll let down the lead again."

I did as he bade me. Again, at a hundred fathoms, the strange look of wonder came into his face. Without being told I again raised the lead, and dropped it, our drift nearly a quarter of a mile from the first try.

"There it is," Thorhall said quietly. "The bottom, as sure as God. It's a great bank of some kind. But which way does it shelve? How can we know but keep lowering the plummet——"

"We'll do that, too, but as a start we'll follow yon sea bird. By heaven, it's a swan, as beautiful as I have ever seen, and what is she doing over salt water, this far from land?"

Not one of my shipmates knew the whole story of Minin and me. Perhaps some of them thought I was daft when I ordered the helmsman to set his course by the flight of a waterfowl, even though the sunlight caused her wings to gleam like silver. All hands that were not busied hung closed and tense, and every face except Helga's was mazed with wonder. Helga's eyes flashed fire.

7

The swan, Minin or some other, perhaps Minin's emissary, could not fly slow enough to keep pace with our fastest sailing. Often she flew so far away that she was only a white speck on the horizon, then she would come flying back, snow white and beautiful, until she was well-nigh over our stem, and then side-slip in the air, reversing her course, then, with triumphant trumpet, wing on again. Her flight was almost straight north. In following this radiant monitor we were sailing directly opposite from our intended course, which had been south by west, yet there was not a man aboard who doubted that we were being guided to some good, and that included hard-bitten Gorm and, more remarkably, Novice Joseph, whose bent of mind tended toward incredulity of the supernatural. He knew that seafowl of various sort, usually albatross or gulls, sometimes precoursed a ship; he did not know that it was almost unheard-of conduct by a fresh-water bird. Thorhall and Starkad were perhaps consoled by the question we three had raised as to whether our ship was too far east to come in sight of great lands lying southward of the lands Ugruk had skirted on his prodigious journey. As for me, I had no need of consolation of any sort. The sight of the guiding swan exalted my soul.

Yet the day died, and twilight dimmed away, and dark night set in without our sighting land. The glimmering dot that was our monitor, whose snowy wings had caught the last rays of the sun, was swallowed up at last, and whether she was still in our van we could not know, although two of my crew thought that they heard her distant call. I took it that she had shown us our true and nearest route to a good landfall, and now she had gone to roost in some fresh-water pond with her beautiful companions. Since it was a clear night, affording us a constant view of that faintly pale but lovely star, the most beloved by sailors of any in the sky, the only star that did not rise and fall with the wheeling heavens, that sate his arboreal throne winter and summer, the wondrous North Star, he remained our pilot; and often the lifting waves caused the great narwhale tusk that was our precursor and our guard to appear to point straight at him, and I thought there was some ancient bond between them and unearthly communication.

The night passed and the light began to clear. I was up early, scanning the northern horizon, but all I could see was low-hanging cloud, and no glint of white wings. I had gone to the bow, and there Thorhall joined me, for no breaking day had ever found him sound asleep, and presently Starkad likewise joined us, and then Novice Joseph. I was at a loss, I told them, as to what orders to give the helmsman. The ocean had never seemed vaster and more gray. My heart bade me continue on this same course at least until noon, but my brain protested, because it was not far from a direct reversal of the course that had fetched us nowhere but to open and illimitable sea. And it was my dream to discover land not in the wintry north but a more southerly land, where spring was in full flush.

"You might try sailing straight west," Thorhall said after a long silence. "If an unknown western continent exists, you could not miss running into it. Still, if I were in your place I would follow the guidance of the Swan Maiden a good while yet."

"The Swan Maiden?" Joseph echoed, a lively interest in his tone. "Oh, yes, I remember now that pagan—I will not say superstition; at last I have gained enough wisdom not to presume omniscience—I'll say that pagan belief that the savants of Padua call lycanthropy. The idea of a swan being able to assume human form or the form of a Valkyrie is a beautiful idea. Unfortunately it is cut from the same cloth as belief in a human soul turning into a wolf."

"I have seen a werewolf," Thorhall remarked quietly.

"I will not deny it. No civilized man would dream of doing so. But Leif, you gentlemen were talking about navigation. It is quite apparent that you are deeply perplexed. Pray continue."

Starkad, Thorhall, and I resumed our discussion. Starkad, who believed we had not wandered far from the south by west course we had set, rather favored returning to it. Thorhall wished to sail till noon, then turn sharply west. I was suggesting that we watch for and pick up any driftwood that we saw, identify it as far as possible, meanwhile hoping that it was unidentifiable to any man aboard, which would predicate its origin in some land unknown to Europeans. At least it would raise our spirits——

"Excuse me, Leif," came Joseph's beautifully articulated interruption, although his voice had a note in it absent from his previous remarks, and unless it was suppressed excitement I did not know what it was.

"Yes, sir. And if you have any idea what course we should set——"

"No, I was only going to say that if my remarks about swans smelled of the academy, the present discussion as to the best course has become likewise academic."

"What in the name of Odin do you mean?" I demanded.

"Ahead of us you will note a bank of low cloud. About in the middle, it becomes thin, and breaks apart, and rejoins. It has just now broken apart and rejoined. I pray you watch it, and the next time——"

He stopped, because even now the cloud was becoming transparent. Through it I could see a shape that might be a darker cloud behind it, but I did not believe this, because my skin began to prickle from my crown to the soles of my feet. And suddenly the last skein was whisked or melted away, and there before us lay a long beach, a beach that seemed to have no end, dotted here and there by what appeared to be white, flat stones. And behind the beach grew green grass or moss, and behind these stood black forests, and above the forests loomed the crests of mountains. Then my soul confided to my heart a wondrous truth, and that truth was that our little company, recklessly venturing in our little ship on a vast immeasurable ocean, had discovered a New World.

CHAPTER FIFTEEN

SOUTHWARD SAIL

I

Except for Starkad, who called needed orders, and for the men who obeyed them more in the mien of sleepwalkers than of brisk and handy sailors, every member of our company stood silent on the deck as we approached the land. As the low-hanging cloud-bank was stabbed and riddled by the almost level rays of the rising sun, we were given ever longer and deeper vistas, and at this distance we could see that the shore appeared to run almost straight east and west, and that it had countless indentations which might be little coves, and which might well be noble bays, where Ragnar's fleet of dragon ships could have been moored, swinging wide upon their cables, and one would not touch another. What we could not see was whether the land was an out-jutting from a continent which I had reckoned ran generally north and south, or whether it was an immense island.

We need change our course only slightly to head into what appeared the largest of the visible bays, and as soon as we passed its headlands Starkad ordered one of the crew to cast and lower the plummet and call out the depths. But the twenty-fathom line would not reach the bottom and Starkad continued to sail before the south wind for a distance of about three miles. Then as depth began swiftly to reduce, from twenty fathoms to fifteen, and then to ten, Starkad ordered the sail furled and the oars manned. And the oarsmen hardly had got hand on the white ash when Gull Eye gave a little grunt, and all hands stopped moving, and the same expression, half wonder, half fear, stole into every weathered, leathered face. And my heart too made one of its greatest bounds, not as high and wild as when I had first seen land, but still hard enough to jar my bosom. Out from what was no doubt a cove in the banks of the bay came forth a fleet of perhaps thirty boats, about the size and general appearance of

Ugruk's kayak, each manned with at least two, and sometimes three, and one at least with four, skin-clad paddlers.

Since they were plainly making in our direction, fast as they could go, and that rate was considerably more than Ugruk and I together could drive his kayak, I called to Starkad to let down our hook. In the first place it was impossible for some seventy men to board us against our wills and weapons, and in the second place our stopping and waiting for our coming visitors seemed an act of courtesy and friendship. And the iron had hardly splashed, its line uncoiling like a gigantic snake, when another notion set fire to my mind.

"Ugruk, would you be afraid to launch your kayak and paddle to meet their boats?"

"Ugruk no afraid," my brother answered.

"We will take no weapons. They would be of no use against seventy."

"Ugruk know. We just blow wind."

This mundane remark took what might be called wind from my sails, because while truly the coming meeting with savages of the New World had not struck me as heroic, or dangerous in the least degree, I was not insensible to its wonder or even its historic significance. As far as I could deem, it would be the first face-to-face meeting of dwellers of the Old World with dwellers of the New, except for Ugruk's and my meeting on the shore of Ericsfiord. The reason we would run no considerable risk was, in the first place, that man of himself is not a quarrelsome animal, that hate breeding hate, revenge breeding revenge, and jealousy breeding jealousy had not yet begun to forge its dreadful chains between them and us, and the first instinct of men who have no deep-rooted quarrel is that of unacquainted children, meeting on a village row, to make friends with one another. In the second place, Ugruk's boat would contain no gear or weapons of a new sort that the strangers might covet. Lastly, if they trembled at sight of so large a seagoing craft as ours, each hiding his own tremors from his comrades, this meeting at a distance from the vessel would quiet all and remove the danger of quick violence that is born of fear.

Yet I was half over the rail, and had answered the little wave of Helga's hand, and was dropping into Ugruk's kayak that he had launched and that lay alongside, before my mind could hit upon any good reason for the parley, Ugruk and I with unknown savages away from the protection offered us by the ship and its crew. Obviously I had acted on impulse or at best was doing what the unprecedented occasion appeared to call for. No, it was not unprecedented in one respect. I remembered from long ago Ugruk's calm approach over wind-tossed waters to the strand where I had stood, both of us utter strangers to each other, men of different skin, language, and ways, our natal places almost unimaginably distant, and how we had grinned. Thinking of the infinite profit of that meeting, boldly I dwelt on profit to be gained from this one, such as fresh victual and the refilling of our water casks. Truly our chances of a mutually gainful meeting with the New World dwellers were far better if all of us sat in little boats, level with one another, than if we visitors stood on a high deck looking down at them, a position preventing all communication except signs.

So it might be, I thought, that in obeying my errant impulse, I was building better than I knew.

"Good boats," Ugruk remarked to me, as we drew within a stone's throw of the strangers, now advancing slowly in a flock, like swimming ducks. I had already noticed the trimness of the crafts, the ease with which they progressed, and now I could see that these were of a different cut from kayaks, their bows and sterns raised and rounded, and none of them decked over. And presently I perceived that they were not skin boats at all, and that their light frames were covered with what appeared to be the bark of birch trees. The men stroked their single-bladed paddles with easy skill.

Soon I had a good view of their faces and bodies. They appeared to be small men, scarcely over five feet, well-formed, brown-skinned, and of no more resemblance to Ugruk than to me. Their eyes appeared dark, not narrowly set or slightly slanted like Ugruk's eyes; though not especially handsome they were far from an ill-favored people, and their facial expressions were as pleasant as was indeed their whole appearance and ease of movement. Their black hair, worn long, in some cases braided, in others flowing free, appeared to have a handsome wave; on this chill late April day all wore jackets and pants of deerskin, the former decorated with what might be bright pebbles or bits of shell. Their footgear was rather like mukluks, and was probably sealskin.

The lead boat of the fleet was manned by two young paddlers and carried a man in early middle age, whose face was striped with red ocher and who wore a large bear claw on a thong about his neck. The gaze of all three was fixed on me and indicated no great fear, but certainly some misgivings. On the other hand Ugruk received only a passing and pleasant glance from them or from the other boatmen now drifting close to us. The reason was not hard to find; obviously they had seen Innuits, or other natives greatly like Innuits before, while a pale-skinned, fair-haired, blue-eyed man, more than a head taller than any of them, was utterly new to their experience. All I could do was look pleasant as possible. Ugruk, however, began immediate communication.

Pointing to himself, he said, "Innuit!"

The man with the painted face nodded in perfect understanding, then pointing to himself said "Beothuk—*Sachem.*"

My first guess was that the first word was his personal name and the second was the name of his tribe. It was the wrong guess, as became manifest when the native pointed at me and repeated the word in a tone of question. Evidently it meant chieftain.

Ugruk waved his arm to indicate the chieftain's followers. "Beothuk?" he asked. All his hearers nodded and grinned.

Now the chieftain went through the motions of paddling a boat, then pointed toward the cove from which the fleet had emerged. His next gesture was to point at both Ugruk and me, and then make a beckoning motion. "*Wek!*" he said pleasantly, with a suggestion of entreaty. Obviously we had been invited to visit their village, and the word "wek" might mean either "come" or "house."

I looked into the cove and could see what appeared to be huts, with green roofs. The distance was hardly half a mile, so I answered the chieftain with a cheerful nod at which every face brightened with pleasure. The chief spoke to the two boatmen; and old paddlers such as Ugruk and I must goggle with admiration at the skill with which they dipped and drew their blades. To display this, they shot forward like salmon at a gait we could not hope to equal, then, with heart-warming laughter, waited for us to catch up. Whatever else they might be, plainly the Beothuks were peaceful, good-natured, and hospitable. Ugruk and I, paddling alongside the chief's boat, with the others in our rear, approached the village without the slightest fear.

The crude settlement, of which its dwellers appeared so proud, gave indications of the kind of life these cheerful little people lived. The houses appeared to be mainly made of driftwood, the holes stuffed with moss and with roofs of turf. Three slaughtered seals lay on the beach; drying on the flat white stones that were such a prominent feature of this coast lay countless fish, resembling smelt. Nearby was a great high-smelling pile of what seemed the inedible parts of shrimps, backbones of fish, and clam and lobster shells. Yet the Beothuks were hunters as well as fisher folk. Fastened on the roof of the chief's hut towered the tallest and heaviest pair of reindeer antlers I had ever seen, so large indeed that I thought they represented a species unknown in the Old World. On the wall of one house I saw a pair of snowshoes of a different style than Ugruk's; their weapons appeared to be harpoons with well-worked blades of flint, well-fashioned but somewhat weak bows, and arrows with bone heads.

Ugruk suddenly bethought himself and pointed first to the north, then to the east, and then to the south, after which he said in a questioning tone:

"Skraellings?"

Half a dozen arms were raised, all pointing southwest.

Ugruk and I both ate some dried smelts, evidently something of a luxury that early in the year, and then the chief made me a lavish offer or at least a most hospitable gesture. Pointing to a young and pretty girl, whose jacket bore more elaborate decoration than any other I had seen, and whom I took for the sachem's daughter, he then pointed to me and made motions with his hands, the meaning of which was unmistakable. The maiden smiled faintly and shyly looked away. I turned to Ugruk.

"Can you make him understand that I have a wife aboard the ship?"

Ugruk, who did not seem at all astonished by the sachem's offer, answered him in some sort of sign language. Some of its coarser passages I myself could grasp; but many of the gestures meant nothing to me. The fact remained that the sachem's nods and grunts indicated a good degree of understanding; and I took it Ugruk was communicating with him by what was a formalized and probably inconceivably ancient means, widely known throughout the New World. Occasionally the chief appeared puzzled, but clapped his hands at the close of Ugruk's silent discourse.

"I tell him you no want girl, you have young, pretty girl. Ugruk no want girl, he want to hurry up, go hunt and fish. But some Ugruk's friends aboard ship, they be mighty glad to have this girl and any other girls and young women men can spare tonight. I tell him Ugruk's friends come to village in long boat, but they no take girls while Beothuks look on, Beothuks must leave houses, one house for each couple, sit around fire until Ugruk's friends get through and go back to ship. Ugruk come with friends, so Beothuk feel good, sit around fires while friends have good time. Sachem say, all right, he glad, plenty women for ten, twenty sailor, young, pretty wives and daughters. Ugruk glad too. Friends be long time at sea."

"That is quite true, Ugruk. I think that if Joseph were here, he would call you, only half in jest, a gentleman and a civilized man."

"Ugruk no understand. And tomorrow give Beothuks barrel of salt fish, for we not need them now, and some spare lines and lumber, and they fill up water kegs and give us fresh fish and meat. Then we go southwest, find Skraellings, hunt, fish, see new country, new rivers, new mountains. Leif, is Ugruk your brother?"

"Indeed you are, Ugruk."

"You Ugruk's brother. Ugruk happy. He stay happy till one of us die."

2

For the ship watch that night, Starkad appointed only men who had shipped their wives, so that the bachelors could attend what he delicately called a feast at the native village. Helga's quick mind lost no time in observing the discrimination and guessing the cause. When, an hour after nightfall, she made an excuse to go out on the deck, my often-thick head was able to perceive her design. I too had heard the longboat being launched and palpably she wanted to see what members of our company were participating in the event.

"I know what you're up to, Helga," I told her. "We have no thralls—only freemen—aboard this ship, and no one has any right to interfere with them or to spy upon them, when they've been given leave of duty."

"I want just one peek, to find out if Novice Joseph is staying aboard, where a man of the cloth belongs, or going to shore with those lechers."

"Joseph is not a man of the cloth as yet. He has taken no vow of celibacy. And I wouldn't call any man a lecher for one night of adventure after more than a month at sea." Then her cheeks flushed, causing me to remember that princesses do not like to be balked, and I made haste to add, "Stay with me, Helga. I'll get out my flute and play your favorite tunes. And after that we will play with each other and then. . . ."

So it came to pass that Helga never knew whether Joseph was among the revelers, nor did I, for men in general and Norsemen in particular are respecters of their fellows' secrets.

In the morning I ordered a brief cruise eastward in order to see more of Beothuk country, and to determine if possible if it were an island. We skirted a coast with innumerable bays, and after four hours' sail we sighted a cluster of long peninsulas jutting westward and southwest, and in clearing these our southward sail brought us in sight of a large island and then of an enormously long coast running southwestward, which seemed a great arm of the land too wide for our vision. We named our discovery

Helluland, the Land of Flat Stones, but it deserved better than this, because it was a land of forests and green plains and towering mountains and immense rivers, and I had no real doubt, although not the slightest proof, that it was about as big as Iceland. Its waters teemed with whales and seals, and fish great and small and innumerable, and often we glimpsed reindeer, nearly as large as elk, as well as wolves and bears.

We came at last to what seemed land's end, and then put in to a cove of a small, uninhabited island lying about three hours' sail to the southwest. And here, visible from the vast wastes of water to the southward, we raised a six-foot cairn of the flat, white stones, cone-shaped and symmetrical, obviously the work of man, and on the top stone I engraved with a sharp flint the runic letters LE, standing for my name. Gorm alone did not assist in the labor. I thought that possibly, despite his protests otherwise, he had joined the revelers at the village and was dog-tired.

"How long before the watch of a ship from Europe sees our cairn, and launches a boat, and the men look at those little marks, and wonder?" Joseph asked, with wonder in his eyes.

"I'd guess two hundred years, but perhaps within ten years if our discovery proves great enough, and knowledge of it becomes known," I answered. "In that case, many a Norse captain will itch to see it, even without an Ugruk to spread the itch, and if nine ships turn back from the monstrous, great, gray seas, the tenth will get through."

"Aye, but it may be the ninetieth ship that spies our cairn," Gorm remarked, in a tone of satisfaction that I did not understand. "Leif, you forget what great seas, and what great island or great land we've stumbled onto. Of this immediate region, the land of the Beothuks, we've seen only a trifle. There are countless bays, with a different entry to every one, and headlands innumerable. I'll abide by your first guess. Within two hundred years a shore party will come and look at your fine cairn, and stare at the runic letters if they're still legible, and puzzle awhile, and then go about their business. Your fame will be built with stronger rock if Ian writes in his fine hand on that great roll of parchment he carries with him, and that writing is copied and recopied, for learned doctors to read and muse upon, and spread word of to their fellows, and for instructing the young."

"What you say, old man, is true in general," Joseph replied. "Little ink marks on parchment wear better than carvings on stone. But supposing this is a one-way journey for all of us, and not one of us ever looks again on the Skaggerak? In good time, others will come here—because men have restless souls and love the lure of the unknown—maybe they'll be Norse, and maybe Romans, or Breton fishermen—but if you want them to know we were the first comers, write the signs large."

"A fresh northeast wind is springing up," I broke into the talk, "so let us stop blowing wind at one another, and set our sail to catch her belly full and run before that wind, and keep on running until we sight new land."

It must be a kind of thrill ran through our sober, long-faced crew, for their faces flushed and their eyes brightened, and they stood with bold carriage, and some of it leaped to me, and my soul rejoiced. In a matter of seconds all were pushing the beached longboat, and in a minute the long oars dipped in rhythm, and in ten minutes we were climbing aboard the *Narwhale*; and in a short space thereafter the boat was hoisted and stowed, and our anchor was being weighed to the creak and whine of our wooden windlass, and the sail popped and crackled as she filled with wind.

Sundown found us out and far on the open sea. Although the moon was yet young and her light puny, the helmsman would be able to see land or even an islet at a good distance, and we took our chance on striking a submerged reef. A greater danger was in hitting a water-soaked, barely submerged tree trunk. Twilight had revealed an unusual number of logs drifting before the northeast wind, which caused me to believe that not far away to the west a mighty river flowed through vast and heavy forest and emptied into the sea. I could picture it as lonesome as the ocean except for prowlings of wild beasts, and silent as the sea in a dead calm except for an occasional outcry.

The night passed, the wind held, the ship sped like a darting gull, and I reckoned we were three hundred miles from our Helluland anchorage when again was raised the cry of "Land

Ho!" As we drew near, we saw that this new land lacked the mountainous grandeur of Land of the Beothuks, and my guess of its highest elevation above the sea was hardly a thousand feet; but it was so densely and darkly wooded that we Norsemen immediately thought of it as Markland, which means the Land of Forests. We were making into an enormous bay, the shores of which ran at a wide angle, north by east, and south by east, from its inmost point. And then to our amazement we gazed beyond the point up a large inlet, the whole conformation suggesting the runic letter K, resembling the Latin Y, the converging coasts representing its outspread arms and the inlet its stem; but no imagination could picture a troll of sufficient magnitude to carve it there. And to the southeast we could see the opening of three other inlets, the largest being about ten miles in width.

By now we had reefed our sail and boldly drifted into the inlet, passed a small island, and anchored in a small bay lying on our left hand. For half an hour we rode there, watching for natives to emerge from the woods and come out in their boats to behold this wonder, the like of which their shamans and their spaewomen had never dreamed. None did so, and our native restlessness soon overcame us, and I ordered the launching of our longboat, wherein to go to shore. Yet when we disembarked, it seemed that instead of visiting a nameless coast virginal to the step of man, I had drifted into a dream most strange; or another realm of being as when I had entered the ice palace after eating daft fish. At first I did not know what caused the spell, then perceived that in a large measure it was the effect of unearthly silence, a silence deeper than amid snowy wastes of Greenland, for there the wind always murmured, or howled, or shrieked, or whished. The huge-trunked spruce trees, their foliage black with a silver frost like some voluptuous fur, stood immensely tall and utterly silent, for in this sheltered place the wind did not wag their tops. They grew so close together that I could not pass between one and another without the aromatic needles brushing my face. It became unthinkable that any human being had ever precoursed us here, as we advanced wide-eyed into unthinkably silent depths. And when we had gone a little way, we stopped, and glanced at one another, and ached to communicate further, but said no word. Then we returned to the longboat, launched her, and quietly rowed back to the ship.

When I looked for Helga on the deck, to my great relief I did not see her, which meant almost certainly that I would find her in our cabin, and there we twain would be alone. And so it came to pass, and a startled look came into her eyes when she saw my face, and she was as beautiful as Minin when holding my hands in the ice palace had bade me call up Isis. And then I put my arms about Helga and held her in wondrous closeness, and I knew not what strange dreams drifted through my mind as clouds of mist drift across the Greenlandic ponds, but it must be that they took vague shape before her eyes as well as mine, because she began to weep. And then as we lay breast to breast on our bed, she was shaken with sobs, and at last she put her arms around my neck and put her tear-wet mouth to mine, and then she whispered of what she had seen.

"No, Leif, we will never see the Skaggerak again."

"Will we pass soon from this New World to some other world, or only into silence?"

"We will live many years. We will bear children, and our children will bear children by mates of a darker race. And when you die I believe you will not pass away, for I seem to see you living on, century after century, in some other form."

"Perhaps in a tale told by the winter fires of home?"

"This is now our home—the New World. The tale will be told, for you will tell it to Ian, as Gorm bade you, and in some fashion I cannot see it will reach across the sea. It will tell of a great storm that I feel, I believe, is yet to break. And the words that I speak to you now break forth from my locked soul, and I cannot withhold them, and I cannot doubt them, for some hand has touched me, briefly, out of the unseen. And now come in unto me, Leif, for it comes to me that if you do, I will conceive, and bear you a daughter as beautiful as Minin, and as beautiful as I am this moment, for a great beauty has come upon me now, begotten of your greatness; and the babe, if you give me one, will be got of both. The Gods await! Odin rides swiftly on his

Eight-hoofed Horse, and gentle Kris rides his cruel Horse of Tree. Now is the time; the appointed hour; do not delay.

"But I cannot promise it will be a daughter. It may be a son, with blue eyes and fair hair. He will not be as tall as you are, and he will not bear upon his shoulders and within his soul the burden of as great a dream, yet he will be worthy offspring of Helga, Princess of Norway, and of Leif Ericsson, the discoverer of the New World."

3

For two days and nights we skirted the coast of this great land on a west by south course. The wind was from west by north, sometimes northwest, and on the whole we made good headway. At best we gained eight sea miles per hour, and at worst about six, according to Starkad's and Thorhall's calculations in approaching and passing headlands. At sunset of the second day we sighted rocks, and soundings showed forty fathoms, then suddenly only twelve, and the pitching clouds might well forecast rough weather; so I ordered that we lie at anchor for the night, in the mouth of a bay between two peninsulas, where soundings made from the longboat revealed no water less than ten fathoms in any swing the ship might make on her cable.

On both days' sail we had seen an enormity of forest, its spruce, pine, fir, hemlock, and cedar being evergreen, with deciduous trees, now in full bud, that we thought were oak, ash, and maple, and, in more open country, stands of high, fine birch trees.

Nor need we borrow Gull Eye's marvelous powers of vision to see game. Usually he found it first and pointed it out and was the first to name it, but even old Gorm saw enough to make his thinned blood leap in his veins. We caught sight of the larger animals in copses of birch or when they ventured out of the heavy forest into low-lying meadows. Here were reindeer of the same large species we had seen at Helluland, and elks that appeared to stand taller and of greater weight than Thorhall Hunter had chased in Norway. Black bears came down to the beach, along with foxes, gluttons, and lynxes; and what excited us most were herds of a dozen or more red deer of a gigantic species, far surpassing the red deer of Scotland, which Thorhall had thought the largest in the world. The stags had dropped their horns in season, but we could not mistake them for hinds, because of the majesty of their bearing.

Birds such as pelicans, beach geese, short-winged ducks who had no aversion to salt water and flew falcon-fast, coots, gulls, terns, and several kinds of waterfowl new to our eyes flocked in prodigious numbers. Whales, sharks, and dolphins were numerous; seals appeared scarce. The greatest scarcity was of any kind of human being. Once we caught a distant glimpse of forty or more who appeared to be casting nets in the river mouth, a taller breed than the Beothuks; and we did not doubt that these were Skraellings, whom Ugruk believed to be the predominant race of the New World. Gull Eye caught a very brief glimpse of three boats rounding a headland, each with two paddlers; and it seemed to him that they wore some kind of blanket, and that their heads were shaved bald.

The heavy blow, perhaps with rain or sleet, which we had expected took some other route than down this coast, and in fact the wind gentled somewhat during our anchorage. So we weighed in the first clear light, and, watching for reefs and skerries, we continued southwest at a slower pace, with the lively but not strong breeze out of the northeast on our port side. Before midmorning we could perceive we were nearing the end of the land, whether a huge island or a projection of the mainland we did not know, and when we sighted a noble cape, I resolved to erect a cairn at its barren southwest tip. Anchoring in its lee, in fourteen fathoms of water, we manned the longboat to gain its beach.

To my astonishment, for he was usually the foremost volunteer on any adventure, Gorm asked leave to remain aboard ship. Our boat crew spent about two hours erecting a monument of black or dark brown stones, crowning it with a flat, white stone on which again I carved the runic initial letters of my name. When again we had hauled the boat aboard, raised our anchor, and continued on our course, it became a wonder at what great distance we could still spy the black, white-topped monument on the gray beach. But at length the last faint line of the land dimmed, and we were again in open sea, an enormous reach of it to judge by the swells shaped by the light wind. And on the supposition that the mainland cut sharply southward, we changed our course from west by south to southwest.

On the following day, out and far from any land, I began to wonder if we were sailing across the mouth of an immense gulf or bay, because our soundings gave no less than a hundred, and never more than two hundred, fathoms of water under our keel. On the next day we must tack, the wind being from the northwest forward of our beam, and hence we must creep instead of fly; yet even so I changed our course to sou'southwest, in fear that a southwest course might carry us wide of any coast, into forlorn and empty seas. On the next day the wind shifted more northerly, whereby we made good way; still we were sick for sight of land when the sun went down leaving us in deepening darkness and what seemed growing solitude and in emptiness forever.

Still the sky remained clear, and we kept to our course guided by the North Star, Hesperian being much higher in the sky, and new stars, we had never seen or dreamed, low on the western horizon. Shortly after sunrise the depth of the sea changed swiftly from a hundred and twenty fathoms to half that number, and then to twenty-four fathoms. Then, peering through a haze lying low on the western waters, Starkad sighted what he thought was land.

So it proved, a long low beach curving northwest. We could see no mountains or hills or woods behind it, and before long we became convinced that it was a long and extremely narrow peninsula, with a hook at its end. For a matter of two hours' sail in a fair wind we saw not even a good cove, let alone a harbor, although the depth of water ranged between only fifteen and thirty fathoms. Still we were resolved to skirt the coast, and not lose sight of it again, short of being gale-blown eastward. Then we came to a shallow bay we dared not enter, and then hugged a long spit running straight south, and behind it we found a well-sheltered bay, although the five fathoms that our plummet gave were too shallow for our comfort. Still we anchored off the head-

land, where I ordered the longboat launched so that some ten of
us could go to shore, where I thought to raise another cairn of
stones.

"Ugruk no see any stones on that beach," my brother remarked.
"See nothing but brown sand."

"What do you see, Gull Eye?" I asked.

"Sand, sir, and plenty of it."

"Ugruk know what we do," the Innuit said, his eyes shining.
"We make pretty landmark. You wait till Ugruk go below."

He returned lugging two planks, one ten feet long and the
other about six. Also he had a soapstone pot of white paint, a
small metal cup of seal tar, a shovel, and hammer and nails. These
he put in the longboat, which we lowered and launched. During
the short ride into shore Ugruk said no word to reveal his design
and took obvious pleasure in our curiosity.

"All right, Ugruk," I told him, when we had gained the beach
and I had chosen the site of the monument, to be visible for miles
from the east, south, and north. "You are in command of our
shore party."

"Leif, you nail short plank across long plank about three feet
from top. Put in plenty nail, drive deep. Connelly, you dig hole
in sand and gravel foot square, and three feet deep. Thorvald,
while Leif nail, Connelly dig, you paint both planks with white
paint. Thorgils and Freyson, while Leif nail, Connelly dig, Thorvald paint, you hunt for biggest stones you can find, for I see some
big as my fist. Fill friz sack and bring to hole Connelly dig."

We fell to our varied tasks. Ugruk walked till he was above
high-water mark and pulled up a little bush that he had found
rooted in the sand, and sharpened some of its twigs with his
knife. In a very few minutes the hole was dug of the required
depth and breadth, the crossbar was nailed securely, and both
planks were painted with a mixture of chalk and deer fat and
caustic that weathered well. About two hundred pounds of stones
and rocks, averaging a pound in weight, had been heaped nearby.

"Now Leif, you take pointed stick, play like it is Ian's pen, and
write Thorhild's name across bar."

So I wrote in large runic letters:

Then we erected the cross in the hole Connelly had dug and filled it in with rocks hard-tamped by a mallet of driftwood. Truly it made a fine appearance; and since the planks had been stout oak, I reckoned it might stand there for a hundred years, a sign to mariners beating in from the stormy sea that civilized men had precoursed them, and they could proceed with confidence and courage. And I reckoned that the soul of my mother in heaven, the abode of the Christian dead she had described to me, would take pleasure in the sight, this lonesome monument to her memory, and perhaps she would call to other angels to look down, and even call it to the attention of gentle Kris, and perhaps Kris would speak of it to his mighty sire.

Gorm had walked down the beach while we were at work, and returned as we were done, but the crusty old fellow said no word of admiration for the handsome edifice and indeed did not look at it at all but busied himself with the boat. He had gone searching for beach pools, he said, hoping to find stranded flounders, but it had been a fool's errand.

"The whole voyage is a fool's errand," he muttered to himself, "or else I'm in the company of fools."

4

We rowed out to and boarded the ship, and we had hardly set sail when I had cause to wonder if I were indeed a fool to have erected a Christian cross, considering that Odin, Thor, and Njord had all three treated us civilly despite our boldness in venturing so far into their wild realms, and had given us a good run of luck in the way of wind and weather. For almost immediately the sounder shouted that he had found five fathoms, a depth too shallow for our comfort and where, by a little more reduction or striking a big rock on the bottom, we might be stranded. Furling the sail and dipping our oars, we crept on with the utmost caution, only to find six and a half fathoms. And soon we could see that we were at the edge of great shoals, and the deeper water lay westward, and for this we made, our hearts thumping and the oars strongly drawn, until the sounder found ten fathoms, when again we could catch our breaths. Spreading our sail, we entered what appeared to be a sound, about eight miles wide, between what we took for a projection of the peninsula we had skirted, now lying northward, and a large island with boulder-strewn hills on the south.

This was the bare beginning of a period of ill fortune and contrary winds. At the mouth of the sound, where we had hoped to find the open and deep ocean, we sailed into a shallow sea, eighteen fathoms being the deepest water that we could find. For three days we made southward, not daring to sail by night and· instead rode at anchor in any lee we came upon. We were so happy to get rid of the treacherous shoals that we again cast our iron, and again lowered our longboat. We had seen what we took for the end of a peninsula eastward of our position, so prominent that I resolved to raise a cairn at its very butt. And this time it would not be a Christian cross but a cairn such as was raised of old in memory of heathen battles and Viking victories.

We had hardly returned to our ship when a blow hardly short of a gale came out of the east. Were we in open sea we would have flown before it, because its way was favorable, not adverse, to our chosen course; but here we were never out of sight of islands with their threat of close-lying reefs. So we had no choice but heave to not more than a mile from a long coast, running east and west on our port side, and barely visible in the blown rain, and without the slightest sign of a harbor. So we put out a sea anchor to slow our drift; and with our heathens shouting now and then to Odin, and the Christians often praying on their knees, we weathered the storm. As for me, I did not shout and I did not pray. I only minded the ship the best that I knew how.

At storm's end, the rain stopped, the sun came out, visibility leaped from half a mile to the horizons, and we found ourselves deep in an arm of the sea, about twenty miles wide, and with

abundant depth, sheltered on the east by the long land we had
seen, either an island or a peninsula, and of utmost beauty to our
sight, and on the west by heavily-wooded shore that I thought
was the mainland. And truly now we were finding what we
sought, a vast, rich, and habitable country, not bleak like Iceland
and wintry and wild like Greenland. Judging by the height of the
North Star at midnight, Thorhall thought that its north and
south position was about the same as the capital city of Asturias
in northern Iberia, which the Viking fleets on the Bay of Biscay
had often raped, and where now and then they had wintered.

The air had a soft feeling, humid instead of dry, the sun was
ardent, and spring was in full flush. We could not feel lonely and
lost, because of the high spirits of the porpoises that played around
our keel, and the constant breaking of water by leaping fish. The
soil must be deep and rich, we thought, to produce such dense,
high forest; and now and then we spied a meadow, the grass green
as Eric's eyes, which were now so far away, unseen for an eternity,
and perhaps darkened by dire death. Again the waters swarmed
with swans, geese, and ducks, many of whose kind I had seen in
Greenland, but many of new feather; and great rafts of them,
half a mile wide and half a mile long, black upon the water,
floated or fed in numbers incalculable. And the beauty of the
floating swans warmed my heart, and I wondered if any of these
were Swan Maidens or Valkyries, so far from Ashargrad and Valhalla's halls.

On the bank we glimpsed deer of two kinds, one being the
immense kind we had seen in Markland, the other very much
smaller, and wonderfully playful, standing in the most graceful
poses as though inviting our admiration. Not one reindeer did we
see, and very few great, black elk, but we had a glimpse of some
sort of wild cattle, not long-haired like the Greenland oxen, but
with shaggy necks and very much larger. We saw no great whales
and not a single seal. Also we saw no wolves, to no one's regret.

We kept watching for signs of human life, and after a while
we spied at a distance what we thought must be a village of the
Skraellings, which was a cluster of low-roofed huts with sticklike
figures walking about and some short sticks, that we thought

were children, running about. Once at the edge of the forest on our left hand we saw two Skraellings who were obviously hunters, since each carried bows and arrows in shoulder sheaths. They were naked except for some sort of loincloth and belts on which hung either knives or hatchets.

I took it that we had come on one of the most choice regions of the New World, but yet we had seen only its merest fraction, unless Thorhall, Joseph, Ian, Starkad, testy old Gorm, and I missed our guesses. I had no notion of stopping, except perhaps for a fortnight's good feel of the good earth under our feet, and to lay in fresh meat and water. I wanted to journey on, all this year and perhaps the next, to the very end of the land, whereby we would have a vague notion of its dimensions north and south, but no inkling of its width east and west. It felt queer to think I might grow old and die without ever knowing.

Just at present the water body on which we sailed began to narrow, with innumerable shallow bays and points on the west side, and far-spaced deep bays on the east. But there would be an egress somewhere to the open ocean, and not far away, as I could tell by the freshness of the wind and the feel of the tide on our bow.

In waters at least five miles wide we moored for the night. At early morning the same prevailing, obliging wind wafted us on, and presently we came on a tidal river, about one mile wide at its narrows, and two miles wide at its full span. In a little more than an hour's sailing we came upon a bay into which the river emptied, about five miles wide at this place, and with great joy we perceived that this was the outlet of a still greater river, flowing from the northwest. The latter was two miles wide as far as we could see up its expanse, and the amount of driftwood that it carried made me believe that it had flown out of vast forests perhaps vastly far away, and that above the tidal flood it had fresh water.

What might be one of its arms, and no puny river, had emptied into our tidal river, near its first narrowing. If so the land on our right hand was not the mainland, but an island lying at its breast. The next day Ugruk and I would launch our kayak, and let our light strokes and the heavy tide carry us back that far, a distance of not more than ten miles, and answer this question. If it were indeed an island, I dreamed of coming to shore, making friends with the Skraellings, and establishing a camp, with wondrous hunting and fishing at our very door, and perhaps remain a fortnight on the land, safe behind the wide waters from any great army of Skraellings that might be at war with our neighbors.

It so happened that we, Ugruk and I, did not take the little jaunt of exploration the following day. Most of the crew, and especially all our women passengers, from Helga and Fatima to the motherly wife of Starkad, became enamored with a campsite in a little cove near the southwest point of what we called West Land, fronting the great river out of the north, and at the same time with the notion of taking leave of the ship and its confines for a fortnight's camping out on dense, soft spring grass gay with flowers under immense patriarchal trees. Truly I had never seen a more enticing spot for campers. A brook, the dark and shadowed holes of which held small spotted trout of a species we did not know, rippled with a pleasant sound through the glade. There was no sight, sound, or track of Skraellings on this part of the land, and indeed the few we had seen had been on the long island we had passed on our port side in approaching the river. The site was in easy walking distance, not more than a mile from the southwest point, the grassy shores of which were a nesting place for a species of wild duck we had not seen before, the eggs being freshly laid and delicious to eat.

So my comrade and I put off our exploration until the following day and helped pitch camp. Our spare sail raised on posts made an excellent pavilion for all the campers, who constituted our whole company except a ship watch of Thorvald, Connelly, and Freyson. Also we raised drying racks and cut fuel, for I intended to lay in a good stock of smoked venison and, I hoped, dried fish, for this was a game heaven such as neither Ugruk or Thorhall Hunter had ever seen.

Two trips in the longboat to our ship, lying in deep, sheltered waters only half a cable's length from shore, landed all the campers and their gear, and in the number were Helga and Fatima, who did not want to miss at least one night, and perhaps several, to be spent in the open whispering forest instead of on the cramped ship. In fact I had proposed to Thorhall that we look for a place where we could beach her, and shore her up and scrape the barnacles from her bottom, and burn rushes to sweeten her bilge, and clean her inside and out; and truly we need not look for more sheltered waters than these, of safe depth almost to their margins, and more sloping and handy beaches. All this represented a month's labor by all hands, delaying for that long our explorations southward, but the latter mattered hardly at all, since the year was yet young, summer and not winter was marching fast, and with fair fortune we could spend the cold months in regions so far south that cold was almost unknown.

At supper we stuffed on fresh baked venison from an immense stag that Gorm had shot a hundred paces from our camp, and which Thorhall declared surpassed in flavor the finest red deer of Ireland. During our jollity, Helga announced that she and Fatima were going with Ugruk and me on the morrow's jaunt, or, if there was no room for them in the kayak they would follow us in the small sailing dinghy, manned by Ian and Novice Joseph and weather-wise Gorm. When I spoke of the possibility of meeting a war party of Skraellings, Helga's only reply was an emphatic and disdainful "Pew!"

I glanced to Ugruk, intending to seek his support in my contention, only to find him stretched on a sheepskin, fast asleep. It did not astonish me, despite his love of fun, for he had been curiously active all day on what business I did not know. He had gone forth in mid-morning with his harpoon and bow and arrows, declaring he was going deer hunting, but had come back wearied and empty-handed except for a large fowl, despite the fact that these forests swarmed with deer. The like of the fowl none of us had ever seen. It had been one of a large flock he had found feeding, apparently on mast from last year's fall, and Thorhall had declared him kin to the cock o' the wood, a heavy grouse he had seen in Ireland, but very much larger, his weight being at least twenty pounds. In color he was like bronze, and he had red feathers on his neck and around the base of his bill, from the top of which hung a red appendage more than an inch long. On being cleaned he resembled an enormous rooster, with a disproportion- ately larger breast. Ugruk had declared his intention to spit and bake him over the fire for the morrow's breakfast, inviting all who wished to sample the new fowl.

But it had not been to shoot giant grouse or deer either that Ugruk had absented himself from camp most of the day. I took it he had been ranging the woods, seeking some tangible sign of danger. Knowing my comrade so well, I had sensed that his heart was troubled, for causes he himself did not know.

He wakened presently, and suddenly sat up. An amazed look remained on his dark face, and when we questioned him, he re- plied that he had had two dreams, one of them a nightmare that he did not remember, and the other most strange. In the latter dream he had dreamed of being on this very spot, but instead of forest giants there had stood giant buildings of iron and stone, hundreds of feet taller than King Olaf's cathedral tower, and seeming to reach to the sky.

"And people—people everywhere," he told us, "thick as wild bees in a swarm."

"People like us?" I asked.

"Some like you, Leif, tall and fair-haired, but most of them black-haired. Some were blue-eyed and some had eyes of brown or gray. A few of the men had mustaches; mostly their faces were shaven; and the women were most beautiful, some as tall as Helga, some with their hair on top of their heads, and some with it cut off like a thrall's, although a little longer. Many had sable and mink skins around their necks, most had woolen coats with fur collars; and their lips were red and their eyes arched like the new moon. And between the rows of buildings where the people did not walk except to cross over, carts of a strange shape scuttled back and forth, in long files, fast as a sea gull flies when he takes it easy, and although Ugruk stare and stare, he no see any dogs to draw carts, or any oxen. And men in blue coats had something like a willow whistle, and always some of them were whistling, and the others waving their arms. And always there was noise, people in the carts blowing some kind of horn, not soft-voiced like the flute but harsh like the caws of crows, and the carts themselves made sound, not loud but like a shaman beating on a skin drum very fast."

"Did the people look happy?"

"No look happy. Sometimes young man and pretty girl walk hand and hand, and they look happy, but most of the people walk alone, with grave faces and look like they mighty worried about something, or mighty lonesome. And how they could be lonesome when so many people, people everywhere, Ugruk not understand."

"It was just a dream," Thorhall said with undue emphasis.

"Ugruk know that. There not that many people as ducks in the fall flight. Besides, Ugruk see red and green lights flash on and off. Ugruk put dream out of his head."

But I could not have put it out of my head, even if I had tried. Too well I remembered the prophecy of the ancient salmon who raised his battered head out of water and spoke to the King of the Ice—that the hordes who would settle the new land were greater than his hordes swarming into the river mouths in spawning season, as well as the hordes of waterfowl blackening the sky in the spring and autumn flights. I had been dreaming when I heard him speak, for I had eaten daft fish. But ofttimes the truth is stranger than the dream.

5

Ugruk and I took off not long after sunrise at the start of the flowing tide. We brought with us our bows and harpoons, our kamleikas against rain and spray, and the plucked fowl on which he had not made his breakfast after all, and instead had saved it for the mid-meal of ourselves and our stout companions. These came behind us in our sailing dinghy—Helga, Fatima, Ian, Joseph, and Gorm, filling it full as an egg of meat, but not in the least troubled by their crowding and all eyes bright with excitement. If Ugruk and I had not wanted them to pass us, we need never dip paddle, such a powerful lift and thrust was given us by the sea.

But Ian spread the little sail of the dinghy, to catch the inshore breeze, and she dogged our heels.

We reckoned the journey to the mouth of the river we had seen on our westward sail at eight or nine miles, and did not miss it far. In an hour and a half we came on it, truly not much more than a deep tidal creek, although when we had progressed about two miles up its rippled length, it widened suddenly to resemble a salt-water lagoon, about a mile at its greatest width, and we entered it amid a veritable thunder of wings, as countless waterfowl took off in sky-darkening swarms. Mostly they were gulls, coots, cormorants, loons, and suchlike fish eaters of salt or brackish waters, but there were thousands of black-headed ducks with white bellies and dark backs, and thousands with ruddy heads and what Joseph called a Greek profile and glossy gray backs, handsome fowls as I had ever seen, and I reckoned they were kin to the pochard duck of Norway, so belting and swift was their flight. After passing its wider waters the river narrowed to its usual span, and perhaps a little narrower than before. Then it made a great bend toward the mighty river of the drifting tree trunks, putting an end to my doubt of their joining each other and of our camp being on an island, not a peninsula.

For two miles more it flowed through salt marsh, flooded by the still-rising tide, and this vista was lonesome and melancholy, relieved only by flocks of some sort of long-legged rails that rose with the wailing cry and slowly winged away. Then again the river widened, and shortly its rising waters were lost in rising tidal waters of the great river. And now the sun had passed its zenith, and we were hungry and tired, yet hard put to it to find high ground on which to build fire and eat our dinner, and on the marshy banks there was no fuel. The difficulty was soon solved by our discovery of some cliffs on the right bank.

Amid the rock we cooked our unknown, nameless fowl; and its eating was one of the most pleasant minor adventures of our journey. The meat of its breast was snowy white when baked, and its gamy flavor, not nearly as strong as that of pine grouse, proved delicious. We were just finishing when a tall, brown-skinned man in a loincloth and a feathered bonnet pushed out of the woods and came timidly toward us. We encouraged him with gestures and calls, and presently we were gazing into the face of the first Skraelling we had seen at close range.

I thought him a fine-looking fellow, with his piercing black eyes, high-bridged nose, wide cheekbones, and severely planed face. Heightening my admiration for him was his dignified manner and proud posture. He seemed friendly enough, but there was no wide grinning as passed between Ugruk and me at our first meeting.

"Innuit," Ugruk said, pointing to himself.

The native appeared puzzled only a few seconds. I could almost guess his thoughts—wonderment whether "Innuit" was Ugruk's tribal or personal name. He took a quick glance at the other faces of our party, noting the difference in color and feature, and when he pointed to himself and spoke, I think he uttered the name of his tribe.

"Manhasset, Algonquin."

Meanwhile his hawk-bright eyes were taking in our raiment, the color of our eyes and hair, and especially our weapons. He was armed with a roughly made bow, flint-tipped arrows in a shoulder sheath, and what appeared to be a new kind of bludgeon. Actually it was merely a stout pole to the end of which was weighted a skin bag full of stones. A shattering blow could be dealt with it, no doubt, but its uselessness except for close fighting, presumably with other natives, gave me an unpleasant start.

I pointed to it, went through the motions of striking with it, and then pointed to the woods with a questioning grunt. At once he dropped on his hands and knees, clawed at the ground with his fingers, and uttered a low growl in imitation of some animal. Whether he meant the weapon was for fighting wolves or bears, or perhaps some ferocious creature unknown in Europe, I could not guess. The wolves I knew in Greenland were rarely bold enough to attack man except in the starving time of deep winter. The brown bears of Norway were dangerous when wounded, Thorhall had told me, but almost always rushed away at sight of man. But certainly some long-clawed beast was commonly met in the woods hereabouts, and which frequently attacked man, or this savage would not be shouldering the heavy, awkward weapon.

Presently he uttered a big grunt and quietly walked away. The sudden mysterious appearance in his wilderness of seven people of skin and speech different from his own had not aroused his curiosity in any great measure. The thought crossed my mind that his manner of aloofness and dignity might stem from stolidity. Certainly he was no match in wit with Ugruk when we had first met on the shore of Ericsfiord.

We hunted deer a little while, waiting for the tide to turn, but did not get in good arrow range of a fat buck or a barren doe. Then we took off down the mighty river at what I reckoned was at least twelve, and might be fifteen, miles from our camp. If only twelve, these were long miles. Ian could not sail the dinghy against the up-river wind, so except for desultory paddling and rowing, he and his mates, and Ugruk and I, relied on the tidal current to bear us home. The shadows began to lengthen and to gloom when we were in distant view, at least four miles, of the prominent southwest cape of the island we called home. And then low in the southern sky, barely above the forest, I noticed a yellow glow in the darkening sky. Nor did I believe for an instant that I had become turned around and that it was the effulgent rising of the moon in the eastern sky.

"What is it, Ugruk?"

"Ugruk not know. Ugruk, he mighty scared."

CHAPTER SIXTEEN

GREAT GALE, STRANGE CALM

I

In a moment we both had full and grave cause for great fear. The yellow glow was turning into an orange and red glare, which in this lonely land could be caused only by fire.

"Ship, she burn up," Ugruk told me, as he began to paddle at top speed. But after a few seconds he lifted his blade, and without a sound or motion waited for the dinghy boat to catch up with us. It seemed to take an hour for the five rowers, heaving at their oars to gain speed, to close the short distance between us. They too did not speak except by their wan, drawn faces. But now Ugruk spoke.

"We no save ship now. She soaked with seal tar to burn so bright. What Ugruk dream came true. Maybe Skraellings come out in boat, push over tar barrel, set on fire, but Ugruk no believe it. Now we go slow, no splash oars, no speak loud. You know where little brook flow into river. No go that far, go to reed bed long arrow cast nearer—Gorm, you know where we saw big flock of white cranes—push into bank and wait. Leif, you get in dinghy and stay till Ugruk come back. I go alone, look and listen, then come back and tell you what. But if Ugruk no come back to reed bed in an hour, you forget about Ugruk, Ugruk caught and killed, so you try to save people Ugruk love."

So in dread hush, into the deepening dark, but with awful visions before our eyes, and with horrid speculation in our minds, my own being the most horrid with good reason, we sped onward with the tide. And we had gone only a little way when the darkness began to dim, for the moon was rising over the eastern forests, and since she had waned but one night from her effulgence, she poured forth a flood of sickly light, glimmering palely on the river, and herself making a rippling bright streak across it to our sight. And now Ugruk sped down river fast as a loon could swim, but we could not keep pace with him without splash-

ings and the knocking of oars in their locks, sounds in eager haste
to carry across water, so we four men did not attempt to row and
used the oars as paddles, which we could dip in silence.

The glare in the sky changed to tongues of flame, fiercely leaping, and shadows ebbed and flowed, and I knew the whole ship
was ablaze, the sail long since a fiery banner, and now fallen
black and crumpled to the deck. What of the ship watch? Were
they given time to get off? It was too weak a hope to which to
cling; perhaps the men had leaped off, in which case they would
be swept away on the tide or devoured by sharks. And then I
asked a question of my soul, which was whether or not I should
have gone with Ugruk, only to decide that my impulse to let
him go alone had been true to him and to myself, because he
knew the ground better than I, he could move in deeper silence,
and by long practice in the rigorous wastes of his native land and
in hunting in Greenland he was the better spy. And my thoughts
could not help but leap to what he would have to tell us, when
we met in the reed bed, and I did not beguile myself with false
and empty hope, because I was almost sure already that the ship
and the camp too had been taken by surprise, and I became certain when, hardly half a mile from the pavilion, I heard no shouts.

We came to the reed bed, about two hundred paces above the
mouth of the brook whose glinting in the moonlight I could
plainly see. There we seized handfuls of the tough stalks so we
would not drift on, and because we could not be sure of letting
down our little anchor without sound.

We waited, I suppose, about a third of an hour. It seemed
longer than that to my mind and spirit, but a hard core in my
brain would not weaken or be softened by either hope or despair,
and I did not greatly overestimate the interval. Then out of the
pale moonlight I saw the kayak thrust, advancing strongly against
the tide, and I heard not the slightest sound from Ugruk's hard-
drawn paddle. In a moment he slid the little boat alongside of
ours.

"Our ship burn up and sink," he told us. "Big tusk, she no
burn, but lay on bottom. A big dragon ship lay two cable lengths
up wind but down tide from where she rode. I think warship lay

behind big island on west side of big river mouth until nightfall, then launched two boats, a sailing dinghy and big longboat. Dinghy sneak up to our ship with hook ladder, men board our ship, kill the watch, set fire in her hold. Meanwhile longboat with fifteen, twenty spearmen, bowmen, sneak around point, land, go through woods to our campfire, capture camp. But Leif, you and Ugruk go see, Ugruk know way to good lookout. No can take others now, make too much noise, but you wait here until Leif and Ugruk come back, then we do best we can. I no think we save any of our people, but we pay blood debt. Leif, we go now?"

"Yes." And I climbed overside into the forward hatch in the skin deck, taking only my weapons.

Almost at once Ugruk and I landed, and in deep stealth advanced toward the glimmer of our campfire. The ground was soft and silent under our feet, and there were few thickets between the mighty boles to rattle and swish, and we twain were stalkers aforetime. The glimmer grew to a gleam, and then we began to catch glimpses of its bright flame between the trees. And when we were still fifty paces from the pavilion, Ugruk led me to the immense butt of a forest giant that had toppled in some gale of long ago because of weak old age or death, tearing out such roots as did not break off, and leaving a pit in the ground eight feet or more deep and in diameter. Still clinging to the broken stubs was enough dirt to make a mound about eight feet high; and finding his footing well, Ugruk led me to its top.

And now the whole dread scene was open and firelit before our eyes. These grew wild and round only for a few seconds, then narrowed to find true, sharp focus, and captured detail after detail of the horrid scene. About the fire, fully twenty-five men wearing horned helmets and broadswords, and one woman, were passing and drinking from wooden bowls that were constantly being refilled from a big cask holding about twenty gallons set at one side. In a few seconds one of the bowls was tipped a little by an unsteady hand, and a little of its contents spilled, and I caught a glimpse of red as it fell, so I knew the drink to be red wine. But another red juice had been spilled which I could see clearly on the firelit ground, and it had poured from the broken heads and slashed sides of five of my shipmates, Starkad, Thori, Stori, Bjarni, and Gull Eye, and I need not glance at them twice to know that they were dead men. And plainly they had died in desperate strife against many times their number, and my soul rejoiced to see the legs of one Viking sticking out of some bushes where his body lay, and my starving eyes searched farther, to reveal three others lying at the edge of the firelight where they had been dragged, their lives ended and their souls dispatched by my brave companions. Still their revenge had been inadequate, and the new-cast souls demanded a greater meed, and it must be these had flitted toward me, for I heard their fierce, imperious cry in my inner ear.

Thorhall must have been attacked in force and complete surprise, and had been knocked down and pinioned before he could make a last, deadly stand, for he yet lived, sometimes moving a little, his feet and ankles bound. Also bound but yet alive were the wives of four of my mates who had been slain. Of the Vikings who quaffed from the bowl there was only one that I recognized, by his build and movements and glimpses of his face, and he was my brother, Thorstein. Of all the rest I knew not the names, although two, who appeared to be officers, I had seen before and in fact had spoken to one of them, on the wharf at Nidaros.

Too well I knew the woman joining wildly in their revels. Her hair was fair, and it contained strands of red that sometimes caught the firelight, and her face was too twisted with hate and exultation to retain its beauy; yet my soul cast back, against my will, and I remembered it as I had seen it long ago.

2

Although I scanned the scene with great care, I saw no thick-bodied man with a red beard.

"We could kill four with arrows before we were torn down by the rest, and perhaps two more with our spears," I told Ugruk.

"We do it if you say so. But what good, Leif, my brother. Plenty would be left to man the longboat, catch our dinghy, and kill out."

"That is true. Then we will lie here, until the drinkers fall down drunk and go to sleep. It won't be long. Then we will cut their throats and set free Thorhall and the four women."

"Anyway we better lie here until they sleep. But Ugruk, think, think, and know better way than to cut throats. I tell you now. After we cut loose Thorhall and women, we push off Thorstein's dinghy and dragon's longboat so they drift off on tide, then our people get in our longboat and paddle to reed bed. Then you and Ugruk get in kayak, the rest stay in longboat, tow our dingy, then we go out to dragon ship. Ugruk see only three lanterns. Think all the rest come to shore to capture our camp and drink wine and kill. We may find hook ladder in boats; if no find, you boost Ugruk, he climb aboard, reach down hand, everybody help everybody, we get on dragon ship all right and kill out ship watch. Then we weigh her anchor and sail her best we can; or drift off with the tide. When Thorstein and Swanhild and devil Vikings wake up from big drunk, they find prisoners gone, us gone, ship gone, and they no have boat to get off island. After while they build raft, but they never can go home, and after while big war party of Skraellings kill them to get their swords. What you say?"

"All you have said, we will do."

"Now Ugruk sneak back to kayak, launch, go to reed bed, tell princess and rest wait, no worry, we come back after while."

"Go quickly as you can, Ugruk, without making any noise. I'll keep watch until you return."

In a moment he had gone. In all the wastes of snow of the Greenland winter that I had traveled alone, I had never felt such aloneness as came upon me at that moment. As I had returned from that dread cliff where I had slain my son, I had felt Thorhild's lovely spirit at my side. But this solitude, as I lay on the mound and gazed at the firelit ring of my enemies, was not the worst and it did not even approach the worst that dread Norne had written in the runes for that night.

Leaning against a tree, I saw the same kind of weapon that the Skraelling we had met earlier had carried—a skin sack of stones fastened to the end of a stout pole. No doubt some shore party from the dragon ship had got it by trade or murder from a Skraelling farther north, when it had put in to some cove to fill water casks. Without the slightest warning, after a long stillness I had not noted but through which I had watched and listened, Swanhild ran and seized the brutal weapon and swung it high.

Instantly I perceived that she was aiming at Thorhall's head. The old Norseman saw the same, but he did not flinch one jot, and instead he spoke two words in his deep, rumbling voice that ever reminded me of the ice pack breaking up far at sea; and well out into the forest his voice resounded, because I heard him with perfect clarity at fifty paces.

"*Bitch wolf!*"

Then Swanhild struck with all her strength. As the red blood gushed, some of it spurting on her dress, she laughed wildly. Meanwhile I had slipped my bow off my back and nocked an arrow.

But I did not launch it. My sole hope of saving Helga and as many as possible of my other shipmates lay in attack by stealth. I could only wait.

The Gods had ordained that I must wait alone through what followed, a grisly and horrid scene, perhaps their punishment dealt to me for the murder of my infant son. Swanhild pointed to the four women lying in a row; and harsh and frantic and drunken rose her voice as she gave an order to her followers.

"Kill them all! If you don't they'll find a way to signal Leif and the rest before they walk into our ambush tomorrow noon. Cut their throats, I say. Are you men, or long-tailed rats?"

My brother, Thorstein, was the first to shake his head. The fiery blood of Eric the Red ran in his veins, and his hate of me had turned it into poison, but he had come out of Thorhild's womb and had sucked her teat, and a lingering trace of its warmth and sweetness was not yet dead within his soul. This action emboldened several other men to shake their heads. Still Thorstein did not seize the momentary advantage; he did not speak; and I reckoned Swanhild had seduced him to her incestuous bed.

"All of you are half-woman," she yelled from her twisted mouth, "and a whole woman will put you to shame."

Upon the piteous line she rushed, and four times the awful bludgeon fell, and blood spurted and gushed copious and scarlet in the firelight; and again I nocked an arrow on my bowstring and indeed half-drew the bow when a hand of iron appeared to seize my wrist. I thought it must be Ugruk's hand until I looked and found myself alone; then I knew it was a hand reaching from beyond earth, perhaps the ghostly hand of Eric whose absence from the party was most likely explained by his having been struck down, not gently, and amid his blazing fury, ere the ship sailed. And I thought of his sea-green eyes being darkened and it seemed to me that the wheel of fate was nearing its full turn.

Screaming, Swanhild dropped the dreadful blood-red weapon and went reeling toward Thorstein. He thrust her away with a gentle arm, yet she tottered and fell. Unable to get up, she rolled on her side, vomited, and lay still.

In a few minutes more a little shaking of the torn roots under the mound caused me to look about, my knife hilt in my hand. Ugruk had returned and was climbing to join me. And after his first long stare at the firelight ring he put his arm about my shoulder and wept, the sign of it being his spasmodic breathing and drops of salt water not out of the sea on his dark face.

"Leif!" he murmured at last. "You mighty good captain, when you stay still."

"I hope the Gods think so too, and let me live to help save those who remain."

"We can move soon," Ugruk told me after a long silence, in which we had watched some of the men reeling or dancing about the fire.

One of them laid down, and then a second, and then a third. Awhile longer the others kept their feet, no longer dancing but staggering about, and soon they were falling fast. The last to fall was Thorstein. I had been half-afraid he had sipped lightly at the wine and would remain on watch, but what seemed his certain victory over me had caused him to weaken, a weakness that I had observed ever since I broke his forearm in punishment for his breaking my great gift from my mother, a maker of music. True, he sat down awhile, trying to fight the poison of too deep draughts now moving against his brain, then he lay down, tossed a few minutes, then stilled.

Ugruk and I waited about twenty minutes more, to see if any of the enemy revived. None did so, and I signaled to Ugruk to climb down. Instead he spoke in flawless Norse, as he could do only when his mind was strongly set on what he wished to say.

"Leif, I will go now alone. I will look along beach and find the longboat from the dragon ship, and her dinghy too and see how many men we will need to push them off the beach and let them drift away on the tide. You wait here?"

Ugruk vanished, but he did not go immediately to the strand to search for the enemy boats. And now I knew why he had asked me to remain here, not only to lessen my danger but his own too, because he was a better stalker than I, and a man alone can always stalk more quietly than when with a companion. Ugruk had a task to perform, I thought, when I saw him steal into the firelit ring where lay the sleeping and the dead. And my guess as to its kind proved true when he tiptoed to my sea chest, and brought out my flute. But he carried it in his left hand instead of the right, suggesting that he might have another task in mind.

He paused, and for long seconds, appeared to be gazing at Swanhild, and my blood ran cold. Although the fire was beginning to burn down, still Ugruk's body cast a long shadow as he stole close to the girl lying in drunken sleep after her soaking in wine and her bath in blood.

His right hand was not now empty. Something that he held reflected a gleam of firelight. He bent down, looking closely at the sleeping woman, and then his arm moved, again casting a black shadow, and again what he held in his hand shone bright, as a spear of flame leaped higher than the rest. Then his hand moved quickly and strongly, and deftly he stepped aside so he would not be splashed by an upbursting, arching jet of scarlet blood.

And now he stole away, his shadow vanished, and the ice melted in my heart, and I felt as though wakening from the dreadful dream. In a short while, not more than ten minutes, Ugruk stood at the foot of the mound, and I climbed down to join him.

"Ugruk find boats easy," he told me. "We no need men to push off dragon ship longboat and dinghy. Dinghy already moored, Ugruk take anchor line hooked on shore, drop into boat, and she float off herself. Longboat on slippery wet sand, Ugruk give shove, big grunt like porpoise, and she slide off. But Ugruk make one mistake," he concluded sorrowfully.

"A bad mistake?" I asked.

"Maybe so," he answered as we made for the strand. "He no look close in dragon's dinghy boat before I turned her loose, and as she drifted between me and the moonlit water I see something in her bow, that filled it full, and it was yellow or brown color. Leif, I know not what it was for sure. But I think it was spare sail for the dragon ship, which Swanhild ordered brought to shore to make pavilion or use as a tarpaulin between cold ground and blankets."

"In any case, she'll not miss it now."

"Maybe we miss it. For soon now all of us left alive try to capture dragon ship."

"We've got a good chance. There's likely to be only a ship watch."

"Ugruk bring flute from chest. You saw him get it. But you saw the rest, too. Leif, Ugruk's knife did what it had to do. But better be my knife than your knife, for she was mother of your blind baby that you killed, and you my brother, and you murmur and breathe hard and toss in your sleep enough. I no want it to get worse and instead I want you to sleep in peace with the beautiful princess, and cut away the past as I cut away Swanhild's life."

"I will try to do so, Ugruk my brother. And we will not speak of Swanhild again."

By now we had come nigh our kayak and Ugruk asked me to sit in the rear hatch, a request that my bestormed mind did not at once understand.

"You want to change places? Tell me why, Ugruk."

"When we get to dinghy boat, Ugruk get in, help Ian, Joseph, Gorm sail her down to our longboat. Then all the people get in longboat, paddle out to dragon ship, coming up on the dark side away from moon. Ugruk sail dinghy. You follow in kayak. We need longboat, dinghy, and kayak too if we capture dragon ship and sail south, hunt, fish, have good time. If we lose each other on dark bay you make sound like whistling swan, I do the same. We come together and all of us board dragon ship at once."

"There may be more men on her than the ship watch. Some of the Vikings might have been ordered to stay aboard, or wished to do so."

"Then maybe Leif need broadsword he find so long ago in Iceland, and maybe Ugruk need knife again, and Joseph need falchion he carry under cloak, and Ian and Gorm need oars, swing like club, and maybe even princess need bejeweled dagger that she carry and Fatima need Moorish knife she wear under skirt."

In a moment we had rowed to the dinghy, which Ugruk boarded. Helga caught my hand and pressed it, but no one asked a question or spoke at all. Ugruk took the tiller oar and the dinghy began to drift with the tide, my kayak close on her stern. When we reached the longboat I directed that everyone board her except Ugruk and me. We too could have boarded, towing the two smaller craft, but there was danger of their knocking and making noise. As it was, we began to move, Ugruk leading the way, in deadly silence. Not one oar, used as a paddle, knocked against the gunwale. The sea slept in the pale moonlight, with only a little moaning in unknown woe. And now all of us paddlers must stroke hard to go slantwise across a powerful tide, and Ugruk must lean on the steering oar, to bring us up on the dark side of the dragon ship.

We came up on her stern, and fastened our dinghy and our kayak to our longboat. And the silence yet held, as I lifted Ugruk until he could grasp the taffrail. Then I tossed him the anchor of the longboat, which he caught deftly and hooked about a stanchion. Then old Gorm scrambled up and boosted Ian and Joseph, and still no lantern light was flung into our wide, wild eyes, and no sound was heard but the murmur of the light wind and the soft splashings of water against the ship's side.

For a moment I wondered whether to leave Helga and Fatima in the boat until we had won or lost the fight that was surely waiting us. If Fatima saw that we were losing, she could cut the anchor rope and drift the Gods knew where. But Helga had guessed my thought, and she feared the dark wastes of water more than our enemies, and rightly since their only hope of rescue would lie in a peaceful tribe of Skraellings who would tow the boat to shore or find it stranded. "Take us with you, Leif," she told me, and held out her arms to me.

I lifted her up, and Ian reached down a long strong arm, and presently she and Fatima became dim forms on the deck, dark gray with moonlight. And then I too climbed and was heaved aboard, and now I bade the girls stay in our rear, while we five men moved forward with bared weapons.

Then a cry of alarm was raised, and two men in the bow came rushing toward us with swords in their hands, and three more spilled out of the forward hatch brandishing axes. So we were five against five, and our enemies were Vikings of no frail breed, and armed as well as ourselves. Nay, we were seven against five, because Helga drew her dagger and Fatima bared her narrow Moorish knife, and both sprang into the fray with the fury of a wounded lynx. And it might have been that except for them we could not have conquered, for Fatima stabbed in the back one of the swordsmen who had pinned Ugruk against the rail, and Helga gave Ian a helping hand in a moment of dire peril. Yet it was Joseph's falchion which, with good cause, the enemy most feared. It slashed back and forth, with gleamings of the moon along its blade, and it sped to Valhalla the other swordsman, a brave and formidable foe, by a clean stab in the breast. Meanwhile Gorm and I had each engaged one of the sailors, our swords against their axes, and the fight seemed long-drawn as a dream, while in fact it was brief, for what Thorhall had taught me stood me in good stead, and so did our fight with the wolves in the fatal cold of our first winter in Greenland. By what maneuver I know not, I dodged a swing of my enemy's ax that whistled by my ear, and while he was overstretched and helpless, I laid him low. And when I looked up, Gorm still stood, his old legs bearing him up well, the body of his enemy at his feet.

So the moon looked down and saw five Vikings lying in blood, four of them dead and the other direly wounded. And she looked down and saw us avengers all on our feet, but amid her wondering glance she saw Joseph sway, stagger a little, and fall. And when I bent over him I perceived he had taken a sword wound in the side. It seemed that it must not be very deep, because only a little blood came out, but it was perilously near his heart and I feared it had punctured his lung.

While the two girls watched over him, Ugruk and I searched the ship for foes who might be in hiding, but there was hardly a place for them to hide in this narrow vessel, the stores being nearly used up, and the water casks on shore, and the cubbies holding only a spare sail for the longboat and some other gear.

And now the time had come for Ugruk, Gorm, and I to heave the anchor, and run with the tide, and leave forever these waters of our woe and loss. Hard work we made of it, only three to haul instead of the customary five or six, but we managed it, and the heavy iron thundered aboard. And even then I felt the ship start, and appear to come alive, as the ebbing tide drove unchecked under her keel and against her stern.

Then, leaving Ugruk at the great rudder oar, I raced back to see if Joseph had died, his mirth silenced forever, or yet breathed. I found him still able to smile, and to drink wine that Fatima had found, and in my joy I gave no thought to the danger of this passage, out of the bay of the great river in the pale dark through a mile-wide exit to the open sea. But in about two hours, so fast we sped, we had passed the cape of the left bank; and the brisk west wind as well as a tidal current swept us along, until I feared we were getting too far from shore, and somehow we must spread the reefed sail of the dragon ship and turned southward.

Only the ardent sun could cure us of this dark and evil chill we had caught by the island of the Manhasset, and only the beaming rays of the southern sun could warm the cooling blood in Joseph's veins.

3

When I had bade Joseph good night, he had told me not to be concerned with him during the dark hours, and if he lived to see the sun rise, he reckoned he could get well. Truly I had little time to devote to him, with standing a four-hour watch at the helm, relieving Ian, and myself catching a little sleep, which my mind and body told me I direly needed, between which spells I visited Joseph, and attended to his immediate needs, and kept him warm. Also I rolled the wounded Viking in a blanket, so he would not die of chill during the night, but it was well-nigh wasted effort, to judge from his deep and bleeding wound.

For the nonce we had four able-bodied men aboard, Ian, Ugruk, Gorm, and myself, and two able-bodied women, Helga and Fatima, whom I intended to do men's work after they had recovered from the exhaustion of their long wait in the rushes and the bloody battle which they had fought at our sides. If Joseph's wound should prove trifling, we would soon have five able-bodied men who might, with the girls' help, and in some fashion I could not quite imagine, man the ship. At present she was making no trouble. She had escaped the strong tidal current running out of the bay, and her slow drift, her headway held by a half-reefed sail, was with the light, northerly wind, parallel to long narrow barrier reefs, whether sand or rock I knew not, but in either case too close for our comfort. My only order to Ugruk, when Fatima had wakened him and called him to the deck, was to keep his rudder oar, which was on our stearboard side, at an obtuse angle from our hull, which would prevent the ship from veering to the right into the reef.

When he had stood that watch for four hours, I wakened Gorm, and together we lowered the anchor in eight fathoms of water. The sun was up and shining, and our spirits raised a little too, despite the dire losses of the night, and I thought to chart some sort of southward course, employing the favorable wind. As it happened, Fatima called me to the side of the wounded Viking, who she thought was dying.

"I have something to tell you before I die," he told me in a weak but audible voice. "I bear you no ill will—our voyage was ill-starred from the first, and cursed by the Gods. At first it was only King Olaf's intention for us to sail to Greenland—this is his flagship in which King Haakon fought the Jomsvikings at Oder Mouth—old but still seaworthy. King Olaf's only purpose was to make new demands on Eric the Red, and to fetch home his daughter Helga if they were not met; and we met Eric at Vesterbig, and were lying there when he sailed to Osterbig to meet Helga, and meet with his fellow chieftains. But at Osterbig some sort of demon rose out of Hel or from a bottomless crevice in the ice, for Eric and his elder son, Thorstein, and the she-wolf Swanhild came flying back to Vesterbig, Eric in a rage greater than those of Harald Bluetooth of old, saying that his younger son had made off with the princess on a westward sail, and we were to set forth in chase. What else could our master do? Eric had a parchment from the king, demanding obedience to Eric of all his subjects in the present matter. And as Eric stormed, his face turned fiery red, and then he fell, clutching his sides, and groaning, and then he lay still, and his face slowly darkened and the green light in his eyes went out."

It seemed to me that the light in the speaker's eyes was going out. In great haste I ran and poured some dregs of wine from an almost empty cask left on the deck, and brought them in a soapstone bowl to the dying Viking, and poured them between his pale lips. Then he revived somewhat, during which I mused on my sire's death by violence of his own making, and then my soul returned to the present moment and scene, for the dying Viking resumed his tale.

"When we had sailed a westerly course, and had not sighted land, and had lost one of our sails in a heavy gale, our captain declared he would go no farther and straightway turn back. But even as he was speaking, the vixen Swanhild stole up behind him and drove her long knife into his back. And our men were mazed, and only Thorstein could give orders, and like sheep we obeyed them, whereby he became our captain with Swanhild ever whispering in his ear, and his orders were that we continue on."

The Viking began to gasp for breath, and his face turned pallid, and I knew that the hand of death lay cold upon his breast, and he had only seconds to live ere it grasped his heart.

"What is your name, my friend?" I asked him. "Speak quickly, so we may speak it when we give your body to the sea."

His lips gaped twice like those of a dying fish, and he tried to speak and could not. And so he died, his name unknown as that of a dead fish, and there was little difference between the two now that had ebbed away the magical fluid, or humor, or what else it be that puts light in a man's eyes and causes his heart to burn and yearn, and his breast to swell, until his heart ceases to beat and he passes away. And straightway I took off the Viking's broadsword of which we might have use, and his haversack, and fastened to his heels a leaden weight that might have served as a spare anchor of the ship's dinghy boat. Then I put my arms about his cooling body, lifted it to my shoulder, and heaved it into the sea.

Then three of us weighed anchor, a heavy haul, and looked to weather and to lee. Then because the land swung westward a little, and our danger of striking a reef was reduced, even though our plumb could find no deeper water than eleven fathoms, sometimes shorting to seven, I dared make a little more sail, not in haste but to ease steering as the ship gained way.

And meanwhile I kept glancing at the stem, and was always startled not to see the glimmering tusk of the King of the Narwhales, and instead saw a dragon's head and neck, ever the dread sign of the Viking, as it bowed and bobbed as in Ian's song.

In late afternoon we came to a big bay, ten miles wide at its mouth and nearer twenty at its greatest span. I craved to enter it, but dared not, against the turned tide, and without oarsmen. Yet we succeeded in rounding the headland, where we lay for the night. Sailing at dawn, we skirted a coast forty miles long with only one bay, that looked of no great size, and then followed an unbroken line of barrier reefs for about fifty miles. After we had anchored for the night in a well-sheltered cove, I began to long for a deep, safe inlet, because we needed fresh meat and fish; and the beaches of the barrier reef seemed bereft of life except sea birds.

Meanwhile there was an advancement and decline, the first most welcome and the second most worrisome. There was no doubt now that we had gained a mild climate, as attested by the rich greenery of many islands lying on our stearboard, and sea birds of bright feather, and whales and sharks whose like were never seen in Iceland, let alone Greenland; and then I was sick at heart for Thorhall. Likely enough he could have named the gay-hued birds and the unknown sea monsters, for he had sailed deep into the Roman sea. And while late spring danced toward early summer, attended by riotous bloom and no doubt the song of birds, Novice Joseph slipped down toward death.

His wound, although not deep, would not heal, perhaps because fever had settled in it, and, although he always greeted me with sardonic smile and something like a jest, he could not hide from me the plain fact he was growing weaker. And the night came that he ceased trying to hide it, and indeed confessed it, but the manner of his confession remained the manner of Joseph, princely, implacably honest, and a little gay.

"Leif, would you mind very much if I depart?" he asked.

"Depart where?"

"Now that is a question I cannot answer. There are many good theologians who would have a pat reply—too pat, too meaningless when well-searched, to satisfy my love of precision. I mean, Leif, to turn on my side and no longer try to breathe, whereupon I will cease breathing. Before then, in the last hour, I will not ask forgiveness of my sins. All of these I committed with full intent, knowing precisely what I was doing and for what gain. Whatever its fate when I have cast my soul, I look it in the face."

"You are some sort of a priest, Joseph, and can you not pray for your wound to heal?"

"Some kind of what? Never in your life have you shot as wild. But put a wine cup at my elbow, if any is left of the little Fatima found aboard and it may be I must ask you to hold it to my lips, to prevent spillage, for although my lips, along with my tongue, are the strongest part of me, else I would not be gabbing like a gray goose, my hands are woefully tremulous and weak."

I did as he requested, the wine being some from a leather

flask we had found in the sea chest of one of the now-departed Vikings. And the first cup he raised manfully, although at great strain, and having accomplished the feat, and downed its contents, he gave me a great smile of victory, and this I put away in my heart to treasure always, because only a few who lived could give smiles of such charm, Joseph's heart being different from any I had ever known. And I thought, with a deep pang in my own heart, there would not be many more.

"I was once a priest, ordained by a cardinal of might and, let us trust, piety. You understand, Leif, my friend, the number of callings open to the best-born young Roman are somewhat few. One is to be a courtier to the emperor and empress of the Holy Roman Empire. Another is to lead men in battle, for in Europe there is always a war in which a brave man can die. The third is to devote one's life to one's own pleasure, such as hunting, wining, dining, and copulating. The fourth is to seek a career in the Church, by which a clever, well-born man can gain power, flattery, wine and dine in great style, and otherwise indulge himself. But mark you, Leif, it will be not so always. John XIX, who ordained me, had spoken of the need of a more pious life than lived by most cardinals and archbishops. He has mused on the notion that no man of the cloth should marry and should indeed remain celibate, sublimating his carnal self into spiritual ascendancy. Enough of that. You wish to know why, since I was once a priest, I am not one now."

"Yes, I would like to know."

"Because, my friend, I was defrocked. I had the misfortune to be caught, sans clerical garb or any at all, in the bower of a cardinal's daughter. Of course that was not the reason given, the girl having been compliant; hence my defrocking on a charge of heresy caused no great stir. So I invented the Brotherhood of Saint Ambrose and went forth to see the great wheel of which Rome is the hub. And I do assure you, Leif, that in respect to thousands of worthy priests traveling to the ends of the earth to spread their faith, or endlessly toiling to benefit mankind, I wore my cross upside down, the sign of Devil worship, and never pretended any piety. Pour me some more wine." I did so and his dim eyes brightened and a faint flush spread and deepened on his sallow cheeks.

"It comes to me, Leif, that you and your followers are precursors of the path that many priests, of the kind I speak of with such respect, will in time follow," Joseph went on. "With stark determination they will seek to convert the heathens of the New World. I would like to have your precursing make their work easier instead of harder. In saying this, I am assuming that you will settle somewhere on these shores, you and your beloved and your friends; and even if you pine for the icy winds of Greenland, which I would not do in your place short of losing my mind—even if you should want to return, Leif, you will not be able to do so in this vessel with a rotten sail. Two ships seeking new land in the west will have disappeared. None other will attempt the search in your lifetime and perhaps not for some hundreds of years. It follows that in settling here you will make your mark here, because you are one of those who make their mark on everything they touch. One reason I deplore this early dismissal from human life is that I will never know what in the Devil—pray you, pardon my mention of one I hate—you will do next. It will be something no one else has ever done, remarkable and dramatic. Therefore I am going to make a final request of you, and perhaps a very odd request to issue from my heretical lips."

"Speak it, Joseph, and I will do it if it is in my power."

"When you touch land where you are likely to see folk, wear a red cross, or several crosses, on your tunic. The people will not know what they mean, but they will remember you by the deathless sign, and remember the deathless sign by you. It will be told in their stories, such as all savage people tell, and such as never die. When they again behold the sign, some decades or some centuries from now, silver or gold, or brazened on a shield, it will not be completely strange and meaningless, but a token whereby priest and savage can make friends. And mark you, the wearing of this sign does not mean that you have renounced Odin, Thor, and the others in your enchanting pantheon. It will mean only that you subscribe to the teaching of one who died on a cross, that all men are brothers."

"Joseph, I will wear the sign gladly and proudly."

"My sins have been venial, not deadly," Joseph told me, with deathbed earnestness. "I have no fear of the future, because if hell exists, which I decline to believe because it would be a paradox in a religion stressing mercy and the forgiveness of sins, I will not go there. Where I will go is a question that stirs my curiosity to its depths. Of all the heavens ever conceived, I prefer the Hesperides—the abode of heroes—but alas, I am no hero. So I will have to wait and see. Or wait and never see."

My throat tightened and I could not speak.

"Now, Leif, will you anchor the ship so that all hands may gather about me, and I clasp those hands? And empty yon water bowl and fill it with the rest of the wine, so all may quaff. And be not too long about it, my good friend, for my soul is behaving strangely, like an uneasy bird that is about to take wing."

I did as I was told, and in a moment the anchor made a great splash and the whining line ran out. Then I collected my companions, and how few there were—Ugruk, the brother of my soul, Gorm, beautiful Helga and her servant, and Ian—six in all to say farewell to a companion departing. We went down to the hole where Joseph lay, and I filled the bowl with wine, and I passed it into his hands, meanwhile supporting them with mine.

"I feel the solemnity of the occasion," he told us. "My part in it is slight—the solemn fact is this journey of exploration of the New World, in which I will not participate from henceforward. You may lay eyes on many new lands and seas; still I have a feeling that you could journey all your lives long and still perceive only an appreciable fraction. And now I will quaff from this bowl, and then it will be passed so all of you may quaff."

He caught his breath with a rattling sound, and I feared he would not live long enough to speak what was on his mind, what rose in his heart, what issued from his soul, his last will and testament.

"May your journey prosper," he said very slowly. "May your little band remain together as long as possible, and when one drops out, drink to his future fortunes, as now you will drink to mine. Remember me, my friends. Hold me in your memories and, I hope, in your hearts as long as they beat on earth, and as my heart ceases my last thoughts will be of you. And I pray you, do not resist the call of adventure, but seize upon one that comes to hand, and strive greatly, and achieve greatly if that is in your fate. What you have already achieved, even the discovery of a New World, is not enough since you all are so young. But in any failure remember this success, and doubt not that in years to come it will be heralded over all the world and it will cause great changes in the lives and minds of men, and in human history. Leif, my captain! Ian, poet speaker, on whom I must rely to trumpet his story to the world. Ugruk, defender and Leif's right arm! Gorm, old sailor once a slave, whose spirit has never weakened, whose head has never bowed! Beautiful Helga, Leif's worthy bride who will bear him children and who will walk and live in beauty! Fatima, a daughter of the brave Moors, and who glorified that heritage by her staunchness and her valiance in the hour of trial! What a worthy company in the great adventure of all time! Now pass the bowl, and take deep draughts, and drink to all our party who embarked with us, living or dead, and deepest of all drink to the New World that we have found, a hope and refuge for generations unborn, and may that hope be fulfilled and that refuge endure forever. Farewell."

He drank a little from the bowl and passed it to Ugruk. And then the rest of us drank in the order that we stood about his bunk, and he watched us with a last brilliance, and final upsurge of his spirit, in his great, dark eyes. Then he turned on his side as he told me he would do, and Helga kissed his cheek, and so did Fatima, and I kissed his hand, and a flame rose in Ian's face, as some great idea, or at least some realization of his part in our adventure, assigned by very fate; and Gorm's weathered face twisted into beauty, and Ugruk knelt before the unfrocked priest and wept.

When we listened for Joseph's breathing, we could not hear it. When Helga brought forth a little looking glass and held it to his lips, it remained clear and cloudness as was often, Joseph had told me, the Roman sky in May. And then Ugruk, Gorm, and I weighed anchor, so the vessel would be under way, intent and bent on the continuance of her great adventure, when we gave Joseph's body to the sea.

4

On the second day following Joseph's death and burial, the same gentle north wind fetched us safely through coastal waters of ample depth about a hundred miles from our last anchorage to one of the finest and boldest capes I had ever seen, evidently the gate to a great bay. My first thought was to erect there a cairn that could be seen by ships plying north or south for about twenty miles. But there was something wrong with that thought, and I did not know why until Ugruk, at my side, uttered a big grunt of self-surprise. Very plainly he had guessed my intention from my admiration of the cape. Very plainly he spoke.

"Ugruk know now why Gorm no help with building cairns all the way from Helluland. They like tracks in the snow of wild bull of Greenland."

"Possibly they were, Ugruk. But I had no notion that Eric the Red, now in Valhalla, would move so fast." More, I could have added that any ship following us now would be friends, not mortal foes. Still I forsook the idea of erecting a cairn.

Our good ship entered one of the finest bays I had ever seen, thirty miles wide at its mouth, so wide at its swell that we could not see either shore, and apparently endless in length. When we had sailed westward about two hours we came to the mouth of a gigantic river, and by then we were so excited that we tacked northward about two hours more to come in sight of what I thought at first was a bay of the mighty bay, but which proved the mouth of another river as great as the first. Then we resolved to explore its whole coast, as far as we could fetch, and camp on one of the numerous islands to hunt, fish, and smoke and dry enough of our catch to see us through a gale that might drive us far to sea.

Truly this was the most lovely region I had ever seen. Back of the silvery beaches lay heavy forests and wild meadows festive with blossom, and we could not sail a mile without seeing white-tailed deer almost as big as Scottish stags, and another stag, with high, sweeping antlers, that was very much larger than Scottish stags, indeed almost as large as a Norwegian elk. Of the flat, palmated horns and black hides and horselike heads of European elk we caught no glimpse. But there were black bears a-plenty, feeding behind the receding tide, a few brown bears, and handsome little beasts with ringed tails that we did not know; and a myriad of ducks, geese, and swans fed on a wild water plant that we intended to gather for our own lean fare.

In all, we passed five rivers on our northward sail up the bay, the fourth being so large that it could swallow up without flooding its banks the great river at whose mouth we had met doom and disaster. There was no longer any doubt that we had discovered a great continent, undreamed of by man, greater perhaps than the Roman Empire in its prime glory, plus all the lands lying eastward known to our outmost voyagers. Here the air was balmy and the winds gentle and warm. An army of ten thousand could not have starved on the fertile, game-thronged banks. And it was during our stay here, a matter of two weeks of easy living and little work, that I began to do as Joseph had bade me, which was to recite to Ian the strange tale of my life, beginning with the fairy gift of the runed sword, and this he wrote down on parchment as fast as his hand could fly. For pens he used sharpened goose quills, split at the tips, and for ink a mixture of water and soot from the oil lamps we had found on the ship.

I had thought that the benevolent north wind would have blown itself out during our long loaf, but he had not done so, and when we again passed the cape into the open sea, right cheerfully he puffed our sail. And very shortly we again encountered barrier reefs, the longest we had ever seen, wherefore on these dark nights with low-lying land on our right hand we dared not sail, and instead anchored in the most sheltered waters we could find. And it came to pass we rejoiced in this provision, for at the outmost point of the endless reef, constituting a cape, a squall broke in the east and would have surely driven us on the sands, had not all hands been up and awake to re-set the sail and tack as fast as possible to sea until the brief storm blew itself out. Even so, I perceived that our sail had split, and although we could mend it with twine, it would never be as strong again.

A north wind, shifting sometimes to the west, seemed the prevailing wind at this time of year on this coast, and I thought it might be because warm air rises, and cold north air rushed in to take its place. After we had passed the easternmost point of what seemed the endless barrier reef, we changed our course to southwest, in order to keep the land in sight, but the north wind still spanked us along. And now the reef lay far out from the mainland, with a great bay between, but at last, after eleven days, we found a beach where we dared enter, and which proved to be the mouth of a noble river. And in this sailing we needed as well as longed for Gull Eye, for a good part of the time we could not spy the mainland or distinguish it from a low-hanging cloud.

Then we came upon a coast flanked by islands large and small. This we skirted, taking another eleven days to do so with maximum safety, because winds were contrary, squalls frequent, currents strong, and the ship's hands grievously short. And in this stretch, which we wildly guessed as three hundred miles by crow flight, we saw great numbers of Skraellings, fishing from their little boats, gathering shellfish, and staring at us from the beach. Also we caught glimpses of many deer, the bucks sprouting horns, but they were of a much smaller species than we had seen farther north.

At the end of this stretch where the southwest curving strand began to run straight south or even a little east, we found the full flush of summer. Here again we entered a noble river, in search of fresh meat and fish, getting all we could use, and in addition gathering quantities of large, blue grapes which we intended to squash and let ferment and make wine. Then again we came on barrier reefs, stretching south by east at least three hundred miles, and surely this was Furder Strandi, the long beaches of Norse myth, wondrous beaches as strange to ice as to us. And I was glad that we had entered what might prove the southern end of the monstrous continent, because the farther south we went, the better and more numerous were Skraelling boats and houses. Still what I most sought might be yet distant. My mother, Thorhild, had told me that the southern lands of the Old World, such as Egypt, Greece, Judea, and Persia, had become civilized centuries before the great forest-grown lands of the north; and I had hoped the same might be true in the New World.

What I wanted to find was a Skraelling city where we might settle if we wished, or at least buy sailcloth and other ship stores for journeying on. In all truth we could not go much farther, until the ship was overhauled and re-readied. There was a great crack in the mast that would cause it to fall in a full-blown gale, and our repeated resewing of its tears had greatly weakened our sail. Nor did our search reveal a spare sail, convincing me that those who lay dead at what we called Camp Terror, or had been eaten in nearby waters, or who still lived like gaunt hollow-eyed ghosts wandering in the woods, had indeed brought it to shore in their dinghy boat to use as a tarpaulin or a pavilion, and Ugruk had caught sight of it too late.

And then, wholly without warning, I was confronted with a decision, appalling in its magnitude. Following a barrier reef, broken by inlets and small islands, we came suddenly to the end of the land, or at least to the end of the coast we had followed ever since we had landed on Helluland. Gazing around the cape of what I thought was a chain of keys, we saw islets beyond counting, and a long shore running straight west. Indeed my mind was getting reconciled to vasty distances, and I thought this land might be linked with another continent, as sailors say the continent of Asia is linked with Africa. On the other hand we might have sailed down the shore of a huge peninsula, and this was the end of it, and nothing lay south of us, or west, but interminable seas. And while I was daydreaming of these possibilities, Ian came up to me and courteously asked to confer with me, and the conference was to be about some mighty issue, as I knew by the depth and solemnity of Ian's eyes.

"You have the longboat and the kayak," he began, "and lately have had little use for the sailing dinghy."

"That is true, Ian."

"She's a stout little vessel. She even has a cubby where a spare sail is stored along with some other gear. Because we used her for sealing and even whaling, she has two hundred fathoms of stout line attached to her iron. Captain Leif, I ask to victual her and go back the way we came and make my way to Norway."

"Ian! Are you in your perfect mind?"

"I thought not, when the notion first struck me. Pray you, let me plead my cause. If need be, I can give five years to the journey. I can sail the boat, as you know well, and she has such shallow draft I can keep in a stone's throw of the coast line, ready to run from any great storm or even a little squall. In all our journey we have found fresh water with the greatest ease; we have touched nothing resembling a desert. We have never failed to find game, which I will cook when I can, but when I cannot, eat raw. When winter comes and the ice thickens I will go to a Skraelling village, or to an Innuit village, and ask to lodge there until spring, meanwhile helping them kill seal through blowholes in ice, Ugruk fashion. It may be that I will sail eastward from Helluland, but that would be a long sail, exposing my little boat to contrary winds and great gales, and me to starvation and thirst; so it is my mind to go on northward from Helluland, following the coast as long as there is any coast to follow, choosing my time to cross inlets and bays, until I come on the narrow sea that Ugruk crossed in his kayak, from what he calls the Long Land to the coast of Greenland. I pray you, Leif, heed me, for to this I have given thought ever since your great discovery."

"Ian, my long companion, I do heed you but why do you want to return to Norway, instead of wandering on with us others, until we find a suitable habitation?"

"Because I have a song to sing."

"What song is of that importance?"

"The song of your life, as you have told it to me. From the hour that Eric killed Kol, the river of your life has flowed with great power and depth, and although it wandered from its bed it always returned there, and in the course of your life you have made the greatest discovery, established the most pregnant fact, in the history of mankind. In Greenland, Iceland, and Norway a few folk will believe me. A very few will venture forth upon the oceans to see for themselves if I have told truth, for, whatever else we are, we Norse are mariners, and eaten up with curiosity about this world on which we have been given life. Some truth will be told by those who come after me, saga and poem speakers, and a great many lies will be told, and the main of the knowledge that we have gained may be lost at last for uncountable years; still in due time it will be proved. And what, if on the vast journey, dire accidents befall me and I die? Still I would have been true to my calling as a poem speaker, and I would have been true to my captain, Leif, and my friends, his followers."

"You realize, of course, that your going would leave only three men and two strong and quick-handed women to sail the ship, one of them with child?"

"I do know that, but judging from what you have said you intend to seek a suitable habitation in the New World, where you may live well and have adventure; and it comes to me you could find it on these very shores, where great piles of shell attest the richness of the waters, and where deer abound, and Skraellings must live in numbers undreamed of in Markland."

"All that is true. But as you must keep faith with your calling, I will seek to keep faith with mine. If yonder headland is not the end of the land, but the beginning of another coast leading the Gods know where, we five will try to sail the ship as long as it lasts. It is my purpose to see as much of the New World as I can in the time given me, and that purpose was waked in me by some God or Gods, for reasons beyond my dreams. Aye, Ian, you may take the sailing dinghy and then take departure. Only wait until we can land, and victual her well with dried venison and dried fish, and Ugruk can fashion for you a harpoon for spearing seals, and lines for fishing, and spare gear of various sort. And we will search the chests of the dead or lost Vikings for articles of use to you, especially warm clothing, and capes against sea spray and rain. But I have no farewell gift for you but this, and I pray that you wear it in your headgear, because I think it is a token of good fortune and of the love of some being of the unseen, as well as a token of my love."

Ian wept as I handed him the plume from the divine swan, still white and beautiful as ever, and then fastened it in his cap. So it came about that we sailed west a short distance, anchored the ship in sheltered waters among some islands, and went to shore in the longboat, proposing to make every provision possible for Ian's unimaginably long journey and for our own journey in the sun. Because by now we were almost certain that the land we had followed southward turned and ran straight north, that indeed it was a peninsula as large as Ireland, and at its northern end it would surely join with some other land, presumably running eastward. In fact a very old Skraelling, his garments adorned with shells and pebbles, and who gave his name as Seminole, drew in the sand the cape we were now on and the northward sweep of the coast until it turned east, and to Ugruk he gave a sign that after its turning it ran on forever.

At last Ian was ready to start his journey and we were ready to continue ours as well as possible with a rag of a sail and a six-hand crew. And he went out with us to the ship for the last time, and there we poured the purple wine that we had made from the grapes we had gathered far up the coast, and filled a great bowl, and drank. And now Ugruk took from around his neck a thong from which hung a little figure carved in walrus ivory that no other than I had laid eyes on in all the years he had lived with us, and I had seen only once or twice. I thought it represented a seal, perhaps the King of the Seals I had seen in the ice palace.

"You keep, wear, have good luck, be welcome at Innuit villages," Ugruk told Ian. "I no need it any more. I borrow what luck I need from my brother, Leif."

And once more I brought forth my flute, one of the precious few of my belongings that had been saved from fire and destruction, and I would not have had this if Ugruk had not picked it out of the baggage when he had returned in stealth to our camp at the river mouth, and there saved me from paying with my own hand a debt of blood. And I wondered what tune to play, but Ian asked me to play once more the Strand Song of the Norse Women to the Departing Fleet, and when I sounded once its haunting notes, I played it over, while Ian sang the words; and the moment became most strange, and the air was fresh in my nostrils as when I had entered the ice palace, and neither Ian nor I had ever before such mastery over our instruments, he his voice fit for wooing the glorious Goddess Siff and I my flute. And Helga wept, because she was a Norse woman of the true breed, and the day of the Viking had passed.

"The sweetest theft you have ever made, or can ever make, was to steal my heart," she told me, changing in only three words the last two lines of the song.

Then Ian took off in his little boat, but as it decreased and dimmed in our sight, the sun peered down from between clouds, and his beam hit with certain aim Ian's small sail, and lighted it as though by flame. And when all sight of him was lost in the great waters, we weighed our anchor and sailed boldly westward to round what we believed was land's end. But it would not be the end of the land for us, for I aimed to sail northward along its coast, and then sail east along another land that we would find. And it might be that our tattered sail would serve us a good while yet, until we came to some harbor, with perhaps a city and a temple visible in the distance, or some equally happy promise, and there the saga of Leif Ericsson would end because there would be no one to recite the latter parts in the old land; but I would still have my four shipmates and my mate; and adventure would not leave me as long as I lived; and sometimes in moments of great peril, or great change, or great dealing, a white swan would circle over my head, look in vain for her gift to me, trumpet her grief, and fly away and dim in the immensity of the sky.

To His Grace,
José de Vierzo y Astorga,
Archbishop of San Isidor.
Greetings:

Your Grace may recall that you honored me, one of the humblest who look to you for spiritual guidance, by the request that I write to you of the wonders of the Aztec kingdom, conquered by that servant of God, Hernán Cortez, and especially to write you of the religion of the yet unenlightened and heathen natives. On this day, October 23rd of the year of our Lord 1519, I take pen in hand.

At last I have been permitted to visit the chief temple of the Aztecs in the great coastal city of Coatzalango.

There I laid eyes on the images of their most powerful gods, to whom woeful and bloody sacrifice is made. But a more cheerful spectacle, although of less spiritual importance, was a large picture writing in a rocky crypt of the Aztec god Quetzalcoatl, whose name appears to mean Feathered Snake. These pictures, seen in the flickering light of a flambeau, were vivid and dramatic in the extreme.

The first picture represents the god, who is often called Son of the Sun, coming into harbor on his first arrival out of the east, which according to legend occurred approximately five hundred years ago. The stem of this ship represents the head and neck of a giant serpent, as did the stems of the Viking ships that harried the coasts of our beloved Asturia at about the same period. At first glance I thought that the sail was not well-portrayed; then I realized that it was not intended to represent a sail and instead the wing of a dragon of which the stem was the head and neck. The connection between the god now coming out of the east, and the name given him, Feathered Snake, became immediately apparent.

The second picture shows the god's landing on the beach. And truly I was so excited by his appearance, and so strangely moved, that I must breathe the name in due reverence of Mary, Mother

of God. Pray believe me, your Grace, that the picture revealed a
very tall man, whose hair, worn long, was gold in color, whose
eyes were blue, and on whose tunic the Christian symbol of the
Holy Cross was worked in red dye. The third picture represents
Aztec priests and other folk prostrating themselves at his feet. Of
the meaning of the fourth picture I am not sure. In this picture
the tall man is shown in conjunction with a crude representation
of a large feathered serpent, with a sword in his hand, brandished
in what seems a threat to a group of priests with stone knives,
suggestive of an adz, but held by a projection at the top of the
blade, instead of by a wooden handle as we know the adz. Behind
him, apparently under the protection of his sword, is a group of
naked boys and men, their faces white and their eyes staring, and
I cannot believe but that they were about to be slain as human
sacrifice to other Aztec gods, and the tall, blond-haired man wearing the sign of the Cross, undoubtedly a Viking gale-blown to the
Mexican coast, had intervened.

The supposition is well-nigh proved by what a very old Aztec
priest told my shipmate Bernal Diaz, also a follower of Cortez,
that during the tall man's long sway over the kingdom, human
sacrifice of all kind was forbidden and completely stopped in the
cities of the Aztecs.

The legend, passed down for five centuries, and assiduously
recorded by various chroniclers, contains detail which does not re-
fute and indeed lends credence to the hypothesis I present to your
Grace. In the first place, the visitor from the Sun was an expert
archer, and your Grace will recall that the Roman God of the Sun,
Apollo, was also a great archer. With our Viking visitor of five
centuries gone was a dark-skinned man, native perhaps to some
northern region of the New World. Also with him was a blond-
haired young woman of great beauty, and her Moorish maidservant, and an old man to whom death came and which he looked
in the face to the last. The other members of the ship's company
presumably had been swept overboard by a great gale, or perhaps
slain in battle by another Viking ship before it was gale-driven to
this coast.

The picture writing as well as the legend has proved of great usefulness to our Lord's work in Mexico, and to Cortez, faithful servant of our Lord. God ordained that Cortez should arrive the very year that the sorcerers and soothsayers had prophesied the return of the living god Quetzalcoatl. Cortez was immediately identified with him, the Son of the Sun. Except for this identification, Cortez' little band of soldiers and Indians would not have been able, short of a miracle, to conquer the great, rich Aztec kingdom, Montezuma its lord, and neighboring kings, and again put a stop to human sacrifice as well as bring to the folk their first knowledge of our Savior.

This letter is already long, still I must add one other detail of the legend, corroborating its truth, and which the scholarly as well as sanctified mind of your Grace will appreciate. In the fullness of time death came to the man whom the natives mistook for a mighty god, as death comes to all men. In the same hour, death came to his dark-skinned companion. And then the fair-haired lady regarded as his wife and priestess, herself in old age, had the two corpses borne to the seacoast, and put aboard the Viking ship of their arrival, now without sail or helm, its double keel well-nigh rotted away. Then she cut the cable and allowed the decaying vessel with its hushed freight to float away on the tide and be caught in the current that streams northeastward from the gulf, and ultimately be driven by the winds into the fastnesses of ocean.

I am happy to report that the Christian faith is gaining many converts among the heathen, and in due course Nueva España may become a see of Holy Church.

With protestations of Christian love for my great spiritual leader, and wishing your Grace a long life and the doing of many more good works, I end this letter.

Yours in Jesus Christ,
Fernando de Riano y Vicente,
Humble Servant of God